THE IDEAL LOCATION
FOR MAKING LOVE...

As Stephanie gazed entranced at the lush meadow—the perfect spot for the next scene—Cade murmured huskily, "We'll have to test the site...." Then his lips were crushing hers, and she was swept away in the rapture of his embrace, unable to stop the tide....

But when harsh reality suddenly pierced the fog of sweet new sensations, she struggled to release herself. "I...I simply can't."

Cade's eyes glittered warningly. "I'll show you what happens to teases," he growled, once more torturing her with kisses that sent shivers through her spent body.

Just as she again reached the point of letting down all barriers, he thrust her abruptly from him. "Get back to work, Stephanie," he snapped scornfully. "I think you've proved a love scene can be done in this setting!"

AND NOW...

SUPERROMANCES

Worldwide Library is proud to present a
sensational new series of modern love stories—
SUPERROMANCES

Written by masters of the genre, these longer,
sensuous and dramatic novels are truly in keeping
with today's changing life-styles. Full of intriguing
conflicts, the heartaches and delights of true love,
SUPERROMANCES are absorbing stories—
satisfying and sophisticated reading that lovers
of romance fiction have long been waiting for.

SUPERROMANCES
Contemporary love stories for the woman of today!

Alyce Bowen
DANGEROUS PROMISE

A SUPERROMANCE FROM
WORLDWIDE

TORONTO · NEW YORK · LOS ANGELES · LONDON

Published September 1982

First printing July 1982

ISBN 0-373-70032-6

CHAPTER ONE

IT WAS A STRANGE LITTLE ROAD for someone accustomed to the sleek Los Angeles freeways. A farm-to-market road, this one was called. Narrow, blacktopped, winding and undulating as it followed the gently rolling and overlapping hillsides of north Texas. Heavy-leaved oak trees grew out of the bright orange red clay that lined both sides of the pavement, their rough-barked trunks often leaning over the roadway, casting flickering shadows along the path Stephanie Lasater was taking.

She should have felt tense, driving an unfamiliar rented car along an unknown road to a place where she was expecting an obstinate old man to blockade her plans. Yet she had seldom had a morning as light-hearted and blissful as this one. The countryside had taken hold of her from the time she turned off the highway northwest of Dallas and began finding her way through the pastoral lanes to the Steele Ranch.

It wasn't only the landscape that had her in its grip, Stephanie realized as she hummed along with the country music pouring out of her FM car radio, but the entire mood of Texas, the state she had been wanting to see ever since she could remember. Texas—the word itself had a mystique that excited her. Visions of vast expanses of cattle ranches, oil wells, the Gulf Coast beaches and metropolitan centers like Dallas and Houston converged in a brilliant image, making her shiver with joy at the fact that she was here at last.

Maybe it was because she had grown up in the middle of New York City, in a high-rise apartment in a crowded building in Manhattan, that she had developed a passion for wide vistas and rolling prairies. Even moving to southern California hadn't eased her desire to see Texas. There she was caught up in the swirl of Los Angeles life, freeway traffic and the constant clamor of the motion-picture industry. Well, she had asked for it, had even pleaded with Jon Jenson for a job as his personal assistant.

It was a job any woman might desire. Jon Jenson had a mystique, too. The renowned producer-director was famed for his realistic motion pictures, for films that depicted life as it was, and it was he who had insisted that his new movie about Texas be shot on location, not in the fake interior of a Hollywood studio.

Jon had hired Stephanie three years earlier, two weeks after she had deserted New York and a broken engagement to start a new life on the West Coast. They had grown up together in Manhattan, although Jon was six years older. Now, at thirty-two, he was acclaimed as a genius, and his reputation had made Stephanie a little hesitant about approaching him for a job. But she had needed work badly, so she'd placed the call to his office, exchanged remembrances of New York and mutual friends and asked if he knew of any work at the studio. She was an accomplished secretary and had served as the executive assistant to the president of a large advertising agency in New York before circumstances she didn't want to recall had led to her resignation.

Jon had hesitated about offering Stephanie the position as his assistant, openly wondering if she was prepared to meet its considerable demands. Critical, concerned with details and inclined to be more than a little impatient with those in his employ, he had seen three assistants walk out on him in the past year, all informing him in no uncertain terms that he was an impossible boss. Jon had warned Stephanie he was afraid their friendship might be ruined by working together, but she had begged for a chance, one that had eventually led to a permanent position not only as his personal assistant but also as the production coordinator for his films.

That was why she had flown to Texas. She had known that Jon would want her to make the trip as soon as she had received the telephone call from Mike Adams, the young man who did much of the advance scouting for Jon Jenson movies, the one responsible for finding the perfect location for shooting each film.

"Steffie, baby," Mike had greeted her on the phone, and Stephanie had instantly known there was trouble. Mike called her Steffie only when he had encountered a problem he couldn't solve. "I've found absolutely the ideal place for the ranch shots."

"Then what's wrong, Mike?" she had asked,

knowing that he wasn't calling to relay good news.

"Well, just one slight problem," Mike had informed her. "The old codger who owns the place won't let us use it."

Stephanie had been irritated by Mike's attempt to thrust the problem onto her, the way he so often did.

"Then find another ranch," she had directed him.

"But this is the one we want," Mike had answered. "It's everything that Jon requested—close to Fort Worth and Dallas, so the crew can stay in hotels there and we won't have to bring house trailers onto the ranch property." Mike's enthusiasm for the site crept into his voice. "And you've got to see the ranch, Steffie. I'm mailing you some pictures today. The eastern section of the property is heavily wooded, and it's exactly right for the early scenes in the movie, but the western half is on the prairie, and it will be ideal for the cattle drive."

He went on to tell her that not only was the ranch physically perfect but it also had a herd of longhorn cattle, descendants of the animals that had made it possible for many Texans to survive following the Civil War. "And he even has a few buffalo on one section of the ranch," Mike had added.

It did sound ideal, just the kind of place Jon would want for his film, and Stephanie knew that once the director heard Mike's report he wouldn't be satisfied with any other location. She was right about that: Jon had insisted she call on the ranch owner personally to try to gain his permission to film on the property.

Jon had smiled in that slow seductive manner of his, the way he could charm anyone when he wanted to, including the most temperamental actresses on his sets; and Stephanie briefly wondered how she had managed to escape falling under his magnetic spell, as most of the women who starred in Jon Jenson films had done. Maybe it was because they had known each other for so long, since the day Jon had come to her aid after she had fallen off a swing in Central Park when she was four and he was ten. She had thought of him as a big brother then, and she still did, even though her friends kept telling her how thrilling it must be to work with the handsome producer-director every day. Watching him lean over her desk and touch the tips of her polished fingernails, she wasn't the slightest bit affected by his considerable charm. She only knew he was planning to send her to Texas.

"You go talk to the owner, Stef," he ordered in his deep voice, making it seem more like a polite request. "You can convince him to let us use the ranch. Old men like to have a pretty girl pay attention to them; you can smile sweetly at him, and he'll be happy to lease the property to us for the summer."

"Maybe he doesn't like pretty girls," Stephanie replied, but the tiny laugh in her voice indicated that she was already looking forward to the trip.

Jon ruffled her honey-blond hair, even lighter than it had been when she was a child, thanks to the southern California sun, and kissed her forehead lightly.

"He'll like you," Jon told her. "Everyone likes you."

Well, Stephanie thought, that wasn't exactly true. At least, it hadn't been back in New York City, when she had thought she'd found love. But that was another story and another time, and she didn't want to remember it. She had Texas to see.

The plane had left Los Angeles early in the morning. Stephanie had made certain her reservation was for a daytime flight because she wanted to be able to see the land over which they were flying. The Grand Canyon spread out impressively before her as the jet soared over Arizona, and the Rocky Mountains loomed up against a background of clouds. But when the pilot announced that they were flying over the Panhandle and the Staked Plains of Texas, Stephanie had pressed her slightly snubbed nose even closer against the window.

The Staked Plains. Llano Estacado. Named, some historian said, because they were so immense, so vast, that the first Spanish explorers had to drive stakes into the ground to be able to find their way back. Stretching for miles and miles of high, almost flat tableland through northwestern Texas, they were broken only by a few natural phenomena, such as the deep canyon of Palo Duro, south of Amarillo. Stephanie had looked at the land and yearned to reach out the plane window to touch the great open spaces below her.

Now she could touch the land and breathe the fresh spring air, free of smog and pollution, carrying with it the scent of recent rains and fragrant aromas of the wild flowers that grew helter-skelter among the trees and underbrush on all sides of her.

To spend the summer here helping Jon film his movie—it was almost too pleasing a prospect to be true. But it still might not be true, she reflected ruefully, remembering her ever approaching appointment with Cade Steele. He had been as belligerent as Mike had reported when she had called and asked for an appointment, telling her in terse words his opinion of movie people. Finally, when Stephanie was at the point of despair, he had informed her bluntly, "If you want to come all the way from California just to hear me say no in person, that's your problem. But I'll warn you now that I don't cotton to frivolities like filmmaking. I've got a ranch to run."

A slight quiver in her stomach shattered Stephanie's lighthearted mood and betrayed her growing uneasiness at the thought of meeting Cade Steele face-to-face. He sounded even more stubborn than Jon Jenson on one of his worst days. She'd have to use all her tact if she were going to succeed in leasing the ranch for Jon's movie.

The road curved abruptly to the left, forcing her to brake and to turn her thoughts toward her driving and away from the encounter that couldn't be more than a few minutes away. Then just as suddenly the road turned sharply again, propelling Stephanie's car out of the woodlands and onto the prairie. She couldn't contain a gasp of pleasure at the sight before her. As far as she could see, for at least ten to fifteen miles, there was nothing but lush green grass and rolling landscapes, broken only by the white-painted rail fences that lined the highway and marked divisions in the pastures.

As she gazed transfixed at the panoramic view, she caught sight of the ranch house. It had to be the Steele place. Even if it hadn't matched the photograph Mike had mailed her, she would have known that this house was the one Jon would want to use for the final scenes of his film, the ones showing Texas in the early twentieth century. It had a majesty about it, a grandeur in its isolation from the city. Set snugly against the fingers of trees that escaped from the confining timberland and crept onto the prairie, the house was large and imposing, three stories high, with a front porch encircling at least three sides of it. Pure white except for the red roof with the old-fashioned wind gauge in the shape of a rooster, it stood like a sentinel against the elements. A windmill at one side whirled briskly in the breeze of the late morning.

Stephanie had to slow the car almost to a stop to pass through the narrow opening between the fences, and the car wheels clanged against the metal poles that lay crosswise above a slight ditch to form the entryway. A cattle guard. She knew its name and the fact that it allowed cars to cross but kept cattle inside, and a smile of delight spread across her face at the realization that again she was actually experiencing something she had previously only read about.

But the smile disappeared as she parked in the driveway at one side of the house and tossed her keys into her oversize navy blue purse. Determined to look professional, she carefully checked her makeup and hair in the rearview mirror, pushed a stray curl back into place, adjusted the collar of her blazer and took a deep breath to prepare for the ordeal ahead.

What kind of a man was this Cade Steele anyway? Would he issue a curt no and throw her out immediately, even after telling her that she could see him? He had been impatient with her again when she had called the night before to confirm her appointment.

"I have very little time to waste with you," he had told her, and she could hear the chill even over the telephone line. "Be here at eleven if you still want to make the trip. Not that it will do you any good...."

She glanced at the tiny hands on her jeweled wristwatch. Ten to eleven; thank heaven she was early. She had left her Dallas hotel long before she had thought necessary simply to avoid any possibility of incurring Cade Steele's wrath by being late, and she had been glad she did, for she had lost fifteen minutes after taking a wrong turn a few miles back.

The house was quiet as Stephanie approached and rang the bell, but she could hear the sound of footsteps almost as soon as the chimes completed their tolling. Her shoulders squared, she prepared to meet the irascible Cade Steele.

Instead she was greeted by a middle-aged woman with a round rosy face and hair pulled back into a bun, only a few salt-and-pepper strands escaping confinement to fall below her shoulders. A trace of flour lingered on her fingertips and forehead, and she hastily wiped her hands on the bibbed apron that covered her red-and-white checked dress.

"Mrs. Steele?" Stephanie immediately assumed the woman was the rancher's wife, for she fit perfectly the image of a Texas farm woman: sturdy, unconcerned with fashion and makeup, her interests limited to cooking and housecleaning.

The woman smiled through the metal woven links of the screen door. "Oh, no, no," she protested. "I'm the housekeeper, Mrs. Martin." She opened the screen door to invite Stephanie in. "And you are the woman from the movies?"

"I'm Stephanie Lasater from Los Angeles," she explained. "I have an appointment with Mr. Steele."

"Yes," Mrs. Martin acknowledged. "Cade said you were coming. But he's not here right now. Will you come in and wait?" She led Stephanie into the comfortable high-ceilinged living room with its polished oak floors and paneled walls. A red brick fireplace covered almost one entire wall at one end of the room, and lounge chairs were placed casually in front of it, their printed fabric adding a flash of color to the room. Overhead an antique brass ceiling fan turned noiselessly.

"Do you think Mr. Steele will be away very long?" Now that she was here, Stephanie wanted to get the meeting over with. Her body was tense as she stood uncertainly in the center of the room.

"I don't think so, but you might be more comfortable waiting on the back porch. There's a pretty view and a nice breeze, and I'll bring you a glass of lemonade."

Stephanie relaxed slightly. "That sounds lovely, thank you." She followed the housekeeper through the informally decorated home, past the kitchen, where the tantalizing aroma of a cake baking in the oven made her remember that she had skipped breakfast that morning because of her determination not to be late for her appointment with the rancher.

Within minutes Stephanie was comfortably ensconced in an old-fashioned wooden porch swing that hung from chains stretching from the high roof above her, a tall glass of iced lemonade in her hand. Mrs. Martin sat on a rocking chair for a minute or two, regarding her with an appraising but twinkling eye.

"Are you a movie star?" she finally asked.

"Oh, no," Stephanie corrected her. "I'm not an actress at all. Just the director's assistant and production coordinator."

"But you're pretty enough to be a movie star," Mrs. Martin insisted. "Your hair looks like spun gold, and your eyes are a lovely shade of blue."

"Thank you." Stephanie blushed at the compliment. She was so accustomed to being around the gorgeous actresses who starred in Jon Jenson films that she thought of herself as very ordinary looking. It was a surprise to hear someone sincerely tell her that she was pretty. In Hollywood lots of men called her beautiful, but that was just a casual expression applied to practically every woman connected in any way at all with the movies. Sometimes, Stephanie knew, when a man called her beautiful or gorgeous it simply meant that he couldn't remember her name.

She always took the compliment with a huge grain of salt.

"I go to the movies sometimes," Mrs. Martin continued, "but Cade never does. He doesn't like them one bit."

Stephanie wasn't astonished to hear that. She realized from her two telephone encounters with the man that he felt life was intended for work and anything even remotely connected with entertainment was simply foolishness. Her stomach tightened again just thinking of him, and she almost wished he would show up, tell her he hadn't changed his mind and send her on her way, so she could return to Los Angeles where she belonged.

But there was something about this land that caught her imagination and made her want to linger and see more of it. When Mrs. Martin excused herself, explaining that she had to complete a couple of chores before noon, Stephanie was glad of the opportunity to be by herself. She knew she would relax when left alone with the almost endless view and the pasture off to one side of the house that was filled with sleek horses, some with frisky colts close by. Soaking in the rich atmosphere of this place was like taking a tranquilizer, soothing to her mind and body.

Half an hour later, however, she was beginning to grow restless, occasionally pacing the length of the porch and stretching her legs, taut with nervous energy. She finally turned back to the swing and resigned herself to the likelihood that Cade Steele was keeping her waiting on purpose, determined to impress upon her that he was a busy rancher with no time for trifles. Mrs. Martin returned once to refill her lemonade glass and offer her a sandwich and a slice of cake, which Stephanie refused. This was a business meeting, and she didn't want to be munching on food when the owner showed up; that is, if he ever did.

It was strange, she realized, that the ranch should be so quiet when Mr. Steele had emphasized how busy he was and how little time he had for her. The only sign of activity she could spy was a lone rider directing his horse toward a barn a couple of hundred yards or so from the porch.

She was actually considering walking to the barn to ask the man if he could find Cade Steele for her when Mrs. Martin returned, informing her that Cade had telephoned to say he had a problem with one of the fences and couldn't get back to the house for lunch or for his appointment with her. He had left word that she could drive to the south pasture if she still wanted to talk, but that he had not changed his mind and she might as well return to California.

"Where's the road to the pasture?" Stephanie leaped to her feet, suddenly certain that Cade Steele was avoiding her deliberately and determined that he wasn't going to succeed.

"I can show you how to get there," Mrs. Martin answered, "but maybe you ought to stay here or go on back to your hotel. We've had a lot of rain lately, and the dirt roads on the ranch property get kind of muddy. They're not paved like the public highways. You'll get your car messed up."

"It will wash." Stephanie smoothed her skirt, took her keys from her purse and smiled at the housekeeper. "Don't worry about my car or me. Just direct me to where Mr. Steele is. I promised my boss that I would speak to him in person, and I'm not going to let him send me back without a chance to plead my case."

Mrs. Martin laughed. "I think you're about as stubborn as Cade is." She glanced at her watch. "I hate for the men to miss lunch. Would you mind taking along a picnic basket of sandwiches for them when you go?"

Ten minutes later Stephanie had the large wicker basket and a huge thermos of coffee in the trunk of her automobile and was slowly guiding the little sports car behind the house and down a narrow road that passed the barn and followed a row of white rail fences. Mrs. Martin had drawn a sketchy map on the back of an envelope, and from time to time Stephanie glanced at it to make sure she was heading in the right direction. With the sun directly overhead, it was easy to become confused amid the frequent curves and turns along the dirt path. In addition, she had to concentrate on keeping the car centered on the road, for Mrs. Martin's prediction of mud had proved correct. Sticky reddish brown clay was even more prominent along the edges of the path, and Stephanie could keep her wheels from getting stuck only by driving in the exact middle of the road.

It was much farther than she'd expected. She had not realized how large the Steele property was. After several minutes of driving she still wasn't near the pasture indicated by the large X on Mrs. Martin's map, and she picked up speed, sending flecks of mud flying from the tires of the car as she entered what appeared to be a long straight stretch of the road. She had seen no other vehicle, and it seemed unlikely that she would meet someone coming from the opposite direction, so she had few qualms about driving faster. Her control of the car was excellent despite the soggy ground, and the auto responded well to the road conditions.

Her mind raced with arguments to use when she finally met Cade Steele, so she didn't notice that she was pressing harder and harder on the gas pedal; not until a cottontail rabbit, startled by the sound of the car engine, dashed across the road in front of her, its ears flat against its head as it streaked to safety. Stephanie caught only a glimpse of the animal, but it was enough to make her slam on the brakes, sending the automobile into a slide. She pulled hard on the steering wheel, and for a moment she thought the car was going to straighten out, but it slid again on the soft slimy mud at the edge of the road and came to rest deep in a soggy batch of ocher clay.

Stephanie rested her head on the steering wheel for a moment, trying to settle her frayed nerves. Then she opened her door to check the damage and was dismayed to see that the tires on her side were at least three to four inches deep in the mire. She started the engine, eased the car into gear and pressed lightly on the accelerator, hoping that somehow the wheels would take hold and she could manage to maneuver the car out of the ditch. But she only succeeded in flinging mud against the rails of the nearby white fence, and the tires settled even deeper in their muddy prison.

She listened for sounds of other cars or of people, but the air was silent except for the occasional shrieks of blue jays, building their spring nests in nearby trees, and she knew that she would have to help herself. No one would be coming to her assistance.

Slipping out of her high-heeled navy pumps and sheer panty hose in an effort to protect as much of her clothing as possible, Stephanie pushed open the door on the passenger side of the car, where the ground wasn't so soggy. But even there her bare feet sank into the mire, sending clumps of damp soil almost to the level of her slender ankles. Taking careful steps, she managed to reach the back of the automobile, only to discover that both rear wheels were securely submerged. Maybe, she decided, if she could find some boards she could place them against the tires and get enough traction to work her way free. A quick scan of the area didn't reveal anything she could use, but after trudging along the length of the fence for a quarter of a mile, her feet all the while becoming more and more soiled and damp from the spongy earth, she discovered a small slab of wood that might work.

By the time Stephanie had the board in place against a tire, not only her feet but her hands, face and clothes were covered with mud. Still she kept working, reasoning that if she could free the car from the trap it was in, she could turn around, go back to the house and ask Mrs. Martin for assistance in cleaning up. There was no way she was going to face Cade Steele looking like this, even if it meant he had to go without his lunch for another hour. It would serve him right anyway; if he hadn't been so obstinate about seeing her, he could have had lunch in the comfort of his own home.

Stephanie was leaning against the car, trying to shake the mud from her hands as she planned her strategy, when she saw the man on horseback at the top of the hill. He was sitting easily in the saddle, almost one with the superb quarter horse he rode, and he was moving toward her and the fence that separated them surely but slowly, as if there was no rush in rescuing her from the mud where the car rested.

When he dismounted and hitched the reins to the top fence rail, Stephanie cast a grateful eye at him. For a moment she had been afraid he might be Cade Steele, and she couldn't let the ranch owner see her looking so disheveled. But this man, likely one of the cowboys employed by Steele, was too young to be the boss; he couldn't be more than thirty-five or thirty-six years old. Nonetheless, there was a definite maturity to his bearing as he strode toward Stephanie—and vitality and virility, as well.

As the rider drew nearer, Stephanie felt the imprint of the years she had worked with Jon Jenson. In spite of her anxiety about her predicament she cast a professional eye over the approaching ranch hand just as she did whenever she helped Jon judge the physical merits of the actors and actresses he was considering for roles in his movies.

That the man was tall Stephanie had known from

the moment he dismounted from his horse. But as he lithely scaled the fence with only one hand on a rail to propel him over the barrier, she took in his entire lean body, from the gray Stetson on his head to the long-sleeved plaid cotton shirt, taut across his broad chest, and the snugly fitting jeans that emphasized his narrow hips. His rugged face was as impressive as his physique.

Stephanie had seen a great many handsome men since she had been working for Jon Jenson, and the producer-director was one of the best-looking of them. But there was a sheer animal magnetism about the cowboy that instantly captured her attention. He had not only the good looks of a movie actor but charisma, as well. Somehow she knew that before he spoke a word.

"Wait until Jon sees him," she whispered to herself, knowing that her employer would want to cast this handsome man in the film. She wondered briefly if he could act, but she decided that was an unimportant detail. Jon could always use him for a role that didn't require dialogue—that is, if Cade Steele would let them use one of his workers and if he would even allow the filming at the ranch in the first place.

The man's mocking glance ended her musing. Autocratically and contemptuously he looked her up and down while he flicked his hat against the side of his jeans to shake off the dust that clung to it. As he did so, wavy coal-black hair fell across his forehead, making his face more appealing by softening some of the chiseled lines of his profile.

"Having trouble?" he asked with a jeering half

smile, causing Stephanie to blush. His steel-gray eyes, with flecks of darker gray around the irises, were appraising her in an intimate way, and she was acutely aware of the fact that she was covered in mud from her silky hair right down to her polished toenails. She had removed her powder-blue linen jacket, tossing it into the car before she searched for the board, and now she realized that her silk blouse was clinging tightly to her body, revealing the full curves of her breasts. She tried to make her way toward the car door so she could don her jacket again and keep the man's cold eyes from undressing her, as he now seemed to be doing.

"Do you think you could help me get my car out?" Stephanie couldn't hide the exasperation in her voice. The man could see that she was in trouble; he didn't need to stand there and leer at her!

"Not the way you're going about it," he replied curtly, not even bothering to walk to the rear of the automobile to inspect the problem.

Stephanie fought to overcome an almost irresistible urge to grab a chunk of damp clay and throw it at him. Damn him, anyway. How dared he look so clean and well groomed when she resembled a homeless waif from a Victorian novel! She tried to flick a wayward strand of hair off her face and found that, like the rest of her body, it was coated with mud.

"No doubt you're one of Cade Steele's employees," she lashed out at him, fatigue from her effort mixing with anger at the cowboy's insolent attitude. "You're about as helpful as he is."

"Probably." The man was undaunted by her insult.

With what little dignity she could manage, Stephanie picked her way around the car, flung open the door, grabbed her jacket and hurriedly put it on before gathering her purse, hose and shoes. She left the keys in the ignition. Perhaps someone with a bit more courtesy could be persuaded to pull her vehicle from the mud; it certainly wasn't going to be this oaf of a man. He simply proved her theory that, with the single exception of Jon, the handsomer a man was, the more likely he was to be a cad. She had placed her trust in a handsome man once before. Never again; particularly not in one with eyes that could bore into her and make even her bones shiver with unexplained anticipation.

She glanced sideways at the cowboy and frowned. He was enjoying this entire scene, she knew, treating her discomfort as a big joke. She could tell from the way he leaned easily against the fence post, even though his face was an expressionless mask, and she was also aware that he sensed her unbidden response to his sexuality.

Stephanie slammed the car door shut with a bang. Let him think what he wanted to about her; she wouldn't give him the satisfaction of begging for assistance. She would manage by herself, without any help from Cade Steele's insolent employees.

Without another look at the man, she began the long trek back to the Steele house, trying to make her way with dignity but self-consciously aware that it was a losing effort when her feet kept slipping in the mud. Behind her she could hear the man's deep-throated voice, but when she turned he was speaking into a walkie-talkie contraption instead of to her. After finishing his very brief conversation with who-ever was on the other end, he inserted the machine into a holder attached to his belt and faced her.

Gray eyes swept over her, lingering on her smudged face and lips. Then, while she stood im-mobile, rage making her blood almost boil at his refusal to help, she saw him retreat toward his horse on the opposite side of the fence and fling himself into the hand-tooled leather saddle. He swung the animal in a semicircle, away from Stephanie, who determinedly started back down the soggy road, care-fully picking the driest sections and ignoring the oc-casional pebbles that jabbed into her soft feet. Under her breath she swore at the cowboy—and at Cade Steele, whose attitude had evidently spread to his employees. Texans were reputed to be courteous, protective of women; well, now she knew better. Blast them all! She was better off in California, where men at least complimented you, even if they didn't mean it.

Absorbed in her fury, she didn't hear the horse ap-proaching, and when she looked up it was almost upon her. Somehow the man had circled around ahead of her to an opening in the fence she hadn't noticed, and he was now barring her path to the house, leaning forward against the saddle horn, wait-ing for her to make a move.

"Get out of my way," Stephanie snapped, not willing to play any games with the insolent cowboy.

"Do you know how long a walk it is?" he asked nonchalantly, his eyes fixed upon her bare feet, his mouth a hard line.

"I don't care how long it is. Get out of my way." She would have fought an army to get past him. His attitude was unbearable.

For answer he touched his boots to the horse's flanks, and the animal moved slowly toward Stephanie, barely clearing her body as it passed on her right. When the rider was even with her, he reached down and lifted her easily into the saddle in front of him, ignoring her flailing arms and legs as she tried to resist. The horse didn't even break stride, but her purse, shoes and hose went flying in all directions. The man ignored the loss of her possessions.

"Let me go," Stephanie screamed, terrified at his sudden attack. Panic was taking hold of her, fear replacing anger at his rough handling. Where was he taking her and what did he plan to do? She knew of the dangers of traveling alone, but she had never been frightened before. Would Jon search for her? Would Mike come looking? He was still in Dallas.

She jerked upright, attempting to twist her body so she could scratch his face with her long nails, but in his confining hold she could turn only fractions of an inch. "You can't kidnap me," she cried out. "I'll be missed. People know I'm here."

His laugh was almost a snort. "Surely you don't think you're appealing enough to kidnap," he informed her rudely. "I like my women to be washed, at least. You look like some kind of ragamuffin."

"I'll show you who's a ragamuffin." Stephanie

tried to leap from the horse, but the man's grip around her waist tightened even more, pulling her close against his wide chest.

"If you'd quit acting so ridiculous and settle down for a minute, I'd explain that someone will be on his way in a few minutes to tow your car out of the mud."

Her fears slightly abated, Stephanie stopped struggling, but her body remained tense, on guard. She was afraid to trust the stranger, but she was also concerned that if she didn't cooperate he might cancel any order to have her car rescued. His self-assurance proclaimed authority, strangely incongruous for a mere ranch employee.

"I'm taking you to the quarter-horse pasture. You can wait there until your car is ready." His breath was warm against her ear, and for a moment she succumbed to the hypnotic appeal of his soft voice and the satisfying feel of his hard arm around her, just below the swell of her full breasts.

"Oh," Stephanie answered in a quiet little voice. But then she began thinking about the man's arrogance, and her fury returned. She tried to wrench his arm from her waist, but it was like trying to fight a lion without a weapon: there was no possible way for her to win. She tried a new tactic. "Does Mr. Steele know his employees are so rude to guests?" she demanded.

"Most guests don't require rude handling," he informed her.

"Well, you can be assured that I'll report you the minute I see him." Stephanie could see the pasture just ahead, with a half dozen or so men working on a broken stretch of fence, so she felt braver than she would have otherwise. He couldn't retaliate with his employer within shouting distance.

He didn't say a word. He merely let go his hold on her waist and allowed her to slide unceremoniously to the ground. Stephanie had to grab the horse's long mane for a second to keep her balance. She glared up at the man, his face half-hidden by the brim of the Stetson, but he wasn't even looking at her. His attention was drawn to the men at the fence.

"How's it going?" he asked as he turned the horse toward them, leaving Stephanie to attempt to tuck the straying hemline of her blouse back into the waistband of her pleated skirt.

"Fair to middling, Cade," one of the men answered.

Cade. A chill swept through Stephanie's body. That couldn't be Cade Steele. There had to be a mistake. She distinctly remembered Mike's description of Cade Steele as an old codger. Perhaps this was a son of the owner; that would explain why they shared a strange hostility toward her. When she saw the Cade Steele she came to see she was going to be dressed properly, not barefoot with mud smeared in her hair and down one cheek. She had to look like someone he would respect, not like what this man had called her: a ragamuffin.

She watched incredulously as the man called to a young ranch hand who was leaving the area in a pickup truck. "When you get the car out, Steve, take it back to the house and clean it up."

"Right, boss."

Boss. My God, it *was* him! No wonder he acted like such an autocrat! Stephanie wanted the earth to open up and swallow her. She didn't want to call attention to herself, but she had to shout, "No, I need the car here."

Cade turned to look at her, his eyes narrowing as he surveyed her from top to bottom. "The car's dirty enough without you climbing into it the way you look," he informed her. "You can return to the house in one of the trucks. They won't mind a little more mud."

She would have liked to tell him what he could do with his trucks, but she had to speak up again. "The men's lunch is in the trunk. Mrs. Martin asked me to bring it."

"Drop the lunch off here, Steve, before you move the car." His gaze raked Stephanie for a moment, a hint of a sarcastic smile curving his lips. "Oh, one more thing, Steve. This *lady* lost some of her belonging on the road. Would you take them to the house when you go?"

Stephanie's pale face reddened at his emphasis on the word "lady" and his reference to her belongings. It was mortifying to think that he'd noticed her panty hose and specifically asked one of his men to pick them up. She waited uneasily to see what new insult he would throw her way, but Cade merely watched the man acknowledge the order and then turned back to the fence repair, as if he had forgotten entirely that Stephanie existed.

She was forced to stand there, trying to avoid the

curious glances of the workmen as they passed by her and noted her disheveled appearance and mud-covered feet. Her eyes focused on Cade Steele's broad back, at which she could cheerfully have slung any weapon she could get her hands on. Violence had never been a part of her nature, but Cade Steele was arousing new emotions, and she didn't like any of them.

CHAPTER TWO

THE PICKUP had returned and the food was being distributed among the men before Cade noticed Stephanie again. He was gathering a couple of foil-wrapped sandwiches from the basket when he glanced at her, still standing awkwardly where he had left her, and tossed one of the packages her way.

"Here—eat this, grab yourself a cup of coffee and let's get on our way. We don't have time to waste."

As hungry as she was, Stephanie still wanted to defy the man, but she meekly unwrapped the sandwich and took a quick bite of the ham and cheese on crusty homemade wheat bread. One of the men brought a heavy mug of coffee to her and invited her to sit down on a saddle that was resting on the ground, but Cade interrupted with a sharp, "She doesn't have to sit. She's caused us enough of a delay as it is."

He leaped into the driver's seat of a nearby Jeep, brusquely threw open the opposite door and motioned for Stephanie to join him. For a minute she hesitated, wanting to remind him that he had said she could wait at the pasture until one of the trucks left for the house. But refusing to go with him would only create a scene and end whatever tiny chance there remained to talk the man into leasing a section of his property to Jon. She had barely settled in her place before he had the vehicle in gear and was careering down the path.

"Aren't you afraid of getting stuck in the mud?" she couldn't help asking.

He glanced at her sideways. "I know how to drive," he informed her coldly.

"So do I," Stephanie retorted.

"I noticed," he replied dryly.

Stephanie stared out the window. An optical illusion made the ground seem to whiz past the Jeep instead of the other way around. Her head ached, the sandwich felt like a stone in the pit of her stomach, and her muscles protested from the unexpected strain of trying to move the car. She had no strength left to fight, and she was grateful that at least Cade Steele didn't prolong the quarrel. He fell into as moody a silence as she did, not indicating where they were going or when they would be back at his house.

After a few minutes the stillness became even more oppressive than Cade's belligerent words had been, and she knew she had to shatter the terrible quiet somehow. Besides, talk was better than thinking. She didn't even want to think of this day again, not when she had failed Jon so miserably.

Would it do any good to mention the movie now, she wondered. A quick glance at Cade's jutting jawline gave her no hope, but Jon was counting on her to try, and when she got out of this Jeep she probably would never see Cade Steele again. This was the only opportunity she would have.

"Mr. Steele—" she tried to make her voice sound calm and pleasant "—I'd like to discuss the leasing of part of your property for the movie."

"Forget it."

He spoke so brusquely that for a moment Stephanie wasn't even certain he had replied. She took a deep breath, silently wishing that Mike could have handled this job by himself, that Jon had made the trip, that anyone had tried to reason with Cade Steele but her. She wasn't sure there was a single person in the entire world who could force him to listen to reason, but she had to make another attempt.

"I think you may have the wrong impression of the movie industry," she continued, as if he had not rejected her first effort at conversation. "I can assure you that all our people are professionals and that we know what we're doing."

Cade swung the wheel of the Jeep viciously, turning the vehicle onto a narrow path leading to a green pasture where some white-faced Hereford cattle were grazing. He hit the brakes hard, snapped off the ignition and was out of the Jeep practically the instant he opened the door. Not even bothering to respond to her comment, he slipped the latch on the gate and with long strides joined a couple of men who were examining a young calf.

While he was gone, Stephanie took advantage of the opportunity to wipe some of the mud off her arms, legs and feet with an old rag that had been on the floor, but she kept an eye out for Cade's return, consciously bracing herself for his attack when she saw him swiftly moving toward her.

He didn't even glance at her, much less speak. Sliding the gearshift into reverse, he maneuvered the Jeep back onto the road and off to another destination, where he again checked on work that was being done on the ranch.

Stephanie tried once more to talk to him as they traversed the twisting paths that skirted the trees. "I'd really appreciate it, Mr. Steele, if you'd at least listen to what I have to say. It's important."

He looked at her for a long moment, then turned his attention back to the road; his eyes were freezingly cold, chilling Stephanie with disdain. "I can't imagine anything about the movies being important." He stopped the Jeep beside a barn in which Stephanie could see large bales of hay stored and honked the horn. While a rotund balding man ambled toward them, wiping his brow with a red handkerchief as he came, Cade added in a tone so demanding that Stephanie knew there was no point in pleading any further, "I told you on the telephone that I have a ranch to run and that I have no use for movie people. Now *I* would appreciate it if you'd keep quiet and let me attend to my business."

She sat stonily silent while Cade spoke to the employee, paying little attention to the conversation except to notice that Cade was displeased because some piece of equipment wasn't functioning correctly and the heavyset man was blaming the problem on a defective engine. "Damn," Cade muttered, returning to the driver's seat, "we've got to have that engine."

As he practically raced the Jeep away from the barn and onto another road that Stephanie hadn't seen before, she began to realize exactly how immense the Steele ranch was and how much effort it must take to direct operations. She had already seen at least a dozen employees, and she felt there must be others elsewhere on the property. A grudging respect for the job Cade handled began to grow inside her. But even if he was overworked, he didn't have any right to take out his frustrations on her.

It had to be more than that, she mused. His objections to movies couldn't have anything to do with the fact that his ranch was a busy place and it was a logistical problem to see that everything was done on schedule. No, his hostility surely stemmed from some much deeper source. She cast a sideways glance at the man beside her in the Jeep, at the strong jawline with a slight cleft in the wide chin. He seemed to bear a grudge against the entire entertainment industry, and there must be some personal reason behind it.

Something to do with a woman, she speculated. Perhaps his wife wanted to go into the theater and he objected. Maybe he had a daughter who aspired to be a dancer or a singer, and he was concerned about the potential negative aspects of that life-style. She couldn't resist an offhand glance at his left hand. There was no wedding ring on his finger, but that might not mean anything; many men didn't wear rings, particularly those working outdoors or around machinery that might catch the ring and cause injury.

She would have liked to ask, but the scowl on his face was so forbidding she remained mutely eyeing the scenery.

At the next stop Cade left the Jeep and motioned for Stephanie to accompany him. She didn't want to get out in front of the cowboys who were at the scene; she looked so bedraggled that she preferred to remain inconspicuous. But Cade insisted, and without her shoes she could only awkwardly pick her way across the rocky hillside to a building that seemed to serve as some type of a shop. A couple of men were busily repairing equipment, and one of them talked seriously with Cade for several minutes about the condition of the engine.

"We'll just have to go get a new part," Cade decided after listening to the explanation of why the engine could not be fixed immediately. "Jake, let's take the truck. Carl, you bring the Jeep back to the house when you finish." He tossed the keys to an angular cowboy who was tinkering with a bit and bridle.

When they departed, Stephanie found herself in the center of the truck seat, jammed up alarmingly close to Cade to make room for the hefty man who accompanied them. The hard muscles of Cade's arm brushed against her sleeve, making her acutely aware of his masculinity.

"This is the woman from the movies," Cade introduced her with a marked lack of enthusiasm, spitting out the word "movies" with disdain, as if it were a curse.

"Pleased to meet you," the man acknowledged

her, not even aware, as Stephanie was, of Cade's debasing tone.

The men talked over her head for the thirty minutes it took to drive off the ranch and into a little town that intrigued Stephanie with its one stoplight and old-fashioned general store. If she had been presentable and if conditions had been right, she would have liked to browse through the place, but she was forced to wait inside the truck while the two men entered the building to purchase the needed part. She could see them through the window of the store, both chatting amiably with the shopkeeper while he boxed their purchase and wrote out a receipt. Once Cade even laughed, startling Stephanie. Somehow she had not associated laughter with the man. He seemed so stern, so imposing, so arrogant, his few smiles only mocking her, that it was a shock to realize he could actually enjoy a conversation.

He was still smiling as he left the store and, with Jake's help, placed the bundle in the bed of the truck. But the curved lines of his mouth vanished completely when he opened the cab door and looked at Stephanie. She was the reason for his anger, she knew, but she didn't know why.

"We'll get out at the house, Jake, and you can deliver the part and see that it's installed," Cade informed his employee as they pulled through the front entrance of the ranch.

"Will do, boss." Jake reached for Stephanie's hand and shook it vigorously. "It was nice to meet you, little lady," he told her, and Stephanie couldn't help but respond with an answering smile.

"You sure are a tiny thing, aren't you?" Jake continued, her grin seeming to encourage his conversation. "Need some good corn bread and beans to fatten you up a little. And quiet, too—you hardly say a word."

Cade's low snort cut off Jake's friendly chatter, but Stephanie merely compressed her lips to contain a harsh retort. It was too late, and she was too tired for any more turmoil. All she wanted to do was to get back to her hotel, take a hot bath and go to bed. And, if possible, forget that this day had ever happened....

But Cade wasn't that eager to free her bonds. When the truck stopped by the kitchen door, he hustled her out of the pickup and into the house, calling for his housekeeper as they entered.

Within moments he had asked Mrs. Martin to show Stephanie to a bath and to wash her clothes. He pivoted and was gone before Stephanie could tell him that she preferred driving back to Dallas as she was. She had been in muddy clinging garments so long now that another hour wouldn't make any difference.

But the housekeeper wouldn't listen, either, and Stephanie found herself stripping off her clothes and stepping into a hot shower in an unusually large bathroom on the second floor of the house. It was surprisingly modern for an older home, spotlessly clean, bright and shining with yellow paint on the walls and a sunflower-patterned carpet on the floor that soothed Stephanie's sore feet. She lingered under the sharp warm spray of water from the shower, letting the drops carry every vestige of mud from her hair and skin.

By the time she had towel dried and wrapped a second cloth around her wet locks, Mrs. Martin had returned with her purse and shoes, cleaned and polished to a high shine, in addition to her panty hose and a long hostess-style robe.

"Steve brought your things back with the car, and I went ahead and washed your stockings and cleaned your shoes," Mrs. Martin explained. Noticing Stephanie looking questioningly at the silky pale blue garment held up before her, the housekeeper explained, "This belongs to Cade's mother. She stays here occasionally when she thinks Cade needs some of her home cooking or when I'm busy canning or freezing the fruit crops." There was admiration in the woman's voice for a mother who cared so much about her grown son.

"Where is Mr. Steele's wife?" The question had been on Stephanie's mind for most of the afternoon, and at last she couldn't contain her curiosity.

"Oh, he's had a couple of close calls, as my husband says, but that man's a hard one to catch," Mrs. Martin answered cheerfully while Stephanie fastened the soft sash of the robe. The pale blue of the silk fabric enhanced the deeper blue of her eyes, giving them added luster and sparkle.

"You mean he's not married." It was halfway between a statement and a question.

"No, Cade's single and likely to stay that way as far as I can see. Not that the women don't want him. They flutter their eyelashes at him all the time, but ever since Merilee he's been immune to their attempts to attract him.''

''Merilee?''

''A girl from his past. From a long time ago. Everyone thought they would get married, but Merilee left here and she's never been back.'' The housekeeper picked up Stephanie's damp clothes and added them to a basket of laundry she was carrying. ''I don't know what happened, and I don't guess I ever will. Cade's not one to talk about his personal life.''

Stephanie removed the towel from her head and shook the long locks before brushing out tangles with the small brush she carried in her purse. Could it be because of Merilee that Cade didn't like her?

''Mrs. Martin, did Merilee look like me?''

''Oh, no, child. She was a redhead, much taller than you and always talking. She chattered like a magpie all the time. My Ben says Cade couldn't have asked her to marry him: she wouldn't have stopped talking long enough!''

Stephanie fluffed her hair, letting the warm air dry her light gold tresses. Her brain raced with conflicting thoughts. It couldn't have been because of the other girl anyway. Cade Steele had been antagonistic even before he had seen Stephanie. His attitude toward her must have something to do with movies—something awful that made him hate the industry and everyone connected with it. Especially Stephanie.

''Take your time getting your hair dry,'' Mrs. Martin advised her. ''It will take an hour or so to get your clothes washed and dried, and supper will be ready by then." She rubbed the fabric of Stephanie's skirt with a rough finger. "Is it all right to put this in the washing machine?"

"Yes, but I won't be here for dinner," Stephanie hastened to correct Mrs. Martin's ideas about her plans for the evening. "I'll be leaving as soon as my clothes are ready."

"I've already got a steak set out for you, and I don't take no for an answer, either. I'm a lot like Cade."

Stephanie paused, her brush in midair. "Where is Mr. Steele?" she asked. "I should tell him goodbye before I leave." *And not inflict more torture on either of us,* she added to herself.

"He's downstairs in the den waiting for you." The housekeeper took the basket of clothes and briskly left for the laundry room.

As quickly as she could, Stephanie applied powder and a dash of lipstick and eye shadow from the small makeup kit she carried in her purse. Her hair was still damp, but at least it was clean, and it would have to do. She needed to see Cade Steele as soon as possible, to tell him she was going. Then, once her clothes were finished in the washer and dryer, she could be on her way back to her hotel. The thought of Dallas had never seemed more inviting.

When Stephanie entered the small den that doubled as the ranch office, she found her reluctant host lounging in a black leather chair. The nearby desk was filled with papers, account books and magazines pertaining to agriculture, and a well-worn veterinary-medicine text sat on one corner. Cade stood when he saw her, and for a moment Stephanie was flattered by the courtesy; then she remembered that it would be an ingrained habit with the Texan, that he was trained from childhood to stand up when women or older people entered a room.

"Do you want a drink?" he asked, his tone blandly cordial.

"No." She slipped into the chair he indicated opposite the one where he had been sitting.

He had showered and changed, too, and was now attired in a creamy silk shirt with tan slacks that hugged his long athletic body as he settled back in his chair. Extending his legs to their full length, he tucked the heels of his dressy boots into the edge of an oval fringed rug that had been placed between the two facing chairs. Though his posture was relaxed, he had a proud bearing that came so naturally it couldn't be disguised; a demeanor that wouldn't allow Stephanie to forget that this man controlled what must be hundreds of acres of rich ranchland and the lives of the men who did his bidding.

Her full rosy lips quivered for a second under his steady gaze, but she quickly gained control, adopting a tenuous air of confidence to assist her in dealing with a man whom she suspected to be totally ruthless.

"You have a few minutes to recite your propaganda piece before Mrs. Martin serves dinner," he told her with a sneer. "Then we can drop the subject of filming at my ranch and have a leisurely meal."

"I'm not staying for dinner." Their eyes locked in battle.

"You're wasting time, Miss Lasater." He twirled the drink in his hand, jarring Stephanie with the clink of ice against the sides of the glass.

"Yes, I certainly am." She felt undressed and at a disadvantage in the hostess gown, although it was not low cut or deliberately seductive. Still, it clung to the sides of her body, revealing the outline of her firm breasts, narrow waist and flared hips. He was so cosmopolitan in his new attire that he would have been at home in Manhattan, and Stephanie felt like a child trying to argue with an adult. "I think I'd better leave."

"In that?" He raked her with his derisive glance, sending a rush of pink color to her face.

"Oh, don't worry, Mr. Steele. I'm not going to run off with your mother's robe. I'll get my own clothes from Mrs. Martin."

"They're probably a bit wet right now." He was so certain she wasn't going to walk out that he didn't even stir from his chair when Stephanie jumped to her feet and started for the door.

"I don't care if they're dripping wet!" she snapped at him. "I'm leaving."

"And not complete your assignment?" His tone was challenging—deliberately so, she knew, but she found herself stopping with her hand on the doorknob. "My, my, Miss Lasater, I would think you were more of a professional than that."

Her voice shook with livid anger when she turned back to him. "And would you listen to me if I stayed?"

He waved a hand imperiously toward the empty

chair. "I told you that you could give me your spiel until dinner was ready."

She hesitated, knowing that he was taunting her but realizing that Jon would expect her to do all she could to win the obstinate rancher's approval. "My briefcase is in the car. It has all the data I need to show you."

Cade leaned forward in his chair, his muscles tensing with energy, like a cougar about to attack. "I don't care about papers. Surely you can talk without reading notes."

"Yes, I can." Stephanie sat down again stiffly, clenching and unclenching her hands. "What would you like me to tell you?"

He shrugged indifferently. "Whatever it is that you came here to say. Just don't take too long; it's been a busy day, and I'll be ready to eat as soon as Mrs. Martin announces dinner."

Stephanie took a deep breath and began to talk, nervously at first, but soon opening up and speaking with ease and enthusiasm about Jon's picture. She outlined the amount of land that would be leased, the proposed working schedule, the number of people involved and some of the logistics of bringing in all of the equipment needed for filming.

"Of course we will make certain that your property is respected and that everything is left as it was before," she assured Cade, who had sat silently watching her for fifteen minutes, his expression obscured by the smoke curling from the cigarette he held lightly between two tanned fingers.

"I'm sure," he responded dryly.

"You don't believe me, but it's true. Jon has a special crew that cleans up every single day. There won't be a scrap of paper blowing across any of your fields."

He extinguished the cigarette with a harsh movement. "Are you telling me that no one will even drop a cigarette butt on the ground?"

"Yes."

He leaned back in his chair, his arms reaching up to rub the muscles at the base of his neck. He must be tired, Stephanie realized, and for a second she felt a pang of sympathy for the man. He carried the responsibility for everything happening on his vast property. Her mood swiftly changed, however, when Cade abruptly caught her hand, pulled her to her feet and half dragged her toward the picture window at one end of the room.

"Look at those fields," he ordered, but Stephanie found it hard to concentrate on a view that at any other time would have intrigued her. His closeness and the heady masculine scent of his body besieged her senses, increasing her awareness of the dark curly chest hairs that lay exposed above the vee opening of his shirt and of the natural sensuality in the way he stood, seemingly at ease but tautly aware of her every action and reaction.

"What about them?" It was an effort to speak.

"Do you know what one carelessly discarded cigarette could do to them, particularly in the summertime, when you propose to bring your crew here?" A strong hand gripped her shoulder. "Did you know we sometimes go for a month or more without any rain in July and August, that the land becomes a tinderbox, just waiting to explode into raging grass fires?''

"Smoking will be controlled. There won't be any cigarettes dropped on the ground.'' She felt paralyzed, unable to escape from the hold he had on her.

"I can't believe that." His hand left her body as quickly as it had touched her, but it took a moment for Stephanie to realize that he had turned away from her, toward the tiny bar, where he was adding ice cubes to his drink.

"Don't you prevent cigarettes from being thrown on the ground by your workers?'' She spoke with a planned insolence and was rewarded by a flicker of anger in his steely eyes.

"Certainly, but my men respect the land, and they take pains not to hurt it.''

"Jon Jenson respects it, too.''

"Ah, yes, Jon Jenson. The wonder boy of motion pictures. I've heard of him.''

"Then you know that he will make a picture to be proud of,'' Stephanie defended her employer and friend. "He has promised that this film will be a truthful account of Texas following the Civil War.''

Cade slammed the glass on the bar and covered the distance between them in two swift strides.

"You don't think I believe that, do you?'' His hands gripped her arms fiercely. "You know and I know that people from Hollywood don't always say what they mean,'' he snapped. "Who knows what your Jon Jenson might do with this movie?''

Stephanie's face turned crimson with anger.

"That's not true," she declared. "You don't know Jon or you wouldn't say that. He is scrupulously honest both with his films and with his crew. He cares about people and places and things." Tears clouded her blue eyes, giving them a brightness that added to the beauty of her oval face and clear creamy complexion.

Why did everyone always believe the worst about movie stars and directors, she wondered. True, the popular magazines promoted an image that wasn't altogether wrong, but Stephanie had a great many friends in the industry, people who were devoted to their families, people who wouldn't stab others in the back for top billing in a picture. Jon was temperamental, of course. His artistic sensibility couldn't tolerate imperfection, and he had received some unfavorable publicity because of it. The columnists said he was a prima donna, but they didn't know the real Jon Jenson. And someone like Cade Steele would be eager to believe the worst.

Her opinion was confirmed when he scoffed openly as he pulled her closer to him, almost burying her face against the soft fabric of his shirt. She could feel the heavy thumping of his heart, like the angry beat of a war drum.

"You certainly defend your employer. He sounds too good to be true." His hand curled through her hair, forcing her face upward toward his harsh jaw. "What is he—your lover?"

Stephanie tried to jerk free of his hold, but the strength of his arms kept her imprisoned.

"I hate you," she cried, amazed to find herself

blurting out the intense dislike she felt for a man she hardly knew.

One arm circled her back, continuing to press her lightly against his hard body, while his free hand skimmed lightly over her face and traced the outline of her lips.

"Now, now, Miss Lasater," he scolded, "is that any way to act?" His touch was like hot metal against her skin, and Stephanie was powerless to stop the fingers that were sliding down along her neck toward the chasm between her breasts. "Isn't it time for your seduction of me?" His lips hovered teasingly over hers.

Rage gave her strength, and Stephanie lunged free of his grasp, toward the door and safety.

"You're an arrogant, egotistical, chauvinistic...." She couldn't find insults rapidly enough to suit her. "What makes you think I'd ever want to seduce you?"

"That's why you came, isn't it?"

"It certainly is not!"

He took a step toward her, and Stephanie turned the brass knob of the door. She had to get away from this despicable excuse for a man.

"I'm not naive, Miss Lasater." He turned away, back to the desk, where he paused to light a cigarette with a gold-plated ivory-inlaid table lighter. "When that young man who was here failed to obtain my blessing, your Jon Jenson decided the assignment needed a woman's touch. That's why he sent his girl friend." His gaze burned into her. "I'm sure he must know how suited you are to the purpose. I might not respond to the offer of money for the use of my land, but I'd be bound to agree if it meant having the pleasure of your lovely body.''

''I can't believe this.'' Stephanie was too upset to flee.

''You can't believe I figured out your scheme.'' Before she could react he was beside her, his tall body looming over her. ''What do you take me for anyway, a dumb hick from Texas? We are educated down here, you know. We even understand the wiles of women.'' His chuckle was harsh and demeaning. ''But getting your car stuck in the mud—that did require some imagination. I have to compliment you on that.''

''I'm getting my clothes and I'm leaving, and I hope I never see you again!''

''Do that,'' Cade advised. ''You'll look even sexier with wet clothes clinging to that curvy little body of yours. That might be exactly what it takes to win me over.''

''You really do have a low opinion of women, don't you?'' she challenged him. ''Well, I'm glad I don't have to be around you any longer. Goodbye, Mr. Steele. It was definitely not a pleasure to meet you.'' She whirled out of the room, almost running down the hallway to the kitchen, half-afraid he would follow and drag her back to the den for more insults. But when she looked back there was no sign of Cade. Apparently he had vented his anger upon her and was satisfied.

Mrs. Martin was every bit as much of a problem in her own nice way. She simply refused to allow Stephanie to depart until her clothes were completely ready, and she insisted that the visitor stay for dinner.

"It's no problem, really," the housekeeper assured her. "We're just having chicken-fried steak and baked potatoes with sour cream. And there's an apple cobbler for dessert."

But Stephanie had no appetite, not after her scene with Cade Steele. How could he possibly think that she would use her body as an enticement? Why did men always think that? It had happened before, and she had fled from the scene—all the way across the country, from New York City to Los Angeles. And now she was running again, back to California and the safety of her friend Jon. He at least respected her as a woman. Jon had never even made a pass at her, treating her instead as an invaluable assistant in his film productions.

"I simply can't stay." The tremor in her voice caused Mrs. Martin to stop tossing the green salad and look up.

"If you're worried about driving back after dark, you can spend the night here," she suggested. "I'm certain that Cade wouldn't object."

"In fact, I insist." The deep voice behind her was so startlingly close that Stephanie almost jumped. "I had already decided you weren't going to drive back to Dallas alone this evening."

"You don't make my decisions, Mr. Steele." Stephanie didn't care if Mrs. Martin was near enough to hear the argument. The housekeeper had probably heard many more if Cade treated everyone in this overbearing manner.

"I'm making this one," he informed her matter-of-factly. "Remember, I have your car keys." Nonchalantly he strode across the large kitchen and poured a glass of iced tea from the pitcher on the long counter that curved around two sides of the room.

"I'll walk back if I have to," she defied him, "but I'm not staying here...not tonight, not ever, and not even another hour!"

"Sit down, Miss Lasater," he responded calmly, pulling out a chair from the round oak table in the center of the room. "I believe dinner is about to be served."

Before she realized what she was doing, Stephanie had obeyed the command and was sitting at the table watching the housekeeper place a platter of steaks, fried in crispy milk-egg-flour batter, on the table. Although the meat was so tender it could be cut with a fork, Stephanie could only find the strength to push it around her plate despondently. She had no appetite and no energy. This day with Cade Steele had left her completely drained.

She eyed him warily. They were eating alone, Mrs. Martin having excused herself to return to her own section of the house to have dinner with her husband. But the endless arguing didn't seem to have disturbed her dining partner's appetite: he had two helpings of dessert followed by a tall glass of ice-cold milk before wiping his lips with the edge of a checkered linen napkin and leaning back in his chair to stare at Stephanie. She glared back at him.

"May I have my keys?" It came out like a question, but she meant it as an ultimatum. Cade Steele would find that he couldn't order her around; she wasn't on his payroll. Examining the gray eyes that hypnotically held hers, she knew he was aptly named. Steele: it was the perfect name for him. He was as hard as the steel beams that held up skyscrapers, and he was, like the powerful foundations, not about to bend with the breeze.

"Are you telling me you don't want the pleasure of my company tonight?" A cutting smile flickered across his face.

"That's exactly what I'm telling you." She rose from the table and held out her hand, palm up, to accept the keys.

"You're not driving that far by yourself at night." It was a flat statement, leaving no room for dispute.

"I certainly am."

"Miss Lasater—" he turned on her viciously "—maybe where you come from women carouse around at all hours, but here we don't let our women go out by themselves at night. It's too dangerous. No telling what might happen, particularly the way you drive."

"I'm not one of *your* women, as you put it." How dared he try to take charge! She dashed through the kitchen to the small laundry room that was adjacent to it and pulled her clothes rapidly from the dryer, barely taking time to separate them from the other items that Mrs. Martin had placed in the same wash. Cade was still in the kitchen when she rushed back through. She didn't say a word to him but just swept up the stairs to change into her suit.

When she returned five minutes later, Cade was waiting for her at the bottom of the stairs. Her keys were in his hand, and a light tan Stetson was on his head. "Are you walking me to my car?" she asked sarcastically. "After all, it might be dangerous for me to step out the front door...."

"It might be even more dangerous for you to stay on this side of the door," was his sharp reply.

She looked up at him, but she couldn't read anything in his bland expression. He took her arm and led her toward the front entrance. "I'm taking you to your hotel."

"Don't be ridiculous." Stephanie tried to stop where she was, but Cade's strong arm propelled her forward. "How will you get back?"

"I'll spend the night at the hotel," he told her, still steering her toward the little red car that stood in the driveway.

"They might not have a room," she objected.

"In that case I'll have to share yours, won't I?" His tone left no doubt that he was firmly convinced Stephanie had been sent to Texas to win his approval for the filming by using her feminine charms.

"You'll never share anything of mine," she replied hotly, trying to turn toward the driver's side. But Cade adroitly maneuvered her to the opposite side of the car, opened the door and almost shoved her inside. She seethed as he strolled around the front of the vehicle and took his place behind the wheel, as if he had the right to be there.

"Don't you have too much work on the ranch to spare the time to drive to Dallas?" she asked bitterly.

"That's right," he answered tersely.

She turned to him. "Then why are you doing it?"

But the only answer she got was a hard appraising look, one that x-rayed her. He started the engine, turned on the lights and began the drive to Dallas.

When they arrived Cade insisted on accompanying her inside the hotel, ignoring her protests, treating her as if she were a six-year-old, and making it worse by doing so with a courtesy that was blatantly false.

At the door to her room he watched as she turned the key in the lock. She paused to think of a way to put him in his place as she said goodbye, but she didn't have the opportunity. He followed her so closely that he was in the room before she could slam the door shut.

"I didn't invite you in." She held the door half open so that he could leave.

"I'm sure you meant to," he commented while he looked around the small but elegantly furnished room. "It was an oversight." Noting the stack of books haphazardly strewed on the dresser, he picked up the top two and scanned the covers.

"I see you're doing research on Texas," he told her.

"I told you that the movie is going to be accurate in its portrayal of the state." She stood with her back stiffly against the door. "The film is based on a novel by Carter Graham, who's a well-known historian and writer."

"I know him," Cade cut her off sharply. "But your movie may not be anything like the book. Most movies aren't."

Stephanie sighed, a deep racking sigh that convulsed her body. Lord, would she ever get anything through the stubborn head of this impossible man!

"The movie," she tried to explain, "is titled *A Passionate Land*. It tells the story of a man from the time he returns to Texas following the Civil War, when he's twenty years old, through the rest of his life."

Cade's eyes were on her, almost daring her to complete the story and prove that she was not taking liberties with history.

"The working script is in my briefcase if you'd like to read it," she told him, still hugging the door.

"No," he replied, settling his large body in the one small chair that was in the room and, amazingly enough, looking graceful in the process. "You can tell me about it."

Stephanie began to speak, and as she became absorbed in the story she started strolling absently around the room. Finally she settled on the bed, one leg curled under her, while, gripped with emotion, she described the hunger and the poverty in the state following the devastating war between the North and the South. The main character, she explained, had come back to find his home falling apart, his father dead and his mother and younger sisters ill. There was no work to be had, but there were herds of longhorn cattle roaming wild and free on the open ranges in the state.

Her eyes brightened as she explained how the hero would work to gather the longhorns and herd them north to Kansas. Slowly he would restore his home, purchase more land and establish his own herds of cattle, switching over in his middle years from the longhorns to white-faced Herefords, more popular with beef-eating Americans for their tender meat. But he could never give up his longhorns completely, keeping a small herd intact for sentimental reasons even as the animals were disappearing from the state.

Naturally the story would have a love interest. Kara Warren, one of Jon's favorite actresses, had been signed to play the role of the woman who comes to Texas to visit a relative and stays to create a new generation with the man she loves.

A Passionate Land had a natural appeal for movie fans, Stephanie knew, and the novel on which it was based had won critical acclaim when it was published three years earlier. She had talked to the author when Jon decided to make the film, and he had been very encouraging when she mentioned that Jon wanted to film in Texas, even suggesting the north Texas area as the best location.

The characters were fictitious, of course, but Carter Graham had made them very believable, basing them, he said, on his extensive research as a historian.

Perhaps some people really were like the strong Texan of the book and the beautiful wife who shared his dreams, Stephanie mused. She almost wished they had been actual people, not just made-up characters in a book. After reading the novel again and again, she had developed a strong affection for the fictional Will Ransom; like the heroine, she might easily have fallen in love with him in just a few days. Her eyes became misty at the thought, but she blinked a time or two and went on with her account of the story.

Stephanie didn't know how long she had been talking, but when she finished she was surprised that Cade had let her run on as long as she must have done. He hadn't interrupted with a comment or question the entire time, but his eyes hadn't left her, and she suddenly realized that her position on the double bed was rather suggestive. She didn't want Cade to have any more reason to think she had been sent here to seduce him, and hastily she rose and smoothed the satiny bedspread.

Cade sat mute for a minute longer. Stephanie wanted to shatter the oppressive silence, but she didn't know what to say. Her anger at him had been dissipated by her account of the movie's plot, so she waited for him to speak while she watched the twinkling lights of downtown Dallas from the window.

"You'll report to me personally every single evening the film crew is on my property," he suddenly announced, and Stephanie whirled in surprise. He was still seated in the little chair, staring at the floor, his fingers intertwined as if he were about to pop his knuckles. She could almost see the tension in his body.

"There will be no charge for using the ranchland, but I want to know each night what you plan to do the next day. I don't want my employees bothered, and I don't want my cattle and horses disturbed any more than necessary. I intend to be present anytime you film the longhorns." He looked up at Stephanie. "Do I make myself perfectly clear?"

Her eyes were wide, but her tongue was thick, and she could only nod her assent. She watched him stand up, pick up his hat from the end of the bed where he had dropped it as he entered the room, and take her car keys from his pocket to toss them onto the dresser.

"You will be responsible for anything that happens," he told her. "Not the producer or the actors or anyone else. I expect to have a complete report by seven o'clock every night."

Taking her stunned silence as agreement, he strode to the door and walked out without looking back. Stephanie stood like a statue, staring at the closed door. She was too numb to feel any exultation at the fact that her mission had finally been accomplished.

CHAPTER THREE

STEPHANIE SHOULDN'T HAVE HAD TIME to think about Cade Steele. Her days and most of her evenings had been filled with preparations for the filming in Texas ever since, after a virtually sleepless night following Cade's abrupt departure from her hotel room, she had called Jon to let him know they had been granted permission to make the movie on the Steele ranch.

Jon had been ecstatic at the news and immediately began listing a variety of jobs he wanted Stephanie to take care of while she was in Dallas. There were so many things to do before production could begin. She had to hire a talent agency to handle the task of auditioning area actors and actresses for the minor roles in the movie, and she had to make arrangements for hotel rooms for the people coming from California. Plus, Jon wanted her to take care of leasing as much equipment as possible from the movie-production companies that had made Dallas one of the largest film centers in the country. And she also had to find a caterer to provide lunch for the cast and crew each day of shooting. Mike would be there to help, but she knew Jon would be counting on her to make certain everything was handled properly.

She had tried to tell him that she didn't think they

should make any definite commitments until Cade Steele actually had signed the lease, but Jon was too involved with plans for the film to listen.

"If he told you it was all right, I'm sure there's no problem," Jon assured her. "Now, could you arrange for some aerial photography of the part of the ranch we'll be using? I want our set designers to build a scale model so I can plan each specific shot before we get to Dallas."

She didn't tell him about Cade's order that she report to him every night by seven and that she was to be held responsible for anything that went wrong. Perhaps she hadn't heard him correctly. Maybe Cade would forget...although she had the uneasy feeling that Cade Steele was not the type of man to forget anything.

By the time she entered the hotel coffee shop for breakfast, she had decided that she would have to find some way to stay in California while the picture was being made. Surely there was plenty of work for her to do there, and Jon could explain, should Cade ask, that he simply couldn't spare her from his office.

Warily she scanned the coffee shop, afraid that she might see Cade, but if he had actually spent the night at the hotel, he wasn't having breakfast there now. Probably he had roused an employee from bed at an unbelievably early hour to drive in to Dallas to get him. That was the kind of thing Cade would do.

He shouldn't have accompanied her anyway. She was perfectly able to take care of herself, and she didn't need him to protect her. But if he hadn't, they might not have talked again, and he might never have given permission for the filming.

Why had he, anyway? Mentally she reviewed the conversation of the previous night while she waited for her order of a cinnamon roll and coffee. There hadn't seemed to be any particular turning point in their talk—her monologue, actually. Cade hadn't said a word until he had suddenly told her it was all right to use the ranch. There was no time she could pinpoint when he had acted interested in what she was saying. All she could remember was his gray eyes on her, eyes that shielded whatever he was thinking.

It didn't matter, though. She had won. She stirred the coffee the waitress placed before her in a beige pottery mug and stared at the unappetizing roll. Or had she won? Cade's harsh face seemed to fade in and out of her vision. Somehow she couldn't believe he would give in on something in which he believed so strongly. And he had definite views about the movies, none of them good. He was an enigma for certain, and Stephanie didn't think she would ever know what had changed his mind. But she had an uneasy feeling that she had been manipulated and that she was about to fall into a trap Cade had waiting for her.

Surveying her hastily scribbled notes from the telephone conversation with Jon, she knew there would be little time to speculate about Cade's decision. She had a busy few days ahead.

It took most of the morning to go over the assignments with Mike and plan what each would do. Then Stephanie settled in the middle of her bed, her legs

crossed under her, and reached for the phone. There
were a lot of calls to make.

By the time she was ready to return to Los Angeles
a week later, she had made virtually all the arrangements. Fortunately, she had been required to call the
Steele ranch only once, to warn Cade that the
photographer would be flying low over the property
to take pictures. As well, she had to arrange with him
a location for storing trailers of heavy equipment
they didn't want to take back to Dallas or Fort
Worth each day—things like the portable generators
that would supply their electrical needs during the
filming.

Mrs. Martin had answered the telephone, saying
that Cade was not at home, for which Stephanie was
grateful. She left her messages for the rancher and
asked him to contact Mike Adams about the storage
facilities.

But that evening the telephone rang just as she
was stepping out of the shower. Wrapping a heavy
towel around her, she dashed to the phone. She was
expecting a call from Jon, and she didn't want to
miss him. The angry voice on the other end of the
line, however, definitely did not belong to Jon Jenson.

"I told you before that I'm dealing with you on
this movie, not with some young kid."

Stephanie felt suddenly vulnerable, embarrassed
that she didn't have her clothes on. It was silly, of
course, because Cade would have no way of knowing
that she was wrapped in nothing more than a towel,
but she couldn't rid herself of the urge to grab her

long silk robe and slip it on, juggling the telephone in the process.

"I thought perhaps Mike would be easier for you to reach," she tried to explain. She had the uneasy notion that Cade knew she really didn't want to talk to him. "I'm flying to Los Angeles tomorrow afternoon."

"Back to Jenson?" His laugh was short, almost scornful.

"Back to finish preparations for the filming, Mr. Steele." She wasn't going to get mad, she told herself repeatedly. She wouldn't let him rile her. She mustn't say one word that might make him change his mind about using the ranch, so she bit her lower lip and made an effort to keep her voice low and soft.

"Did you understand the message I left?"

"Certainly. You want to haul in a bunch of equipment that's going to tear up my pastureland."

He was going to be impossible to work with. Obstinate, stubborn...even worse.

"I promised you we wouldn't harm your land, Mr. Steele, and we won't. One of the reasons for my call was to find out where the best place would be to put the equipment so it would not disturb you or your pastures."

There was a moment of silence before Cade replied, and Stephanie wondered what was going through his mind.

"Tell your people not to bring one iota of machinery on this land without an appointment. I'll assign one man to meet the trucks and show them where—and only where—they can park." His tone was so authoritative that Stephanie shuddered. "They're not to go anywhere else."

"I'll tell them, Mr. Steele."

There was another silence, disturbingly long to Stephanie.

"Do you need to see me again before you go back to California tomorrow?" he asked.

"No, I don't think so," she replied, but the idea did sound somewhat appealing. She shook it hastily from her mind. "Jon will be in touch with you about the exact time of filming and any other details he needs to handle."

"I have no intention of discussing anything with Jon Jenson," Cade reminded her. "You will be the one to get in touch."

"Yes, sir." She couldn't hide the sarcasm in her voice. Cade would have made a great general: he certainly knew how to give orders.

"So, when will you return?" He ignored her tone.

"I'm not certain, Mr. Steele. I don't make the decisions, you know. I'm only an employee of Jon's."

"Are you sure about that?"

"Goodbye, Mr. Steele. We will contact you as soon as Jon has all his plans finalized." She hung up the telephone before he could respond and wiped her hands on the towel that had fallen to the floor when she'd slipped into her robe. She hadn't realized how damp her palms had become from holding the telephone... from one brief conversation with Cade Steele.

JON MET HER at the airport when she arrived in California.

"I knew you could do it, Stef," he exulted, giving her a big hug and swinging her off her feet while they waited for her luggage to be brought into the terminal building. "Remind me always to have you handle negotiations with stubborn old men."

Stephanie sighed. She felt terribly tired from the strain of the past week plus an unavoidably bumpy flight caused by thunderstorms over Arizona. Her dusty-rose pantsuit was limp, hanging on her body lifelessly, and her long blond hair had little sparkle. She hadn't bothered to shampoo it that morning as she should have done. She had been too eager to get away from Texas, as eager as she had been to go there in the first place.

"Cade Steele's not an old man," she informed Jon abruptly. "Just stubborn."

His eyebrows lifted suspiciously. "I see," he murmured. He gathered her larger pieces of luggage while Stephanie picked up the makeup kit, then steered her toward the exit and his waiting car. "And how did you charm this stubborn not-so-old man?"

Stephanie almost slammed her case to the ground, regardless of the breakable cologne bottle inside. "Good grief, Jon, you know me better than that. You don't think I went to bed with him, do you?"

"Now, honey, don't get ruffled; that wasn't what I meant." He unlocked the trunk and began stowing the suitcases inside.

"Then what did you mean?" Stephanie wanted to

get the air cleared right away. She knew about Hollywood rumors: once something was started, there was no way to get it stopped.

"I just wondered how you got him to change his mind, and I was surprised when you said he wasn't old. I had the impression he was about sixty or so."

"He's only three or four years older than you, Jon." She glanced at her handsome friend. His light brown hair framed a face that was both sensitive and strong, and his greenish gray gaze was often alarmingly direct. "Actually, you two should get along very well. You both like to have your own way."

Jon laughed. He was tyrannical, and he might have resented the comment coming from anyone else, but Stephanie knew she could be perfectly honest with him. He did like to have his way, and he knew it. That's why his pictures were so good. He wouldn't compromise on quality, insisting that a scene be absolutely perfect before going on to the next one.

"This Mr. Steele seems to have made quite an impression on you," Jon remarked. "Did he make a play for you?"

"No." She stared at the traffic ahead of them as Jon pulled out of the airport parking lot and began the drive to her L.A. apartment. "Look, Jon, can we discuss something else? I've had my share of arguments the past few days, and I'd appreciate talking about another subject for a change."

"Then I'll tell you that I've hired Robert Grant to play the leading role in the picture."

Stephanie sat up straight, her spirits lifted. "Really?" She was delighted. Robert Grant was her favorite actor, the one she had immediately suggested for the part of Will Ransom, but she had assumed he would be unavailable. He had been making a movie in Europe for the past several months. "Oh, Jon, I'm so glad. He'll be great. He *is* Will Ransom, you know, tall and dark and strong."

"He'll make a good match with Kara, too," Jon added, and Stephanie nodded her agreement. Kara Warren was a tall redhead, and sometimes leading men were too short for her. But not Robert Grant. He was at least six foot three, and in boots he would tower over the lovely actress. Jon was right, too, about their looking good together: Robert's dark handsome features would complement Kara's pale translucent skin and light red hair. She was a true beauty, turning people's heads everywhere she went. But she could also act and take direction well, two qualities that had induced Jon to star her in his film.

Their conversation throughout the rest of the drive swung from one aspect of the film to another, both being careful not to bring up the name of Cade Steele or even to discuss the location shooting. They merely talked about the people who would be working on the movie and the stack of paperwork that littered Jon's desk and needed to be put in some kind of order.

"I simply can't function in that office without you there," Jon complained. "I can't find a thing on my desk."

It was nice to feel wanted again. Cade Steele had bruised Stephanie's ego with his derisive treatment of her and his insulting insinuations about her relationship with Jon. But she was safely back in California now, and if she could figure out a means of staying, she wouldn't return to Texas. She didn't think she could stand the effects of Cade's belittling attitude again.

Two weeks later Stephanie was feeling more wanted than she cared to be. Jon was demanding more and more of her time as he worked on final preparations. It had taken two days just to sort out the clutter on his desk, and then Stephanie had been required to spend several evenings at home typing correspondence and script-change suggestions that Jon had dictated into that abominable recording machine he carried with him even in his car.

She accompanied him to wardrobe fittings for the film's stars and checked the costumes against her research material on what was actually worn in Texas during the period covered. To her relief, only a few slight revisions were required. The costume designer had done a good job of research on her own.

There were conferences about the construction of sets, the handling of animals and the employment of the stunt man who would do the dangerous job of working in the stampede segment of the cattle drive as well as double for Robert in other action scenes. Stephanie took copious notes and distributed them to the assistant director, the lighting director, the sound man, the cinematographer, the stunt and livestock coordinators, and even the attorney and the accountant who oversaw the business activities of the production.

Mike reported daily from Dallas and mailed in the measurements of the extras who were being hired in Texas and would need costumes brought from Los Angeles for their roles. He asked once if he should go out to the Steele ranch to check things out, but Stephanie told him not to. She didn't explain that Cade refused to discuss business with anyone but her. How could she explain Cade Steele? No one would have believed her anyway. Even Jon teased her a couple of times before her belligerent expression made him realize that she had no sense of humor where the Texan rancher was concerned.

Each morning she made up her mind to ask Jon about staying in California during the filming, but she never found the right opportunity. There was always a rush job to be completed, and Jon Jenson wasn't one to sit around with his feet propped up on a desk. He dashed from one appointment to another with Stephanie trailing behind, trying to keep up with her energetic employer.

When, for a change, he was alone at his desk one morning, sorting through his mail, Stephanie decided the time was right to bring up the subject of staying in California. She'd been checking the airline schedules to Dallas and thought of wandering into his office with the schedule folder to suggest that she make reservations for the others but not for herself. If Jon protested, she could tell him she would try to fly out later, when she had caught up on her assignments. It might take a long time to catch up, she smiled to herself. Certainly Jon would have to admit that there was plenty of work for her to complete in California: her desk top was covered with assorted papers to file and letters to type.

For a few minutes she tried to think of better ways to approach the subject and had just decided that the direct method would be the best when Jon called to her.

"This is the strangest thing I've seen in a long time," he remarked, waving a sheaf of papers at her as she entered his large private office, stenographer's pad in hand. Even before Jon handed it to her, she recognized the contract the attorney had drafted for the lease of the Steele Ranch property. "Look at the changes Steele has written in," Jon told her. "I've never seen anything like it."

The attorney had included a rental fee for use of the land in the contract even though Stephanie had explained that there was to be no charge. "He'll take the money," the lawyer had insisted, "and this will make it a binding legal arrangement."

The amount had been a generous one, and Stephanie had agreed that it would be difficult for even someone like Cade to turn it down. But the obstinate rancher had boldly run a line through the figure and changed it to one dollar.

Stephanie shook her head. "He's a hard man to figure out," she reminded Jon. "I don't understand him."

"If you think that's odd, take a look at the clause he's added on the final page," Jon advised, watching her reaction as she flipped the pages and read the note that Cade had written in before signing the document.

An express condition of this contract is that Miss Stephanie Lasater is to report to Cade Steele each evening during filming on the Steele ranch and that she is to be held totally accountable for any damage done to the ranch property by her or any person employed to work on the movie or by any equipment used for filming purposes.

Stephanie stared at the page long after she had read the paragraph. She knew Jon was eyeing her intently, waiting for her response, but there was nothing civilized that she could say. If Cade had been present, she might have reacted. She might have yanked a chunk of that wavy charcoal-black hair from his head. Her trembling hands shook the papers, and she finally had to place the contract on Jon's desk and clasp them together in an effort to gain control. Was there no way to escape from Cade's looming presence this summer? Was she really going to have to see him every evening and argue about what had happened on the ranch that day? But now, at least, she knew why he was allowing the filming: so that, for some perverse reason, he could have the opportunity of humiliating her.

She glanced up at Jon. "He said something to this effect, but I didn't really think he really meant it." To actually insert it into the contract...! She was furious. Stephanie reddened and looked down at the floor again. Cade had known she would try to get out of returning to Texas, and he had made certain that she would be there. Well, two could play at that game. If she had to go, she'd give him as much trouble as he provided her. He'd regret the day he wrote in that clause.

"What did happen between the two of you?" Jon asked.

"Nothing...nothing at all." She picked up the contract and thrust it back at Jon. "Go ahead and initial the changes he wrote in. I'll report to him every evening. It will be a joy to announce each day that nothing has gone wrong." She pounded the desk. "That's what he's going to be waiting for, you know—an excuse to kick us off the ranch." She stared out the window behind Jon's desk, not wanting to look directly at him. "Cade Steele has this thing against motion-picture people. I don't know what it is, but he hates all of us, and he thinks you sent me there to seduce him into giving permission for leasing the ranch."

Jon was around the desk and beside her in a minute. "Oh, Stef, why didn't you say so? I'll handle the dealings with this Steele man. You don't have to be involved." He rubbed her shoulders with his strong hands, and Stephanie tried to relax, but it was impossible. "Leave Cade Steele to me, Stef. I'll take care of things."

"No." She sat up, determined now to make the trip to Texas. "Mr. Steele wants me to report to him, and I'll do it. The picture's important, Jon, and I can listen to his derogatory remarks about the movies for a few weeks. I want to do it."

"Are you sure?" Jon asked, his hands still on her slender shoulders, his thumbs digging into her collarbone.

"Absolutely," she told him.

STEPHANIE PACKED CAREFULLY for the trip, scrutinizing every dress, blouse and pair of jeans she took. She wanted to avoid any possibility of looking like Cade's preconceived idea of someone in the motion-picture industry. Her brightest garments were rejected; no doubt Cade would expect her to dress flamboyantly, and he would comment on anything that hinted of California casual. But her wardrobe had to be serviceable: three years on film locations with Jon had taught her that. The hours would be long, and the work would be tiring, so she needed to take jeans and tennis shoes. There would be little occasion to wear her few long elegant-looking gowns, but she couldn't resist inserting two of them into a garment bag and packing the silver-toned slippers and small purse that accessorized the outfits. Perhaps she could celebrate her last sight of Cade Steele by enjoying a night out in a Dallas or Fort Worth nightclub with Jon and some of the others who would be working on the movie. And there was also the traditional cast-and-crew party that marked the end of filming of a Jon Jenson production.

It was ridiculous, she realized, to base her wardrobe on what a virtual stranger might think of her, but she couldn't help it. No more than she could prevent the jarring distraction of Cade's deep baritone voice or his calculating eyes unexpectedly interrupting her thoughts as she crept into bed at night or applied her makeup in the morning. He seemed to be nowhere and everywhere, and he was as stubborn a ghost as he was a man, refusing to vanish from her mind for long. Perhaps, she hoped, his eerie presence would no longer plague her once she had to face the vibrantly alive man at the ranch again.

There were a dozen or more members of the cast and crew on the flight to Texas, so Stephanie didn't have the opportunity to enjoy the panoramic display of land and the occasional rivers and lakes beneath her as the jetliner sped across the southwestern states. Jon was taking advantage of the chance for a conference with his people on the first scenes to be shot, and he spent an hour or more, while Stephanie took notes, conversing with Robert Grant and Morgan Anderson, the stunt man and double who would do the dangerous segments of the movie in Robert's place. Stephanie had worked with Morgan before and enjoyed his company. He had a lighthearted outlook on life and seemingly disregarded the perils of his career, although he always checked all the equipment at least twice before beginning a stunt.

This was her first opportunity to meet the male star of the picture, and in spite of her previous dealings with celebrities, Stephanie couldn't help feeling a bit awed at his presence. He was so famous that the flight attendants and the other passengers kept besieging him for autographs, making it difficult for Jon to discuss the picture.

Robert's size and dark coloring startled Stephanie

when she saw him in person for the first time at the airport, and initially she credited the fact that she thought she knew him to having watched him so often on the screen. Yet his actual appearance was different from his movie image. He looked a little younger in person, more rugged, without the cosmopolitan air he often had in sophisticated roles. Maybe she felt a kinship with him because he fit so perfectly her idea of the hero of the story they were filming.

It wasn't until the ninth or tenth request for an autograph came that Stephanie realized why Robert looked so disturbingly familiar. They were in the middle of a detailed description of how a difficult scene would be shot when a fan interrupted, thrusting a napkin at Robert and asking for his signature. A look of annoyance crossed his face before he composed himself and smiled at the elderly woman, but the fleeting expression was enough for Stephanie. She had seen that same irritation on the face of Cade Steele.

She leaned back in her seat, studying the actor while he murmured a few words to the fan, who insisted on telling him that she had seen every one of his movies. Stephanie hadn't realized how much Robert did resemble Cade. Both were unusually large men, powerfully built, with deep tans and dark hair. Cade's eyes were gray while Robert's were brown, but otherwise the resemblance was amazing.

Actually, she mused, Cade probably fit the model of the fictional Will Ransom even better than Robert did. He had been born to the role of a rancher, while

Robert had been required to take riding lessons for the past two weeks so that he could handle his close-up shots in the cattle-drive scenes.

She turned back to her notes. It was better not to think of Cade as the hero of the story. She might come to admire the man, and so far she had found almost nothing to even like about him. She preferred it that way. It was better, she decided, not to think of Cade at all.

That was difficult to do, however, for as soon as they were on the ground at the Dallas-Fort Worth Airport, Cade's name seemed to be a part of every conversation. Mike was there with a small bus to transport the newcomers and their luggage to the hotel in Dallas where they would stay until filming actually began. At that time most of the group, Stephanie included, would move to a more convenient location on the outskirts of Fort Worth.

"We really need to go over some of the plans with Mr. Steele," she heard Mike tell Jon as he was helping to load the baggage. "I thought you might want me to make an appointment for tomorrow, and I knew you'd want to see the ranch yourself as soon as possible."

Jon glanced at Stephanie, who turned quickly away, hoping that he wouldn't inform Mike about Cade's demands concerning her. To her relief, he didn't. "I do want to go out to the ranch within the next few days to make certain that the scale-model set the designers built from the aerial photographs actually matches the real site." He loosened the patterned silk tie around his neck in an unconscious acknowledgment of the warmth of the Texas summer, even if it was just the first day of June. "But first," he informed Mike, "I need to meet with the talent agency and with the production firm we're using here." His eyes strayed toward Stephanie, who had already found a place in the bus and was leaning her head against the glass windowpane. "I think we'd better send Stephanie to the ranch tomorrow while I handle things in Dallas."

"Whatever you say, boss," Mike agreed. "Do you want me to call Steele and see about setting up a time for Stephanie to go out there?"

"Let's just let her handle the call," Jon decided. He smiled at Stephanie, who could hear everything he said. It was a small smile, a sympathetic one, and one she needed. Anyone dealing with Cade Steele needed all the sympathy she could get.

It was evening before Stephanie dialed the number of the ranch. She told herself it would be better to wait to make certain that Cade was in, that she needed to make sure she had all the information from Mike about business she had to discuss, and that she should freshen up before she handled the assignment. Anything but the real reason: that she wasn't quite prepared to hear his voice again.

The line was busy the first two times she dialed the number, and the delay, once she finally worked up enough courage to place the call, was frustrating. She was in Jon's suite, and there was a meeting going on. With Jon there was always a meeting going on. She should have returned to her room, where it was quieter, but Jon kept asking her questions or wanting her opinion about something, so she didn't leave. She did try to muffle the noise by using the telephone in the bedroom of the suite, shutting the door to the living room, where five or six people were all talking at once.

On her third try Cade answered the phone almost as soon as it rang, and the quick lifting of the receiver startled her. She became unnerved, not remembering what she had intended to say, and she stuttered a bit as she began to talk.

Cade, however, had no trouble finding the words he wanted—what few he did want.

"What time?" he asked when she finally blurted out the fact that she needed an appointment with him.

"Whenever it's convenient for you," she replied. "I'm at your command."

"Is that so?" His tone changed for a moment, teasing her, challenging her to rise to the bait he offered, but she remained silent.

He asked where she was staying, and when she told him he wanted to know if Jenson was with her.

"He has a suite at the same hotel," she informed him, "and so does Robert Grant. Actually, there's an entire group of us here," she added, wanting to dispel any notion he might have that she was sharing Jon's quarters. Someone opened the door, allowing the noise from the living area to spill into the bedroom, and she had to cover her free ear with a hand to hear Cade.

"I have business in Dallas all day tomorrow," he explained. "I can meet you for dinner about six-thirty in the evening; that is, if you're through with the wild party you seem to be having."

"That will be fine," she replied, reminding herself of her vow not to argue with the rancher.

"I'll pick you up at your hotel." Cade paused for a second, then added, "You will manage to stay out of the mud tomorrow, won't you?"

He hung up before she could answer.

STEPHANIE PACED NERVOUSLY back and forth on the dirt road that led to the site where Cade had agreed the trailers could be placed. The trucks were late, and the man at her side was growing as impatient as she was.

"I can't stay much longer, Miss Lasater," he told her. "Cade expects me to move the colts to new pastures for the summer."

"I'm certain they'll be here soon, Ray," she responded. At least the rancher wasn't present to complain about the delay, and Stephanie was equally thankful that he hadn't sent one of the employees who had seen her barefoot and muddy during her previous visit there. She glanced at her watch for the tenth time in the past fifteen minutes.

Cade had insisted that they stick to their announced schedule. He had emphasized that point again and again, demanding that his employees not lose any more time than absolutely necessary because of the movie.

She kicked a rock that jutted out of the red dirt. For certain the paths were dry, so the trucks couldn't be stuck in mud anywhere. Probably the drivers were lost. She had gone over and over the directions, had given them maps showing the way, and they had promised to be on time. But she had been waiting for more than an hour, and still no one was in sight.

At first she and Ray stood near the trees, where the equipment was to be placed, but they finally walked out to the road itself, hoping to see some sign of the missing vehicles. This was all she needed—something going wrong. After all her promises. She had committed herself twice to Cade, on her first visit and again at dinner three days ago.

That had been some evening, she reflected ruefully. She had been the one late that time, and it was all Jon's fault. They had been to a final audition for the actresses wanting to play the part of the hero's mother, and Jon had insisted on hearing two of the women repeat their lines several times before making up his mind. Then, after he'd made his selection, he'd spent another half hour talking to the actress, going over his ideas about the role and having Stephanie obtain the necessary information for placing her on the payroll. The woman had been excited about being cast in the film, for even though she had appeared in television shows shot in the area, she had never had a movie role before. She kept asking questions and expressing her excitement at winning the job while Stephanie tried to encourage Jon to return to the hotel.

Cade was waiting in the lobby when they rushed in, Jon's arm casually draped around Stephanie's shoulders. She blushed when she saw him and self-consciously pulled away from Jon. She tried to apologize for being late and to introduce the two men at the same time, failing miserably in both tasks and finally excusing herself to go to her room to change clothes.

By the time she'd returned to the lobby twenty minutes later, after a fast shower and an even faster application of her makeup, Cade was alone. He had probably insulted the director, she mused, and Jon had stalked off to his suite. But she didn't ask where Jon had gone, and she certainly didn't comment on how handsome Cade looked in a dark gray business suit, accented by an almost matching gray tie and silvery silk shirt. She had been wrong to think he looked like Robert Grant: Cade was much better looking than the movie star.

Cade had been polite throughout the evening, not actually participating in her business talk but allowing her to discuss what she wanted to. He did agree with her suggestion that she, Jon, the assistant director and a couple of key crew members tour the section of the ranch they would be using, and he gave his permission for the equipment to be moved onto the property.

Otherwise he'd had little to say, paying more attention to the steak he was eating than to Stephanie. He hadn't said a word about the chiffon dress she wore, one she knew was unusually becoming to her figure. It was almost the same shade of gold as her hair, and it made her feel sunny just wearing it. Usually, that is. With Cade she might as well have been wearing sackcloth. She had chosen the dress on purpose, to prove to him that she didn't always look as bedraggled as she had been when he first saw her, but he didn't seem to notice the change in her appearance.

As soon as they'd finished eating he'd returned her to the hotel, where they had a quiet drink at the small bar just off the lobby.

"You do understand," he told her at the time, "that you must keep your promise about not disturbing my employees or my animals any more than necessary, and you must keep to the schedule that you provide for me."

She had promised to make certain everything went perfectly.

And now here she was, waiting for trucks that she had guaranteed would be on time. She hoped Cade wouldn't find out. He didn't appear to be taking any interest in their activity, for he hadn't shown up yesterday when she had toured the property with Jon and the others. They had spent virtually the entire day inspecting the grounds they would use, deciding on camera placements and the location of the fake log cabin they would erect for one scene. But they had never seen Cade. Ray had dropped by once, informing them that he'd been assigned to answer any questions they had, and Stephanie had made arrangements with him to meet her for the arrival of the trailers full of equipment.

"I'm sorry, Miss Lasater," Ray apologized now, "but I simply have to go back to work. I'll drop by later if I can, when I've finished moving the colts."

"I'm sorry, too, Ray, and thank you," Stephanie

murmured. She watched him walk toward the pickup truck, the same one Cade had used that day she'd accompanied him to town for the engine part, when she'd been forced to sit uncomfortably close to him in the cab. "Wait, Ray!" she hollered suddenly as he was almost at the pickup. "I see them coming now."

Ray glanced back down the road at the caravan of trucks slowly making its way toward them. "Since they're here," he told Stephanie, "I'll stay a little while and help get the trailers in place." He waved at the lead driver to indicate where to turn off the road and onto the grass.

Two hours later the sun was close to sinking in the western sky and the parking of the trailers still wasn't completed. A lock holding a door on a trailer had snapped, strewing bits of sound equipment over the ground, and there had been a long delay while microphones and booms were carefully put back in place. By the time the work was done, the night guard, hired to protect the equipment during the filming period, had arrived, and Stephanie was ready to retreat to the sanctuary of her hotel room. But before she could she had to report to Cade.

It was all she could do to force herself to drive to the old but elegant home that served as headquarters for the ranch. Mrs. Martin took one look at her and offered to prepare dinner for her.

"You look so tired," she insisted when Stephanie refused.

"I'm too tired to eat." Stephanie tried to laugh, but she was so exhausted it was impossible. "As soon as I see Mr. Steele I'm going back to the hotel to rest."

"I think he's at the barn, but I'm not sure," Mrs. Martin explained her employer's absence. "Let me go check."

She didn't have to. They both heard the back door slam and the heavy thump of Cade's boots coming through the kitchen and the hallway toward them. Listening to the angry sound, Stephanie knew she didn't have to tell Cade about the delays. He already knew.

"My colts didn't get moved today." No "hello...how are you?" or anything. Just, "My colts didn't get moved today."

"I know, and I'm sorry," Stephanie apologized. "The drivers got lost and then there was an accident. Ray helped us longer than he should have."

"Didn't you tell the drivers how to get here?"

"Yes, but they still got lost."

He opened a small wooden box on an antique table in the living room and removed a small cigar. Angrily stripping the plastic cover and biting the end off, he paused to glare at Stephanie before striking a match and lighting the cigar. A cloud of smoke enveloped his face, hiding his hostility for a moment.

"I don't want something like this happening again."

Stephanie closed her eyes for a minute, then opened them and looked at the man. Even when angry he was handsome. Vitality swept through him, creating a sensual appeal that was strikingly strong, and she had an irrational impulse to smooth the knitted heavy brows above the eyes that glowered at her. But all she did was murmur, "It won't happen again."

He didn't walk her to the door, and she didn't expect him to. It was enough that he hadn't canceled the lease.

CHAPTER FOUR

FILMING A JON JENSON MOVIE was never simple, and shooting on location always complicated affairs even more. The trailers filled with sound and lighting equipment, the makeup tent, dressing areas and the canopies set up to provide shade for the cast and crew cluttered the ranch site. Grass that had been vividly green before the film crew arrived was now either brown or simply beaten away, victim to the onslaught of traffic that traversed the area. Stephanie noticed the destruction every day, but she didn't know what to do about it. They couldn't build sidewalks, and wooden planks across the grass would have done the same damage. She would just have to arrange for the budget to include reseeding the land once the picture was completed.

The first few days were absolute chaos despite the organization and planning that had taken place in California. It took a while for people to discover where they needed to be at certain times, and more than one actor had been late for shooting simply because he had failed to find the makeup tent. As a result, only six short scenes, none of which was particularly important, had been completed by the end of the first week. Yet Jon had fussed over each one, particularly the one showing the yourg Will Ransom returning from the Civil War. Time after time, Robert Grant trudged down a small path in the thickest area of woods on the ranch while Jon directed the filming. Once Jon didn't like the way a branch blocked the actor's face momentarily, so they stopped while adjustments were made. Another time Robert forgot to pause at the right spot to wipe his brow with a red bandanna. Before every take, the wardrobe woman made adjustments to his outfit, and the makeup woman sprayed his face with a fine mist of water to simulate perspiration that was supposed to dot his brow. It had been a long afternoon.

Keeping sightseers away had also proved to be a problem, much greater than they'd anticipated. Jon had budgeted for only one guard at the main ranch entrance to check on people trying to enter the filming site, but he had to add three others to control visitors trying to come through all the side roads, as well.

Kara had been to blame for that, although she hadn't meant to be. A news photographer had spotted the actress arriving at the airport and had asked why she was in town. She had not only told him she was making a movie but mentioned the Steele ranch by name.

Stephanie was furious when the information appeared in the paper the next day. She had requested that the talent agency, the production company and the people hired in Dallas not publicize the filming, and all of them had cooperated. When Stephanie complained about Kara's actions, however, Jon hadn't blown up the way she'd expected him to do, merely shrugging his shoulders and informing her that they had to tolerate sightseers. He had greeted the actress warmly, inviting her to come out to the location site the next morning, even though her first scene wasn't scheduled for another few days.

Kara's arrival at the ranch caused the stir Stephanie had expected, bringing work to a halt temporarily while fans fought to enter the site and extras rushed to get autographs. Without a complaint the star accepted the compliments, the requests for her signature and the pleas that she pose for snapshots with members of the company. She had grown used to being treated as a celebrity, and she didn't object to the extra demands her fame made on her.

Stephanie waited until order had been restored before offering to show Kara to the private trailer that had been set up for her use as a dressing room. Only she and Robert received such privileges, and only they had limousine service to the film site. Jon drove a rented car, but everyone else, Stephanie included, rode on one of the chartered buses. One brought the local people hired for the film from Dallas, while two others carried the California group from the Fort Worth hotel where they were now staying.

Watching the effect Kara had on even the most blasé crew members, Stephanie couldn't help wondering if Jon might find a way of assigning the beautiful actress to report to Cade each evening. Surely the rancher couldn't bring himself to ridicule movies in front of such an exquisite woman. She wondered if

Cade would come to the site to meet Kara. He hadn't been interested when she'd offered to introduce him to Robert, telling her rudely that he had no use for movie stars.

Stephanie was almost sorry that she had met Robert, and she already regretted the fact that she had suggested him for the movie. Certainly he was a competent actor, and he was always on time, his lines memorized. But he insisted on wine, fresh fruit and other delicacies for lunch instead of the sandwiches provided by the catering truck; he made passes at several of the women in the company; and he complained about the hot weather and the poor air conditioning in his trailer. He complained once too often to Jon, who turned to him in fury, reminding him that he hadn't been forced to sign up for a Western film and that he couldn't expect to shoot all of his scenes on a Hollywood sound stage. Robert had muttered his disapproval to others after that, and Stephanie had been forced to listen to him more than she wanted to. Between Robert and Cade, she was losing her normal enthusiasm for filmmaking.

Mostly, though, she was feeling exhausted. The burden of Cade's demand that she be responsible for damage to the property was taking its toll. Long after the first bus left in the evenings to return the cast to town, she was surveying the location, making certain that the cleaning crew didn't miss a scrap of paper. Only then did she borrow the keys to Jon's car and drive to the ranch house for her ritualistic report to Cade.

Why she was doing it she didn't know. After that

first night, when Cade had been enraged about the delay in moving his colts, he had become completely disinterested in the activities of the movie people. He seldom asked a question and granted whatever request Stephanie made regarding the next day's shooting plans. He didn't even object when she informed him that they would be erecting a partial log cabin to represent the hero's home immediately following the Civil War.

She felt foolish standing there each night, to report like a schoolgirl to her teacher, with her hair and clothes showing the ravages of a day in the warm Texas sun. The first time or two Cade had asked her to sit down and have a drink, but she had refused, and now he didn't even extend the invitation. He simply listened to her report, nodded and told her to see him again the next evening.

Always, however, he escorted her to the car, a rite that Stephanie dreaded. His tall lean body dominated her tinier frame, reminding her of the day he had held her so tightly against him on the horse, and his casual but expensively tailored clothing evidenced that he had been able to shower and change clothes following his day's work. Stephanie was still an hour or more from getting the sand out of her hair and the Western boots she had purchased in Fort Worth off her aching feet. Even then, she had paperwork to handle, call sheets to type and scripts to check.

On Wednesday of the second week of shooting, Stephanie rode the first bus from the hotel, the way she often did. Generally the technical people made the trip at the same time, and the second bus was used to pick up actors and others who didn't need to be there until later.

Stephanie wanted to be especially early this day because the false front and side of the log cabin were going up. It wasn't necessary to build an entire house since the camera would show only the two views of the structure. The two sides, one with the front door and a small porch, would be propped up from behind with long boards that were hidden from view.

But she didn't get to see it until they were ready to shoot. As soon as she arrived, Jon handed her another script change, to be typed immediately, so she rushed to the trailer that served as an office and prepared the new pages for him. Then there was a problem with the lighting equipment, and she had to find the gaffer, the chief electrician, who had just left for a coffee break.

As a result, it was almost noon before she could take a look at the actual set. Jon was lining up the cameras when she arrived, and several crew members were arranging the microphones and finalizing the light placements. To one side, a woman was adding dark smudges to Robert's face with a long-handled brush, and another woman was adjusting the crease in the hat he would wear in the scene.

"Let's get on with it," Jon ordered as Stephanie took a sweeping look at the scene in front of her. "I want this scene wrapped up before the lunch break."

One by one he called on the lighting technicians, the sound men, the wardrobe people, the actors, and all of them responded that they were ready to shoot. Stephanie had a terrible sense that something was wrong, but she couldn't put a finger on the problem. The costumes were right, the lighting setup was perfect to enhance the natural light of the day and block out an unwanted shadow, and the sound equipment was in position. Just as a final run-through rehearsal began and the actress playing the hero's mother opened the door of the cabin and stepped onto the porch to find her son returned from the war, Stephanie snapped her fingers.

"You can't do it, Jon," she called out. "The cabin's not right."

Jon slowly turned to look at her, impatience showing in the set of his mouth.

"What do you mean, it's not right?"

The set designer was at his side in an instant. "My dear Miss Lasater," the man protested, "this is a log-cabin front. What more could you want?"

"You didn't use vee-shaped notches for the corners of the cabin."

"And what difference does a notch make?" The man was offended by her criticism. "I have made the cabin look like pictures of log cabins in many books."

"But not in this part of Texas," she informed him, determined that she wasn't going to let him get away with a mistake in the picture. She turned to Jon for assistance. "Remember the book, Jon? There were a couple of pages about the building of the family's home, and the author described it. The logs were notched at the ends in vee shapes. They weren't just stacked on top of each other." She was having trouble making Jon understand, too. "By cutting vee notches in the ends of the logs, they could be fit snugly together and the cabin would be sturdier. Most of the log cabins in north Texas were built that way.''

Jon glared first at Stephanie and then at the designer. ''This should have been handled a long time ago,'' he told them. ''I'm sorry, Stef, but it's too late now. We simply don't have enough time to rebuild the front of the cabin.''

''But you can't let a mistake go through when you can prevent it,'' she argued. ''I know it means a delay, but can't you shoot something else while a new cabin front is being built? You know you want everything to be accurate historically.''

''I can't wait that long, Stef. We're already behind schedule.'' He turned back to the camera and eyed the scene he was about to shoot. ''I'll move the camera closer, so the end of the cabin will show only for a brief second or two at the most. No one will notice.''

''I will.'' Furious at Jon's uncharacteristic failure to insist on perfection, she whirled around, away from the director and the designer and the rest of the crew who were watching her losing battle. The people around her moved aside as she strode away from the cameras, giving her room, wanting to avoid a confrontation with her themselves. Only the man leaning against an oak tree, his arms folded in front of him, stayed where he was.

Stephanie glanced up and stopped in mid-stride. Cade had never visited the shooting site before, and now he had to come just as she was fighting. No doubt he'd think even less of her than before. She swept past him, not paying attention to the slight smile on his face or noticing that he walked up to speak to Jon as soon as she was beyond him.

She was sitting on the ground, her back against a tree, too angry even to watch the filming, when she heard footsteps approaching.

"Go away," she muttered. "I'm having no part in shooting that cabin."

"Then come with me, and I'll show you one you can use."

Her head shot up. Cade was standing above her, a hand extended to help her up. She hesitated to accept his offer. "What do you mean?"

He reached down for her, bringing her to her feet without a hint of effort, and his hand lingered on hers while he spoke. "You were right about the cabin, you know."

"I know, for what good it does." She cast a savage glance at the shooting site. They must have finished in a remarkable hurry. Everyone was scattering for the catering truck, except for a few hands who were dismantling equipment.

"I told your director friend that there is a log cabin on the ranch," Cade informed her, guiding her toward a nearby path with a firm hand on her shoulder. "It was the one my ancestors built when they first came here. I'll show it to you if you like."

"Oh, I'd like that." She smiled at Cade.

He grinned slightly in response. "I didn't know you could smile, Miss Lasater."

"This is the first time you've given me anything to smile about, Mr. Steele," she replied formally, but she couldn't help the tiny laugh that escaped her throat.

"Perhaps I should find other ways to make you smile," he mused. "I wonder what would work." His hand slipped farther around her shoulder, bringing her closer to him. A surge of electricity swept through Stephanie's body, and she had to pull free to avoid the temptation of leaning her head against his virile chest.

He took her hand as he led the way down the narrow path toward a small stream. Stephanie eyed the water skeptically, wondering how deep it was. There was no bridge anywhere around, but the path continued on the opposite side.

"Are you afraid of getting your feet wet?" Cade asked, but before she could reply, he had lifted her in his arms and was carrying her across. When they reached the other shore, he continued to cradle her against him. Stephanie had automatically clung to his neck while they crossed the hollow stream, but now she realized how intimately entangled they were. Her hands slid down from his neck until they rested against muscular arms that didn't seem to be straining under the weight of her mere hundred pounds.

"I can get down now," she told him, reluctant as she was to lose the delicious contact with his firm male body.

"Do you want to?" he murmured in her ear, his lips moving to her throbbing temple and over her fluttering eyelashes.

It took all of her willpower, but Stephanie nodded, and Cade set her on her feet. The tender mood was shattered, and he was all business as he directed her farther down the path to a small clearing where the little cabin stood.

Someone had loved that old house, Stephanie knew at first glance. It had been maintained for more than one hundred years. The mortar between the logs was still in place, the roof was solid, and the porch might have had a chair and an old churn sitting on it. The cabin looked lived in.

She turned to Cade. "You've preserved this, haven't you?"

"It's a part of my heritage," he answered, leading her toward the ancient front door and into the single room that had once housed an entire family. "I can't let my history die." He surveyed the room. It was furnished with an iron bed covered with a feather mattress and a patchwork quilt, a small table with four chairs and an old loom standing in the corner. A large black pot hung from a hook on the fireplace, and a delicate porcelain statue of a shepherdess held a place of honor on the mantel.

"That was brought all the way from Tennessee in a covered wagon," Cade told Stephanie when she admired the statue, "and before that it was shipped from England to Virginia and then overland to Tennessee by mule train." He set the piece back on the mantel. "It's been in my family for more than two hundred years."

"Then why don't you have it in the big house?" Stephanie asked. "Wouldn't it be safer there?"

"It belongs here," Cade stated flatly, and turned back to the door. "You can film the outside of the cabin, but I don't want anyone messing around in here."

"I'll tell Jon that only the woman playing the mother can come in," Stephanie agreed. "She has to walk from the inside onto the porch in the scene." She stared at Cade, wondering why he was being so helpful. It wasn't like him to be of any assistance in the making of a movie. And why had he held her so gently and brushed her face with his lips? As far as she could tell, he didn't even like her!

She'd probably never know. Cade wasn't the type of man to let a stranger share his feelings. Even his housekeeper didn't know the details of his shattered romance with that Merilee, so why would he explain any of his actions to Stephanie? It was better not to speculate about Cade or his motives. She could only appreciate that he had suddenly provided a means for her to keep the movie completely authentic.

"How can we bring the equipment in here?" She wanted to keep the conversation on a business level.

"I'll have Ray guide them this afternoon," he said. "Right now I think it's time for lunch." He eyed Stephanie's slender body, her figure emphasized by the jeans and form-fitting T-shirt she wore. "Do you eat lunch, Miss Lasater?"

"Sometimes," she murmured, wishing he wouldn't undress her with his eyes. She glanced around the clearing, framed by the heavy cluster of post oaks and blackjack trees. "I can't remember the way back to the film site."

"I have a better idea," he suggested, and she followed him away from the little road that led to the cabin, going down a hillside along the edge of the rows of trees instead. They must have hiked a half mile or more before arriving at a fenced area where a few horses grazed on the green grassy pasture.

Cade scaled the fence easily, but Stephanie couldn't manage, and he had to pull her across the top rail, an indignity that sent a flush of color to her cheeks. There was a small building nearby, filled with equipment, and Cade quickly saddled a sorrel gelding and turned to pick up a second blanket and saddle. He stopped long enough to ask, "Do you ride, Miss Lasater?"

She admitted that, except for her experience with him, she had been on a horse only twice in her life, but she didn't add that she had fallen off both times. "I'm not sure about riding one of your horses," she confessed. "Are they very gentle?"

He shrugged and put the second saddle back on the rack. "You can ride with me," he told her. "You've done it before."

"I think I can manage on my own." She didn't want to remember her previous humiliation at his hands, not when he had been so nice this day.

Cade edged closer to her, and she backed up, moving away from him until she collided with the planked side of the building. He leaned his arms against the wooden structure, effectively trapping Stephanie in front of him. "The question is, Miss Lasater, are you more afraid of me or one of these horses?" His steel-gray eyes held hers for a moment, and she found herself trying to avert her gaze to break his hypnotic hold on her.

His laugh came low out of his throat. "I think you're more afraid of me, but I can't take a chance of your breaking a leg falling off a horse. We'll ride double."

He gave her no opportunity to protest, sweeping her into his arms and depositing her in the saddle before settling his body immediately behind her. She had to grab the saddle horn for balance and to keep from leaning heavily against Cade, but the rocking motion of the horse as it made its way toward the main house made it impossible for her to stay out of the range of Cade's huge body. She was flung against his chest in rhythmical fashion, and her temple brushed against his rugged jawline with each movement.

They didn't speak during the ten-minute ride to the house, and it wasn't until Cade had tied the horse to a fence railing and had sent word to Ray about the plans for the afternoon that Stephanie thought to ask why he had visited the movie site that morning.

"I didn't think you were interested," she pointed out to him as they turned toward the house.

"I'm not," he told her bluntly. "That man running your security force was responsible."

"Was something wrong?" Stephanie asked. The guards were good at their job, and fans hardly ever got past them to interfere with the shooting schedule.

"My mother drove out this morning, and they wouldn't let her in," Cade said, helpless to control the tiny smile that escaped at the irony of his mother's predicament. "She was quite incensed," he added. "She drove to the nearest telephone, called me and complained loud and long about being kept out of her own family ranch.''

''Oh, dear,'' Stephanie responded ruefully. ''That was my fault. I never thought to put your mother's name on the list of people who were allowed in. I'm sorry, Mr. Steele, I really am. When I got the list of employees from you, I should have asked about your relatives and friends.''

He opened the screen door. ''Forget it,'' he advised. ''It only ruffled her feathers for a little while. After she did get in and to the house, she was still a bit upset, so I took her down to the filming location and asked your buddy Jenson to introduce her to that drugstore cowboy who's supposed to be the hero of this picture. She was thrilled, and the last time I saw her she was getting everyone's autograph. I think she even has the signatures of those kids who pick up the trash.''

Mrs. Martin was in the kitchen when they entered, and she immediately poured large glasses of iced tea and offered lunch. ''Would you like a fresh salad, Miss Lasater?'' she inquired. ''I've heard that your lunch truck just brings sandwiches, and I wondered if you'd like something different for a change.''

''That would be simply wonderful,'' Stephanie exclaimed.

For the first time she was enjoying the prospect of a meal with Cade. He was actually being human—warm, witty, friendly. They even joked while Stephanie ate her chef salad and Cade dined on a thick roast beef sandwich and a large slice of peach pie.

''Do you have to go back to work right away?'' he

asked as Stephanie handed her empty salad bowl to Mrs. Martin and got up to leave.

"In a few minutes. Why?"

"I want to discuss something with you." He indicated the back porch with a sweep of his hand. "Let's go out on the porch."

He sat uncomfortably close to Stephanie on the swing where she had waited for him on that first visit to the ranch, and his arm rested on the back of the swing, his trailing fingers occasionally flicking against Stephanie's neck and shoulder.

"I'd like to know why you were so insistent about the log cabin," Cade asked her, stretching a leg to full length and letting his booted foot control the movement of the swing.

"The picture should tell the real story," Stephanie tried to explain. "You can't do that if you start making substitutions."

"And you'd fight for that?"

She turned to face him, and his arm moved to enclose her back. "Of course. Wouldn't you?"

"I'm not making a movie," he replied.

"But if you were?" she insisted.

Cade's eyes roamed over her, resting on the outline of her full breasts, making her regret that she had tucked her T-shirt inside her jeans instead of allowing the garment to hang loosely over her upper body. "I'm not, so I don't have to decide what's real and what isn't." He pushed the heel of his boot harder against the wooden floor of the porch, sending the swing into a higher arc. "But since you are, if you need more facts, I have a lot of books about the early days of Texas. You can look at them if you wish, and there's a collection of varieties of barbed wire you might find interesting.''

"Thank you, Mr. Steele. I appreciate your offer.'' She dragged her feet against the floor, forcing the swing to slow until she could rise. "Now I really must get to work. Jon's already upset about the delay in filming the log-cabin scene, I'm sure, and I'd like to get back and help him get organized.''

Cade rose in an instant. "Then I won't keep you from your *friend*.'' His emphasis on the word was clearly suggestive. "Ray should be ready to head back to the location now. I'll ask him to give you a ride.''

Stephanie was a little disapointed that Cade himself wouldn't take her back, and he observed her questioning look.

"Or would you rather ride double with me again on the horse?'' he asked. "Actually, my car is still down there and the other ranch vehicles are in use, so I have no transportation available here except for the horse.''

His voice had turned cold, and Stephanie found it difficult to accept the change. She led the way around the porch to the front driveway, walking as quickly as she could without seeming to run. Ray was just arriving in the pickup, so she extended a hand to Cade and prepared to go. "Thank you for letting us use the cabin, Mr. Steele, and thank Mrs. Martin for the salad.'' She tried to withdraw her hand from his grasp, but he held her fingers tightly. "Would you like me to bring your car to you?'' she added.

He let her go while he opened the door to the truck, touching her elbow to steady her as she stepped up into the vehicle. "No, that won't be necessary. I left the keys with my mother, and she'll bring it back; that is, if she ever gets through collecting autographs. Her own car is the one in the back of the drive, but I don't have keys to it, or I'd enjoy the pleasure of your company for a few more minutes." He gave a mocking laugh and closed the truck door. "Remember what I told you about the cabin. Only you and the one actress are allowed inside." Stephanie had barely enough time to nod before Ray took off for the film site.

Stephanie couldn't help looking around for Mrs. Steele when she arrived back on location, but she didn't see anyone who might be the rancher's mother, and there was no time to ask. The entire crew was busy loading equipment for the move to the new site, and Jon was hurrying everyone, determined to finish the scene and go on to another one before the day was over.

"Just those involved in this particular scene are to go on the bus," he stated, turning to his assistant director to order that preparations be made for the next scheduled shooting, a scene Robert freely and loudly admitted he was dreading. He would have to pretend to chop down a tree, and he complained that he would have the tree felled himself before Jon would be satisfied and let the double take over for the long shots.

Morgan Anderson was already dressed in an identical outfit, ready to do the actual chopping once close-ups were completed. A dead tree had been selected at Stephanie's insistence, for she had known Cade would never approve the destruction of a live one. But she had been surprised when he suggested they fell an entire clump of trees.

"They're mesquites," he had said, "the bane of ranchers." He explained that mesquites had spread from south Texas to take over much of the prairie land in central and north Texas. The ranchers had to burn them out.

Stephanie had protested. "They're grotesquely shaped, but they're kind of pretty in an odd way. They must be good for something."

He had scoffed at her defense. "The old-timers used to say you planted tomatoes when the mesquite tree budded and cotton when the leaves appeared. The Indians used mesquite gum for everything from cement, candy and dye to dressings for wounds, but now we mostly curse its thorns and its rapid growth. Once it takes over, you can hardly make it through the brush." He had deliberately surveyed her feminine curves, so casually revealed in the jeans and shirt. "Only a city girl would like a mesquite tree," he had decreed.

Jon suggested that she stay behind to help the assistant director prepare for the tree-chopping scene, but Stephanie insisted on watching the cabin filming.

"I promised Mr. Steele that nothing would go wrong, and I intend to keep my word," she told him. Jon merely shrugged and motioned her onto the bus.

When they arrived, Stephanie explained the rules

and stationed herself inside the cabin, making certain that no unauthorized person entered. She could hear the turmoil of noise outside, but it didn't disturb her. Years of working with Jon had enabled her to tune out the disrupting sounds of movie making. Instead she spent her time wandering around the room, imagining how life would have been when the people who lived there first came to the area.

They must have been poor, at least for a while. They had not added a second room to the cabin, making do with the single room for all of their needs. Her fingers explored the dainty stitchwork connecting the patchwork designs on the handmade quilt, and as her gaze roamed she wondered what cooking in the fireplace had been like.

Indians had probably been a danger then, she realized, although her research had told her that the Comanche usually avoided the wooded Cross Timbers area of Texas, preferring to stay on the open prairie. But even if there were no Indians, the life must have been lonely. There would have been few neighbors and only limited opportunities to socialize.

The door swung open while she was still admiring the designs on the quilt, and she looked up to see not the actress she expected, but Cade.

"I decided to watch over the cabin myself," he told her.

Stephanie nodded, understanding why he would want to take personal charge of this special part of his heritage.

They remained silent for a few minutes while the actress portraying the mother rushed in and waited just inside the door until Jon called for quiet and the first take. Outside they could hear the clapper board strike and Jon's call for action. Even without seeing what was happening, Stephanie knew the scene by heart. Robert Grant, as Will Ransom, was staggering up to the house, his clothes ragged, his face dirty, but home from battle. As he fell exhausted on the steps, the actress, her clothes almost as ragged as his, opened the door, dashed out onto the porch and cradled him in her arms, sobbing with joy at the return of her son.

They did the scene over and over until Jon was certain that it was right, and then they did it again from another angle, and then from a third angle, and later they worked the close-up shots, first on the son and then on the mother. There was a long pause each time while the lights and microphones were shifted.

"Isn't it ridiculous to spend three hours filming something that will take up about one minute in the movie?" Cade asked during one particularly long delay in the shooting.

"That's how it's always done," Stephanie replied. "You learn a great deal of patience making movies, and the actors spend a lot of time sitting around waiting for the scene to be set up and trying not to be bored."

"I can't imagine a worse way of making a living," Cade scoffed at the whole idea. "This," he added, indicating the room, "is what life is really about, the struggle to carve a home out of a wilderness."

"It must have been difficult," Stephanie agreed, "and from what I've read, it was especially hard after the Civil War."

Cade sat on the bed beside her, rubbing his hands together. She felt a sudden great rush of sympathy for the man, and she didn't know why. He had never experienced the hardships of the pioneers, but he seemed to share their agonies and their pain.

"There was practically no money in this part of the country after that war," he explained. "The Confederate money was no good, and many people had lost all that they owned." He told her that earlier the federal troops stationed at the frontier forts to the west had been called back by the Union to take part in the war, and the people of the area were left to protect themselves against the Indians who took advantage of the opportunity to raid villages and farmhouses. Some settlers were burned out and had to leave. In his own family, he continued, the men left to fight for the Confederacy, and the women stood alone against intruders and the elements.

"Sort of like the story we're filming," Stephanie mused.

He glanced sharply at her. "Sort of," he agreed.

While the men were away, he continued to explain, women often dressed in men's clothing so that Indians watching from a distance would not realize they were alone. Then, after the war, when the men returned, many of them crippled or ill, there was no money for necessities, much less luxuries. People had to make do with what they could obtain by themselves.

"My folks lived on prairie chicken and wild turkey and the small fish they caught in the streams around here," Cade stated. "Coffee was out of the question.

They used parched barley instead." He strode around the small room that was filled with his presence. "Do you see any candleholders?" he asked, and when she noticed the omission he told her that his ancestors couldn't afford candles following the war. They had to produce their light by soaking various things in oil. He pounded a huge fist on the sturdy wooden table that stood close to the fireplace.

"But they survived, and they fought back," he exclaimed. "They never gave up, and they found a way to make a living." He gripped Stephanie's shoulders. "That house I'm living in now is the proof. It's the result of a lifetime of effort by someone who wouldn't let poverty and disease and war defeat him."

Stephanie was silent while outside the door Jon again called for quiet and for the cameras to roll. Her mind was whirling with Cade's revelations. She was delighted to know that the book they were filming was an accurate account, after all, of what had really happened. But even more she was elated at Cade's opening up to her, at the resulting thrill she felt deep inside her. She wished she could tell him how she felt.

"Cade," she began when filming stopped, not realizing that she had called him by his first name and not seeing the tiny smile on his face that indicated he had noticed, "did your family round up longhorns on the open range?"

"Of course," he answered, "That's why my longhorns are so special, and that's why I intend to be present anytime they're used in this movie."

"Next week," she told him. "That's the first time we're scheduled for that part."

"I'll be there," he told her, "and you will be, too."

They sat silently, each lost in private thought, until they heard Jon call for a wrap-up of the scene. "If we hurry," Jon told the crew, "we'll still get the tree-cutting shot before dark."

There was a cyclonelike whirl of activity outside, but inside the little cabin the air was still and warm, lulling Stephanie into a lazy languorous mood. She didn't want to hurry; she'd rather sit in the stuffy cabin and think.

A deep sigh racked her body as she reluctantly rose and picked up her shoulder bag, slinging it across her to keep her hands free. She looked back at Cade, still standing by the fireplace staring at the old black pot.

"I'm glad you told me about your family, Mr. Steele," she said quietly, clutching her arms to her body to resist the impulse to reach out and touch him. "It's a story you should be proud of, and it's one you can hand down to your own children."

He looked at her for a long time, his face a mask, then nodded and turned back to the fireplace. Stephanie walked to the door, glanced back for a moment and went on out to catch the bus. Cade was still in the cabin when the bus pulled away.

STEPHANIE PRACTICALLY WHISTLED as she parked the car in the driveway of Cade's home. It had been a good day of filming, but more important, she was happy to be reporting to Cade. Her normal dread of his wrath had disappeared with the openness he had shown at the cabin and at lunch a few hours earlier. Perhaps now he would be more agreeable to the plans of the movie company, and that would certainly make her life easier. He might even tell her that she needn't bother reporting to him each night.

She frowned as she turned off the ignition, startled at the unexpected sadness she felt at the thought. Her dealings with Cade were purely business, and there was no need to report to him if production remained on schedule, but now she had an overpowering need to know what the man was really like.

The glimpse of himself he had provided at the cabin had only whetted her appetite to learn more. It was an intellectual curiosity, she told herself. Certainly there was no romantic interest on the part of either her or Cade. She preferred a gentle man, and Cade was anything but gentle. If he had any interest in her, it was only to see how far he could push her before her temper ignited into a fiery battle with him, to punish her for his unexplained hatred of the motion-picture industry.

He was waiting for her when she stepped onto the front porch. Stephanie hadn't noticed him standing in the shadows. It was late, much later than usual, and the sun was already gone from the western sky. She couldn't stay long. Jon had gone to get a hamburger with the talent agent, and she was supposed to meet him almost immediately at the café in the small town south of the ranch. But when Cade invited her in, telling her he had something to show her, she couldn't resist. Thoughts of meeting Jon quickly fled her mind, and she nodded her agreement.

They sat in the intimate little den where she had confronted him the first time she visited the ranch, but now the atmosphere was so different it was as if they were in an entirely different location and as if Cade were a completely changed man.

He was relaxed this time, talkative, almost bursting with enthusiasm at the opportunity of telling her about the early days of Texas and the roles his ancestors had played in the development of the ranching business. When his steely eyes rested on her this night, there was no mockery. It was as if he accepted her as another history enthusiast.

That was all it was, she reminded herself. He wasn't thinking of her as a woman. He merely approved of the research she had done. It was not a pleasant thought.

The old photo albums and scrapbooks Cade brought out for her to see made her wish she'd had access to them earlier, when she was first doing her research. They provided much more detail than the novel on which the movie was based.

She sat in one of the two facing leather chairs in the room while she turned the pages of the book. Cade leaned forward in the opposite chair for a while, watching her face intently, gauging her interest in the material.

When she asked a question about a particular photograph, he moved to her side, settling his large body on the arm of the chair where she sat, draping one arm around the chair back so that it seductively grazed the nape of Stephanie's neck. With his free hand he pointed out details in the pictures and in the old newspaper articles carefully pasted into the books. Once or twice his arm brushed Stephanie's breast as he reached across to indicate an item in the books.

She wished he would move. He was too temptingly close, and she couldn't think clearly—not enough even to ask an intelligent question. His masculine cologne assaulted her senses, and the warmth of his body against hers raised her temperature to a dangerous level. She knew she should close the books and hand them back to him, but she couldn't do it. All she was capable of was listening to the sensuously deep voice that spoke when she couldn't utter a word and turning the pages automatically at his bidding.

She lost track of time. They could have sat there ten minutes or ten hours; she wouldn't have known which. She did know that she didn't want it to end, and when the last page of the last book had been turned she couldn't move, couldn't even hand back the leather-bound volumes that rested in her lap.

Cade took them from her and gently replaced them on a shelf of the bookcase, which covered two walls of the room. She was still sitting in a daze when he returned, still feeling the delicious imprint of his arm on her back and his chest against her side. He stood before her for a minute, his large body looming over her small one, but Stephanie didn't shudder the way she once had when he was near. When he held out his hands, she grasped them and allowed him to pull her to her feet and into the warmth of his embrace.

His touch was surprisingly soft for a large man. His hands cupped the back of her head, fingers twining in her hair, while he explored every inch of her face with his fathomless eyes. Then his lips followed his gaze. Stephanie shivered, and her own hands reached around his waist, imprisoning him as much as he held her. His mouth took possession of hers, his tongue exploring her lips, which parted at his touch, while his hands moved to her shoulders and downward, caressing her breasts and enveloping her waist.

Her body ached, not from the pressure of his hands but from the fire inside that his touch kindled, and she didn't protest when he lifted her off her feet. Still holding her lips with his magnetic attraction, Cade settled in the chair, cradling her in his arms as if she were a child. But his seductive murmurs belied that impression. He was whispering to her about the sweetness of her mouth and the lushness of her breasts, erotically hard under his grasp. Stephanie couldn't reply, couldn't do anything but moan and trail her fingertips across his chest, catching her fingers in the wispy hairs that were revealed in the opening of his shirt.

"Will you spend the night with me?" she heard him ask, as if from a distance, but her mouth wouldn't form an answer.

He seemed to take her silence for acceptance, pressing his lips hard against hers, letting his hand drop below her waist to her sensitive inner thigh. In spite of the heavy denim of her jeans, his touch sent electrical sparks through her body. She wanted to tell him she wouldn't stay, she couldn't stay, but he was giving her no opportunity to refuse, keeping her defenses so low that he could practically have his way without a single objection.

Lost in the ecstasy of his embrace, Stephanie didn't hear the telephone ring, and when Cade moved, rising from the chair and gently depositing her in it, she could only call his name hoarsely. Her hearing and her eyesight seemed diminished, overwhelmed by the new emotions surging through her body, so she didn't hear his conversation, and it took Cade's tug on her arm to bring her back to her feet and her senses.

"Jenson wants to know what's keeping you," he informed her, cold ice replacing the warm glow in his gray eyes.

At first she didn't understand what he was talking about. Her face was still flushed from the ardor he had aroused in her.

"I should have told him you were doing what he had sent you here for in the first place," Cade continued. "You do know how to stir up a man, don't you, Miss Lasater?"

Tears she couldn't check overflowed her eyes and streaked the makeup on her cheeks. "I don't know any such thing," she cried. She looked around for her purse and grabbed it off the desk, knocking over a pen-and-pencil set in her haste. She didn't stop to pick it up; she had to get out of that room and out of that house. "I've got to pick up Jon," she announced as she fled.

Cade followed her to the car, grabbing her arm before she could close the door of the vehicle. His eyes were narrowed, she could tell even in the dim light reflected from the porch lamp.

"If I've insulted you, I apologize," he told her, "but if I spoke the truth, I think you owe me an apology."

Stephanie fought back the tears still welling in her eyes. "I don't owe you a thing, Mr. Steele." She jerked free of his hold, slammed the door and started the engine. Swinging the car around in the circular driveway, she sped down the narrow road away from the house. When she glanced in the rearview mirror, she could see Cade still standing in the drive, hands thrust deep into the pockets of his dusty brown slacks. The image remained with her long after she fell into bed and into a restless sleep.

CHAPTER FIVE

THE SUN was filtering into her hotel room when Stephanie finally opened her eyes on Sunday. She stretched, pulled the top sheet higher, tucking it under her chin, and smiled. A morning off. She could hardly believe it.

Actual filming might be only a five-day-week operation, but working for Jon meant being on duty practically every day. He never seemed to get tired, and she had spent all Saturday morning watching him going over and over next week's scenes with the technicians, using the scale model they had shipped from Los Angeles. Exact placement of lights and cameras was determined so that there would be no possible excuse for error.

Jon had called for a rehearsal Sunday afternoon in his hotel suite for Kara, and Stephanie knew that meant she'd have to be there, too, but at least she had been able to sleep later than usual. It had been comforting to know she didn't need to leave a wake-up call with the operator or have to ride the bus to the ranch. She needed a change of scenery. . . particularly from the sight of Cade.

He had been even colder than usual when she had reported to him the past couple of days, and only the appearance of his mother on Friday evening had made that visit bearable. Mrs. Steele had charmed Stephanie immediately. She had startled her, too.

The woman might have been the mother and the widow of ranchers, but there was nothing countrified about her. Her makeup was impeccable, and her clothes had the styling of designer originals. If she had lived much of her life on the ranch, she must have gone into the city to do her shopping. At Neiman-Marcus, probably.

There was little resemblance between her and her only son, just a similarity in the straight lines of their noses and the natural waves in their hair. Mrs. Steele's hair was a lighter shade than her son's, but, as she confided to Stephanie, "I have no idea what color it really is. I haven't seen the natural shade in years."

She had taken a great interest in the filming and had invited Stephanie to stay at her condominium in Dallas if she grew tired of hotel living. Stephanie had turned her down. She needed to be close to the crew so that Jon could call on her when he needed her help.

"I'm so anxious to meet Miss Warren," Mrs. Steele admitted. "I haven't had a chance to see her yet."

"You will soon," Stephanie told her. Scenes with the gorgeous Kara Warren were coming up quickly.

Today's rehearsal was the actress's first, and by the time Stephanie arrived at Jon's suite, still yawning in spite of ten full hours of sleep, Kara was already there, waiting to go over her lines with the

director. As usual he was on the telephone, and a
projector was going at the same time, showing rushes
of the previous week's work. Stephanie didn't want
to look at them. She nodded to Kara, took out her
copy of the script and a notebook to record changes
and settled in a chair until Jon was ready.

When the last conversation was completed, Jon
ruffled Kara's red tresses with an affectionate caress,
one he almost always used with actresses working for
him, and asked if she was ready to begin. Her answering smile was so tender that Stephanie caught
herself wondering whether Kara Warren was falling
for the handsome director. If she was, Stephanie felt
sorry for her. Being in love with Jon was a losing pro-
position. He loved only his work, and more than one
actress had failed to win him over. Even the beaute-
ous Kara would find she was doomed to heartache if
she cared too much.

Stephanie wanted to warn her, but she decided it
would be useless. She had done that once, with another leading lady, and the woman had become very
angry with her. Her well-meant gesture had caused
problems on the set, and Stephanie had vowed never
to interfere again. She shrugged, picked up her script
and ignored the affection gleaming in Kara's wide-set
eyes.

Nevertheless, she couldn't help thinking, *never fall
in love with a man who doesn't know how to love in
return*. She tried to conjure up a picture of the fiancé
in New York who had fit that description so well, but
he had faded so much that it was difficult to remember even what he looked like. Each time she tried to

recall him, she kept seeing a flash of dark wavy hair and steel-gray eyes, and her fiancé had been a brown-eyed, sandy-haired man.

The rehearsal quickly turned into a farce. Jon was reading the lines of all the other characters in the scene, and while he was a fantastic director, he was a complete flop at acting. They were convulsed with laughter every few minutes, and Stephanie was still chuckling when she answered the telephone as it rang for the fourth time in forty-five minutes.

"I thought I'd find you in Jenson's room when no one answered in your own."

Her laughter caught in her throat at the sound of Cade's voice.

"Is something wrong, Mr. Steele?" She racked her brain trying to think of what could have happened. Everything had been under control when she had reported to him on Friday evening, and there had been no shooting on Saturday.

"Would I call just to ask the correct time?" He was obviously in no mood for casual conversation. "Of course something is wrong!"

Stephanie could feel her heart sinking, and she sat down on the rose-patterned couch. Her legs didn't want to hold her up any longer. Around her, Kara's and Jon's laughter seemed incongruous, out of place, and she wished they would be quiet. "What's wrong?" she asked, crossing her fingers in a superstitious hope that the problem could be easily solved.

"Someone didn't put on the emergency brake on one of your trucks," he informed her. "Sometime last night or this morning, it rolled down a hill, hit a pasture fence and knocked it down, and now I have horses scattered all over this ranch." He paused as if refueling his rage. "Would you like to come round them up, Miss Lasater?"

Stephanie tried to apologize, but Cade wouldn't listen. "I've had to call in my men on their day off to find the horses," he told her, "but you had better get out here and get this truck out of my pasture in a hurry. We can't even repair the fence with that monstrosity in the way."

"I'll find the man who handles the trucks and send him to the ranch as quickly as possible," she offered.

"I said for you to get out here," Cade corrected. "You're responsible for damage, if you recall. Now, you get the keys, you get out here and you remove that truck from my pasture." He was silent long enough, Stephanie guessed, to glance at his watch. "You have two hours to get here, Miss Lasater. I realize you don't want to tear yourself away from your *friend*, but don't be late."

She hung up the telephone and sat dejectedly until Jon noticed her swift change of mood. Hearing what had happened, he was instantly on the phone trying to reach Dave Wilkes, the man in charge of the vehicles. Dave was nowhere to be found, but Jon did manage to find the keys to the trucks after talking an assistant manager into allowing them into the man's room at the hotel.

"I'm going out there, Stef," Jon told her. "You're not facing Steele alone." He thrust the truck keys into his pocket and thanked the assistant manager for letting them into the room. "We should never have accepted that condition in the contract about your being personally responsible for damage." He took her by the arm and led her toward the elevator. "That's my fault, and I'm going to let Steele know that from now on he's dealing with me."

"It won't do any good, Jon, and you'd both just get mad." Stephanie leaned against the back wall of the elevator, her eyes on the crisscrossing leather straps of the sandals on her feet. She was wearing white shorts with a yellow halter top that tied around her neck, leaving her back bare, and she knew she should stop at her room to change into something less skimpy, but Jon wasn't stopping for anything. He propelled her and Kara, who had accompanied them on the search for the keys, through the back lobby and toward the parking area.

Stephanie sat in the back seat of the luxury automobile Jon had rented for his use while in Texas, silently cursing Dave Wilkes and Cade Steele with equal venom. She refused to accept Kara's murmurs of sympathy and assurances that the damage probably wasn't as great as she expected to find.

"You know how men exaggerate when they want to make an impression," the actress remarked encouragingly.

"Oh, do they?" Jon questioned, a light tone in his voice for the first time since hearing of Cade's call.

Kara laughed. "Well, present company excepted, of course." She smiled brilliantly at Jon, and the director returned her smile before turning his attention back to his driving.

The brief exchange distracted Stephanie from her dark cloud. She was already suspecting that Kara was more than fond of Jon, but could he possibly be interested in her romantically? She shook her head. It seemed unlikely: Jon made such a point of never becoming involved with his leading ladies, often telling Stephanie that he didn't want to be accused of playing favorites with an actress in his movies because he was dating her. Sure, he flattered them, hugged them after a particularly satisfying performance in front of the cameras and sent flowers after the final day of shooting. But as far as she knew he had never dated one of the actresses in his films. He was usually too involved with work to go out much, and when he did, he mostly dated women who were not in the business.

But right now Stephanie didn't have much time to mull over Jon's possible change of mind. She needed to prepare herself for the approaching confrontation with Cade. Maybe Jon, in his usual diplomatic manner, could calm the rancher and blunt his anger. But that wouldn't work: she knew Cade had no use for Jon, dismissing him as an artistic director with no sense of reality.

Perhaps Kara could smile at the brooding rancher and he would succumb to her beauty. Most men did when they met the gorgeous redhead. But Stephanie wasn't sure she wanted that to happen, and in any case, it struck too close to Cade's suspicions about herself. Somehow facing his wrath alone seemed a better solution.

There was no sign of Cade when they arrived at the site of the accident, for which Stephanie was grateful. A couple of men were at the scene, carrying boards, hammers and sacks of nails, ready to begin the repair work as soon as the truck was removed. It had crashed almost completely through the fence, stopping so that the back wheels were practically even with the boards that had been knocked down. A rise in the rolling prairie had slowed the truck enough that it had stopped just short of a large oak tree at the edge of the pasture.

Stephanie, Kara and Jon were taking a look at the damage when Cade rode up on his quarter horse, leading two other horses behind his. Slowly he dismounted, flipped the reins of his own horse around a rail of still standing fence and made his way toward them.

Stephanie was uncomfortably aware of her scanty attire when Cade's eyes raked her, particularly since Kara was immaculately outfitted in a crisply fresh sundress and wore a wide-brimmed straw hat to protect her delicate skin from the powerful summer sun. Cade didn't seem to notice either the actress or Jon. He had eyes only for Stephanie, and his dark expression told her that his mood had not lightened since their telephone conversation a little more than an hour earlier.

"Isn't this what you promised me would not happen?" It was less a question than an accusation.

Jon tried to soften Cade's attack on Stephanie. "We are truly sorry, Mr. Steele. There was no way of knowing that the emergency brake wasn't on and that the truck would roll."

Cade ignored him. "You're responsible, Miss

Lasater. Let's see you undo your damage." He folded his arms, waiting for her to take action. "Once you've removed the truck from my pasture, perhaps you'd like to round up some horses. Two of them are still running loose around here."

Jon pulled the keys from his pocket. "I'll get the truck out, Stef. You stand at the back and guide me so I don't hit anything coming out."

"No." Cade stopped both Jon and Stephanie instantly. "I don't mean to be rude to you, Mr. Jenson, but this is between Miss Lasater and me. I want her to move the truck."

For the first time, his gaze encompassed Kara, who was silently watching the scene, her mouth slightly agape with wonder at the activities going on around her. He turned away, then pivoted sharply and stared at her again.

Watching him, Stephanie wondered what had so arrested him about the actress. As she took the keys out of Jon's hand and walked toward the truck, she kept an eye on Cade with her peripheral vision. He had clearly been jolted by the sight of Kara, for he was paying no attention at all to Stephanie, standing there instead like a simple fan awed at seeing a famous movie star in person.

Jon introduced Kara to the rancher, and the actress offered her hand. For a moment Cade seemed too stunned even to take her slender fingers in his, but then, almost physically shaking himself back to life, he suggested that Jon drive Kara to the ranch house so they could wait in air-conditioned comfort while the truck was removed.

Jon didn't want to leave, pointing out to Cade that since he was the producer as well as the director of the movie, anything that happened was his ultimate responsibility, and he couldn't let Stephanie take the blame for what he should have handled.

"I assure you I have no plans to beat her up," Cade announced, unmoved by Jon's statement. "I only want her to see that when she makes a promise, she must be prepared to keep it."

"It's all right, Jon," Stephanie called out. "Really."

Jon's brows knitted, and that obstinate look that she had learned to know so well appeared. It was exceeded only by the stubborn expression on Cade's face. She'd have to take action on her own to break up this stalemate, she knew.

"Kara?" she almost whispered, and the actress, knowing what she wanted, nodded. Taking Jon's arm, Kara murmured that the hot sun was bothering her and that she really would appreciate it if he'd escort her to the house for a little while. Jon's frown deepened, but finally he nodded, and they departed. Before he started the car engine, Jon searched Stephanie's face.

"Are you sure you want me to leave?" he asked, and she nodded.

Cade didn't give Stephanie the opportunity to move along the outside of the fence to the broken segment, where she would be able to walk into the field. He picked her up and unceremoniously dumped her on the other side of the fence, then leaned against the railing while she self-consciously picked her way through the ankle-high growth of grass. She yearned for her jeans, a dress, anything that would cover her legs, because she could feel his eyes on her every stride.

It took four tries before she could get the engine started and three attempts to get the truck into reverse gear. Although she had driven standard-shift cars before, she had never had occasion to tackle a vehicle of this size. Nervous as she was, she couldn't seem to coordinate the clutch pedal and the gas pedal, and the truck repeatedly stalled.

Her face rosy more from embarrassment than from the heat of the midafternoon, she waited for Cade to make a sarcastic comment. No doubt he was enjoying this show of ineptitude on her part. She couldn't even back up a truck. When she did get the vehicle moving, it lunged backward so quickly that she brushed against the broken fence rails on one side, leaving an ugly scratch along the entire length of the truck. She hit the brake as quickly as she could, and the engine died again.

Before she could attempt to restart it, Cade was yanking the door open and pushing her to the passenger side. "Where did you take your driving training?" he asked. "At a demolition derby?"

He eased the truck onto the road and repositioned it with the other trailers and trucks parked nearby. Jerking the emergency brake on, he pulled the key from the ignition switch and tossed it at Stephanie.

"I'll have my people repair the fence," he told her, sarcasm giving his words a bitter edge. "I'm afraid you couldn't figure out which end of the hammer to use.''

Cade was out of the truck and issuing instructions to his employees before Stephanie could even reach for the door handle on her side. She warily watched him talk to his men while she wondered how she was supposed to get back to the house, to Jon and Kara. For certain she wouldn't ride back with him on that horse of his. She'd rather walk, although it was a long hike and she didn't have on the right kind of shoes for such a trek.

It was a relief when Cade indicated that they would make the trip in a ranch truck, and she heard him ask one of the men to return his horse to the barn when they had completed the repairs and found the two missing horses.

"I really am sorry," she said again on their ride to the house. The apology was sincere, but she spoke simply to break the hideous silence between them. "I'll try to make it up to you for putting you to so much trouble."

Cade kept his eyes on the road, but one hand reached out to touch her bare knee, massaging it before she flinched and scooted out of his reach. "I suppose I'll have to think of a way to make you repay me for my trouble." He glanced at her, his probing gaze revealing nothing. "Don't you think so?"

"I'll do what I can as far as your property is concerned," she answered, averting her eyes and staring out the window.

"What about as far as I'm concerned, Miss Lasater? What are you going to do to ease my problems?''

"If you're saying what I think you're saying, Mr. Steele, you can just stop it right now." She was furious at the implication she assumed he was making.

He laughed, a harsh sound that rumbled from deep in his throat. "It's just that knowing what you are, I thought you'd make an offer to soothe my anger at your stupidity." He stopped the truck in the driveway and reached for her chin, holding it firmly in a viselike grip. "Don't women trying to get ahead in show business usually trade their sexual favors for whatever will help them?''

His other hand slipped behind her neck, keeping her locked in his rough embrace.

Stephanie defiantly turned to face him. "You've been reading too many gossip columns, Mr. Steele."

He held her a minute longer, watching the sparkle that anger brought to her vivid blue eyes. "Perhaps," he admitted at last, "but only perhaps." Then as suddenly as he had taken hold of her he released her. "Shall we go inside and join the others?''

Jon, clearly concerned about Stephanie, was pacing the living-room floor as they entered, while Cade's mother, overwhelmed at being so close to Kara, was chatting away with the actress. Mrs. Martin was there, as well, offering more coffee and tea and additional supplies of fresh-baked cookies.

Stephanie could tell from Jon's expression that he wanted to make an issue of the truck, but Cade didn't give him the opportunity, turning aside Jon's furor with a joking remark.

"She's not much of a truck driver, I'm afraid," he laughed. "Jenson, you're going to have to show Miss Lasater a thing or two about shifting gears."

His humor broke the tenseness in the room, exactly as he had planned, Stephanie realized, and she had to smile a little, too, at the thought of her efforts at moving the truck. She had deserved being forced to try to drive it out of the pasture after all of her promises to Cade, and she didn't resent that. But she didn't deserve his remark about women in the motion-picture industry trading sex for roles or promotions.

There were some who did, she knew. She had met a few, but there were many others who made a success of themselves through hard work and real talent. Kara, for example. Stephanie had never known her to use her beauty to win movie roles, and she never looked twice at influential producers. Maybe that was because she was interested in Jon, Stephanie mused. Perhaps she had been interested in him since the first picture in which he directed her. If not then, it was obvious she liked him now. At least, it was obvious to Stephanie. She racked her brain trying to think of any time she had seen them together apart from business meetings, but she couldn't think of any. She had never run into them in any Los Angeles restaurants or clubs.

Maybe she was mistaken. They weren't acting like lovers now. In fact, they almost ignored each other. Kara devoted her full attention to Mrs. Steele; that is, until Cade sat beside her on the long couch. Then she turned to him with an enchanting smile and proclaimed how thrilling she thought it must be to run a ranch.

That was all the encouragement a man would need, Stephanie reflected wryly. She sat by Jon on the opposite side of the room while Cade and Kara lightly discussed the ranch and the animals he raised. Cade seemed entranced with her; he was smiling, laughing, immediately noticing when her cup of coffee was almost empty and offering to refill it.

Stephanie glanced sideways at Jon. If he was jealous, it didn't show. He chatted with Mrs. Steele and Mrs. Martin as if Cade and Kara weren't even there. Stephanie was certain that she had been mistaken. If he really loved Kara, Jon would have torn her away from Cade by now. Cade wasn't the type of man you could safely leave with a woman you loved. He was the kind who would steal a girl's heart without even trying and without even wanting it when it was won. She knew that much about him.

Stephanie didn't want to watch Cade and Kara any longer, so when Mrs. Martin gathered the dishes and carried them into the kitchen, she trailed behind her.

"It's such a thrill having you all here," the housekeeper enthused as she placed the fragile bone-china plates on the kitchen counter. "I'm so excited. And Miss Warren is as beautiful in person as she is on the screen, isn't she?"

Stephanie nodded her agreement. She couldn't deny that fact, and she couldn't feel much envy, either. Kara was not one to flaunt her good looks.

Most of the time she seemed genuinely unaware of how striking she really was.

"I think Cade kind of likes her," Mrs. Martin confided, although it wasn't news to Stephanie. "I haven't seen him smile so much in a long time. Not since Merilee left." She stopped wiping a silver tray in mid-motion. "That's it!" she exclaimed. "That's why Cade is so interested in Miss Warren. She looks a lot like Merilee."

Stephanie could feel a sinking sensation inside her.

"She does a bit, you know. The same light red hair and fair complexion. And they are both tall." She began rubbing the tray again. "I don't think he ever completely got over Merilee."

The matchmaker instinct in the housekeeper began taking over. "Maybe we can find a way of getting Cade to that movie site more often," she suggested. "Kind of let him see more of Miss Warren. Who knows? We might have a movie star in the family in a few months." She laughed at the idea. "Wouldn't that be something?"

"It certainly would." Stephanie didn't know what else to say. This conversation wasn't going the way she wanted it to, so she hastily excused herself and returned to the living room, suggesting to Jon that they depart so they could get back to Fort Worth in time for dinner.

Mrs. Steele overheard and urged them to stay and eat at the ranch, but Jon, to Stephanie's relief, turned down her invitation.

"We've got a rehearsal to finish," he explained, and his eyes fell on Cade as he remembered the cause

of their interrupted practice session. "And I've got to
make certain my leading lady gets to sleep early
tonight," he added, turning his attention to Kara.
"She goes before the camera first thing in the morning, and we can't have her photographed with dark
circles under her eyes."

"Miss Warren would never photograph any way
but beautiful," Mrs. Steele protested. "Don't you
agree, Cade?"

His gaze rested on Stephanie's bare legs for a moment before he answered. "I'm sure Miss Warren
always looks perfect." Then his eyes roved sugges-
tively up Stephanie's firm thighs to her breasts and
on up to her full lips. "Mr. Jenson knows how to
select beautiful women."

Sure that he was mocking her, but unable to retaliate, Stephanie stiffly shook Mrs. Steele's hand,
called goodbye to Mrs. Martin, who remained in the
kitchen, and headed for the front door. Deliberately,
she didn't say a word of farewell to Cade.

He followed them to the car, and Stephanie saw his
eyebrows lift at the fact that she flung open the back
door instead of taking a place by Jon's side. He kept
his thoughts to himself, however, and merely opened
the front passenger door for Kara. He didn't shake
hands with Jon, and Jon didn't offer a hand, either.
There was still too much hostility between them
for more than an uneasy truce. The men nodded
brusquely to each other before Jon started back to
town.

"Now, that was a strange experience," Kara commented before they were even off the ranch property.

"Cade Steele is a very strange man," Jon agreed.

"There's nothing strange about him," Stephanie argued, glancing back toward the house, even though she knew it was out of sight by now. "He's just a simple rancher with a big ego and an obstinate nature."

It wasn't completely true, she knew. He might be egotistical and stubborn, but he was also very well-read and highly educated. Stephanie was ashamed that she had categorized him so quickly as a simple rancher. There was absolutely nothing simple about Cade Steele.

CHAPTER SIX

THE LONGHORNS were reluctant to make their movie debut. Time after time, the stock coordinator had tried to turn them toward the prairie where the cameras were trained.

The scene was supposed to be the one in which the hero first sights the animals on the open range. Later he would round up the longhorns, brand them and drive them back to his own property before joining a cattle drive to Kansas along the brand-new Chisholm Trail, which came from the San Antonio area through Fort Worth on its way north.

The animals, however, didn't want to leave the sanctuary of the fenced pasture where they were comfortable, and they were still wild enough to resist the people who tried to prod them along the way. Cade stood silently by and watched, not offering any suggestions except a warning about the danger of getting too close to the curved horns that twisted away from the animals' faces. He demonstrated vividly by placing an unopened sack of oats in the pasture, near one of the bulls. The beast slit the sack with a horn as easily as a man could have done with a knife.

Stephanie was impressed at her first meeting with the longhorns. Their hides were reddish brown relieved with spots of white, and they stood taller than most cattle she had seen. They had a dignified air, almost a haughty grandeur, as if practically daring the men to come near them.

"It's the long legs," Cade told her when she questioned him about the height. "Longhorns are noted for their long legs."

He squinted at a bull that warily eyed the group from behind the fence rail. "That fellow's ancestors arrived in the New World with Columbus on his second voyage in 1493, and by the late 1600s and early 1700s the Spanish were crossing the Rio Grande into Texas and bringing the cattle with them."

"And when the Spanish left," Stephanie continued his story, "the cattle stayed, roaming free on the land."

"Right," Cade agreed. "And that's what saved my people and many others."

Jon was standing nearby listening to them, and he joined in the conversation. "As I understand it—" he looked to Cade for confirmation "—there was a market for beef in the North after the Civil War, when millions of longhorns roamed the unfenced Texas range." He openly admired the animals. "I've heard of as many as ten million longhorns being trailed north by the drovers just between 1870 and 1890."

"That's about right," Cade confirmed, looking at Jon with new respect. He pointed out the lean look of the animals and noted that longhorns were particularly suited to the long drives to market. They could travel long distances without special care and could survive cold, desert sun, floods and sparse food and water conditions.

"They do look tough," Stephanie remarked as she gazed at the animals.

"They're tough through and through," Cade answered. "That's why they're not raised much anymore: their meat was tough and stringy, and when cattle with more tender meat became available, the customers didn't want the longhorns."

"But you still raise them," Stephanie commented.

"And I always will," Cade agreed. He turned to Jon. "Now, let me show you what to do."

Calling to a couple of his employees who were watching the activity, he reached for a rope, formed a lasso and swung it around the horns of an especially large bull. Then, swinging himself into the saddle of his sorrel horse, he gently led the animal to the area where the cameras were waiting. With a little urging from the cowboys, the other longhorns quietly followed, and once they were in position, Cade and his employees quickly rode out of camera range. The scene was shot in only two takes.

Jon was elated as the animals were herded closer together for a second scene. "I hope you'll stay around for the rest of our work with the cattle," he complimented Cade, "particularly when we do the cattle drive and the stampede."

"I intend to," Cade answered, but some of the harshness was gone from his voice, Stephanie noticed. He was seeing a new side of Jon, and she wasn't too surprised when the director and Morgan Anderson were invited to have lunch with the rancher.

The three men were all talking at once when they returned, involved in a discussion of how a couple of the horses had been trained to fall on command for the rougher scenes of the movie.

"There are a very few horses in Hollywood·that can do it," Jon was telling Cade. "We've been fortunate to be able to hire these ones and have them shipped here for the film."

Morgan explained that some directors had used wires to trip the horses, resulting in serious injuries to the animals, but that practice had been stopped. One of the reasons he liked to work with Jon, he said, was that the director took such pains to ensure the safety of every animal involved in his films.

He went on to talk about how trainers also used Pavlov's classical conditioning technique to train a horse to act as if it were sick or injured for a scene. When pricked with a pin on its flank while it was lying down, the animal would lift its head in surprise. After a few times, it would raise its head as if in pain when the trainer merely pointed to its flank.

Cade nodded, but his gaze had already strayed from Morgan to Kara, who was coming out of her dressing room costumed for her next scene. Jon was staring at her, as well, his practiced eye checking to make certain that she was dressed exactly as he intended. Or was he simply admiring her, Stephanie wondered as she watched the men from the shade of the tent where the crew was finishing lunch. Were both he and Cade admiring the actress's delicate beauty?

She'd never know what Cade thought about Kara,

she realized, but she intended to question Jon if she had the opportunity. It would be something new if the director were falling for his star, and she hoped he might be. It was about time for Jon Jenson to think of something besides business all the time. He needed a woman in his life, and Kara would be the perfect choice, she decided. Besides, if Jon captured the heart of Kara, that meant Cade couldn't have her. It would serve him right to lose out to Jon.

Stephanie blushed at her wayward thoughts. Who cared what woman Cade had or didn't have, anyway? It was none of her business except that she felt sorry for any woman in love with him. A woman would have to be crazy to want to spend her life with that insufferable man...even if his kisses could ignite such a raging fire inside of her.

When Jon called to Kara and then started looking around the film site, Stephanie knew he was hunting for her. She took a final swallow of her cold drink and deposited the empty can in a trash barrel at the edge of the lunch tent. She was reluctant to face Cade again but curious to watch how the two men would act with Kara. She knew that Morgan wasn't affected by the actress. He was a happily married man with four children at home in California, and he never looked at any of the women on the sets of the movies in which he worked.

When Stephanie joined the group, Jon immediately threw his arm around her, virtually ignoring Kara, who stood between Cade and Morgan. His fingers were tight against her arm, but they didn't send the prickly tingles of electrical sparks shooting through her body the way that Cade's touch did. Without thinking, she looked up at the man she wanted to avoid, and his icy glance chilled her to the bone.

She tried to wiggle out of Jon's embrace, but he kept holding her as he discussed plans for the afternoon's shooting. She wished Jon wouldn't be so affectionate. It was his nature: she had seen him hug and kiss dozens of women, Kara included, and it never meant a thing. But Cade didn't know that, and Cade, she was acutely aware, believed Jon was her lover.

There had never been a lover, but she wasn't going to admit that to Cade. Let him think what he wanted to about her; she had no reason to explain anything to him!

If she had been willing to have an affair, she might never have left New York. Her fiancé had been an account executive at the advertising agency where she worked. He had wanted her to move in with him and had given her a hard time when she refused, scoffing at her old-fashioned reasons for putting off total intimacy. Later he had tried to persuade her to go to bed with one of his prospective clients in the hope of landing the account, and she had realized then how shallow his love really was. Depressed and confused, she had fled the city, ashamed that she had even thought of marrying such a man.

But her past was none of Cade Steele's business, and she didn't have to feel guilty because Jon, a good friend, casually hugged her. It spoke of the comfortable supportive relationship between them. He had firmly taken her under his wing when she arrived in

Los Angeles, and he had taught her about the movie industry, instilling in her confidence in her professional ability.

He had tried to help her socially, as well, constantly introducing her to men who worked with him, but she had found them all disappointing in some undefined way, and shied away from involvements. Certainly they were sophisticated, familiar with the best restaurants and the correct wines, but they lacked the quality of strength she intuitively sought in a man. Actually, she didn't know if she ever did want a man in her life again. After what felt like a long time, her bruises had barely healed, and she was reluctant to take the risk of allowing love into her heart.

When everyone's eyes were on her, waiting for her reply, Stephanie realized she hadn't even heard what Jon had asked her, and she had to have him repeat his question about the tentative shooting schedule for the rest of the month.

Hastily she outlined the program the director had worked out a few days earlier, which she had typed and distributed to everyone involved. He planned to work with the longhorns for the rest of the week, and then he would go on to other scenes before filming the stampede segment.

"I think it's better to let the animals get settled again," he told Cade, who nodded his agreement, "before we do that scene." He explained that Morgan would do the major stunts and would be the one who had to turn the herd at the last moment by riding dangerously close to the animals.

"The delay will give Morgan more time to plan his

action," Jon added. "On this type of scene I let Morgan do most of the figuring. I just tell my cinematographer to aim the cameras at him."

Cade was becoming interested in spite of himself, Stephanie could tell. He was soon wandering off with Morgan toward the range where the longhorns were calmly grazing.

For the first afternoon scene, the hero was to be shown displaying to his bride his new herd of cattle, which he was going to drive to market in Kansas. Kara grew increasingly anxious about going near the animals, and Jon patiently explained that she would not be very close to them, that he would shoot her close-ups completely away from the herd and that she would have to be only about three feet from one, a longhorn bull that Robert would bring close.

Robert was almost as skittish with the longhorns as Kara, but he did manage to do his close-ups once Morgan, dressed in identical clothing, performed the long shots, corralling the animals into a designated area so that, as the cameras photographed them from various angles, the herd looked larger than the two dozen cattle actually involved.

But when it came time for the largest longhorn to be displayed before the hero's bride, Kara couldn't go through with her part. She would start toward the animal that was supposed to bring the end of hard times for the fictional family, then scream and run back behind the cameras, making the animal even more nervous than it already was with the crowd of people gathered around and with Jon calling instructions for the crew.

Finally Jon gave up, and one of the extras, who was the same height as the star, put on Kara's costume and did the scene, her back turned to the cameras so that the moviegoers would never know a different actress was being used.

During all of the filming Cade stood to the side, silent except to suggest a way of turning the cattle for a better camera angle. He watched Kara's attempts to do her scene without saying a word, and Stephanie wondered if he was feeling sorry for the actress or merely confirming his theory that movie stars didn't know what the real world was about.

By the time the afternoon's shooting was over, everyone was exhausted, and Stephanie could barely face the thought of staying late to oversee the cleaning crew, much less having to report to Cade. She realized she wouldn't have to, however. He had been with them all day long, so he knew everything that had happened. For once she might be on time for the early bus.

But when she walked over to the rancher and suggested that she didn't need to visit his house that evening, he knitted his heavy brows and frowned.

"You're supposed to report every night, Miss Lasater." He glanced at the gold watch on his wrist. "I'll see you in forty-five minutes." Then, dismissing her, he turned back to Jon. "Now, Jenson, I've been thinking. It's inconvenient for you to drive back and forth to town every day while you're shooting here. I've got that big house—why don't you stay at my place on nights when you're working late?"

Stephanie's mouth was agape as she listened to

him. She couldn't believe Cade was actually inviting the director to stay at his house.

"Your man Anderson might want to stay, as well," Cade added. "And Miss Warren, too. My home is large and my housekeeper will be more than happy to fix your meals." He removed his Western-style hat, brushed back a stray lock of hair that had fallen over his forehead and replaced the hat on his head.

"That's very kind of you, Cade," Jon responded, walking off with the rancher toward the office trailer. "I'd be delighted myself. It would save me a great deal of time right now when we're on such a tight schedule. Of course, I can't speak for the others."

"Then it's settled," she heard Cade proclaim. "Why don't you come to the house with me now and have a drink." He glanced over his shoulder at Stephanie. "Your...assistant can pick you up when she's finished here."

"Fine," Jon answered blithely. "Let me wind up a few details first." And the two men walked casually into the office, closing the door behind them, leaving Stephanie fuming outside.

Cade was really something, she thought, picking up a rock in her path and tossing it away with a vengeance. He managed to get his digs in at her while smoothly charming anyone he wanted to. He was even smoother than Jon, whom he already had eating out of his hand. Why, he'd have Kara enthralled in no time.

Stephanie frowned, not wanting to think of that

possibility. She tucked her T-shirt inside the waist-band of her jeans as she wandered to the tent area, where trash was being collected and removed from the site. Her mind wasn't on the details she was supposed to be paying attention to; she couldn't focus on whether the crew was doing its job properly or not. Her brain raced with conflicting ideas.

There were endless possibilities involved in this situation, she mused. Cade was probably already attracted to Kara, and Kara was likely in love with Jon, but Cade would sweep her off her feet, and she would forget about Jon, who might be in love with her and then be rejected. And then Stephanie herself wanted.... She hesitated, muttering a savage, "Nobody," loud enough that one of the crew stopped his work to ask if she was speaking to him.

Stephanie perched on a redwood table, letting her feet rest on the matching bench, and stared at the office trailer across from her. Let Jon and Cade be friends; it was fine with her. They'd soon discover they were both after the same woman, and they'd have to fight it out themselves. Stephanie wouldn't be involved. She hoped Kara wouldn't be hurt in the struggle over her, but men had probably fought over the beautiful actress before. They weren't likely to compete for Stephanie, that was for sure.

Briefly Stephanie considered paying a visit to Kara's dressing room and warning her of what might lie ahead of her, but she remembered that the actress had departed in her limousine as soon as Jon had released her for the day. She had been so upset at her failure to do the scene with the longhorns correctly that she hadn't lingered to take off her makeup, delaying only long enough to slip out of the long dress, bonnet and high-buttoned shoes that comprised her costume and send the outfit to the woman who doubled for her in the action.

Before the area was cleaned and prepared for the next day's shooting, Jon and Cade had departed. Stephanie found Jon's car keys waiting for her on the desk when she entered the trailer. She also found a list of assignments, all of which needed to be done immediately. Jon had discovered, he wrote, that rain was forecast for the day after tomorrow; therefore, he had decided to alter the schedule to avoid having weather delay the outdoor scene he had planned for that day. Instead he wanted to film an indoor scene, the one in which the two principal characters meet for the first time.

It would be a party setting, although a most unelaborate one in keeping with the economic conditions following the Civil War. According to the script, the heroine visits relatives in the area, who arrange a gathering for their neighbors to meet the guest. The hero takes his mother and two sisters to the event to give them some chance at gaiety, even though he doesn't feel like partying himself. He has had more than he can handle trying to clear away the underbrush that has grown up during his absence and hunting for food to keep the family from starving. He appears at the party in mended but clean clothes and at first glance is bewitched by the daintily groomed woman he meets. But, ashamed of his attire and his poverty, he is afraid to speak to her. She must make the initial move to be friends and win his love.

There would be several actors involved in the scene, all of whom had to be notified of the change in schedule. But first Stephanie had to get in touch with the people who operated the production studio in Dallas, to make certain the facilities there could be utilized on that day.

At least the sets had already been constructed and the backdrops completed, so that wouldn't be a problem. She hoped all the costumes were pressed and ready, but she made a note to check on that as soon as she returned to the hotel and found the wardrobe mistress.

By the time she had finally located the notebook with all the phone numbers she needed and gathered the supplies she would have to use to type new call sheets once everything was finalized, the entire crew was gone from the site. Stephanie would have liked to go straight to the hotel, too. She would have to be on the phone for a while, she knew, and it would be late before she could relax with a hot shower and shampoo. She might as well forget about dinner. She seemed to be doing that a lot lately, and her waistline was becoming smaller each week. She had already adjusted her belt to a tighter notch.

If there was ever a night, she thought, when she didn't need to see Cade, this was it; but at least Jon would be there. Maybe she could honk and he'd come out so they could go directly back to Fort Worth. Or maybe she could wait for him on the front porch. She could always use the telephone calls as a reason to be in a hurry.

When she parked in the driveway of Cade's house, she did pause long enough to quickly brush her hair and dash on some lipstick and powder. It was something she couldn't help doing. Ever since the first week, when Cade's eyes had mocked her bedraggled looks, she had taken pains to comb her hair and apply fresh lipstick before seeing him. There was nothing she could do about the chocolate stain on her T-shirt—courtesy of the melting ice-cream cone someone had handed her during a break in the afternoon session.

Cade probably thought she owned no other clothes than jeans and T-shirts, she reflected. He hadn't noticed her chiffon dress at dinner the night he had met her in Dallas, and she hadn't worn many of her other clothes for the outdoor shooting sessions. It was far more practical to be in jeans and shirts, the way the crew members were.

Besides, the T-shirts were part of Jon's organization scheme. Each group of technicians wore a particular color of shirt, so it was easier for him to find whomever he needed in a hurry. The cameramen wore yellow, the sound engineers were in green, the wardrobe and makeup people dressed in orange, the grips had red shirts, and the electricians were outfitted in blue-and-white stripes.

Even Jon wore jeans to work, although they were designer models, and his shirts were casual even if they were custom tailored. In contrast, his hat was an old straw creation he had picked up in a border town in Mexico years before. It had once been striking, but now it was in terrible shape, and Stephanie often threatened to hide it or burn it. But Jon insisted it brought him good luck, and the straw hat went with him on every movie trip. She hoped he'd have his hat in hand, ready to depart, when she rang the doorbell.

Mrs. Martin let Stephanie in, informing her that Cade and Jon were in the study and that Cade had said she should join them when she arrived. The housekeeper put the phrase nicely, but it sounded ominously like an ultimatum to Stephanie.

The two men were discussing the Chisholm Trail when she entered the room, relaxing and conversing as if there were no other jobs to do this day. For them, there probably weren't. But Stephanie still had calls to make, and she mentioned her work as soon as Cade rose and invited her to sit down. She didn't want to sit where he indicated: it was the chair in which he had held her to him so intimately and from which he had pulled her so violently when Jon had phoned.

"We do have telephones here, Miss Lasater," Cade informed her. "Have a drink and then make your calls. I'm sure Jon will wait for you."

So now it was "Jon" not just "Jenson," she noticed. They had certainly become good friends quickly. It was going to be two against one from now on, and she was the one. She slid into the chair and accepted the glass Cade offered.

He insisted she make her calls from the office, offering her the use of his desk and moving a couple of ledgers out of her way. She didn't want to call from there because she didn't want Cade listening to her conversations, but she couldn't argue with Jon's logical statement that it might be too late to call if she waited until she was back in Fort Worth.

"But these are long-distance numbers," she protested.

"Charge them to our credit card," Jon told her, and so she resignedly picked up the receiver and dialed the first call.

For a while she was acutely aware of Cade's eyes on her as she talked, but later she forgot him, so absorbed was she in making arrangement after arrangement, double-checking the availability of the studio, establishing the hours they could work, checking out the fact that credentials would be issued only to those authorized to enter the building. Every detail took time, but the effort was necessary; Stephanie had learned a long time ago that if she left out even one item, something would go wrong.

She called the wardrobe woman and then the set designer. He was still angry with her about the log cabin, but Stephanie couldn't help that. She made him describe in detail the way the interior of the house set would look, since she hadn't had an opportunity to see it yet.

The prop man was more difficult to track down, but she finally reached him and was assured that he had practically all of his arrangements done. The only thing he lacked, he told her, was the food that would be served for the guests in the party scene.

"Remember, Brad," she told him, "these people are supposed to be poor. They aren't going to have a lot of fancy food." Her eyes strayed to Cade, who was leaning back in his chair, his hands clasped behind his neck, watching her intently. "They would probably serve turkey or chicken with corn bread and maybe have watermelon for dessert."

Mentally she pictured the cabin on Cade's land. "And, Brad," she added, "I think you should have a loom in the corner and some type of ornate clock or porcelain statue on the mantel." She listened to Brad's objection, then insisted. "It's the kind of thing the pioneers would have brought from their old homes, a reminder of the days when they or their parents had the luxuries they were forced to leave behind. Something of beauty in a harsh land."

She confirmed another prop or two and hung up, closing her little book of telephone numbers and propping her chin with an elbow on the desk.

"Sounds good to me, Stef," Jon complimented her, but she looked to Cade. It was his approval she wanted. He didn't say a word, but he did nod his head: only a fraction of a nod, but enough to let her know he respected her insistence on accuracy.

It was another half hour before they left, during which time Stephanie sat almost silently while Jon and Cade returned to their discussion of cattle trails and then went on to plans for Jon to stay at the ranch a couple of nights a week.

"And, of course, the offer still goes for Anderson and Miss Warren," Cade reminded the director.

Stephanie noticed that Cade hadn't invited Robert Grant, but she didn't point out the omission. She was wondering if Kara would accept and stay at the ranch. Both Jon and Cade appeared anxious to have her close by.

Poor Kara, she thought, having to fight off two beaux at once. At least *she* didn't have that problem. Right now she didn't even have one. Jon's recent demands on her time hadn't given her much chance for a social life, but she didn't regret the loss. A man was the last thing she wanted; a man was the last thing she needed.

Take Cade, for example. He had kissed her and held her and aroused in her desires she hadn't even been aware of; but he hadn't acted out of love or even affection. He no doubt simply thought she was the type of woman who would go to bed with any man; he was interested only in having a sexual encounter and then discarding her. It would be a way of getting back at a woman for what one had apparently done to him. Merilee had left him, and now he wanted revenge on all women. Stephanie could understand why the woman had wanted out of Cade's life. *She* certainly did.

But when he took her arm as she was about to leave, swinging her around to face him, she forgot that she didn't want any part of him and she let herself slide sensuously against him, touching his hard broad chest and laying a hand on the strong arm that held her.

"You did a good job on the phone, Stephanie," he told her, and her heart pounded hard inside her chest at the use of her first name. "I appreciate the fact that you insisted on the right props and food."

So that was it. He touched her only because he wanted to tell her she was efficient at her job. She had hoped he was going to say something else. Normally she would have been happy at his praise, at even the fact that he took notice of what she was doing. She had looked to him when she finished her calls, and her emotions had soared when he had nodded. But that wasn't enough. Anyone could be good at her job. There were many people in the film company who were every bit as competent as she was.

Suddenly she knew what she wanted. She wanted Cade to clasp her in a tight embrace, to caress her face with his lean brown fingers, to let her taste his firm male lips and feel his hard muscular thighs against her own, now aching with a longing to know the strength of him.

Stephanie stared determinedly at the floor, hiding her eyes from his omniscient gaze. She didn't want him to read the yearning in them. He'd laugh at the thought that she was emotionally involved. He would accept sex, of course, but she didn't want sex, not without love, not without yielding her entire heart to a man and having him do the same for her. Cade would never give his heart to her, just his body, and that wasn't enough. It wouldn't fill the void inside her that cried out to him.

Saying a hasty goodbye, Stephanie dashed to the car and waited for Jon to shake hands with Cade and tell him he would see him the next day.

The director was in a good mood on the drive to the hotel, excited about the rancher's change of attitude and his offers to help. "It will really make a difference, Stef, having him on our side."

She mumbled an inaudible reply.

"You know, he said he would work with us to get

even better locations for some of the scenes we'll be doing."

"We have locations," Stephanie answered.

"But Cade knows of even better ones," Jon told her. "I mentioned the love scene that takes place in the woods, and he says he knows the ideal spot. I thought maybe he could show it to us sometime tomorrow."

"Whatever you say, Jon." She wished he would quit talking about Cade. Every mention of the man's name stirred raw emotions inside her, feelings she still needed to sort out. She had a terrible suspicion she might be in love with him—but surely she couldn't love a man who didn't care about her? That had happened once, and it wouldn't happen again. Or maybe she hadn't really loved her fiancé. He had never been able to send goose bumps up and down her arms with a look or a touch, and he had never brought her practically to the point of surrender with a sultry embrace. Her love for him had been more intellectual, a sharing of common interests, of ideals, of plans for the future; or at least she had thought they shared those things. She shared nothing with Cade except her growing love for his state and its history, but she wanted him with a longing that made their different backgrounds seem inconsequential.

For a moment she thought of using feminine wiles to attract him, but she discarded the idea immediately. Compared to Kara, she didn't have any to use, and she wouldn't know how anyway. It wouldn't matter what she did: Cade might want her to satisfy him sexually, but when it came to his emotional needs he would turn to Kara. Indeed, he likely already had.

She studied Jon with a sidelong glance, wondering if she should mention the actress. Why not, she finally decided. It might get him off the subject of Cade.

"Jon," she queried, "are you really going to ask Kara to stay at the ranch?"

"Certainly," he replied.

"Do you think that's a good idea?"

"I guess you're right, Stef," Jon sighed. "Maybe Kara and I shouldn't both stay at the house. People might jump to conclusions about us."

"Should they?" She kept her eyes on his face, hidden in the darkness except when occasional headlights flashed on them from approaching cars.

"Stef, you know I've always had a rule about not going out with the actresses I direct. It's a good rule and I've always abided by it."

"But you're in love with Kara," Stephanie stated simply.

"You can tell?" Jon was aghast. He paused as if deliberating, then seemed to reach a decision. "Kara doesn't realize how I feel," he confessed, "and it's driving me crazy because I can't say anything to her. I can't ask her out even in a casual way because someone would see us and the news would be in all the gossip columns." He shook his head ruefully. "And you know what problems that would cause on the set. If I took Kara's side in a disagreement with Robert, he would accuse me of playing favorites. That's show-biz politics; I just can't take a chance."

"You should speak to Kara," Stephanie suggested.

"No, I don't dare say a word." He laughed softly. "When I'm positioning her for a shot and I have my hands on her shoulders or her face, she smiles so sweetly that I want to crush her in my arms, but I have to control myself and keep my mind on business. You know how many people watch her constantly anytime she's on the set."

Stephanie gazed at the lights of downtown Fort Worth, visible in the distance. Two lost souls, she thought. She and Jon, both aching for people they wanted. But he had a chance of success, for Stephanie felt certain that Kara returned Jon's love or, at least, had some growing affection for him. For herself there was no hope.

"Is there anything I can do?" she offered.

Jon took her hand in his, bringing her fingers to his lips. "I'll see if I can think of something. Thanks for listening, Stef. You're a real pal."

SHE DIDN'T FEEL LIKE A PAL the next morning when Jon called her to his side during a coffee break. Cade was sitting next to him in the lunch tent, and he nodded at Stephanie, who self-consciously tucked the pink-and-white print blouse deeper into the waistband of her jeans. She wanted to shake him, make him speak and say something kind, something that would give her hope for some kind of affection, but she could only return his nod and listen to Jon.

Cade, he told her, was going to show her where the site was that he had suggested for the love scene. Jon himself had planned to accompany him, but he had to work with the actors on a scene that wasn't going

right. "I'm trusting you to make certain the place is
suitable, Stef. You know what we need: lots of long
lush grass, trees filling the background, a sense of
solitude but with enough space for the cameras and
equipment."

"Don't you want me to stay and finish typing the
call sheets?" she asked, but Jon sent her on her way.
Reluctantly she followed Cade to his truck, unable to
tear her eyes from his broad back and the wisps of
thick dark hair that strayed over his shirt collar.

It was a short drive to the site, only a couple of
hills over from where the company was stationed, but
it seemed light-years away in atmosphere. The grove
of trees shielded an open grassy space that was a hundred yards or so off the road. Cade helped her over a
fallen log, holding her hand as he led her between the
trees and into the clearing.

His hand was still clasped around hers while she
admired the scenery. The spot was ideal, she knew,
exactly right for a love scene, and she turned to Cade
with shining eyes to confirm the selection.

"It's right," she told him. "I know it is."

"You need to make sure," Cade suggested, turning her body in a slow circle so that she could take
another long look.

It was difficult now to concentrate on the landscape because he was so close to her. She felt him
breathing deeply, and her own breath was heavy,
too. She trembled at his nearness, and when he
spoke, his voice came from some faraway place.

"How will you know this is the right place unless
you test it?" he asked huskily. His hand was on the

back of Stephanie's neck now, and his fingers were working their way through the long curls and tantalizing her with soft strokes on the sensitive areas behind her ears. A tremor shook her body, and she tried to move away from his overpowering presence, but she couldn't. He had her in his grasp as much as if he had placed her under lock and key. When his hand tightened on her spine and he turned her toward him, she didn't resist. Her body ached with hunger for him, and her lips parted moistly as his mouth descended upon hers.

He took her greedily, devouring her lips, holding her face still with both hands while his long hard legs curved against her slender pliant figure. When she sighed with the passion she hadn't known fully existed, one of his hands moved down her back to her hips, pulling her even closer to him until her clothes felt like a painful barrier that had to be cast aside.

Without her willing it, without any conscious effort, Stephanie's hands swept across his chest, undoing the top buttons of his shirt so she could kiss the soft curly hair on his chest. When she did, he moaned softly and pulled her with him to the ground, the tall green grass softening their mutual fall. His lips were everywhere, and she almost cried out with the sheer joy he aroused in her. Taut breasts, exposed to his seductive gaze, swelled under his erotic touch, dark nipples hardening as his mouth descended upon them. Then he raised his dark head to find satisfaction again in the moistness of her mouth.

He was above her, leisurely touching the swell of her breasts with the tip of his tongue. But she didn't feel the weight of his hard body, only the electricity that was flowing up and down her spine, curling her toes with tingling sensations. "I want you," he whispered softly in her ear, "here, now," and she could feel the insistent strength of his manhood pressed against her.

Yes, yes, she wanted to cry out, but she couldn't talk. Her whole energy was caught up in the rapture of his embrace, and she could only cling mindlessly to him, lifting her mouth to his to continue the passionate thunder that was rolling through her. Was it thunder or the sound of her heartbeat...Cade's heartbeat? It didn't matter. The intense sensations were carrying her to new heights of frenzy, and she couldn't let go, couldn't stop the tide.

She wanted to tell him she loved him, she wanted him and she would share his embrace and his bed for the rest of her life, but he wasn't giving her time to recover enough to talk. His hands were touching her again, encompassing her waist, moving toward her hips, caressing her inner thighs, forcing her surrender.

He shed her jeans without even taking his lips from hers, and her body quivered in the sheer ecstasy of his movement. Her own hands began to fumble with his shirt, striving to strip it from him under the guidance of his experienced hands. But when he led her to the belt of his jeans, the cold metal of the fancy buckle awakened Stephanie from her trance, making her pull her aching body away in shock at her weakness.

"What am I doing?" she asked in a breathless whisper, confused by how far she had gone in the heat of her emotion.

His low laugh tickled her ear. "Making love to me."

Putting it into words brought the hard reality home to her, and Stephanie pushed him away while she groped for her clothes.

"I can't. . .I simply can't."

He caught her with a hard arm. "Don't you know better than to tease a man?" She could see the violence in his eyes and the strain of holding back his powerful physical yearning.

"I wasn't teasing." She fought back a tear before he could detect it. How could he be so cruel when he had been so warm and loving only minutes earlier?

"I ought to show you what happens to teases." He grabbed her waist and yanked her into the confining prison of his arms, holding her so tightly that she couldn't breathe. His mouth was punishing now, torturing her with deep kisses that forced her lips apart and sent shivers through her spent body.

When she again was almost at the point of responding, of letting all her barriers down, of giving him all that he wanted, he shoved her away, looking at her as if she disgusted him. "Get on back to your work, Miss Lasater," he ordered. "I think you've proved that a love scene can be done in this setting."

CHAPTER SEVEN

STEPHANIE GRABBED her discarded clothing and struggled into her jeans and blouse, trying to fasten buttons with trembling hands that barely managed to do her bidding. Shame, humiliation and rage tore at her until she felt physically sick. All the while Cade stood over her, his expression so hard that Stephanie couldn't get the image of him out of her mind hours after she had fled, across the hillside, through the trees and back to the sanctuary of the film location.

But when she was in sight of the tents and trailers, she stopped, holding onto the thick trunk of a rough-barked oak tree while she caught her breath and tried to stop the flow of tears that poured down her cheeks. In the distance she could see Jon setting up a scene, darting from one position to another as he made certain every detail was exactly right. Farther away, the assistant director was supervising the loading of more equipment for a scene he would handle, to be shot about a mile from the main location.

Stephanie didn't want any of them looking at her. She wiped an arm across her face, brushing away salty tears, but she couldn't do anything about her disheveled appearance. Her hair had stray blades of grass caught in it; her blouse was buttoned unevenly, but she couldn't seem to figure out how to fix it; and her lips, she knew, must be swollen from the bruising effect of Cade's hard demanding mouth on hers. Her stomach became queasy at the thought of the man, and her eyes couldn't focus. Everything looked fuzzy, turning, until she felt she would faint and she had to slide to the ground, leaning against the tree and holding her head in her hands.

She never knew how long she sat there, but when she looked up, Jon had completed the scene he was working on and was busily beginning the next action. He'd be looking for her soon, wanting to know if the place she had investigated was suitable. It might be perfect for him, but she'd never go there again. She couldn't stand the thought of seeing that lushly rich grassy area, the remembrance of the hard ground under her and Cade's strong body above her, of looking up and seeing his tanned face, eyes burning with desire, framed against a cloudless blue sky.

Stephanie waited another half hour before she spotted Brad, the prop man, tossing some equipment in the back of a small van and taking keys out of his pocket. If he was going to town, maybe she could ride with him, Stephanie thought, and she rapidly adjusted her clothing, shook her hair to let the bits of grass fly free and raced down the hillside toward him.

Escape was easier than she'd expected. Brad accepted her explanation that she was ill without a question and kindly didn't talk while he drove to Fort Worth. Stephanie leaned her head against the windowpane and closed her eyes. There was no hope of relaxing. She'd probably never rest again.

When Brad let her out at the hotel, she did manage to think of her job long enough to ask him to tell Jon she had become ill and hadn't wanted to disturb him while he was shooting. Brad told her he was returning to the ranch as soon as he ran an errand and that he would make sure the director got her message.

"Is there anyone else you need to send word to?" Brad asked before driving off, but Stephanie mutely shook her head. She wasn't about to let Cade know she wouldn't be there that evening. She couldn't have faced the man. He'd never hear from her again if she could help it.

Stephanie shed her clothes as soon as she reached her room. Stepping into the shower, she let the beads of hot water sting her skin. But even that didn't wash away the imprint of Cade's touch on her body, and dousing herself with cologne couldn't keep her from breathing the masculine scent of him.

She lay in bed all afternoon and evening, unable to sleep but incapable of getting up and doing anything. The phone rang about dinnertime, but she ignored it the way she was ignoring everything except the sickness inside her.

It took a banging on the door to rouse her from inertia, and slipping a robe around her weary body, she rose long enough to let Becky McAllister in. Becky was the continuity girl on the film, and her room was next to Stephanie's.

"I heard you were sick," Becky told her, "and I wanted to make sure you had something to eat and had called the doctor."

No doctor could cure Stephanie's illness, but her

pallor made Becky insist that she try to get in touch
with one. Stephanie assured her friend that it was
likely only a twenty-four-hour virus and that she
would be better after a day in bed.

Becky agreed and promised to tell Jon that Stephanie wouldn't be at work the next day and shouldn't
be bothered with any assignments from him. "I'll
put out the Do Not Disturb sign for you if you'd
like," she added. "You need a good night's sleep."

She offered to check on Stephanie in the morning
before leaving for the Dallas studio, but Stephanie
declined, insisting she preferred to sleep late. "I
know what you mean," Becky laughed. "I'm ready
for a day of sleeping in, too. This location shooting
is tough on me."

Becky's job was a hard one, and as busy as Stephanie herself always was, she never envied the continuity girl her responsibilities. Becky had to keep a
sharp eye on every scene that was shot and take
notes on each detail so that when a scene was done
several times, from different angles or distances,
nothing changed. If an actor picked up a glass with
his left hand and brought it halfway to his mouth
before he began to speak the first time the scene was
shot, Becky had to be certain that he did it exactly
the same way every other time. She was usually as
exhausted as Stephanie by the time the day was
over.

Becky announced that she was heading for the
restaurant for dinner and offered to bring back a
bowl of soup for Stephanie, but the thought of
eating was so repugnant Stephanie had to decline,

giving the excuse that she could always order from room service if she wanted something.

After her friend had left, Stephanie fell back into bed, lying in semidarkness staring at the ceiling. When the room became dark after the sun completely set, she was still staring. Outside she could hear faint sounds of revelry at poolside, and she cursed the fact that her room was so near the swimming area. She didn't want to know that some people were having a good time, laughing and enjoying themselves. They were people who didn't know Cade Steele. She wished she could be that lucky.

Stephanie spent a fitful night tossing and turning in the queen-size bed in her room, throwing a pillow on the floor in frustration when she couldn't get to sleep. She did doze off at times, only to wake to the knowledge that she had been dreaming of falling into a lush meadow, into the arms of a tall dark man who held her tenderly. The man in her dreams would kiss her lightly on the nose, then touch his lips to her eagerly awaiting mouth. His lips were warm, sensual, electrifying her, melting her. But while she was eagerly returning his kiss she would feel a chill enveloping her and realize that the man caressing her had turned into a metallic robot. Her eyes would fly open in shock, and she would find herself twisted in the covers, drenched with perspiration although the air-conditioning system was providing more than enough cool air.

Stephanie spent most of the next day in her room, listening to the dismal sound of rain against her window. The gloomy weather matched her mood. She did manage to get out of bed when a maid tentatively knocked and asked if she could change the sheets, and she ordered coffee for breakfast, working up to a bowl of soup at noon and a light salad by evening.

She knew when the film people began returning from the Dallas studio. Most of them were housed at her end of the hotel, and she could hear them going up and down the hallway, opening and closing doors. She'd have to face Jon soon, she realized, and she sat in a chair by her window, waiting for him to stop by.

It was late before he did, and he teasingly blamed her for the delay, claiming that he had been required to type the call sheets himself that afternoon. When he joked about having done more of her work by reporting to Cade Steele the night before, Stephanie looked away, not wanting him to see the hurt in her eyes at the mention of the rancher's name. If Cade had asked why she hadn't been there herself, Jon didn't mention it, and Stephanie didn't want to know if he had spoken of her and what he might have said.

"You've been working too hard, Stef," Jon told her, and she let him believe that was the reason for her illness. "You never get out and relax, never go anywhere except to the ranch for filming." He took one of her hands in his, forcing her to look at him. "Now, I want you to have some kind of social life, get away from here and go out to dinner, go to a movie or a play, something to get you away from this constant work."

"The way you do?" she asked, knowing that Jon

put in longer and rougher hours than anyone connected with the film and that there hadn't been a day yet when he had worked fewer than sixteen hours.

"Well, I'm not going to work this weekend," Jon told her, "and neither are you." He eyed her intently. "You did promise to help me, didn't you, Stef?"

"With Kara?" She sat up straight, a sparkle in her eyes for the first time. "Oh, Jon, you know I will. What can I do?"

Jon confided that he had invited Kara to go out to dinner Saturday but that he had included Stephanie in the invitation. Anybody seeing them would assume they were having a business meeting, and as he explained, he had let Kara think they would be discussing the movie. He stood up, stretching and easing the aching muscles from a long day of directing. "I couldn't ask her for a real date," he added. "There were too many people standing around."

Stephanie laughed. It was a strange sound coming out of her throat, one she'd thought she'd never hear again. "And when we are at dinner, I'm supposed to find some excuse to leave you two alone for a while?"

"Well, Stef, you know I enjoy your company, but I wouldn't object if you had to turn in early."

"I'd be delighted to do it, Jon."

"Good." He walked to the door to leave, but turned to her while his hand rested on the doorknob. "As a way of saying thanks, I want you to take tomorrow off, too. I'll see you at work Friday."

"Are you sure you don't mind?" She hated to take another day off, but she wasn't prepared to see Cade so soon.

"It's fine," he said. "I want you to have plenty of strength to be able to announce that you have to return to the hotel immediately after dinner."

"So you can play your own love scene." She smiled at him, hoping he would be able to win the gorgeous Kara.

"We'll see if it works," Jon told her. "By the way, Cade tells me that the location he took you to is perfect for a love scene. Is that right?"

Stephanie looked at the floor, at her toes stuck into the slippers she had half on and half off. "It's exactly what you want, Jon."

"Great." Jon glanced around the hallway to make certain no one from the company was in hearing distance. "Maybe I should take Kara there and rehearse with her."

He said it as a joke, but Stephanie couldn't laugh. She kept her eyes on the floor while Jon wished her good-night and closed the door as he left.

IT WAS A MISTAKE to take another day off work. Stephanie had too much time to think. She sat by the pool, trying to read a magazine but unable to concentrate. Then she attempted a letter to her cousin in New York, but she tore it up before it was completed. How could she write about filming on the ranch without talking about Cade Steele? And how could she write about Cade without pouring out all her aches and pains and love for the man?

She did love him; there was no doubt about it. Somehow she had thought realizing you were in love would be an exhilarating experience, but this wasn't. This was a searing pain that tore at her heart. She found herself scribbling his name on the stationery in her lap and angrily tore the page from her pad. She wondered if he regretted trying to make love to her in the grassy clearing. He had called it making love, but it wasn't. Not for Cade Steele. It was only a chance for physical lust, for taking what he wanted of her body without involving his emotions. If he had got his way, he probably would have closed his eyes and pretended that she was Kara Warren. Or the mysterious Merilee. Or any of the other women he had likely had in his life.

A tremor swept through her body at the thought of how close she had come to yielding to Cade. Her longing for him had been so great that it had been all she could do to pull away; but she couldn't subject herself to the humiliation of being a sexual release for a man's frustrations. If he didn't want all of her—her heart as well as her body—he wasn't going to have her at all.

Cade no doubt assumed she would be happy to please him sexually because he still clung to the belief that every woman in Hollywood went to bed with anyone. He probably thought she was having affairs with all the male members of the company, not just with Jon, as he had already accused her of doing.

By the time Friday arrived, Stephanie had worked herself into such a rage against Cade that she was almost looking forward to reporting to him that night so she could tell him exactly what she thought of him. He wouldn't kick them off the ranch now. That would mean Kara would depart, and Cade wouldn't want that. She hoped Jon would win Kara over before filming was completed so Cade would realize he'd never had a chance with the actress.

She didn't see him during the day except once, briefly, in midafternoon, and then only from a distance. Stephanie was in the office typing some letters, and she glanced out the window to see Cade standing next to Kara as the actress waited for her next scene to be prepared. They were talking animatedly, and though she couldn't hear them, Stephanie could see that Cade was enjoying the conversation. He threw back his head once as he laughed. Stephanie looked around for Jon, wondering if he realized the rancher, too, was trying to win Kara's affections, but she couldn't see the director. She turned back to the typewriter, and when she looked out the window again, Kara was performing the scene and Cade was gone.

Stephanie's resolve to tell Cade off began to fail when she drove up to the ranch house that evening. It required all of her energy to get out of the car and walk to the front door of the big home. She braced herself for Cade's appearance, telling herself that she couldn't let her emotions show, couldn't let him know that she loved him.

No one answered the doorbell, and Stephanie walked around the porch to the back door, where Cade's huge German shepherd lay comfortably against the steps. The dog, accustomed by now to her visits, wagged its tail at her, and she leaned down to scratch its ears. "Well, someone's glad to see me," she teased the animal.

There was no answer at the back door, either, and Stephanie wandered again to the front, not knowing whether to leave or stay. Whatever she did, she decided, would be wrong in Cade's view. The sky was starting to grow dark, and she was becoming nervous at the delay, particularly since she knew that Jon was still at the office and couldn't leave until she returned with his car. Poor Jon, she thought. He was so tired.

A car swung into the driveway while Stephanie stood leaning against the porch. She stiffened, preparing herself for the sight of Cade, but Mrs. Martin and her husband were the ones getting out of the car.

"Stephanie, I didn't know you'd be here," the housekeeper exclaimed. "I heard you were ill. Are you better now?"

"I'm fine, Mrs. Martin," she replied. "I'm here for my nightly report to Mr. Steele."

The housekeeper frowned. "But Cade's not home, and I don't think he'll be back until late." A sudden idea erased the frown from her face as she considered her employer's possible plans. "Cade didn't say where he was going, but he was all dressed up. Do you think he might have a date with Miss Warren?"

"I wouldn't know," Stephanie replied tiredly, relieved and disappointed both that she didn't have to face him tonight and also wondering if Cade might be with Kara. Juggling her car keys in her hand, Stephanie told the Martins good-night as quickly as she could, excusing herself to go meet Jon.

She didn't suggest to Jon that Cade might be out with Kara. Why worry him, and after all, she didn't know for certain. Jon was distracted anyway. Some equipment hadn't functioned properly, and they were going to have to reshoot a scene Monday that should have been already completed.

"The dolly shots," he told Stephanie. "It happened while you were in the office this afternoon. The dolly wouldn't work right." Dolly shots were taken from a moving platform on which the camera was mounted. Timing was essential on that type of shot, with the camera dolly moving at a precise and constant speed and the actors coordinating their movements just as exactly.

They were at the hotel before he mentioned dinner on Saturday.

"Are you sure you don't mind doing this, Stef?" Jon asked. "I've been thinking that the evening won't be much fun for you, especially if you leave early, and I have been suggesting that you should get out more."

"I don't mind a bit, Jon," Stephanie responded, wanting him to know it would be no sacrifice to help bring him and Kara together. "And I will get a good dinner before I suddenly become very ill and have to come back to the hotel, won't I?"

"The best," Jon laughed. Stephanie watched him go down the hall, whistling to himself, after he left her at her door.

BECKY WATCHED Stephanie dress for dinner on Saturday.

"You're certainly taking great pains for just a meal," she remarked. "I didn't know Jon was that special to you."

"He's not, and it's not a date. I'm going with Jon and Kara so I can take notes about the film, but I'm tired of wearing jeans all the time." Stephanie surveyed herself in the floor-length mirror. Her hair was glistening from a shampoo and thorough brushing, and her makeup had been artfully applied. Usually she took time only for powder and lipstick, but for a change she'd utilized some of the techniques she had learned from watching the makeup experts on the set. The result was that she had a natural glow, almost as if she wore no makeup at all.

Her dress was a simple summer outfit done in three tones of blue with a low-cut back and spaghetti straps over the shoulders. She added a fringed shawl in the event that the restaurant's air-conditioning system should be too powerful. When she had finished placing plain gold earrings on her small earlobes and delicate high-heeled sandals on her feet, she pirouetted before Becky, who nodded her approval.

"You look sensational, Stephanie," her friend complimented her. "You'll turn everyone's head at that restaurant."

"You've got to be kidding! Kara's going to be there, too," Stephanie reminded the continuity girl.

"In that case," Becky laughed, "when Kara is in the rest room or out of sight somewhere, you'll be the center of attention."

"You're right. There's no one around who can compete with Kara."

Becky plucked a piece of lint from Stephanie's dress. "Don't sell yourself short, Stef. You're beautiful, too. I've heard a lot of people say you should be in front of the cameras instead of behind them."

Her comment was virtually echoed a few minutes later when Jon stopped by for Stephanie. The director managed to look distinguished in the casual Western clothes he wore, and Stephanie teased him about his Texas image. "You know, Jon, you really should have a scarf around your neck and a beret on your head," she joked. "Then people would accept you as a Hollywood eccentric. What are you trying to do, look like a normal person?"

"Well, you look gorgeous enough to be a movie star tonight, Stef, so you can make up for my bland appearance." He held her hand, squeezing it tightly as they left the room and said goodbye to Becky. "In fact," he added, after Becky had gone into her own room and closed the door, "you're much too pretty to miss out on a full evening of fun, so I'm glad I arranged for you to be with us the entire time."

"What are you talking about, Jon?" Stephanie asked. "You know what the plan is. We'll all have dinner, and then I'll plead illness and return to the hotel. You and Kara will have the rest of the evening to yourselves."

"But that isn't fair to you, Stef. You need your night out, too."

Stephanie laughed. "Being the fifth wheel is not

my idea of a good time, Jon. I'd rather come back to the hotel than keep you and Kara from being romantic.''

"Well, don't worry about being in the way. I've asked Cade to join us, so we can double-date.''

Stephanie was in such shock she was speechless, but Jon went on blithely, "Actually, Cade doesn't know about my hopes for getting Kara alone, either, so I'm counting on you, Stef, to talk to him and dance with him and give me the time I need with her.''

"Y-you shouldn't have done that, Jon,'' Stephanie finally managed to stutter. He was playing right into Cade's hand, providing him with another opportunity to be with Kara, and he didn't even realize it. How could she tell him what he was doing?

Jon obviously misunderstood her meaning, and she didn't try to explain. She simply listened to him suggest that although she didn't get along well on a day-to-day basis with Cade, they might actually like each other in a social context.

"You never talk to him about anything but business,'' Jon explained. "This will give you a good opportunity to get to know him.''

Stephanie knew more than she wanted to about Cade, but she couldn't tell Jon that, either. She shrugged, swallowed hard to rid herself of the dry taste in her mouth and muttered, "What if Cade wants to talk to Kara instead of me?''

"You can charm him, Stephanie,'' Jon insisted. "You're a beautiful sexy woman, and he can't help but notice you. In fact, I've seen him watch you on the set several times.''

"If he was, it was only to see if I would make a big mistake," Stephanie argued, hoping that Jon wouldn't notice her flushed face. "I really am going to be sick, Jon. I won't have to pretend."

His arm went around her waist. "You're not going to be sick," he told her firmly. "You're going to have a good time, and you're going to stick to Cade's side like glue."

He led her into his suite, where Cade was waiting, and left to meet Kara and bring her to join them. Neither Cade nor Stephanie spoke during the almost ten minutes that Jon was gone.

They made the trip in Cade's car, and Stephanie had no option but to sit beside him in the front seat. Jon made sure of that by opening the back door for Kara and then sliding in beside her. The director was in an affable mood, and so was Kara. Their humor and chatter contrasted with the sullen silence in the front of the car. Cade, Stephanie felt, was annoyed that Kara was not sitting beside him, and his occasional frowns as he glanced at the couple in the rearview mirror only confirmed her suspicions.

Their first stop was a little Mexican restaurant on Fort Worth's north side. It was an informal place, looking more like a house from the outside, and they had to walk through the kitchen to reach their table. Their entrance drew the reaction that Stephanie always expected when Kara was around. The natural murmur from the crowd suddenly grew louder as the diners realized the movie star was in the restaurant, and all eyes were on her as she elegantly made her way between the tables, following the hostess, who was leading the procession. All eyes, that is, except Stephanie's. Her gaze, from the corner of her vision, was on the dark face of Cade Steele, who was walking by her side, evidently detesting every minute he had to spend in her company.

They didn't order from a menu. The waitress simply counted the number of people at the table and brought food in large bowls so that, except for the enchiladas placed on individual plates, the diners served themselves the tamales, Spanish rice and refried beans.

The conversation naturally turned to Mexican food and comparisons between the types served in Mexico and those in California and Texas. "Tex-Mex," Cade called the food they were eating, and to Stephanie it was certainly delicious. A little hotter than she was accustomed to, but very appetizing. She especially liked the jalapeño-flavored nachos.

They were interrupted several times with requests for Kara's autograph, and on a couple of occasions someone thrust a pad and pen at Stephanie, as well. She had to explain that she was not an actress—an answer that must have satisfied them, because the pens were quickly withdrawn. A few people recognized Jon from photographs that had appeared in newspapers and magazines, so he had to sign his name along with Kara. One woman stared at Cade for a long minute, not sure whether to ask for his autograph or not.

"Are you anybody?" she finally asked.

"No one you'd want to know," he retorted.

Rebuffed, the woman consoled herself with a smile and signature from Kara.

"This is ridiculous," Cade announced as they made their way from the restaurant. "Can't you ever have a peaceful meal in public?"

"Not often," Jon informed him. "Not with Kara, at least." His eyes lingered on the actress as he spoke, and Stephanie remembered that she was supposed to be distracting Cade from Kara, an impossible task. She didn't even want to try.

Dinner had been awkward enough. She had sat there while Cade was across from her, and neither had spoken to the other. Jon was going to have to come up with a new plan, she decided, and no matter what he did, he might be doomed to failure.

If Cade was out to win Kara, there might be nothing Jon could do to prevent it. Cade was not accustomed to losing to anyone. Perhaps he had been on a date with Kara the night before. Stephanie hadn't been able to resist calling Kara's suite when she had got in on Friday, not after Mrs. Martin's speculations about Cade's activities. There had been no answer—as good a reason as any to assume Mrs. Martin was correct.

They drove through a restored section of north Fort Worth, with storefronts resembling those of the days when the town had been a center of the cattle industry and had earned its nickname of "Where the West Begins." But though the nightclub that was their destination was near the center of the nineteenth-century buildings, it was definitely a modern institution, mechanical bull and all for the city residents to show off their Old West skills. It was noisy and crowded, and the small party wasn't recognized in the confusion of so many things going on at the same time. Cade led them through the building, pointing out the various activities while he held on casually to Kara's arm. Jon and Stephanie trailed behind, both wondering how they had managed to be paired.

When at last they were seated in the main section of the club, Stephanie noticed the lifting of Jon's eyebrows, his signal to her to give him some time alone with Kara. How could she? It would mean asking Cade to dance, and she hated to ask anything of him. Besides, she didn't want to dance with the man, to feel the warm disturbing touch of his hand on her flesh, to be aware of the handsome dark head so close to her own. . . .

Knowing that she would rather be sick, she ignored the signal, even when Jon announced that the music sounded perfect for dancing and Kara agreed. Although Stephanie knew that Jon preferred to sit in a dark corner with Kara, he settled for dancing under the bright lights.

"How about the two of us trying some of those steps they're doing out there?" he asked Kara. "Do you know how to dance the Texas Two-step and the Cotton-eyed Joe?"

"I thought you wanted to talk about the movie," Kara reminded him, but she smiled enigmatically and followed him from the table.

"The movie will wait," Jon said softly in her ear. "It's much too nice a night to waste on business."

Stephanie and Cade sat silently at the table, mutely watching the couple. Kara was a superb dancer, gracefully moving to the beat of the music, and Jon kept up with her, his feet incredibly light for a tall man. They were smiling and flushed when the music ended, but instead of returning to the table, they immediately began another dance as the band started to play a new tune.

Stephanie glanced sideways at Cade to see if he would show his frustration at the fact that Jon was monopolizing Kara, but he was as bland as ever, staring at the couple through a cloud of cigarette smoke.

He smashed his cigarette into the glass ashtray and turned to Stephanie. "You don't want to dance?" he asked.

"I don't think so," she replied in a tiny voice.

His eyes were on her, on her shoulders and bare arms, and she reached for her shawl to hide herself from his probing gaze. Was he remembering, she wondered, how she'd looked when he undressed her? How her body had quivered at his touch?

"That's right, you've been sick, haven't you?" He scoffed as he spoke, well aware of why she'd been unable to come to work. "Tell me, Miss Lasater—" it wasn't "Stephanie" anymore "—does it make you sick to see your lover out there with another woman?"

She didn't answer, and he jerked her to her feet, her shawl falling onto the chair as she rose. "Let's go out there and dance, so you can be closer to them, so you can see how your lover enjoys the company of other women."

He propelled her onto the dance floor and swung her into his arms, holding her against him so tightly that she couldn't resist. She had no choice but to follow his lead as he swept her around the floor in time to the music. He wasn't gentle, far from it. It was as if he wanted to punish her even more for rejecting his sexual overture as his hand gripped her back, forcing her head against his chest and her legs against the hard lines of his own powerful thighs.

Stephanie wasn't aware of when the music stopped, only that Cade released her from his hold, making her stagger for a second as she regained her balance. She darted back to the table before he could begin another dance.

Jon asked her for the following dance, and she accepted, as much to get away from Cade as to tell Jon she couldn't go through with the plan they'd agreed upon.

"What's the matter, Stephanie?" he asked as soon as they were away from the table. "You're not helping out very much."

"Oh, Jon," she cried, and he was instantly solicitous.

"Stef, I shouldn't have brought you out tonight. You're still sick, and that Mexican food plus this dancing can't be helping you very much." He brushed her hair back from her face, and Stephanie couldn't help glancing at the table to see that Cade had noted the gesture. "Do you want me to take you home?"

"No, I'll stay," she promised, knowing that she couldn't leave Kara in Cade's clutches. It would be like the old saying of leaving the foxes to tend the chickens. She did owe Jon that much. "I guess it was the food and the activity, but I feel better now," she lied.

"You're super," Jon exclaimed, his face lighting up with a broad grin, "and I'll make it up to you one of these days." He whirled her around extravagantly as the music increased in tempo. "In fact, when you find the man you want, you can count on me to help you out with him."

Stephanie smiled, reflecting on the irony of his remark. She had found the man she wanted, and she couldn't stand the thought of being alone with him. Not if it meant dealing with his insinuations and suffering his touch.

They stayed long past midnight, and Stephanie clenched her teeth and tried to keep her promise. She didn't want to dance with Cade again, but she did manage to ask him to come walk with her by the rodeo arena in another part of the huge club, explaining to him that it would be valuable research should she ever be involved in a picture about rodeos.

She thought for a moment that Cade would refuse, and her cheeks burned in embarrassment, but after taking a long hard look at Jon and Kara he excused himself and followed Stephanie from the room.

The bulls seemed ferocious and the horses appeared wild to Stephanie, but Cade was bored with the activity and soon led her away into one of the shops that were also a part of the nightclub. He asked if she would like a souvenir of her trip to the state.

Stephanie already had her souvenir—an encounter

with Cade that would forever remind her of Texas—
and she didn't need a trinket to put on display in her
efficiency apartment in L.A. But she lingered, picking up a few things and looking them over, reminding
herself that she had promised Jon time alone with
Kara. Cade's looming presence made her nervous, so
she was careful not to handle anything breakable,
and she was grateful when he excused himself for a
minute, leaving her to browse by herself.

By the time Cade returned, she had looked at
everything in one shop at least twice and had moved
on to an adjacent location. He touched her arm as
she stared at reproductions of Remington and Russell
paintings of Western scenes.

"You like those?" he asked, watching her nod her
approval.

"You should see the real thing, then, while you're
in town," he advised her. "One of the museums in
Fort Worth has a collection of paintings by both
Russell and Remington, and also some Remington
bronzes."

"I'll try to do that," she responded. The two
painters were probably the most famous portrayers
of the American West, and both used vividly realistic
settings in which to depict cowboys, Indians and the
animals that roamed the prairies and the mountain-
sides.

Stephanie realized that Cade must be wanting to
return to Kara and that she couldn't keep him away
much longer. But as she turned to go he stopped her,
holding out a small box..

"Here's your souvenir of Texas," he announced.

Shakily she accepted the package, opening the box to find a delicate gold chain with an equally beautiful and obviously expensive gold charm made in the outline of the state.

"Oh," she whispered, speechless, as she lifted it from its satin nest.

Cade helped her put it on, and she held her hair up while he fastened the clasp. His warm fingers lingered on the nape of her neck even after he had released the chain, and Stephanie could feel the familiar rush of tingles up and down her spine. She swiveled out of his reach and faced him.

"Thank you, Cade." She used his first name automatically; formality somehow seemed out of place, especially since by force of circumstance she was spending so much time in his company. "It's beautiful."

She wondered about his motives. Had he presented her with this lovely gift because he liked her and truly appreciated her interest in his state? Or was it his way of apologizing for the indignity to which he had submitted her when he brought all her emotions to the surface and then threw them back into her face?

She had to know; she couldn't stand the uncertainty. While they were walking back through the club to rejoin Kara and Jon, Stephanie found the courage to put her questions into words.

"Is this your way of saying you're sorry about what happened the other day?" she asked timidly.

Cade turned on her in fury, and this time there was no problem knowing what he was thinking. "You really believe I'm apologizing because you're a tease?'' His voice boomed, and a couple of people turned to stare at them. ''You're the one who owes me an apology.''

Offended, Stephanie struggled to remove the chain from her neck, for it was burning into her skin. But she couldn't unsnap the catch, and Cade watched her efforts with disdain.

''Keep the charm,'' he ordered. ''I bought it for you as a remembrance of your visit to Texas, but it can also serve as a reminder that someday a man might not let you get away with teasing. You can push a man only so far, you know.''

He shoved her toward the dancing area, where the strains of the music were incongruously merry, and when they reached the table he took Kara's hand asked if she was ready to depart.

The foursome rode back to the hotel in silence. Cade summarily opened the front door of his car and motioned for Kara to take a seat beside him, leaving Stephanie and Jon with no choice but to share the back. The others appeared stunned by his action and made no resistance. Stephanie herself couldn't talk, and Cade wouldn't—not until they arrived at the hotel and he suddenly suggested a final drink in the bar. Again, he gave no one a chance to refuse.

Stephanie managed to put on a pleasant, if not delighted, expression and take Jon's arm as they walked into the bar. Several of the other members of the film company were already there, so she had to act as if she were Jon's date. She strolled close by his side through the dimly lit room and to an unoccupied corner table. Cade and Kara were immediately in front of them, and Stephanie couldn't help overhearing the speculative comments about Kara and the handsome rancher. Jon had to be listening to the talk, too.

By the time the drinks had been ordered and then served, Stephanie was a nervous wreck. Her chain felt like an albatross around her neck, the weight made heavier when Kara noticed it and asked where she had got the jewelry.

"At the nightclub," she answered noncommittally, her eyes carefully avoiding Cade's.

"It's beautiful," Kara commented. "I'll have to get one, too, before I leave town."

Cade will be happy to buy you one, Stephanie thought, but he would no doubt present it with affection, not with a sarcastic remark about her morality. She wondered why he hadn't given this one to Kara. Perhaps it was because he wasn't planning on Kara's leaving Texas. He probably would try to keep her here, and she'd have a wedding ring instead of a mere charm. A choking sensation clogged her breathing, and Stephanie knew she had to get away.

"I'm sorry," she said to Kara and Jon, ignoring Cade. "I'm not feeling well, and I think I'd better go to my room."

"I'll take you there." Jon started to rise, but Stephanie motioned for him not to get up.

"No, stay and finish your drink. I really don't need any help."

Cade rose, his long body lunging upward like a rising skyscraper. "I was going to buy a pack of cigarettes anyway. I'll see that Stephanie reaches her room safely and then rejoin you in a minute or two."

There was nothing to do but leave the bar with as much dignity as possible. As soon as she was out of view of the others, however, Stephanie quickened her pace to leave Cade behind. His long stride caught up with her in an instant, and he held her arm as if he were trying to keep her from falling should she faint.

When they reached her door, she started to thank him for the charm and for escorting her to her room, but she couldn't be such a hypocrite, so she said nothing.

Cade leaned against the door, blocking her from unlocking it and disappearing inside. His arms were folded across his chest. "Let's see," he murmured, his gaze traveling down the front of her dress to take in the curves of her slender body. "I'm substituting for your lover, so I should say good-night the way he would."

His eyes narrowed until he was almost staring at her through narrow slits. "I'm sure he would come in with you for a long lingering good-night, perhaps one that would last all night." Stephanie went rigid with fury. "But I promised to be back at the bar in a minute or two, so I can't do that." His arms unfolded swiftly, capturing her in an embrace that surprised her with its suddenness and intensity. "I'll have to settle for giving you a good-night kiss in his stead."

His lips took hers before she could protest, his tongue forcing her lips to part, probing deeply, harshly. Again the shivers crept up and down her spine as she responded to his ardor. She couldn't breathe, but she couldn't break away, and she didn't want to. She gave herself up to the passion that gripped her, her arms slipping around his strong back, holding him to her.

When he let her go, she was afraid to look at him. She was too afraid of seeing the loathing that had been on his features before.

"Good night," he whispered, stroking her face. "Good night from Jon."

He turned from her, and she slipped the key into the lock while she was still able to control herself, slamming the door shut as soon as she was inside.

"I hate you..." she whispered, but there was no one to hear—and no one to believe her.

CHAPTER EIGHT

Jon WASTED NO TIME getting to work Monday morning, and Stephanie stayed on the run most of the day. Friday's scene that had been ruined was reshot, and then they went on to complete the full schedule of work originally planned for the day.

The production couldn't afford to fall behind. Every day on location cost money, and the budget was tight. Besides, the Fourth of July holiday was practically upon them, and Jon didn't want anyone to have to work during the Independence Day celebration.

He made that announcement at the beginning of work on Tuesday morning, saying that he appreciated everyone's efforts and that the entire cast and crew would enjoy a long weekend for the Fourth of July provided every scene planned was completed as scheduled. He even changed the order of shooting to put off the cattle-drive sequence another week because it was long and involved and he didn't want to take the chance of making people work on a holiday.

There were cheers at the prospect of a three-day weekend, and there were more cheers when Jon announced that everyone was invited to an Independence Day barbecue. Most of the people from California didn't have the time or the extra money to fly home for such a short period, and they hadn't been looking forward to eating hotel food on the fourth.

It was news to Stephanie, who hadn't heard of any plans Jon had made for hosting a barbecue dinner; but with Jon she could never be sure of what was going to happen. Likely he had just thought of it, and she'd soon be on the phone trying to find a place to hold the party and arranging for the food. But she couldn't help raising her hand when he asked how many people would want to attend. She needed another break from the ranch, from Cade, and she couldn't use the excuse that she was sick all summer.

When she had visited the rancher Monday evening, he hadn't even listened to her report, dismissing her almost as soon as she arrived, telling her he didn't have time for her but adding, as she left, instructions for her to return the next evening. She tried again to convince Cade she didn't need to see him each night, particularly this week, since Jon was spending every night at the ranch house, but Cade merely repeated his order for her to come back the following night.

Cade didn't come to the movie set, but Ray dropped by once on Tuesday to see what was happening. The ranch was busy, he told her, but he hadn't been able to resist taking a minute out to see how the movie was going.

The ranch people, he explained, were getting some

horses ready for a sale that would be held soon, and then the hay had to be cut and baled and a dozen other things accomplished, because it would soon be time to harvest the grain sorghum that would provide food for the cattle the following winter. "Plus, we're trying to get organized for the barbecue," Ray added as he was leaving.

"Are you having one on the fourth?" Stephanie asked. "We are, too. I think it will be a lot of fun."

It wasn't until after Ray had left that she began putting two and two together and realized that Jon might have been inviting them to a barbecue at the ranch. Surely he wouldn't—that would be Cade's responsibility. But Cade might have asked him to do it since he was too busy to make the trip to the movie location himself.

Stephanie made a mental note to remove her name from the guest list should the party be at Cade's. That would be a day she'd rather spend in the solitude of her hotel room.

In the rush of all her work, she forgot about the barbecue. On an ordinary week she could have spoken to Jon about it on the drive to Fort Worth, but since he was staying with Cade for a few days, she didn't have that opportunity. He had given her the keys to his car, and she drove back and forth from the hotel each day. Occasionally some members of the crew rode with her, but usually her trips were too early in the morning and too late in the evening to suit them.

On Wednesday evening Jon was with Cade in the den when she arrived at the ranch house, and her worst fears were confirmed. They were discussing the barbecue.

"There's one thing you can do for me, Stef," Jon informed her as he and Cade went over the list of guests. There seemed to be a lot of names, more than the number of people who'd signed up from the film cast and crew. "Cade has this barbecue every year for his employees and their families, and they haven't had a chance to meet most of our people or to know what a talented group we have." He glanced at the paper again. "What I'd like for you to do is to organize a little talent show that we could put on for these people who've been so nice about letting us work undisturbed."

"I wasn't planning to attend, Jon," Stephanie protested, but Cade reached over, took the list from Jon's hand and scanned it hastily.

"Your name is here," he commented tersely.

Stephanie stuck her hands in the pockets of her jeans. "I thought I would be coming, but I find now that I can't."

"Why not, Stef?" Jon asked, genuinely perplexed. "Are you going to fly back to California for the weekend?"

"No." Why did he have to pressure her for details, Stephanie wondered. She didn't have to explain what she planned to do on the holiday. Jon was her employer, not her master, and she didn't have to account to him—or to that glowering man behind the desk.

They were waiting for her to say more, both watching her and making her nervous. She didn't want to lie, but she couldn't tell the truth, so she simply refused to elaborate. "I'll ask around tomorrow," she promised, "to see if anyone would like to sing or perform, but that's all I'm going to do." She ran from the room, out the door and to the car before either man could react.

When she thrust the list of entertainers at Jon the next day at the lunch break, he eyed her inquisitively. "Have you changed your mind about coming to the barbecue?" he asked before studying the slate of names she had provided.

"No."

"I wish you would, Stef." His eyes remained on the list. "It's important to maintain good relations with Cade on this project, particularly since he invited us to take part in his Fourth of July celebration." Jon glanced at her. "He didn't have to do that, you know."

"He only did it for his employees' sake, not for us," Stephanie retorted. "His people and their wives and children want to meet the movie stars. Well, they can meet them. Robert's going to attend. Kara said she might be there. I'm not a movie star, and no one's going to care whether I attend or not."

Jon folded the paper and handed it back to her. "I can't order you to attend, Stephanie, but I'd like to count on your being there."

She sat wearily down in the chair across from his desk. The window air conditioner hummed loudly in the background.

"Why, Jon?"

"Because for some reason you're having trouble

A compelling love story of mystery and intrigue... conflicts and jealousies... and a forbidden love that threatens to shatter the lives of all involved with the aristocratic Lopez family.

Mail this card today for your FREE book.

getting along with Cade. We've got work here for another few weeks, and you've simply got to stop quarreling with him while we're filming.'' He took a long swallow from his cold drink and leaned back in his chair. "I think it might be a great help if you took the trouble to attend his barbecue.''

"That sounds suspiciously like an ultimatum, Jon.'' Stephanie was irked by his tone of voice.

"I told you earlier, Stef, I can't order you to go.'' And he reached for his script, silently and effectively dismissing her.

She didn't slam the office door as she left, the way she wanted to, but she almost knocked down a teenager who tried to offer her a sandwich as she rushed into the lunch tent.

JON HAD ARRANGED for the buses to transport the California group from the hotel to the ranch on the Fourth of July, but neither he nor his two stars rode in the vehicles. He sent word that he would take them in his own car.

Stephanie didn't take a bus, either. One of the area people working on the picture had flown to the Gulf Coast of Texas for the holiday and had offered her the use of his car for the weekend. It had been a great help because she hadn't been able to find anyone with the time to drive to the airport to meet Lance Fraser, the young man who would play the hero's teenage son in scenes covering the late nineteenth century. It was the youth's first movie, and he questioned Stephanie all the way from the airport about what he would be expected to do. She had to admire his enthusiasm and energy, and she knew he was destined to become a major star. At eighteen he had a definite sexual appeal that was going to make him a hit with young girls. His few television roles had already proved that.

She thought Lance would want to relax at the hotel after his long flight, but he was eager to attend the barbecue, anxious to meet the people he would be working with in the movie and to see the ranch site. When he heard about the talent show, he immediately offered to sing.

They stopped at the hotel only long enough to unload his luggage and give him the chance to change into fresh clothes, then began the drive to the ranch. Lance chatted all the way, making Stephanie's silence not quite so obvious.

There was already a crowd when they arrived, and the tangy aroma of a side of beef slowly barbecuing over a hickory fire reached them even before Stephanie parked in an open area at the back of the house.

Cade strolled over to meet them as they got out of the car, and Stephanie hurriedly introduced Lance. Then she took the friendly teenager by the arm, explaining that she would find some of the film people for him to meet, as well.

But it was difficult to rid herself of Cade as she had planned. He was with them every step of the way, waiting until she had introduced Lance to Morgan Anderson and the two had begun a conversation before whispering into her ear, "Are you robbing the cradle now, Stephanie?" He'd resumed his use of her first name, all right, but the taunting way in which he spat it out almost made her cringe.

Before Stephanie could think of a suitably caustic reply he had stridden off, stopping occasionally to shake someone's hand and play the part of the engaging host, leaving her to seethe inwardly. She hid her anger as best she could, but Morgan glanced at her rosy face and looked over his shoulder speculatively at the departing Cade. A touch of a smile flitted across his mouth before he turned back to Lance to inquire about the young man's flight from Los Angeles.

In spite of Cade, Stephanie began to enjoy the barbecue. After his initial barb he stayed out of her way, leaving her to chat with some of his employees and their families. She spent a long time explaining how movies were made to a handful of star-struck youngsters, and Morgan, who was sitting nearby, described in great detail how stunts were done to a couple of boys who sat gazing at him in unabashed awe.

"I'll bet you didn't know you were such a hero," she teased Morgan when the youngsters finally left to check out the food.

"I won't be after Robert arrives," he replied with a laugh. Morgan wasn't jealous of the actor, she knew; he was satisfied with his role as a stunt man and double and had no aspirations to become a star.

They talked for a while about Morgan's family, home in California this holiday, and the stunt man's disappointment that he was not with them for the occasion. Telling Stephanie that she would have to substitute for his wife as his date for the day, he escorted her to the serving line where plates were being heaped high with thick slices of barbecued beef covered with sauce, accompanied by red beans, potato salad, thick chunks of Texas toast and slices of purple onion.

They sat at one end of a long table, apart from most of the crowd, trying to keep their conversation away from business and failing to do so. Each time they mentioned the movie they would vow not to talk about it; then two minutes later one of them would say something about an upcoming scene or a change in the script. They were giggling like a pair of school kids before they could finish their meal.

The day was hot, but large canopies had been set up to shield the guests from the sun, and a pleasant breeze was blowing on the hillside where the tables had been placed. Most of the female guests were in shorts, but Stephanie had worn slacks with her frilly peasant blouse. If she had to attend, she'd reasoned, she wasn't going to wear something Cade might consider provocative, so she had ignored Becky's suggestion that she dress in something less warm for the day ahead.

"I wear jeans every day at work," she had told her friend, "and my slacks are lighter and cooler than the jeans. I don't intend to parade around in shorts."

"Suit yourself," Becky had said. "But I'm going to be comfortable."

Stephanie wasn't the only one not to wear shorts. When Kara arrived, she was attired in a shocking-pink cotton dress that seductively followed the curvaceous lines of her body. On any other redhead the color would have been a mistake, but Kara wore the bright shade magnificently. Her hair was swept up off her neck, caught with decorative combs. She was instantly mobbed by the families of Cade's employees, most of whom hadn't had a chance to see her before.

Robert and Jon were with her, and both received their share of attention. It was several minutes before the celebrities could make their way through the crowd to say hello to their host.

Stephanie began another conversation with Morgan so she wouldn't have to see Cade greet the beautiful Kara. She should have known that the actress would be dressed sensationally today: Kara had confided in her a few days earlier that she was so tired of the drab costumes she had to wear in the film she could hardly wait to wear something pretty. Her turquoise dress at dinner last Saturday had been lovely, but it hadn't revealed her ripe figure the way this outfit did.

Morgan glanced at the scene and remarked on Kara's appearance, forcing Stephanie to look in the actress's direction. But she managed to turn back before she glimpsed Cade's face, for she could not bear to see the longing no doubt reflected there.

The stunt man went on to talk about Kara's work in the movie and to chuckle about her failed effort to go near the longhorn.

"I can tell you who really helped us that day," he recalled, "and that was Cade Steele. That man has a way with animals. I could learn a lot from him."

Stephanie murmured some noncommittal reply.

"You know, gossip around the set has it that he's dating Kara." Morgan gazed intently at their host. "Somehow she doesn't seem his type. . . ."

"Why not? She's a beautiful and sexy woman," Stephanie responded lightly.

Morgan lifted an eyebrow. "You're not jealous of Kara, are you, Stephanie?"

"No." She really wasn't. It was difficult not to like the actress: she was not at all pretentious, and she never made impossible demands the way Robert did. It was just that Stephanie wished Kara weren't quite so beautiful. . . that she weren't quite so attractive to Cade.

Stephanie used the excuse that she wanted to try the watermelon, now being cut into luscious juicy red slices by Mrs. Martin, as a means of leaving the table and ending the discussion of Kara and Cade.

Kara and Cade. They were paired already in her mind, the same as they were for everyone else in the movie company. Their engagement seemed a fait accompli, even if it hadn't been announced.

She had to admit that Cade wasn't overwhelming Kara with attention, but then he had his employees to consider. He probably didn't want them to know about his love for the actress until he was ready to proclaim their marriage. Likely, however, they already knew, thanks to Mrs. Martin and her fervent wish for the union of the two.

The guests spent a leisurely afternoon enjoying a supply of appetizing food that never seemed to end. There were kegs of beer and tubs full of cold drinks, and by the time the sun was lowering itself in the west, many of them were able only to sit around and chat. The children hadn't lost their energy, however: they chased one another up and down the hillside, pleaded with Morgan to show them how to do stunts and shyly stared at Kara and Robert.

Robert was spending too much of his time around the beer kegs, and Stephanie hoped he'd slow down his drinking. She had seen him drunk once before, at the hotel, and he had been so obnoxious that she had wished she had enough strength to push him into the pool.

A few of the families departed shortly before dark so that they could take their children to the public fireworks displays marking the Fourth of July celebration in Fort Worth and Dallas. There would be no fireworks at the ranch. Cade wouldn't take the risk of a stray spark setting off a range fire.

For the rest, the tempo picked up as colored lights, strung around a wide area of the hillside, were turned on and a bandstand was set up at the very top of the hill. The picnic tables were moved to the sides, and large boards were set in place to form a dance floor.

The band had a difficult time at first. It was composed of some of the crew members plus a drummer from Dallas and a lead guitarist from Forth Worth. But within minutes the players had adapted to one another's style and begun tunes that had the crowd clapping in unison.

"Our guests of honor should have the first dance," someone called out, and heads immediately turned to find Kara and Robert. She was sitting in a lounge chair with both Jon and Cade at her side, but Robert couldn't be found.

Kara glanced at the men with her, and they looked at each other. Then Jon led the actress onto the dance floor, holding her a little less close than Stephanie knew he wanted to. He was trying, she also knew, to keep his feelings for her from showing on his face. It wouldn't do to let everyone in the crew see how much he cared for his leading lady.

When that dance ended, one of Cade's employees gave him a resounding whack on the back and hollered, "Now it's the boss's turn!"

Cade hesitated for a second, then strode onto the dance floor, taking Kara from Jon's grasp—the way he would do in life, Stephanie realized. She would have liked to flee the area, but that would have raised eyebrows, so she sat and stared at the man she loved dancing with Kara.

His arm was around her back, and Stephanie wondered if Kara was experiencing the tingles of electrical sparks that always occurred when Cade touched her. Could the actress stay within his embrace as they danced and not feel an aching desire to be there forever, to move closer and closer until they were merged into one? She shuddered at the thought, not fully aware that Morgan covered her hand with his and murmured, "It's all right, Stephanie."

Her eyes were dark with pain when she looked up at her friend. "It's all right," he repeated, patting her hand. "It's just a dance. They aren't getting married."

She wanted to shout, "They will be," but she couldn't say that to Morgan. Instead she merely muttered, "I don't know what you're talking about."

"Like hell you don't." He took her by the shoulders, forcing her to face him. "I can see it written all over your face, Stephanie. You're in love with that man, so don't try to con me into believing you're not."

"Of course I'm not!" A flush of color in her cheeks denied her words.

"You are, so quit telling me you don't care."

"Oh, Morgan, leave me alone." She tried to turn away from him, but he wouldn't allow it.

"I'm not going to let you sit there and feel sorry for yourself," Morgan insisted. "Now, tell me straight. Do you love Cade?"

She nodded, and a tear trickled out of the corner of one eye.

Morgan leaned over to brush it away and kissed her on the tip of her upturned nose. "Then you just let ol' Morgan here take care of your troubles. I'll see what I can do to get Cade over here and away from Kara."

Stephanie was shocked at the idea. "No, Morgan, please. Don't do anything. You'd just make it worse."

Morgan laughed. "Don't have any faith in me,

huh?'' He took her hand, massaging her fingers, which were cold in spite of the heat that lingered even after sunset. "Let me tell you a thing or two, Stef. I have a daughter who's twenty years old and another one who's eighteen. I know all about young love." He chuckled. "You think I'm too old to remember what it's like to be in love and to hurt, but I'm not. I'm in love right now with a woman I've been married to for twenty-three years. I'm not the old codger you think I am."

Stephanie smiled despite herself. "You're not old at all, and I didn't mean that." She looked closely at the stunt man. He must have married very young because he barely looked forty years old. "You don't understand the situation, that's all."

He waited for her to speak.

"You see, Cade—Mr. Steele—doesn't like me. He's made that very plain." She looked around to see if Cade and Kara were still dancing, but the floor was now filled with people, and she couldn't find them in the crowd. "He wants Kara, and—" she had to catch her breath before she continued "—he'll get her, too."

"Maybe," Morgan mused, "and maybe not."

Stephanie grasped at both his hands. "Please, Morgan, promise you won't interfere. Please." She waited for him to make a commitment, hoping, praying that he would.

He smiled slowly. "I should be Cupid with a stack of arrows to shoot into his heart, shouldn't I, Stef?" He stood up, eyeing the dance floor. "Come on and have a dance with me. I'll spin you around that floor so fast you'll have to cheer up.''

It didn't occur to Stephanie that he hadn't promised anything.

When the first of the entertainers from the film crew made his way onto the bandstand, the crowd broke into spontaneous applause. Stephanie knew the visitors would enjoy the acts. They had a very talented group on this film. Many of the crew had gone to Hollywood with hopes of becoming singers or dancers or actors, but they had used their technical skills to earn a living while they waited for their big break. Now most of them had decided they preferred being part of the crew and had given up their previous ambitions. But they still enjoyed entertaining, and there had been several informal songfests around the pool at the hotel late at night and on weekends.

The first performer was a sound man who did a clever imitation of a popular Western singer. He was followed by a guitar-playing camera operator and then by another cameraman, who did a saxophone solo. The wardrobe woman sang a popular song while two other crew members acted out a comedy routine.

When Lance strode onstage to sing, Stephanie anticipated the squeals from the teenage girls in the audience, and she didn't have to wait long. He had barely begun his song when the girls began jumping up and down in delight, crowding to the front of the stage to be closer to the young performer. Stephanie looked around for Jon, to wink and let him know he had chosen wisely when he selected Lance for a small but important role in the film. The teenagers were going to want to see more of him in the future. He had to sing three songs before the audience would let him go, and then the girls followed him into the crowd, begging for his autograph, a handkerchief, a lock of his hair, anything.

"I think we'd better rescue our young star before he doesn't have any hair left to photograph," a voice behind her said as hands came down on her shoulders.

Stephanie looked up at Jon. "I think you're right," she had to agree, "unless you've stocked up on wigs."

"I'll go get him," Jon volunteered, leaning down first to whisper in her ear, "Thanks for coming, Stef. I know you didn't want to, but it really means a lot to me, and I think to Cade, too."

When he left, Stephanie wandered around the hillside, wanting to stretch her legs and get away from the noise and confusion of the crowd. She needed time alone, time to think. If Morgan had figured out that she loved Cade, did anyone else know? She didn't think Jon had any idea, but then Jon was often surprisingly obtuse about things right under his nose. After all, he barely suspected that Kara might in fact return his feeling for her—something Stephanie considered a definite possibility, if she was reading the signs right. But then there was Cade: he might be quicker than Jon to declare his love for Kara; and how could she resist him? Stephanie decided she would have to do something about that situation. Give Jon more of a push. Give Kara a shove, too—toward Jon and away from Cade. That would be nice.

From a distance she stared at the flickering lights of the party. It was a pretty site, but not as beautiful as the natural setting. She remembered the first time she'd seen it, when she had sat on the porch swing that day in April, so long ago, waiting to meet Cade for the first time. Well, she had met him all right. She had met the enemy, and he had conquered her. He had won her heart without wanting it.

If she had known then what she did now, she would never have made the trip to Texas in the first place. She would have told Mike to find another ranch and never have given this place another thought. Her father used to say something about being wise too late, and that fit her to a tee. She was always learning the cruel facts of life after she had been hurt. From now on she'd have to be a bit more callous, more skeptical. She'd grow a thicker skin to protect her from men like Cade Steele.

It did no good, however, to stand out in the dark and speculate about what she should or shouldn't do. Stephanie slowly made her way back toward the lights and the music.

She was almost there when she heard Robert's voice. "Hey, beautiful," he called to her. She reluctantly turned to see what he wanted. Robert was another of those men who never remembered her name, calling her "beautiful" or "sweetie" instead. She could barely stand it.

He was drunk, of course. The smell of beer assaulted her senses as he practically staggered toward her, throwing an arm intimately around her shoulders and touching her face with a rough hand.

"Why don't we get out of here, honey?" he proposed. "You've got a car, haven't you?" His hand roved across Stephanie's face, and she flinched in an attempt to avoid his caresses. "I know a nice little bar we could visit, and then later...." His gaze strayed to her breasts, and his arm followed immediately. "We could go to my room."

Stephanie wrenched herself free, but Robert grabbed her again. "You know, I could be a big help to you if you were nice to me." His lips were close to hers, and Stephanie had to duck her head to avoid his kiss. She struggled to free herself, not caring that her blouse was falling off one shoulder, just wanting to get away from the man and his unwanted attentions. "You'll be nice to me, won't you, baby?" he was saying, clawing at her body as he spoke. "You want to be nice to me; I know you do."

Suddenly Stephanie was free, unexpectedly released, flung backward until she almost lost her balance, and Cade was between them. She couldn't see his face, for he was turned toward Robert, but she could tell he was angry by the tight muscles of his neck and the rippling of his shoulders through the soft blue Western-style shirt.

Before she realized what was happening, Robert was on the ground, clutching his face with two hands and claiming that Cade was killing him.

Cade looked at him in disgust. "I only hit you

once," he told the actor, "but if you aren't off my property in ten minutes, I'll be after you again."

Turning away as swiftly as he had appeared, Cade placed an authoritative hand on Stephanie's arm, and she cringed under his tight grip as he forced her to attempt to match his long irate strides. They were near the barn before he stopped, jerking her around so she could see the cold disdain written on his features.

"Didn't I tell you what could happen to a woman who teases men?" he growled. "Haven't you realized yet that a man isn't going to put up with your tormenting him without expecting something in return?"

Stephanie was flushed with outrage. "I didn't do anything!" she screamed. "I never made one attempt to flirt with Robert."

Cade scoffed. "You're really something, to expect me to believe that. I see you in his arms, and you tell me you weren't flirting." His face condemned her without a trial. "It was only when he asked for more than you wanted to deliver that you started to pro-test."

"That's not true." But what was the use of de-fending herself anyway? Cade wasn't going to believe her. He had already made up his mind about her, had done it before he ever saw her, all because of his preconceived notion of the kind of woman she must inevitably be.

"Listen, Miss Prim-and-proper." He was as angry as she was. "You come here today with one man, one who's still a boy. I suppose you're going to teach him the ways of the world. Then you forget about him and start flirting with older men. I saw you holding hands with both Anderson and Jenson." He let her go, discarding her as if he couldn't stand to be near her anymore. "Playing one man against another. Flirting with a man who's married and has children just because you're upset about your lover dancing with another woman."

"It's not true." Her voice grew weaker now as she gave in to the realization that to fight Cade was a losing battle.

"It is true, so don't deny it." He walked away a half dozen steps or so before he stopped. Not looking back, he added, "From now on, Stephanie, I expect you to behave respectably while you're on my land. Save your extracurricular activities for else-where."

Stephanie wanted to run after him, throw her arms around him and beg him to listen, to let her explain the truth, but her pride wouldn't allow her. He could think what he wanted. It didn't matter, and she would learn not to care.

She remained in the darkness until she could compose herself and until, she hoped, Robert had departed. She could imagine the talk now. Having the star of the film in a fight with the owner of the ranch would provide gossip fodder for days, and Cade's name would be bandied about everywhere. She wondered if Robert would say the fight had been over her and accuse her of leading him on, as Cade had assumed. It didn't matter. Nothing did, as long as Cade didn't believe her.

The music was still playing when she finally worked up enough courage to walk shakily back to the edge of the lighted area. She didn't see Robert, and she wondered if he had left and who might have given him a ride. Probably Jon had taken his star to the hotel, and he likely had been required to leave Kara behind...prey to the waiting arms of Cade Steele.

She couldn't see Kara or Cade, either, but that might mean they had gone off together somewhere. It was better that she leave and not consider what might be happening with those two. She looked around for Lance, to see if he could be talked into departing, but when she mentioned it to him, the teenagers hanging around him groaned and protested until the young actor grinned at Stephanie and asked if she minded waiting a bit longer.

There was little she could do but accept his decision or make him ride the bus. If she insisted they leave, it would require explanations that she wasn't prepared to make. She dragged a lounge chair to the semidarkness at the edge of the lighted area and sat stiffly, tapping her fingers impatiently on the sides of the chair.

When about fifteen minutes had passed she signaled Lance that she had to go, but after a hurried conference with his new friends he told her that he had been invited to visit the home of one of the teenagers, where the party was going to continue. The parents would give him a ride to the hotel when they were through visiting.

"If that's what you want to do, Lance," Stephanie agreed. "I'm going to leave now."

"We're going, too," he told her. It was a good time to depart. The band members were putting their instruments into the cases, and a couple of men were folding lounge chairs and moving tables while the remaining food was being covered and carried back into the house.

Stephanie walked with Lance, the young girls and their parents toward the parking lot, but she fell behind when she saw Cade standing by the graveled section shaking hands and thanking his guests for coming.

Not sufficiently recovered to face him, she fled back to the party area. If anyone questioned her, she could say she had lost her car keys and needed to hunt for them. But no one saw her. She wandered past the rows of folded chairs and stacked tables, on toward the barn, where the night would shield her from view until Cade had finished saying goodbye to the departing men and women and she could slip quietly to the car and drive back to the hotel.

The moon slid in and out of view with the movement of the clouds, illuminating her face and then obscuring it again, so instead of standing with her back to the barn the way she had been doing, she slipped to the ground to avoid being noticed. Crouched partially behind a bush, hugging her knees to her chin, she gazed at the activity in the distance. She didn't think Cade would ever finish telling his friends good-night. He chatted with them as if he hadn't seen them in months, and she wished he would hurry. It was late, and she was tired, and she wanted desperately to get off the ranch and into her bed at the hotel.

Stephanie occupied her time thinking of what she would do when she did return. First she'd soak in a hot bath filled with scented bubbles. Then she would crawl between the cool sheets on her bed, shut her eyes and force Cade out of her thoughts. A bath, her bed and sleep: something good to look forward to after a traumatic day. Sleep. She wanted it. She needed it. Her eyelids wanted to close even now, and she had to blink occasionally to keep herself awake. Tonight she was too tired to dream. She could sleep soundly without visions of robotlike men, and she could sleep as long as she wanted to. There was no need to set an alarm for tomorrow. She had a long weekend, and she might sleep through it all.

She tried to look at the parking area again, but the image was fuzzy and she couldn't tell if Cade had left or not. Better not take a chance, she reasoned. Better wait a few minutes longer. She stretched out on the ground, propping her head up with an elbow. When her head fell to the ground, she knew that her arm had given away and that she should prop her head up again. Actually, she should get up; it must be safe now to go. But she couldn't move. And she sank into sleep without even being aware of it.

There was a dream, a slightly hazy one, of a dark man standing over her, looking down at her lithe body curled up on the grass. She felt him pick her up, cradling her in his arms, close against his chest, carrying her somewhere, she wasn't sure where. There was a house, a room, a bed. She knew it was a dream, but it was so vivid that she could feel the soft breath of the man against her face as he gently placed her on the bed. His hand brushed against her hair, and his warm lips settled lightly on her own. She heard him sigh, then move to the foot of the bed and slip her sandals from her feet. The next thing she could remember dreaming was being covered with a sheet and sinking her head into the depths of a plump pillow as she turned on her side and snuggled into the bed.

CHAPTER NINE

SUNLIGHT STREAMING INTO THE ROOM and onto her face awoke Stephanie. She stretched, taking her time to open her eyes and face the day. She felt relaxed, rested, much more than she had thought she would. It was a good feeling, and she wanted to enjoy it before the telephone beside her bed began to ring with messages from Jon, who wouldn't hesitate to disturb her with movie matters—even on a holiday weekend.

She pulled the sheet higher over her face, shielding the light from her eyes. It was strangely bright. Usually the heavy draperies covering her single window in the hotel room kept out much of the morning sun. Probably the unusual intensity of the light this morning was due to her having slept later than she normally did. She wondered what time it was. There were no sounds of activity at the pool, but perhaps everyone else was taking advantage of the opportunity for lying in bed, too.

It was funny also that she was hungry. She had eaten so much at the barbecue that she thought she would never want anything else again. The barbecue. The fight. Cade. By now the story would have made the rounds of her co-workers. She hated to go to the

coffee shop and listen to the talk. Maybe she should
call room service and forget about seeing anyone today. She shrugged, pushing the cover away from her
body and opening her eyes.

Stephanie was halfway out of the bed before it
dawned on her that she didn't know where she was.
Fighting to make sense of her surroundings, she
glanced from the old-fashioned dresser against one
wall to the heavy oak four-poster bed where she had
spent the night to the windows, where a panoramic
display of open fields appeared in her view.

It couldn't be, she told herself. Not the ranch. Not
Cade's house. She tried to remember the events of
the previous evening. It wasn't difficult to recall
waiting by the barn, but she couldn't remember what
had happened next.

A jumble of images appeared before her, hazy
dreamlike pictures of being held and cuddled and
carried into the house. Was it Cade who had found
her? Had she actually fallen asleep beside the barn?
Had he carried her into his house and placed her in
the bed? My God, she thought. Was it his bed? Had
he taken advantage of her in her sleep? That was impossible. She would have been roused from her slum-
ber if he had tried, and besides, her clothes were still
on. Except for her sandals, which were placed neatly
on the floor at the foot of the bed.

She jumped to her feet, slipped into her shoes and
rummaged through her purse, which was on the
dresser. Hastily brushing her hair and straightening
her blouse, she dashed to the door and opened it a
crack. She listened, but there was no sound of activ-

ity, no harsh voice criticizing her and blaming her for leading men on.

She went back into the room, made the bed as quickly as she could and ran back to the door, slipping out without making a sound and shutting the door behind her. It took a minute to get her bearings, but she soon saw the stairway and crept down to the front hallway. Within seconds she was out of the house and had reached the car, shakily inserting the key into the ignition. She didn't look back to see if anyone was around, but she hoped Cade wasn't there to see her flee from him.

Her telephone was ringing when she entered her room at the hotel, and she nervously picked it up, almost afraid it would be Cade calling. Jon was on the line instead, impatiently demanding to know where she had been and pointing out that it was already close to noon.

"It's a holiday weekend, Jon," she evaded his question. "I didn't think I had to keep office hours."

"Sorry, Stef, but I'm upset." She was able to tell that without having him say so. "We're going to have to change the shooting schedule to work around Robert. That idiot got drunk last night, and Cade had to deck him for trying to get fresh with one of the women at the party. He's got a beautiful black eye now."

So Cade hadn't told Jon that she was the woman involved. At least, he hadn't said anything yet. Probably Kara was around, and Cade was waiting to get Jon alone. It occurred to her that Jon had stayed at the ranch all week and that he might have been there last night, as well. She wondered why Cade hadn't mentioned that he had deposited her into the big double bed sometime during the night.

"Are you calling from the ranch?" she asked.

"No, I'm in my suite." Jon explained that he had driven Robert back to town after the incident at the barbecue and had decided to stay at the hotel. "Look, Stef, I know it's the weekend, but I really need your help figuring out the changes we're going to have to make. Cade certainly knows how to punch. Robert's face isn't going to look normal for a week."

"Give me a half hour, Jon," she told him, not wishing to discuss the fight. "I'll be there."

Hanging up, she dialed room service, ordered a light breakfast and stripped out of the blouse and slacks she had worn for twenty-four hours. There was no time for the bubble bath she had envisioned last night. Instead she quickly showered and shampooed her hair. By the time her breakfast arrived she had slipped into a one-piece yellow jump suit that hugged her body. A towel was wrapped around her long hair.

She didn't bother with much makeup, simply applying a dash of pale lipstick and a touch of mascara after she ate. Removing the towel, she shook her hair, letting it fall freely across her shoulders. It was still damp, but it didn't matter. She ran a comb through the locks to keep the tangles out and tied her hair back with a yellow ribbon that matched her outfit.

Jon was fussing with schedule sheets and consulting his script when she knocked on his door. He didn't look as though he'd had a good night's sleep, and he hadn't even taken time to shave. Stephanie felt responsible for that. If it hadn't been for her, Robert wouldn't have been hit by Cade and Jon wouldn't be rearranging the schedule.

"How dare you look so lovely!" he growled as she walked into the room. His robe was loosely tied around him, covering the pajamas he still wore. The room was as much of a mess as he was. Papers were everywhere, and rolls of film were stacked haphazardly on and around the projector.

"I think we need to get organized, Jon, before you can plan anything." She began to pick up papers from the floor, but the director stopped her.

"No, don't fool with that. Just tell me how we're going to shoot a cattle-drive scene without our leading man."

"It won't be so bad, Jon. Do the long scenes now and fill in the close-ups later when Robert is able to work."

"But he needs to be in some of the scenes we have to do." He flung a script down in disgust. "I know we can use Morgan for a lot of the action, but not for all of it. The public expects to see that handsome face of Robert Grant when they go to one of his movies. We can't do the whole thing just showing his back."

"Have you talked to the makeup people?" Stephanie suggested. "They can do wonders, you know."

"They can't do that much. You ought to see him, Stef." Jon shook his head in amazement. "I slipped over to his suite a while ago, hoping he might look better than I thought. Cade really decked him. His eye is swollen shut, and it's going to be all kinds of glorious colors before the bruises subside.''

Stephanie preferred not to think of Robert's black eye and the reasons for it, so she picked up the script off the floor and thumbed through it, trying to think of how the schedule could be changed. Jon fussed and paced while she looked at the thick bound volume.

''Have you thought of writing in a fight scene that would explain Robert's black eye?'' she suggested.

Jon nodded. ''He didn't go for that. It seems he doesn't want to be photographed until his face is healed. He's refusing even to come out to the site.''

The director sat beside her, wearily rubbing his hand over his unshaven face. ''There's nothing to do but figure out how to work around him for a while.'' He picked up a long yellow pad and pen. ''I know I could insist he work and point out the conditions of his contract, but frankly I'd rather not discuss it with him any more than I have to. Robert has made his last film with me.''

''I hope so,'' Stephanie agreed. For a second she was afraid Jon would question her about her remark, but he merely assumed she didn't like the trouble the actor caused.

They began to figure out the best course of action, and an hour later the schedule was finalized. It would mean more work for Morgan because he'd have to portray Robert not only in long shots and stunt scenes but also in the medium shots. A large-brimmed hat, worn low on his head, would help disguise him, and the cameras would never photograph him straight on. They would make certain that the close-up shots to be done later with Robert would not have any cattle in the background so that they could be shot whenever the actor returned to the set.

"Make sure that Becky keeps good notes about the sunlight and clouds," Jon reminded Stephanie. "We can't have a clear sky in the long shots and clouds billowing around Robert in the close-ups."

"Right." Stephanie scribbled a note in her book.

She watched Jon stand up and stretch, and she regretted the trouble she had inadvertently caused him. "Is that everything, Jon?" she asked.

"I think so." He looked around the room, still strewed with papers. "I tell you what," he suggested. "Let's forget about this mess and take the rest of the day off. You wait right here, Stef, while I shower, and then I'm taking you out for a drive and for the biggest steak we can find."

"I'm not dressed for going into a restaurant," she advised, pointing out the informal jump suit she was wearing.

"You look super, and we won't go anyplace fancy. Now don't argue with me, Stef; you deserve it." A knock on the door interrupted him. "Answer that, will you, Stephanie?" She was turning the doorknob as he continued, "That's probably Cade. He called this morning to say I had left a briefcase at the house and to ask if I needed it. Since he was coming to town anyway, he told me he would drop it by."

Cade's eyebrows shot up when he saw Stephanie open the door. His glance strayed from her to Jon, still in pajamas and robe, and back to her. Silently he handed Stephanie the briefcase and turned to go.

"Stay awhile, Cade, if you can," Jon requested. "I'm going to shower and get into some clean clothes and take Stephanie out to wine and dine, but we won't leave for a little while." He smiled at Stephanie. "I owe Stef a good dinner. She's just done me a big favor."

"I'm sure," Cade remarked dryly. "The lady seems to have many talents."

He stood massively in the living room of the suite while Jon took off to the adjoining bedroom, and Stephanie nervously began picking up the stray papers, trying to bring some type of organization to the chaos.

"Tell me, Stephanie," Cade began, armed for battle. "Did you sleep well last night?"

Her cheeks flushed at the remembrance. "Did you find me?" It hurt to ask, to think that he had picked her up and carried her into his house.

"It took a while," he informed her, settling on the large couch and watching her stack film reels on a table by the window. "It was after midnight before I happened to notice there was an extra car in the driveway and to recall that you had been the one driving it. Then it took another ten to fifteen minutes to locate you." He was off the couch and close behind her. "You sleep the innocent sleep of a baby, Stephanie." The harsh laugh she had grown to know so well escaped his throat. "Incongruous, isn't it? Anyway, I couldn't allow even you to spend the night on the ground, so I took you in and put you to bed."

Stephanie kept her face away from him. "Did you...?" She didn't know how to form the question she wanted to ask. "Did you try...?"

Cade did it for her. "Did I try to make love to you?" His mouth was against her hair now, and she could feel his muscular arms about to envelop her. "No, Stephanie, I didn't." He turned her around, cupping her face between two strong hands. "If I had, you wouldn't have slept through it, believe me. You would have remembered every detail."

"You have to reduce everything to sex, don't you?" She stayed immobile, knowing she couldn't escape from his hold and not willing to humiliate herself with a useless attempt.

He let her go, discarding her to reach into his pocket for a pack of cigarettes. "Why not, when I'm dealing with you? You certainly do." Cade lit the cigarette while the impact of his accusation sank in. "I don't want to keep you from Jenson. Tell him I had to leave." And he walked out the door, shutting it firmly behind him.

Stephanie was glad Jon hadn't overheard the conversation. By the time he returned, nattily attired in a sports shirt and slacks, she had recovered enough composure to smile and agree to accompany him on a drive and for dinner. "What about Kara?" she asked. "Don't you want to ask her?"

"I think Kara has other plans," he commented. "It will be just the two of us today."

Stephanie wondered if Kara's plans involved Cade, if that was the reason he had come to town. He had been dressed appropriately for a date with the actress. His lightweight pinstripe suit was exactly right for taking Kara to an intimate dinner at an expensive restaurant.

She yearned to ask Jon if Kara had stayed at the ranch after he left the barbecue, but she didn't. There was no point in discouraging him, too. Instead she took pains to point out how he could succeed with the actress.

"I'm really certain Kara likes you, Jon," she told him, not daring to use the word "love." "I've watched her on the set. She smiles at you in a special way. I don't understand why you don't make your feelings known to her right now." *Before Cade has the chance,* she added to herself.

They viewed the sprawling countryside as Jon drove away from town. He followed a state highway for a while before turning off onto one of the side roads and idly following it past old barns and idyllic pastures full of grazing cattle. They crossed a dam and stopped in a charming little park overlooking a lake, where sailboats and motorboats competed for space. He circled the lake, a trip that required more time than they had thought it would, and they were both ready to eat when they finally stopped at a lakeside restaurant specializing in catfish. Their table by the floor-to-ceiling windows afforded an excellent view of the skiers and sailors enjoying an afternoon on the water.

Stephanie brought up the subject of Kara again. "I don't understand you, Jon. You've certainly never been shy with women before."

"I know," he admitted. "I've had women offer

themselves to me, and I've taken some of them up on those offers. I'm certainly not a saint where women are concerned; and I've gone out of my way to seduce one or two," he added jokingly, dipping a bite of crisply fried catfish into tartar sauce. "But Kara's different. I'm not sure where I stand with her."

"You shouldn't feel that way," Stephanie told him. "You're a handsome charming man, and you've got everything to offer her."

"She's different from the other women I've dated," Jon tried to explain. "She's so sweet to everyone, and so beautiful. . . I just don't know." He took a sip of iced tea. "After all that maneuvering to arrange to go to the Mexican restaurant and the nightclub, I was practically tongue-tied when you left us alone. I could talk to her easily about the film and the movie industry, but whenever I wanted to find out if she'd see me after the film is completed and there's no chance of anyone complaining about favoritism, I couldn't do it."

Stephanie shook her head in wonder. "Jon Jenson, brilliant, famous, the child genius of the movies, afraid to ask the woman he loves for a date." She leaned forward. "Jon, what am I going to do with you? I would shake both you and Kara if it would knock some sense into your heads."

"All that fame doesn't mean a thing." Jon spoke softly. "Kara's more famous than I am. She's not impressed by any work that I've done."

"How do you know?" Stephanie challenged him.

Jon shrugged. "I think I'm going to drop any

plans to be with Kara, at least until we get back to California. Maybe I'll speak to her then.''

Stephanie was alarmed. "But it might be too late by then," she blurted out.

"Why?" Jon looked at her quizzically.

Stephanie hesitated. She couldn't tell him he was giving Cade free rein to court Kara and that if he didn't push his suit she would be lost to him forever. Jon was too trusting of Cade. For an experienced man he was incredibly naive about some things.

"You're not going to wait, Jon. You can't. You never know when someone might come along and sweep Kara off her feet. After all, if she thinks you don't care about her, she's liable to turn to the first man who comes along."

"You mean Robert," Jon scoffed. "No, Kara won't fall for him. She can't stand the man."

"He's not the only man around. . . ."

Jon stared at her for a long time. "I see," he finally said. And Stephanie hoped he understood.

When they had finished their meal and left the restaurant, Jon turned to Stephanie, catching her hands in his. "Stef, would you mind terribly if I cut the day short and took you back to the hotel? I need to get in touch with my leading lady and see if I could meet her for a rehearsal of her next scene."

"Kara's not in any of the scenes we're doing next week," Stephanie pointed out, but she couldn't prevent the slow smile that spread across her face.

"You can never get in too much rehearsal time," Jon explained.

They laughed, and he turned the car in the direction of the hotel.

The smiles faded, however, when they arrived to find that Kara had gone out for the evening and was not expected back until late. Jon immediately headed for the bar, and Stephanie joined him, hoping to comfort him with the suggestion that his leading lady had probably accepted an invitation from some of her new friends to visit them in Dallas. She didn't want him to remember that Cade had been dressed up when he stopped by the hotel room.

There wasn't much chance to continue their conversation, though, because a number of the crew members were already there, enjoying their final days off before work began again. In the background Stephanie could hear the murmured speculations about the previous night's altercation between Cade and Robert. If Robert himself was drinking tonight, he was having liquor sent to his room, for he didn't make an appearance in the bar.

"Hey, Jon," someone called from across the room. "You ought to hire that Steele fellow as a stunt man for the movie. He does a fight scene better than Morgan here ever did."

"That's right," Morgan agreed, joining Stephanie and Jon at their booth. "I pull my punches so no one gets hurt." He called for the waitress and ordered a ginger ale. Morgan seldom drank liquor when he was working on a film. "Boy, would I have liked to see that fight! What happened, Jon?"

The director shrugged. "I don't know for sure. Cade just said that Robert insulted a woman and that he hit him before he thought. It was a reaction." Jon signaled for a refill of his bourbon and water. "Robert was drunk, so I'm not surprised he did something like that.'' He smiled wryly at Morgan. ''You know this means more work for you the next few days, don't you?''

''I figured that,'' Morgan commented, indicating the ginger ale being placed in front of him. ''That's why there's no booze in this.'' The stunt man glanced at Stephanie. ''Did you talk to Cade about why he hit Robert?'' he asked her.

She looked at him sharply, but his expression was bland. ''Robert deserved it, I'm sure,'' was all she said.

Morgan turned back to Jon. ''I hope Cade will be around next week. We can use his help with the long-horns.''

Jon nodded. ''He promised he would be.''

Stephanie could almost hear the wheels turning in his head as he thought about Cade. ''Stef, since Kara won't be in any of this week's scenes, why don't you ask if she wants to fly back to Los Angeles for a few days? There's no point in her coming out to the ranch when she'll just be standing around.''

Morgan quickly agreed, too quickly to suit Stephanie, who was afraid he would let Jon know that he, too, wanted to keep Cade away from the actress. ''She'd really be in the way,'' Morgan explained.

''I'll speak to her if you want me to, Jon,'' Stephanie said, ''but I do think you ought to be the one to discuss the matter with her.''

He nodded. ''I'll go call her room now and see if she's back from wherever it was she went.'' And whomever it was she was with, Stephanie added to herself.

Jon returned within minutes, the frown on his face telling Stephanie that Kara was still out. He tried to call her twice more during the evening, once while they were still in the bar and again after they moved to poolside.

Stephanie stayed up late, keeping Jon company while they awaited Kara's return. She wasn't sleepy; she'd had more than enough sleep the night before, she realized with a shudder. At midnight they agreed to give Kara one more hour before they called it a night and quit trying to reach her. And at ten minutes before one the actress finally answered the telephone in her suite.

Stephanie could hear only Jon's end of the conversation, but it was enough to know that Kara didn't agree with his idea.

"There's simply no reason for you to be here all week," he tried to coax her into going. At last Stephanie heard him mutter, "If that's what you want to do, Kara, then of course it's fine with me."

He hung up the receiver and looked at Stephanie. Before she could say anything, he shook his head, stating emphatically, "It's no use, Stef. She insists on staying in town, and she says she'll be at the ranch Monday to watch the shooting."

"Oh, Jon," Stephanie murmured sympathetically.

"Kara says she likes to watch other scenes being shot because it gives her more of a feel for the entire picture, but you and I know why she wants to be there, don't we, Stef?"

Stephanie nodded, too discouraged to try to deceive Jon into thinking he might be wrong.

She yanked the ribbon from her hair and fluffed the locks out around her face. "I've got to get to bed, Jon. Tomorrow's going to be a long day."

When she was almost at the entrance to the hotel, Jon called to her. "Cade's not going to get her, Stef. Not without a fight."

For the first time in an hour, Stephanie smiled. "Good for you, Jon." She went on to her room, happy that he had agreed to fight for his love. She wished she had the same determination, but there was no strength left in her to try to win Cade. She'd have to forget and console herself with the thought that the rancher might himself lose out with Kara.

CHAPTER TEN

THEY WORKED on the cattle-drive scene for days, long dusty tiring days in which little seemed to get accomplished but somehow under Jon's driving direction reels of film were used up.

The expression of "hurry up and wait" never seemed more true to Stephanie. It took hours to get the equipment in place and what seemed like more hours to position the herd so that it would look larger than it was. Whenever they were almost set, a recalcitrant steer would head in the wrong direction, followed by other cattle, and the shot would have to be postponed while the animals were returned to position.

Coffee breaks were a thing of the past for Stephanie and Jon, who was growing hoarse from shouting orders through the battery-powered megaphone he carried.

Time after time the extras, all dressed in the style of nineteenth-century cowboys, rode with the herd, and Morgan, who had been made up to look amazingly like Robert, went through his part, moving his horse between the cattle, throwing his rope to lasso them. Of course, he wasn't good enough to actually rope a steer, so other shots had to be taken of the cattle being lassoed; the picture merely showed the rope settling around the animal's neck, bringing it to the ground.

Cade became an unofficial technical adviser, showing Morgan how to handle the running iron used to brand cattle on the open range and how to hold the rope so that it would appear he really knew how to throw it. The rancher kept a careful eye on his longhorns, and whenever he felt they were becoming too nervous he refused to let shooting continue, moving the animals away from the cameras and the crowd of people, letting them be soothed by grazing on the vast pastureland on his property.

As a result, the filming took much longer than Jon had predicted, and by the end of the week they still hadn't done the stampede scene and the chuck-wagon segment, or taken the crane shots that would show the herd from a camera high above their heads.

There was little time to think of Cade, but Stephanie couldn't help watching him as he expertly guided his quarter horse, moving the longhorns to the exact place he wanted them. It was the same horse he had ridden with her, a gorgeous animal that was as much at home herding cattle as was the man on its back. It had the speed and endurance of a horse that earned its keep on a ranch and more than enough "cow sense," an ability to anticipate a cow's movements, as she heard Cade say to Morgan one morning.

That's what the quarter horse was for: it had been the principal type of horse used by the early cowboys as they drove their herds of cattle to market, and the men valued their mounts highly. It was obvious that

Cade thought a great deal of his horse; yet he had taken a keen interest, too, in the specially trained horses shipped in for the action scenes in which they would take hard falls without an injury. He watched Morgan rehearse time after time until both he and Jon were satisfied and shot the scene. It was one in which the drovers were supposed to be overtaken by outlaws determined to steal the herd; during the action the hero's horse would be shot out from under him. The stunt horse Morgan rode wasn't solid black, like the horse that was being used for the other scenes; this one had a white blaze on its head, but the spot was dyed black before the animal went before the cameras. The horses, it was said, knew their parts better than some of the actors, for they never failed to fall on cue.

All of the scenes involving the three trained horses were completed by late Friday so the animals could be sent back to California. They had served their purpose well, and the representative from the animal protection society could find no fault in Jon's treatment of them. They were as lively and energetic the day they left as they had been when they arrived on the ranch.

On Saturday Stephanie spent most of the day with the prop man, checking on the equipment for the chuck wagon, which would be set up and filmed on Monday. She had her research material with her, and she carefully matched the descriptions and photographs in her books with the items Brad had chosen to use. The oversize coffeepot was of special interest to her. It was so dented and aged that she wasn't sure she could drink anything brewed in it, which the actors would have to do.

Their last job was to take the props to the ranch. Jon wanted everything there before Monday so there wouldn't be any delay in getting under way with the week's shooting schedule. Normally Stephanie would have dreaded the extra trip and the possibility of running into Cade, but on the way Brad regaled her with stories and gossip.

"You shouldn't talk about people that way," she protested, but she couldn't keep from laughing at his outrageous tales about their co-workers. She only stopped chuckling when he got around to Robert's black eye.

"You know that no one's seen him for a week," Brad pointed out. "I hear he won't leave his room until he looks like a matinee idol again."

"We got by without him," Stephanie responded. She had to say something.

"Actually, it was great with Robert gone," Brad agreed. "Morgan's much better. Or maybe Jon should have hired Cade Steele. He's just as good-looking, and he sure can ride a horse a lot better than Robert."

"I don't think Mr. Steele would be interested," Stephanie muttered. "He doesn't care much about movies."

"Just about movie stars," Brad laughed. "Or should I say one movie star?"

Stephanie quickly turned the discussion back to business and the week's work ahead, making sure that Brad had duplicates of any items that might break during filming. When they arrived at the ranch she quickly helped him unload the gear, wanting to be gone again before Cade noticed their presence. It was only a slight possibility, since his ranch was so large and they took up such a small part of it, but she didn't want to chance running into him. She had carefully avoided him during the week, or perhaps he had avoided her with equal fervor. At any rate, they hadn't had occasion to speak to each other.

She had the big coffeepot in her hand when she heard a truck pulling up behind theirs, and she didn't have to look to know that Cade had arrived. Brad rushed to shake his hand and tell him how much his advice had been appreciated. The prop man looked at Stephanie for confirmation of his compliment, but she couldn't comply. She fiddled with the old pot and finally held it out for Cade to see. "Aren't you glad you don't have to use something like this for your morning coffee?" she asked, trying to force a small lighthearted laugh.

He took it from her, his fingers overlapping hers for a second, barely long enough for her to realize that they had touched her but long enough for the shiver of excitement to tingle down her spine.

"Where did you get this, Brad?" he asked, genuinely interested in the antique and forgetting about Stephanie's quivering presence. He sat on the edge of the table where they were lining their props up for a final count to make sure nothing had been left behind.

"Oh, I've got lots of old things." Brad appreciated Cade's unspoken compliment. "Some of the things came from the studio in Hollywood, but I've been haunting the junk stores here. I found that pot in a little place on the edge of Dallas."

Cade caressed the tin pot with the touch of a lover. He looked up at Stephanie. "Do you know the recipe for making coffee in one of these?" he asked. She had to admit that her research hadn't included coffee recipes, adding that she hardly could brew any in a modern percolator and usually relied on the instant variety.

"You start by boiling two gallons of water," Cade told her, setting the big pot on the table and staring at it as he tried to remember the way he had heard the recipe. "After the water boils, you throw in two pounds of coffee."

Stephanie flinched. "Sounds a little strong to me," she stated.

"I'm not through yet," Cade said, his eyes twinkling with amusement. It had been a long time since he had looked at her without condemnation in his eyes, and she stood silently enjoying the rare sight. "You're supposed to boil the coffee and water for two hours and then check to see if it's done."

Stephanie folded her arms in front of her chest, glad that she had, for some unknown reason, worn a dress today instead of her customary jeans and shirt. "And how do you test it?" she asked.

"Throw a horseshoe into the pot," Cade announced. "If it sinks, the coffee's not done." He laughed, and Stephanie didn't know whether he was teasing her or relating an actual trail recipe.

"I'm going to look that up when I get back," she

proclaimed. "I don't think you're telling the truth."

"Would I deceive you?" The flicker in his eyes let her know that there was an edge to his remark, a question as to her own possible deception.

"It's none of my business really," she retorted stiffly, her good humor gone, as she turned back to finish her count. "I think all the stuff is here, Brad. We can lock it up in the office and be on our way."

Cade watched them put the props away, and when they were about ready to leave he asked Brad if he was planning to use authentic sourdough biscuits for the breakfast scene. Brad replied that they would substitute packaged biscuits.

"And this is supposed to be an accurate account of a trail drive?" Cade sneered at Stephanie. "You have to have sourdough biscuits."

"But no one here would know how to make them, and I believe they look like regular biscuits." Stephanie was ready to leave, and she didn't want to argue.

"And you're the one who complained about the notches on the log cabin being wrong," Cade reminded her of her insistence upon details. "I can see I'm going to have to teach you children about old-fashioned cooking."

They had no choice but to follow him. Stephanie watched the dirt flying up from beneath the wheels of his truck just ahead of them and wondered why she had bothered to dress so carefully. She would be dusty again before they reached the house.

Cade led them through the back door and into the kitchen. He fumbled through the refrigerator until he found a little jar that was tightly covered. It held the starter, he explained, made with yeast, sugar, flour and water. The mixture was saved, he told them, and when it was time to make biscuits most of it was put into a pan with soda, salt and more flour. The dough was kneaded, pinched off into small balls, partially dipped in fat and placed in a baking pan to cook. The starter was also used, he said, for sourdough flapjacks.

Brad encouraged Cade by asking questions, so he told them about such other trail delicacies as a dessert made with flour, vinegar, sugar, cinnamon and water, and a stew known among the drovers by a name he was reluctant to repeat in the presence of a woman.

"I didn't realize you were such a culinary expert, Cade," Stephanie teased as they were leaving. "Perhaps we should have hired you to cater the lunches."

He leaned against a post on the back porch. "I'm afraid I'm not a cook at all, Stephanie, except for breakfast. As a matter of fact, I cooked a particularly delicious breakfast the morning after our barbecue. There was plenty for two; you should have joined me." She ignored the thrust, but Cade wouldn't stop needling her. "Or do you sleep late every weekend?"

"When I have the chance." Her cheeks were flushed from embarrassment, but Brad paid no attention. Engrossed in trying to make friends with the German shepherd, he was not even listening to the conversation.

On the trip back to town, Stephanie mentally calculated the number of days left for shooting at the ranch. There were far too many. She wished they were ready to move to Dallas to finish up with the studio shots. There would be no reporting to Cade Steele then.

On Sunday she did exactly what Cade had accused her of doing: she slept late, not stirring from her bed until noon. Then she joined Becky for a leisurely afternoon at a nearby movie theater, followed by an evening of lying around by the pool. For once Jon didn't bother her; in fact she didn't know whether he was working or not. Fleetingly she wondered if he was with Kara, but then put all thoughts on such matters out of her mind. She was going to have at least one day free of dealing with other people's problems—and her own.

It almost worked. Not until Morgan dropped by to ask how she was doing did the haunting specter of Cade appear before her.

"I'm great," she smiled at Morgan, who eyed her skeptically. "Really. Life couldn't be better." They both knew she was lying, but neither admitted it.

"Are you ready for tomorrow?" she asked.

"As much as I can be."

They both fell into silence, thinking of the day ahead. It would be the most difficult of all—the stampede scene. No matter how many times Morgan worked it out in his head, no matter how often he practiced, actually doing the work was going to be a dangerous venture, and they both knew it. But Morgan was experienced. He had fallen off roofs onto small but thick pads three floors below, and he had crashed through fake glass windows in previous movies. He felt confident about his part, he told Stephanie. He was only concerned that the longhorns be as sure of their role.

Morgan did wish that the scene was scheduled early in the day, but that was impossible. Stampedes rarely took place during the daytime, when the cattle could see what was around them. It was at night, when darkness hid the dangers from them, that they became edgy and likely to run.

Jon had planned the chuck-wagon scene first, and then he had scheduled a break before action would resume in early evening. At that time there would still be sufficient light for filming, but the illusion of night could be created more easily with filming techniques.

Morgan didn't have to report to the set until late afternoon, since Robert was scheduled to handle his role by himself during the initial shooting. It was the leading man's first time back since Cade had struck him, and Stephanie knew the gossip would start up again once the actor made his appearance. Everyone would be speculating about what would happen when Cade ran into him again, for they all knew that the rancher planned to be around for the stampede scene.

Luckily, perhaps, for Robert, Cade wasn't there for the early shooting, but Robert must have been uneasy and worried that the rancher would show up. He forgot his lines, forgot where he was supposed to stand, forgot when to reach for a tin plate. Filming the scene took twice as long as it should have done, and Jon had thrown one of his famed tantrums before the work was finally done to his satisfaction.

Even though they were behind schedule, there was a long pause before they were ready to shoot the cattle. Jon and the cinematographer held conferences, adjusted the crane, rechecked all the angles. At the same time, Morgan was conferring with Cade, going over in great detail exactly how the longhorns would be run across the prairie and how the men would move to slow the animals down at the place Jon indicated.

Stephanie was drawn to them, fascinated by the talk but well aware of the problems facing Morgan and the ranch employees who would serve as the extras for this scene. They might not have been in a movie before, but they knew how to handle cattle, and Cade had insisted that his men work the animals that evening. He had seen for himself during the past week that the professional actors weren't experienced enough with cattle for his satisfaction.

There would be only one take. Cade had made that a condition for shooting because he didn't want to subject his animals to any more stress than was necessary. Jon had agreed and ordered additional cameras, all of which would film at once. They had to be positioned carefully so that each would shoot a specific segment of the stampede. One, high on a crane stationed atop a hill, would do the overall scene.

They began by showing the cattle being moved down the trail to the spot where they supposedly would stop for a night of rest during the drive. Stephanie walked to the top of the hill to get a better view as Jon called for action to begin.

It was going perfectly, she noticed from the beginning. The longhorns walked steadily across the prairie in exactly the formation the director wanted. Stephanie had done enough research to know that a herd on a drive was not supposed to be kept too close together. The animals walked better with space between them, tending then not to stop to graze.

The point riders, in this case an employee plus Morgan dressed in Robert's costume, led the way. The point men on a real cattle drive, Stephanie knew, were the ones who actually pointed the cattle in the right direction, who led the herd to market. They were usually the most experienced of the riders. The swing and flank men worked the sides of the herd, keeping the cattle from scattering and moving them along at the proper speed. The drag men had the worst job. They rode in the dust at the back of the herd, prodding the slowest cattle along and keeping stragglers from straying.

Once the cattle had made their way to the site where the chuck wagon was located, Jon stopped the cameras and boomed his thanks to the riders over the megaphone. The herd milled around while final details were worked out to start the stampede. If the riders did their jobs correctly the cattle would run the way they had just come, and Cade spent a long time preparing his men to make certain everyone knew what he was supposed to do.

These cattle didn't know what it was to stampede. Modern cattle weren't as likely to be spooked as the old range longhorns because they were handled more now, but Cade refused to let the crew set off any type of noisemaker, a firecracker or a gun, to get the herd on the run. Instead he placed a saddle upside down on a horse and told Morgan and Jon that when the horse ran flying through the herd kicking at the flying stirrups, the cattle were as likely to run as if a gun had been fired.

By the time instructions were completed, one camera still wasn't ready. Everyone stood around nervously waiting. They hated this kind of delay, the rush of trying to get everything ready in a hurry followed by a helpless sense of not being able to do anything. The adrenaline was flowing, and most of the crew wanted to get on with the action of the film.

Morgan was one of the few who appeared relaxed. He pulled his personal camera out of his bag of supplies and started taking snapshots of the longhorns and the film preparations.

"Hey, Stephanie," he called when he saw her perched on a stool at the fringe of the commotion. "Let me get your picture."

"Not now, Morgan." She was too anxious to think of posing for a photograph, and she didn't see how the stunt man could get his mind off the action ahead long enough to use his camera.

"Just one." He pulled her off the stool, telling her he wanted to find a better light. Before she realized what he was doing, he had her standing beside Cade and was asking Cade if he would be in the picture, as well.

Cade glanced at Stephanie, and she knew he didn't want to be bothered with a picture, either. He was concerned about his men and his cattle and not about posing with a woman he didn't like. But Morgan insisted, and it was difficult to turn down his charming appeal.

Stephanie stood stiffly beside Cade while Morgan looked at them through the viewfinder. She knew what his purpose was. He didn't care about getting a picture of her and Cade; he only wanted to throw them together, if just for a brief moment. Hadn't he promised not to interfere? She tried to remember what he had said at the Fourth of July barbecue.

"You two look like a pair of wooden Indians," Morgan called to them. "Relax a little bit. Cade, put your arm around Stephanie—and, Stephanie, look at him and smile."

Stephanie felt Cade's arm settle stiffly around her waist, but she didn't look at him. She stared at Morgan's camera, and with a shrug he snapped the shutter.

"I'll have a print made for both of you," Morgan advised them as he wound the film to the next number.

"That won't be necessary, Morgan," Stephanie told him. "Save your money."

"No trouble at all, Stephanie," Morgan responded with a sly grin at her. She hoped he wouldn't say anything else, and she walked swiftly away before he wanted her to pose with Cade again.

At last they were ready to film. The men, in their rough-looking cowboy outfits, gathered around the campfire by the chuck wagon. Morgan had to stand in the shadows so that his face wouldn't show in the long shot. Becky checked her notes to be certain they were all in the same places they had been that morning when Robert had done the close-up and medium shots.

When the clapper board was struck and the call for action was given, the scene unveiled itself quickly. From off camera, Cade sent the horse with the saddle on upside down into the center of the herd, and the animals responded as he had predicted, quickly taking off. Just as swiftly, the men were on their horses and after the longhorns.

The plan was for the herd to be circled, just as a stampede was stopped in the cattle-drive days. The leaders of the herd had to be thrown back among the drags, and the best way to do that was to make them run in a circle. That meant that the riders on one side of the cattle had to turn the front-running animals back and keep them from running straight ahead. Morgan and Ray had that job. The riders opposite them fell back slightly to allow the longhorns to be turned, but Morgan and Ray rode closer and closer to the animals, determined to get them into a circle before they were out of range of the cameras.

Just in time Stephanie saw the cattle turn, and she breathed a sigh of relief. Once the leaders were under control, the rest of the animals would follow naturally. She relaxed and looked at Jon to see if he was satisfied. The excited smile on his face told her that he thought he had good shots, but he kept the cameras turning, ensuring that all the action was on film until the herd was completely stopped.

The longhorns didn't stop as quickly as they had hoped. Instead they circled again and again, the leaders determined not to settle down once they had a taste of running, and the riders had to move closer to the herd than they'd planned in order to cut them off.

Morgan wasn't supposed to get nearer to the cattle than he was; that was the job of the ranch employees. But he instinctively turned his horse toward the stampeding animals the same way the other men were doing.

The big black horse he rode wasn't used to the longhorns' unusual action, either, and it kept trying to pull back and not respond to Morgan's touch on the reins or his spurs on its flanks. When the stunt man insisted, the animal whinnied in protest and flung its front legs high in the air.

Morgan hadn't fallen from a horse since childhood, but he had been so intent upon watching the cattle that he'd become careless in the way he sat on the horse, and he slid from the saddle before he could regain his balance. The gelding sped off, and Morgan fell hard onto the ground while the longhorns swirled dangerously near him.

Cade had been watching from horseback, and he spurred his own mount into the scene without a second's delay, scooping Morgan off the ground, but not before he had been pounded by the hooves of a large steer. Leaving the settling of the herd to his men, Cade turned his full attention to the stunt man, stretching him out on the ground once he was safely out of the way of the cattle and ripping the shirt from his body to check the extent of his injuries.

Luckily, Morgan had worn a protective vest underneath the costume, but even that couldn't prevent the nasty-looking marks that covered his chest. And nothing but a felt hat had protected his head from the hard ground as he fell.

"He has some damaged ribs and probably a concussion," Cade told the group gathering around. His diagnosis was confirmed by the nurse who was always on duty during action filming. She advised that Morgan go to a hospital for observation and treatment.

"I'll take him," Cade announced, asking a bystander to drive his truck back to his home and bring him his car instead. He tossed the keys at the teenager, who nodded and took off for the parking area as fast as he could run. The nurse offered to drive Morgan or to accompany Cade on the trip, but the rancher declined, asking her to stay and treat one of his employees, who was limping toward them. One of the longhorns had stepped on his ankle as the men were calming them down and putting them into their pasture for the night.

The car was brought to the site, and Morgan was gently placed in the back seat, where he could lie as flat as possible during the long ride to town. Jon had suggested calling an ambulance, but Cade had replied that it would take too long to get one to the ranch. He preferred to drive the stunt man himself.

Morgan was conscious, if a bit woozy, and he kept trying to speak as he was lifted into the car and covered with a blanket. Jon leaned over to hear what he was mumbling.

"Stephanie, too," Morgan muttered. "Have Stephanie come with me."

"He wants you to go, too, Stef." Jon turned to her. "Do you mind?"

"Of course not. I want to go with Morgan."

Jon looked at Cade, who was about to get into the driver's seat. "Thanks for the help, Cade. I'll wrap things up around here and get over to the hospital as soon as I can."

Cade nodded and slid into the car beside Stephanie.

They didn't talk much during the drive. Stephanie leaned over the back of the seat, checking on Morgan, talking to him, trying to keep him awake. She was afraid that if he became unconscious he might slip into a coma and never wake up.

"Do you think he'll be all right?" she whispered once to Cade, concern in her voice.

"I think so," he replied. "We'll have to wait and see."

They did wait. Stephanie paced the floor outside the emergency room while Cade sat stiffly on a hard wooden bench. Someone offered to bring them coffee, but Stephanie declined. She only wanted news of Morgan. She wanted somebody to tell her he would be all right, and she wanted to be comforted while she was waiting for the news.

She looked at Cade. There would be no comfort from him. He was as uncommunicative as a statue, and she gave a sigh of relief when she saw Jon hurry through the emergency-room door. Rushing to the director, she flung her arms around his neck, crying out her relief at seeing him. She didn't stop to consider Cade's inevitable reaction.

The physician came out to tell them that Morgan had suffered three broken ribs and a concussion, just as Cade and the nurse had thought. "The ribs aren't a problem," the doctor reported, "except that he will be sore and uncomfortable while they heal, but I am concerned about his head injury, and I want to keep him here for several days." He scribbled notes on the chart he carried. "It's likely a simple concussion, but you can't be too careful."

Jon took care of the details of admitting Morgan to the hospital while Cade and Stephanie waited. They were standing there, lost in their own thoughts, when a nurse informed them that Morgan had asked to see them.

The stunt man managed a weak smile as they approached. "Did the scene get finished?" he asked.

"I'm sure it did," Stephanie told him. "I didn't think to ask. But don't worry about that. How do you feel?"

"Like I've been kicked by a longhorn." He tried to laugh, but it hurt too much. The medication he'd taken had made him drowsy, and he had trouble thinking of what he wanted to say. Stephanie told him to rest, but he clasped her hand, keeping her at his bedside.

"How long will I be here?" he wanted to know.

"A few days, that's all."

"Stephanie, will you call my wife and tell her what happened?"

"You know I will. I had already planned to do that."

"Tell her not to worry."

She touched the white bandage on his head. "You can count on me, Morgan."

"Thanks." He smiled and looked from her to Cade. "I hope the longhorns are all right."

Cade nodded. "They're fine."

Morgan was silent for a minute, and Stephanie thought he was drifting off to sleep, but he opened his eyes again and looked at her intently. "Will you come back to visit me?"

"I'll be here tomorrow," she promised.

"Bring Cade with you," he said. "I'll feel more like talking to you then." His eyes shut, but he continued to speak. "Be sure to bring Cade with you."

CHAPTER ELEVEN

JON AND STEPHANIE said good-night to Cade in the parking lot of the hospital, and Stephanie felt guilty as she followed the director to his car for a ride back to the hotel. Cade's expression had changed from the concern he had shown for Morgan to one of skepticism as he watched her depart with Jon's arm firmly around her shoulders.

She was glad when Jon suggested she take the next day off to stay with Morgan at the hospital while filming continued at the ranch. She didn't mention that Morgan wanted Cade to visit him, too, because she didn't want Jon to suggest she ride with the rancher. She merely proposed calling a taxi when she was ready to go to the hospital so that she wouldn't interfere with anyone's schedule.

But Cade arrived at the hotel before she could call for the cab. She saw him framed in the entrance to the restaurant as she nibbled at her plate of bacon and eggs; and as she always did when she looked at him from a distance, she took the time to admire his muscular physique, the long lines tapering from his broad shoulders to the flat waist and strong thighs. He was wearing a business suit in place of the jeans and boots she had seen him in recently. If there had been a briefcase in his hand he might have been going off to the stock exchange or a banking institution. She was afraid, however, that he might be planning a day at the hospital.

Fortunately, everyone else had departed for the ranch, so no one saw her blush as he joined her, inquiring casually if she had slept well. She never knew whether he was being serious or simply needling her, but she had to ignore him either way. It did no good to rise to the bait he dangled before her, and assuming he was sincere would only raise hopes inside her that would be dashed to the ground as swiftly as Morgan had fallen hours earlier.

"Could I help you with something?" she asked, sipping the orange juice, which tasted slightly bitter this morning.

"Are you going to the hospital?" When she nodded Cade continued, "I am, too, so I'll give you a ride if you have no other transportation."

"I was getting ready to call a taxi—there's really no reason for you to bother."

"It's no bother, I assure you, Stephanie. I was going to visit Morgan anyway."

His vision suddenly shifted to Kara, who was entering the coffee shop, her red hair hanging loosely around her shoulders, enhancing her fair looks and complementing the solid white pantsuit she wore. "Is Kara going with you?"

"I don't know. I mean, I haven't asked." She wasn't sure she wanted Kara along. True, it would divert Cade's attention from her, but it would also give him time to work his charm on the actress. Already she was giving him that enchanting smile of hers as she strolled across the room.

Cade stood up as Kara reached the table, taking her hands in his and telling her how beautiful she looked. He hadn't said anything of the kind to Stephanie, but then she was wearing a simple green wraparound cotton skirt with a flower-patterned sleeveless blouse. Her legs were bare, and she had flat white sandals on her feet. She had dressed for comfort, for sitting in a hospital room, not for impressing a man. But now she wished she had found something a little nicer looking, something that would not make her feel out of place beside a man in a blue business suit.

They spoke of Morgan's accident, which Kara had not seen. She did plan to visit the hospital, she told them, later in the day, but she had already made an appointment to spend the morning in Dallas, for a photograph session that her publicity man had arranged and to tape a television interview for a local station.

They lingered over coffee while Kara talked about moving to a Dallas hotel on Friday. The entire cast and crew would transfer to Dallas in two weeks, when the ranch shooting was completed and all that remained would be the interior scenes to be shot on the sound stage of the film production company. But Kara was going early since she had completed all of her outdoor scenes.

"I guess that means I won't be back at the ranch anymore," she told Cade. "I have to spend most of this week rehearsing with the assistant director, and

I'll be in Dallas after that. I may not see you again."

"Oh, you'll see me again, Kara," he stated firmly, and they both laughed. "I'll make certain of that."

They seemed to be sharing a private joke, but it was one Stephanie could easily decipher. They were pretending for her sake that they were casual acquaintances, but Cade was telling her how much a part of his life she would be, and her laughter was an admission that he was correct. Stephanie couldn't stand to watch their flirtatious behavior. She pushed her plate away and announced that she had to leave for the hospital.

"And I must go on to Dallas," Kara said. She held her hand out again for the rancher to hold. "Maybe I will see you again, Cade."

Stephanie looked away, not wanting to see the eye signals Kara was no doubt exchanging with Cade. She picked up her check and walked to the counter to sign her name and room number on the ticket while Kara and Cade continued their farewells. Very affectionate ones, she assumed.

Cade might have been friendly with Kara, but he was stern on the drive to the hospital, and Stephanie had to search for topics of conversation. She asked about the employees and the animals and was relieved to know that all were well. There had been no damage to the ranch property, and the one employee injured had merely required an elastic bandage on his ankle.

"That's good news," she commented.

"For your sake it certainly is," Cade responded as he switched lanes on the freeway.

"You'll be rid of us soon," she reminded him, "and I'm doing my best to make sure that everything goes well these last weeks of shooting. You're not going to have any reason to be upset."

"I'd better not." He kept his eyes on the road, but Stephanie felt that he was looking at her. The hospital was in sight before he spoke again. "I can't blame you for Morgan's accident," he admitted. "He went too close to the herd, and he was lucky he wasn't killed. He's a plucky man, and I have to admire his courage. I wish he weren't quite so rash, though."

Stephanie nodded. "Morgan has always sacrificed his safety to get the right shot. This isn't the first time he's been injured. His wife wasn't too surprised when I called her last night. She's prepared to hear that he's been hurt even if she doesn't like it."

"He did a good job of working the cattle before he ventured too near," Cade complimented the stunt man. "If he ever needs work, he'd make a good ranch hand."

"Well, Cade, I'm glad you've finally found something to like about movie people. We're not all bad now, are we?"

She knew she had made a mistake when he swung the car into the driveway and into a parking place and then turned his huge body to look at her.

"It depends on your definition of what's bad, now, doesn't it?"

Stephanie glared at him. "I don't consider myself bad, and I'm not ashamed of anything I've done," she retorted.

"I didn't think you would feel any remorse." He opened his door. "Shall we go visit Morgan?"

The stunt man was in pain when they saw him, but he insisted they stay, and Stephanie sat in the small chair in his room while Cade stood at the window. Their talk was sporadic until the physician came in to see Morgan and the visitors had to leave while he examined the patient. They retired to the coffee shop and stared at each other from opposite sides of the small table where they were seated.

"How long will you be filming in Dallas before you go back to California?" Cade asked once they had been served.

"Three or four weeks. The indoor scenes always go quicker than the outdoor ones. We don't have to delay for weather or things like that. The people at the production studio are a big help, too."

Unlike certain people she had been dealing with, she added to herself. But she had to admit that Cade had been better lately. He had become less strident in his dealings with them, and he had seemed to form a genuine friendship with Jon, one that would come to a quick end when he discovered they were after the same woman.

Poor Jon hadn't had much opportunity to see Kara. He had called a couple of extra rehearsals for her, and they had gone out to dinner once or twice—for business, he had made certain everyone knew. No one had thought to start any gossip about them. The entire company was certain that Kara and Cade were the ones who were involved; and for a change Stephanie couldn't disagree with the gossip.

She talked about the movie to keep her thoughts from straying to Kara and Cade, telling the rancher that only a small number of people would be at the location site for the next two weeks. The basic work was completed, and the only filming left involved shots showing the ranch house itself and a few miscellaneous ones that were needed for transition scenes. Many of the people would go on to Dallas to work on preparations for the indoor segments.

"Will you be sorry to leave, Stephanie?" Cade asked, and she didn't know how to answer him. It would be a relief to escape his all-encompassing gaze and his sharp questions about her private life, but the thought of not seeing him again was anguish to her. She would miss the ranch deeply, too. She had grown even more passionately fond of the land than she had been the first time she saw it. Something about the country called her back—and something about Cade was equally compelling.

"We always have mixed emotions about completing filming," she finally stammered. "But there will still be months of work ahead with the editing, the musical score, all that kind of thing."

"And you work on that?" He was watching her so closely she couldn't hold her coffee cup steady, and she set it back down on the saucer.

"No, not really," she replied. "There are experts who handle that. Under Jon's direction, of course. All I do is take notes on what he wants done."

"You must be with him day after day."

"With Jon? Of course. There's not much time off while a film is being made."

He continued to question her about her job with Jon, and she found it strange that he wanted to know so much about the work in Los Angeles. It didn't concern him; once filming on his ranch ended, he'd have nothing more to do with the movie.

"And how do you relax once you've finished a film? Do you go off on vacation?"

She smiled. "I like to," she responded, "when there's time—when Jon's not already jumping into another movie."

"You go on vacation with Jon?" he asked, and she looked up to see the hard lines forming on his face.

"No, as a matter of fact, I don't." She stood up to leave. "I hate to disappoint you, but I usually go somewhere on my own or with a relative. Not that it happens very often," she added. "I simply don't get much time away from work."

He grabbed her arm before she could flee. "Then you should take a few days off while you're here," he announced.

"That won't be possible," she retorted. "I'll be going back the day the filming is completed."

"Surely you can take a day off," he insisted. "Take a sight-seeing tour or something. Get away from that phony world you live in."

Stephanie wondered if he was inviting her out, and a warm excitement swept through her. "What would you suggest?" she dared to ask.

He shrugged, his gaze on her as they waited for the elevator to take them to the floor where Morgan's room was located. "Kara hasn't seen much of Fort

Worth, either. Perhaps you could both take some time off and I'll give you a tour.''

Stephanie didn't answer, and as she stood lost in thought, deflated, the elevator doors slid open without her noticing. Cade gave her a nudge, and she darted inside. His casual invitation was obviously only an excuse to see Kara, to woo her before she returned to California. But if so, why did he want Stephanie to go along? She'd be in the way, and there was no reason to use her for camouflage, as Jon had wanted to do. Cade didn't have to pretend he was dating someone else: everyone knew he had eyes only for Kara.

THE REST OF THE WEEK passed in a flurry of activity. Stephanie spent her days on the set and her evenings at the hospital until Morgan's wife arrived to keep him company. He asked about Cade whenever she visited, and she usually attempted to change the subject.

"I tried my best to get the two of you here at the same time,'' Morgan reminded her.

"Even when you were in pain, lying on the back seat of the car,'' Stephanie pointed out, "you were still trying to be a matchmaker. It won't work, Morgan, so you can quit trying. Cade is interested only in Kara.'' She gave a harsh laugh, amazingly like the skeptical sound that Cade uttered, except in a higher register. "He actually wants me to accompany the two of them on a tour of the city this weekend. Have you ever heard of anything so ridiculous?''

"Maybe he wants to be with you, Stef.''

"Fat chance. I wish you could see the way he practically drools over Kara. It's embarrassing."

Morgan started to laugh but caught himself when he felt the resulting pain in his ribs. "You're too sensitive," he advised. "Now, let me tell you what you should do."

A slow smile spread over Stephanie's face as she listened to the stunt man. It was such a brilliant idea—and it would be the perfect way to get back at Cade.

All she had to do was to invite Jon to make the tour with them. Between them they would see that Cade never had a minute alone with Kara. Besides, it would give Jon the opportunity to be with Kara again. There was only one problem: Stephanie would have to do what Jon had requested of her when they went to the restaurant and the nightclub; she'd have to try to keep Cade's attention on herself. It wouldn't be easy, but she would take great delight in seeing his face when he figured out what was happening.

She was right about it not being easy. Cade raised an eyebrow when she mentioned that she had taken the liberty of asking Jon to go with them. His face darkened, and she thought for a moment that he would cancel the entire trip. But he gained control of himself and simply shrugged, telling her with a hint of a sneer that he wouldn't want to be the one to keep her away from her friend.

The day began incredibly early. Cade picked them up at the hotel and headed north, avoiding the interstate highway and taking the state roads instead, talking easily about the history and the geography of

the land they passed through. At Gainesville he
turned west, stopping at a small but magnificent
church that stood in the middle of a prairie in a tiny
town. Stephanie had never seen anything like the
structure, which had been built by the descendants of
German immigrants. Built in Neoromanesque style,
the building was a replacement for an earlier structure destroyed by a tornado. The inside had unusual
frescoes, stained-glass windows and carved altars,
and Stephanie was intrigued to discover that old
windmill towers had been used as reinforcements in
concrete.

Cade drove on, through another little town that
had served as one of the stopping points on the
Chisholm Trail, and then he maneuvered down roads
that were hardly wide enough to be paths to within
yards of the Red River, which formed the boundary
between Texas and Oklahoma. He pointed out the
historical marker that identified the place as Red
River Station, and they crawled under barbed-wire
fences to go down to the river itself.

Stephanie could understand how the river had got
its name. Accumulated sandy silt had given the water
a red tinge, and Cade pointed out the abrupt bend in
the river that slowed the flow and made the location a
natural crossing spot. Red River Station, he pointed
out, had been a frontier post and the main crossing
on the river for the Chisholm Trail herds, but the
town had been abandoned since 1887, when it was no
longer good business to trail cattle overland through
the area. But in its prime Red River Station had been
so busy that sometimes the cowhands would walk

across the river on the backs of the large herds of cattle that were crossing.

On the return trip he told them about Jesse Chisholm. The man may have given the trail its name, but scholars said he wasn't a trail boss or even a Texan. He was a part-Indian trader who hauled trade goods from Kansas to what is now southern Oklahoma around 1866. When the first cattle drives began, the drovers followed Jesse Chisholm's wagon tracks from the Indian territory north to Kansas.

Stephanie thought Kara might be bored with the recitation of history, but she expressed as much interest as the others, only mentioning that she was tired after the hike from where they left the car down to the riverbank and back again. Stephanie suggested that on the return journey Kara sit in the back seat, where she could stretch out more, and she hopped into the front beside Cade before he could talk the actress into staying at his side.

There wasn't much he could do, but Stephanie could sense the questions he didn't ask about her sudden move. She waited for him to remark about her desire to sit by him, but he didn't say a word to her, instead relating more of the history and the land development, telling them how the first settlers obtained grants from the government and how the railroads were provided free land, also, to encourage them to lay tracks along the vast expanse of the state.

It was late afternoon when they arrived back in Fort Worth. Cade had asked them to bring along a change of clothes, explaining that it would be simpler if they stayed in a downtown hotel overnight. He planned to take them to a musical following dinner.

Kara and Stephanie practically raced each other for the bath in the suite they shared. Both of them were covered with dust, and Kara was complaining that she felt as if she hadn't left the filming site. She was as gritty as a day at work on the ranch normally left her.

Stephanie would have liked to talk to Kara about her feelings for Cade, but they had to rush to be ready in time to meet the men. She shampooed her hair and carefully dried it before using her curling iron to make the ends swirl toward her face. Her dress was a cornflower blue, almost the same shade as her eyes, and the outfit made her eyes appear even larger and more expressive than usual. A touch of eye shadow and mascara emphasized what she considered to be her best feature.

Kara was also in blue, and they joked about looking like twins, but Stephanie knew there was nothing in her own appearance that would appeal to Cade as much as the sparkling redhead who was attaching a simple string of pearls around her neck.

Jon whistled when he saw them, but Cade said nothing about their beauty, merely pointing out that they would have to hurry to be on time for dinner. They were a few minutes late arriving at the exclusive restaurant, but the headwaiter didn't complain—not after he saw Kara. With great flourish he escorted them to the best table and proclaimed that champagne would be served with the compliments of the management. It had been a long time since lunch, and the champagne made Stephanie giddy, even to the point that she covered Cade's hand with hers when she wanted to tell him something. He stared at her, glanced at Jon and turned back to Kara.

If the actress minded being the center of all the attention, she didn't show it. And to Stephanie's surprise, neither Jon nor Cade gave the slightest indication of being jealous of each other. It was almost as if they took turns with her. Jon escorted Kara to the door while Cade paid the bill, and Cade led her into the theater when they arrived for the musical.

After the show was over and they returned to the hotel, both men joined Kara and Stephanie in the women's suite for another bottle of champagne, which Cade ordered to be sent to the room. Stephanie wanted to give Jon time to say good-night to Kara alone, but she couldn't budge Cade. He simply stayed put, ignoring her subtle hints that he should leave. It was after two in the morning before they finally departed, and Stephanie had to use the excuse of having Cade help her get a bucket of ice from the machine in the hallway to give Jon even two minutes with Kara.

She couldn't sleep after the men left, and Kara, tired as she was, stayed awake, as well. They propped themselves against the plump cushions of the couch in the living room of their suite and talked. Their conversation naturally turned to Cade, and Stephanie was shocked when Kara explained that she didn't understand him, that he didn't say very much to her.

"He's probably awestruck and tongue-tied,"

Stephanie excused him. Her lips curved in an ironic smile. Cade was certainly not tongue-tied with *her*. He let Stephanie know exactly what he thought of her. Why couldn't he tell Kara how much he loved her?

"No," Kara answered, "it's nothing like that. He doesn't particularly like me, and I really wish he'd quit showing up when I want to be with Jon."

Stephanie sat up straight. "Jon?" she exclaimed. "Then you do want to be with Jon?"

Kara smiled dreamily. "Oh, yes. He's so wonderful, so tender and strong at the same time. Everything I always thought I'd never find in a man in this crazy business."

"I thought so!" Stephanie proclaimed. "When you were first here this summer, you looked at Jon in a way that made me think you might care for him. Oh, Kara, I'm so glad I was right. You're going to make him so happy."

"You're wrong about that, Stephanie." She picked up a magazine and threw it listlessly back down on the coffee table. "I've done everything I can think of to make Jon notice me. I've chased him like a silly schoolgirl, but he acts as if I'm just another actress he hired to work for him."

"But that's just on the set," Stephanie tried to explain. She had to make Kara understand that Jon loved her. "He's afraid of being accused of favoritism." She couldn't make herself clear. "You know he's always had this thing about not dating his leading ladies."

"Don't I know it," Kara moaned, collapsing onto

the couch. "I'll never work for him again. I can't stand seeing him every day and not being able to reach out and touch him. Do you know what I mean?"

Stephanie nodded. She understood more than Kara would ever know. It was the way she felt about Cade, the reason she planned to leave for Los Angeles as quickly as she could. She had to keep him out of her sight, or she'd go crazy with yearning for him.

"Today, for example," Kara continued. "All morning long I had to sit there beside Cade while you were in the back with Jon. Oh, Stephanie, I was so jealous of you."

"Of me?" Stephanie found that hard to believe.

"You were right there beside Jon, and he took your hand to help you down that hill going to the river." She paced the floor as she let out her pent-up emotions. "Oh, I realize you two are just good friends, but I saw it all, Stephanie, and I couldn't help wishing I was the one with Jon."

"Jon was wishing the same thing," Stephanie tried to console her.

"No, he didn't pay any attention to me. Not even when I rode in the back seat on the return trip."

Stephanie sighed. How was she ever going to get these two together when they wouldn't believe anything she said? But she was determined to do it. Someone was going to find some happiness out of this miserable summer—and Kara and Jon were going to be the ones.

Gently she made Kara sit down on the couch and

told her exactly what Jon had admitted about his feelings for her. Perhaps she was breaking her friend's confidence, but that couldn't be helped. He needed Kara, and she needed him. Stephanie explained about the evening at the Mexican restaurant and the nightclub and how she had promised to keep Cade away so that Jon would have time alone with the actress.

"He was nice," Kara remembered, "but nothing more. We danced and we chatted, but mostly about the film. I thought he just wanted to keep me in a good mood while I was on location."

She looked wistfully off into the distance, and Stephanie kept quiet while Kara was lost in thought.

"Are you sure?" Kara asked at last, and Stephanie smiled and nodded.

They were silent again for a few minutes. Stephanie didn't move a muscle, merely sitting and watching the expressive face of the actress begin to light up with realization that her love was returned. She smiled at the thought of the happiness in store when they saw each other the next day. She'd have to make certain they were alone. She'd have to keep Cade out of the actress's way, not allow him to interfere and break up what Stephanie felt was destined to be a great love. If his feelings had to be sacrificed, it couldn't be helped.

Stephanie felt a tinge of sympathy for Cade because she knew the pain of losing, but it was better that Jon should win Kara. They were suited to each other. Cade wasn't suited to anyone.

That wasn't true, she had to admit. He was exactly

right for her, she knew intuitively, but he would never want her. He might recover someday and find another woman to replace Kara, the way he had chosen her to take the place of the lost Merilee, but the woman he found would not be Stephanie. She would be someone soft, beautiful, appealing, not anyone he clashed with constantly. And no matter how much natural beauty people said she had and no matter how many makeup tricks she learned from the studio people, she could never match Kara's ravishing good looks. Very few women could.

Kara interrupted her rambling thoughts with a panicky question. "What are we going to do about Cade? He's supposed to take us sight-seeing all day long." She pounded a couch pillow with a delicate fist. "I can't take another day like this one," she admitted, "having to walk at Cade's side and pretend that Jon is only a friend."

She thought a minute longer, then asked the question Stephanie knew was coming. "Would you go with Cade, Stephanie? Tell him I'm sick or something, and find an excuse for Jon to be with me instead of going with you two?"

Stephanie stared at Kara for a long moment, then nodded. "I'll try, Kara, for your sake and for Jon's sake, but I can't promise I'll succeed. If Cade Steele wants to be with you, he'll probably knock the door down before he'll be willing to go anywhere with me."

"Thanks, Stef," Kara smiled, "although I really can't see that he's all that interested in me." She leaped gracefully to her feet and pirouetted around

the room. "I'm so excited I can't sleep now." She
paused to smile at Stephanie. "Do you think Jon's
still awake?" she asked with a laugh.

"I don't know." Stephanie couldn't help smiling
at the actress's change of mood. "But if you don't
get to bed soon, you're going to be too tired to tell
him you love him."

"You're right," Kara admitted. "And tomorrow—" she glanced at her watch "—today, really, I
want to be very well rested. Jon's going to know that
I love him if I have to tie him up to make him listen."

"I'm sure that won't be necessary," Stephanie
promised. "He'll be telling you how he feels about
you before you can say a word. I intend to see to
that."

Kara did a few dance steps to take her to the bedroom door. She smiled brilliantly at Stephanie.
"Thanks, Stef; I won't forget it."

She was gone before Stephanie could acknowledge
her words, but it was a long time before Stephanie
managed to find the energy to go to bed herself. She
kept wondering if she should tell Cade that he was
losing the woman of his dreams....

KARA WOKE STEPHANIE UP before eight, not letting
her get away with piling a pillow on top of her head
but insisting that she get out of bed.

"Do you know what time it is?" Stephanie grum-
bled. "I just got to sleep."

"You don't have time to sleep now," Kara insisted, excitement shining in her lustrous eyes. "You
can catch up later. If today goes the way I want it to,

I'll insist that Jon give you a week off to do nothing but sleep.''

"I'll start now," Stephanie replied, falling back onto the bed. But Kara firmly pulled her upright, reminding her of her promise to help.

"I can't do anything this early," Stephanie protested. "Jon and Cade won't be up yet."

"We can't take a chance." Kara was in no mood to put up with her roommate's pleas to go back to bed, so with a muttered oath Stephanie reached for her slippers and robe.

She felt terrible, for the night had brought little rest, and it didn't help to look at Kara, who radiated beauty like sunlight. Already the actress was dressed in a particularly flattering outfit, a summery dress of almost the same shade as her hair, and her makeup was carefully applied.

"There's no man who could resist you, Kara," Stephanie told her sincerely. "You'd better not let Cade see you looking like that. He'll never let Jon have you."

"Don't be silly." Kara flushed at the compliment. "I told you that Cade doesn't care a thing about me. He just hangs around, sort of like an overprotective big brother."

"You'll think he's a big brother when he hears about you and Jon," Stephanie continued. "He'll probably kidnap you to keep you and Jon apart."

Kara gave Stephanie a shove toward the bathroom. "Now quit talking nonsense and get dressed. I know exactly what I want you to do."

Thirty minutes later Stephanie was on the telephone, asking Jon if he could come to their room with the excuse that Kara needed to see him. When Jon asked if she was ill, Stephanie laughed and said, "Just the opposite, Jon. She's never felt better." She couldn't help adding, "And you'll feel the same way when you get here."

He hesitated, letting the weight of her words sink in. "Stef, are you telling me that. . .?" He was afraid to say it, and Stephanie wondered if Cade might be within listening distance.

"I certainly am, Jon," she announced. "Now lock Cade Steele up so he can't get out of the room and get yourself over here. It just happens that I'm on my way out the door."

She hung up, reminded Kara to take her suitcase back to the suburban hotel when she and Jon checked out, and gathered her purse and straw hat.

"I'm going to have a cup of coffee," she informed Kara, "and then I'll call Cade, explain the change of plans, walk around town for a few minutes and take a cab back to the hotel. Cade Steele can go straight back to his ranch."

Kara nodded. "Thanks again, Stef." She was so happy it hurt to look at her, and Jon's smile was almost as brilliant when Stephanie bumped into him at the elevator a minute later. He grabbed her and swung her around, giving her a huge kiss.

"I don't know what you did, Stephanie, but I'm grateful. Whatever you want in return, just ask."

She wanted to say, *Cade. . . give me Cade and I'll be satisfied,* but she merely laughed and remarked predictably, "Well, Jon, I could use a raise."

"You've got it," he agreed, and took off almost at a run for the room where Kara awaited him.

Stephanie was still smiling about their happiness when she reached the lobby and found the little coffee shop tucked away in one corner. She waited ten minutes, longer than she had planned, before working up enough courage to call Cade and cancel the day's schedule. It was going to be difficult to explain Kara's and Jon's sudden absence, and she cared too much for Cade to want to see the hurt in his eyes if she let it slip that their friends were likely discussing marriage plans. Once she had thought it would be delightful to watch him squirm at hearing such news, but now she didn't want revenge. She didn't want him to feel the same pain she suffered. She would have to be very tactful.

Actually, she didn't tell him anything except that Kara was unable to continue the weekend plans and Jon was taking care of her. His tone was indecipherable over the telephone, and she couldn't tell if he was suspicious or not. He merely asked where she was and announced that he would meet her in the lobby in five minutes, then hung up before she could tell him she would soon be going back to her own hotel.

Cade looked devilishly handsome when he arrived, and Stephanie noted the glances of the women in the hotel lobby, many openly admiring his tall trim figure and his tanned face with its strong jaw and penetrating eyes.

He almost smiled when he saw her, and her heart fluttered at his attention. Unconsciously, one hand smoothed the lines of the tan skirt with patch pockets she wore with a light beige blouse. Her open-toed shoes were high heeled, but she still wasn't a match for Cade's towering size, and she felt small in comparison with the man who took her arm and led her toward the front door.

"Is Kara sick?" he asked, and Stephanie's disappointment stung fiercely. She should have known that his first thoughts would be of the actress he loved.

"No," she honestly replied. "Something came up." She let it go at that, and to her relief, Cade didn't press the point. Instead he led her across the street to the water garden she had noticed from her window the previous day. They wandered up and down the steps, admiring the clear water and green plants that provided a pleasant oasis in the midst of the downtown buildings.

From there she unquestioningly followed Cade toward the heart of the downtown area, listening while he told her stories about Fort Worth and its "cow town" nickname. He reported that it was sometimes called the panther city because, more than a century earlier, a man from Dallas had reported that he had actually seen a panther sleeping in the streets of the slow-moving town.

It was a more sophisticated city now, but it still retained its Western image, and he reminded her of the restored area they had seen when they went to dinner and to the nightclub earlier. She remembered; what she remembered, however, was not the buildings with their Western fronts, but Cade escorting Kara into the restaurant and Cade presenting Stephanie with a gold charm and then insulting her. She had tried to get rid of the charm, but she hadn't been able to, and even now it was in the depths of her jewelry box at the hotel.

It was easy to lose herself in her thoughts, and she had to make an effort to listen to Cade and to answer his occasional questions. He announced that the area they were walking through was once known as Hell's Half Acre and asked if she had ever seen the movie *Butch Cassidy and the Sundance Kid*.

"Of course," she replied.

"Supposedly much of their activity took place here," Cade reported. "Their Wild Bunch gang had its formal picture taken here, and it was in Hell's Half Acre, a section of town dominated by gamblers and prostitutes, that the Sundance Kid actually met Etta Place." He paused at a red light, and his arm slipped around Stephanie's shoulders. "When she returned from South America, Etta is supposed to have made her way back to Fort Worth to live the rest of her life here."

They walked to the far north end of the downtown section, around the granite courthouse and to the little park behind it, on the bluff overlooking the Trinity River. It was the site of the original town, and the panoramic view of the prairie had made it an ideal choice for defense against attacking Indians.

Stephanie didn't want to hear about the history of Fort Worth. She wanted to talk to Cade about Kara, to offer a few hints about what was happening between the actress and her director so that the shock wouldn't be so great when he learned she preferred another man. But she couldn't. Every time she opened her mouth to speak, Cade would mention some other facet of history, until she wanted to scream at him to shut up while she let him know he had lost his love.

They walked to another hotel for Sunday brunch. The menu was wide and appealing—omelets, eggs Benedict and Florentine, smoked salmon, roast beef, salads, vegetables and pastries served with complimentary champagne—but Stephanie found it difficult to work up an appetite. She simply asked Cade to order for her.

They lingered over the meal, Cade enjoying his food while Stephanie picked at hers. It wasn't until after they finished and were about to leave that Cade looked searchingly at her for the first time.

"You've been trying to tell me something for the past hour or so," he announced flatly, and Stephanie looked up in shock. How could he have known that she wanted to speak? She hadn't said anything, and he had seemed almost uninterested in her. She was only someone to whom he could recite the history of the area. Cade leaned forward, propping his arms on the white linen tablecloth. "What is it, Stephanie?"

It was time to tell him, but when she gazed at his face, looking sensitive instead of harsh for a change, she couldn't bring herself to dash his hopes.

"Nothing," she whispered. "Nothing at all. I guess I'm just restless and wanting to get back to the hotel." She picked up her purse. "You know, I do have a lot of work to prepare for."

"I didn't think you were going to tell me you were enjoying my company," Cade replied. He threw some bills on the table for a tip and scraped the chair legs harshly against the floor as he rose. "Let's go, then. You're not through with me yet in spite of your longings to return to Jon."

CHAPTER TWELVE

ANY PRETENSE OF FRIENDLINESS vanished as Cade escorted Stephanie from the dining room and out into the midday sun. His stride was longer, and Stephanie had to quicken her pace to keep up with him. By the time they reached the hotel where they had spent the night, she was practically panting from the effort of matching his lengthy steps.

Cade offered no sympathy, and he didn't give her the opportunity of ducking into the hotel and escaping his company. He ordered his car from the parking garage and kept a firm grip on her arm while they waited for the attendant to bring the vehicle to them.

Concentrating on his driving, he didn't stop to point out the sights as he had done earlier. Where they were going, Stephanie didn't know. It wasn't to the hotel where the company was staying, she knew, for Cade had turned the car toward the west instead of the north. A few minutes later he came to a halt near a complex of buildings and led her into the first one, the Kimbell Art Museum, a contrast of such magnitude from the cowboy talk of the morning that Stephanie was almost staggered.

They wandered through the museum for an hour or more, and Stephanie forgot her anger at Cade in her appreciation of the artworks she saw, mostly European paintings by world masters including Rembrandt, Picasso, Monet, Rubens, Hals, El Greco and Goya. But there was more, and Stephanie found herself lingering over the arts of pre-Columbian America and of Africa and the Far East.

The building itself amazed her with its unusual cycloidal vaults. The paintings could be viewed safely in natural light through the use of plastic-filtered and shielded skylights that extended from the top of each vault.

They moved on to the adjacent Amon Carter Museum of Western Art, with a completely different perspective on art. Here were the works of Charles Russell and Frederic Remington that Cade had mentioned earlier, the oils and bronzes of Western life, along with other paintings housed in a building made of native Texas shell stone.

It wasn't until they had visited the third museum in the complex, the Fort Worth Art Center with its modern paintings, and a fourth, this one featuring science and history displays, that Stephanie remembered Cade's lashing out at her.

He was silent during the tour of the museums, contenting himself with serving as her escort, but as they left the last of the exhibits she had the uneasy feeling that she was about to become the target of his anger once again.

He glanced sideways as they sped down the freeway toward the main part of the city. ''Do you need to check out of the hotel?'' he asked.

''No, Kara and Jon are taking care of that.'' She

bit her tongue, knowing that she should have told him she needed to go back. Then she could have eluded him and taken a taxi to the sanctuary of her own suburban hotel.

"Do you want to go to dinner?" His tone almost dared her to agree to his invitation, and she immediately declined.

"We have a busy week ahead of us," she reminded him. "After all, it *is* our last week of filming on your property. I'm certain you'll be glad to see us go." She couldn't hide the bitterness in her voice. "Kara was going on over to Dallas today, and the rest of us will move next weekend."

Stephanie turned away from him. She hadn't meant to mention Kara's name, and she didn't want to see if he flinched.

"Who was taking her to Dallas?" he asked after a pause, and Stephanie felt he was speaking through gritted teeth.

"I really don't know. She didn't tell me," she could truthfully reply. "Kara does have the use of a limousine during the week, and she may have ordered it. Or Jon might be taking her." She was practically certain that Kara wouldn't be going anywhere without Jon from now on, but Cade didn't know what she did. She sighed as she reminded herself she really should break the news to Cade. He misinterpreted her sigh, however, taking a strong hold of her arm with one hand while he steered the car with the other.

"Are you upset about the fact that your lover is alone with another woman?" he asked. "Kara's very beautiful, you know. A man could get interested in her without any trouble. He could be with her right now.'' Cade stopped suddenly, and Stephanie realized he must have recognized that his tormenting of her had backfired. He was only torturing himself by thinking of Kara with Jon.

"I'd like to go home,'' she announced tiredly.

"I'm sure you would, to check up on Jon, but we have another stop to make first.''

He was heading in the direction of the hospital. "I want to see Morgan before he's dismissed. As I understand it, he's going straight home to California.''

Stephanie wanted to see Morgan, too, but not with Cade at her side. When she had visited the stunt man the past two times, he had suggested she bring the rancher with her, but she had refused. Now Morgan would think they were together because Stephanie wanted him to act on her behalf and find some way to make Cade feel differently toward her. He didn't know that was impossible.

She did wish she could tell Morgan about Kara and Jon, but it was their responsibility to break the news, and if she knew Jon as well as she thought she did, he would wait until filming was completed before publicly announcing their plans.

Morgan was sitting in a chair when they walked into his room, and he glanced at them with a sly grin. "Don't you two look nice together,'' he commented, and Stephanie frowned.

He shook Cade's hand and ignored Stephanie's silent plea to change the subject. "I didn't know that you were such friends. What have you been up to?''

He offered Stephanie the chair and sat on the edge of the bed, smiling broadly at her.

Neither Cade nor Stephanie answered his question. Both immediately asked how he felt and when he would be leaving the hospital. Cade volunteered his home if Morgan and his wife wanted to rest for a few days before flying back to California, but the stunt man insisted that they needed to get back to the three children who still lived at home.

"They're teenagers," he remarked, "and I suppose they can take care of themselves, but we want to get home and make sure they're all right." He glanced from Stephanie to Cade. "Just wait until you have children of your own. You'll see how difficult it is not to be overprotective of your little ones...even when they're no longer little."

Stephanie suggested that she and Cade leave. She knew she couldn't take too much more of Morgan's obvious attempts to link the two of them, but he urged them to wait until his wife returned from having dinner in the hospital cafeteria. Cade had never met her, and he readily agreed to stay. Stephanie liked Morgan's wife, but she would rather have waited to see her another time, when Cade wasn't around.

It was only ten minutes before Paula Anderson returned to the room, but to Stephanie it seemed like an hour. She had to listen to more of Morgan's unsubtle conversation, and she wondered if Cade was as embarrassed by the talk as she was.

Morgan introduced his wife to Cade, and she immediately exclaimed, "Well, I've certainly heard a lot about you in the past few days.'' Her gaze strayed to Stephanie, who couldn't keep the blood from rushing to her cheeks. ''Morgan was right: you do make a handsome couple.''

Stephanie never understood how she managed to get through the next few minutes and to leave the room without falling apart. She couldn't believe Paula had said such a thing. Morgan must not have made it clear to his wife that there was absolutely nothing between herself and Cade. There was only an irrational longing on her part, which she resolutely repressed whenever it flowed to the surface.

She said her farewells with dignity, she thought, wishing Morgan a good trip home and advising Paula to take good care of him until he was completely recovered. But when she was outside the door, while Cade was continuing to talk to the Andersons, she leaned against the wall and trembled so badly a passing nurse asked if she was ill.

''I'm sorry about what happened,'' she apologized to Cade as they drove away from the hospital.

He eyed her questioningly.

''What Paula said about us. It's ridiculous, and I can't imagine how she came up with the idea that you and I were....'' Unable to complete the sentence, she stared morosely out the window instead.

She knew that Cade was watching her, but he didn't comment, and she was grateful when they reached the hotel and he let her out at the front entrance. He didn't linger over goodbyes, and she stood miserably under the canopy watching his car speed off into the distance.

Ignoring the greetings from her co-workers milling around the hotel, Stephanie went straight to her room and flung herself on the bed. One more week, she told herself over and over. Five more working days and she'd be rid of Cade Steele. The crew would move on to Dallas, and there would be no reason to see him again. She wouldn't have to make those dreadful nightly reports, feel his warm masculine presence beside her as he escorted her to the car each evening, look at his rugged face or listen to the low haunting vibrations of his baritone voice.

Stephanie fell asleep, not waking until her telephone rang. She stirred then, only half-conscious, to discover it was dark outside; but Jon's voice when she lifted the receiver brought her back to life in a hurry. It had a lilt she hadn't heard in a long time, and she was delighted when he revealed that a wedding was being scheduled.

He was calling, he said, to request that Stephanie tell no one about the engagement. There was still more filming to be done, and he and Kara had agreed to pretend to be only friends until the final day of shooting. At that time, the party he always threw to celebrate the end of filming would also be the occasion for announcing their plans.

Stephanie agreed happily. She was glad everything had worked out for them, but after she hung up the phone she stretched back out on the bed, wondering again how Cade would take the news and if he would still be trying to romance Kara before he learned the truth.

Since Kara wasn't at the ranch, it was easy to keep

the news from the crew during the week. And Jon was so busy trying to wrap up the remaining shots that he had no time even to talk to Stephanie about his newfound love. He didn't stay at the ranch, as he had often done during the past few weeks, instead returning to town and working until midnight to make certain the schedule would be met. He did take one afternoon off to drive to Dallas, to check on the work being done there, he said, and the assistant director replaced him at the ranch. Stephanie alone suspected that the trip to Dallas would include a long cozy visit with Kara.

Stephanie felt a growing sense of sadness as she reported to Cade each night. She was delighted to let him know there had been no damage to his property each day and that the filming was on schedule, but every time she looked at him she couldn't help thinking that this was the last Monday she would see him. Then it was the last Tuesday... and the last Wednesday. She drank in his image, as if storing it to be pulled out and savored late at night after she was back in California.

Cade apparently felt no such desire to see more of her, for he practically shoved her out the door each night. Since Kara was not on the set, his interest, she felt, had waned, and he told Stephanie he simply was too busy to be involved in what they were doing this final week. His longhorns were once more in the pasture, and he didn't care particularly about the rest of the work, only cautioning her about the changes the set designer planned to make to his front yard and driveway.

The last scenes to be shot featured the three-story house, and the designer had pointed out a few modern touches that would have to be hidden to make the home fit into the required early-twentieth-century setting. The gravel drive was covered with a grasslike carpet, and a simple path was created to go over it, to make it more in keeping with the tracks that would have been left by horse and buggy.

Cade made it clear that he wanted the material removed as soon as filming was done, and Stephanie reminded him that she had agreed to all of his conditions weeks earlier.

It was strange working at the house, and she kept expecting Cade to walk out the front door at any minute. But he evidently was up early and out with his animals or in the fields, because she never saw him while they worked. If he returned for lunch, he did so quickly and quietly.

Mrs. Martin, on the other hand, was almost always in attendance during the shooting. She took one look at the cold sandwiches served from the catering truck and told the man running it not to bother to show up on Friday. That day she prepared her own lunch for the crew: fried chicken, hot buttered corn on the cob, potato salad, fruit salad and three types of desserts, including a pecan pie that Stephanie simply couldn't resist. She had two slices before returning to work.

The crew was so grateful for the treat that they huddled together and came up with a present of their own for the housekeeper. She was outfitted in a costume the wardrobe woman provided and used as an extra in one of the final scenes.

"My grandchildren will be so impressed," she giggled as she took her place on the porch and operated the butter churn that was being used as a prop. Jon made certain the cinematographer took plenty of shots of her, and he promised she wouldn't end up on the cutting-room floor. The still photographer, the man who took publicity pictures for the film, also snapped Mrs. Martin from a variety of angles.

They were all becoming lighthearted as the afternoon wore on and it became evident that they would finish this day's work after all. By six o'clock all that remained was the panoramic shot that would be the last scene in the picture.

The crane was brought in and stationed so that the camera operator would be able to shoot from the basket on the machine's extended arm. He would begin his shot with an overhead view of the ranch house, then would gradually pull the camera back and swing it around until he showed as much of the ranch as he could get in the picture. The sun setting in the west, covering the vast prairie, would provide the ending for the scene.

There was a delay while the cinematographer got set, and the crew members took advantage of the opportunity to pack as much of the equipment as they could. Everything that might possibly show was moved out of sight, and in fact one bus had already departed for Dallas, carrying the actors from that city and many of the supplies that would be used in the studio the following week.

Stephanie sat in the shade of an oak tree while Jon

and the cinematographer held conferences, adjusted the crane, rechecked all the angles. There seemed to be a disagreement of some kind about the crane, with the cameraman claiming he couldn't get the scope the director wanted even if he extended the crane to its full length.

"Now, if I could shoot from that windmill," he told Jon, pointing to the tall structure at one side of the house, "I could get a wider shot, a better view of the entire area, from the woods in the east to the sunset on the western horizon."

Stephanie could see Jon's eyes lighting up at the suggestion. She looked at the windmill uneasily. Nothing had been said about using it, and she wasn't going to ask Cade for permission, especially since this was the final day of shooting. It was no time for something to go wrong. But she heard Jon announce that he would speak to Cade, and she saw him go off to find the rancher.

They were back within a half hour, and Stephanie sensed that Cade's approval had been given only reluctantly. While visions of a wrecked windmill flashed through her head, she hoped desperately that everything would go right.

While they were raising the camera in place, using the crane as much as possible instead of carrying the equipment the complete length of the fragile-looking ladder attached to one side of the windmill, Stephanie stood transfixed, unconsciously crossing her fingers in a superstitious good-luck sign. She was afraid the cameraman would be blown off the structure, but he tied himself to the top portion of the windmill. From far above she saw his signal to Jon that he was ready for the cameras to roll.

The director cleared the area, then called out over the megaphone that shooting could begin. The crew stood silently, waiting for the scene to be completed. They were huddled together on the back porch, keeping out of range of the all-seeing camera as it panned the home and then swung out to show the extent of this passionate land.

Stephanie knew the name of the movie was appropriate. This was a passionate land, a loving place, and she didn't want to leave it. The intense heat of the afternoon summer sun and the inconvenience of occasional mosquito bites when she ventured too near the creek seemed minor in comparison with the lusty hold the ranch had on her. Or perhaps it was the lusty appeal of the man who controlled its destiny—and her happiness.

When the filming was done there was a shout of joy from the crew members who were still at the site. Stephanie worked busily, helping to load the trucks and the final bus so that they could be on their way before dark, but she couldn't keep her thoughts on the job. She wandered instead to a grove of trees on the far side of the windmill and watched the cameraman lower his equipment to the waiting crane. Then the man used the ladder to reach a lower level where the crane could pick him up.

Stephanie breathed a deep sigh of relief when he leaped into the basketlike contraption at the end of the machine. It had been frightening to see him on the ladder. He'd looked so small and fragile.

She had turned away to take one final look at the prairie when she heard the crunch. The crane operator had miscalculated, turning the extending arm the wrong way and propelling it into the side of the windmill. While Stephanie swiveled in horror, afraid the entire structure was falling, the operator of the crane, somehow reacting instinctively, swung the equipment around, letting the arm rest against a broken crossbar, propping it into position to act as a brace before any other strips of wood could crack.

Cade had been watching from the porch of his house, but he was at the windmill almost as soon as the onlookers realized what had happened. He surveyed the damage from all angles before barking out orders to get his employees. A crew member raced for the barn, and while they waited for the men, he consulted with Jon.

Stephanie was too far away to hear, and she didn't know if Cade could tell the extent of the damage or not. She glanced at the windmill, worrying that it would give under the stress and collapse to the ground. Cade looked serious, but he wasn't rushing around the way that Stephanie might have done under the circumstances. He calmly waited for his men and for the carpenters who had been taking up the false path in front of the house, and when they arrived he indicated exactly what he wanted them to do.

Somewhere in the back of her mind Stephanie knew that she should be offering to help Jon, but she couldn't budge. Her eyes couldn't leave Cade. It was impossible to tell if he was furious or not; he was too

far away, and twilight was settling over the countryside. His expression was unreadable from where she
stood on the fringe of the commotion.

Vaguely she heard the trucks and bus depart, but
she still couldn't move. Her eyes could only follow
the massive figure of Cade Steele as he stationed
high-intensity lights in place for the workmen to use
as they finished replacing the broken board. Only
then was the crane gently moved away. Stephanie
held her breath as the operator backed up the
machine from the windmill, afraid that without the
crane's support the structure would fall. But it held,
and she breathed a gigantic sigh of relief.

Cade nodded to the men, and they began to leave.
Before Jon departed he had a long conference with
Cade, and Stephanie hoped the director was making
all the apologies that needed to be said. She hated to
have to face the rancher and admit that she had been
unable to keep her promise. She shuddered as she
thought of the possible damage caused by the accident.

The closing of the car doors didn't register as she
kept her gaze fixed on Cade, who still stood staring at
the windmill after everyone else had gone. In the dim
light she watched him pick up a lamp and begin a
slow but steady climb to the top of the windmill.
Once there he minutely inspected the upper area for
damage, shining the light on every segment of the
building. She trembled as he came back down the
ladder, afraid the windmill would give way and crush
Cade under its massive weight.

When he reached the bottom he stood for a long

time gazing at it, checking it out from underneath with a practiced eye before he finally wiped the sweat from his brow and turned to leave.

He saw her then, standing alone beside a tree.

"Did everyone go off and leave you, Stephanie?" he asked, one eyebrow raised. But there was no sarcasm in his voice, only disgust.

She looked around to see that she was indeed alone, and then she remembered hearing the vehicles departing. But she remained immobile while Cade strode past her toward the house.

"Are you going to spend another night sleeping on the ground?" he asked harshly. He was standing a hundred feet from her, impatiently waiting for her to come to him.

"Is Jon inside the house?" she asked timidly, for she hadn't noticed if he had left with the final group of workers. "I'll have him take me to the hotel."

"I believe he is on his way to Forth Worth, if he's not already there by now," Cade informed her. "I told him to leave earlier. There was no point in having him hang around here when there was nothing more to be done tonight." He looked back at the windmill as he spoke.

Stephanie slowly crossed the grassy lawn toward Cade.

"I didn't realize that everyone had gone," she murmured. "If I can use your phone, I'll call Jon and ask him to come for me."

"You will come to the house, Stephanie," Cade ordered, and she could see the loathing behind the exhaustion in his eyes, "but you won't call Jon to come get you. This is one night you're not going to run to your lover.'' He jerked the door open savagely and waited.

There was no point in arguing with Cade when he was in this mood, and actually Stephanie couldn't blame him for being mad. After all the promises she had made, to have something like this occur...! And on the final day of shooting, too.

When he went to change out of his dusty jeans and shirt, she decided, she could slip to a phone and call Jon. Then she would do her best to blunt Cade's anger until Jon could drive to the ranch and retrieve her.

Cade must have sensed her plan, for he didn't allow her a moment alone, first stalking into the kitchen to inform Mrs. Martin that he didn't feel like having a complete meal, asking her instead to prepare something simple for him and his guest. The housekeeper had already heard about the accident and was full of concern, but Cade didn't want to talk about what had happened, and he quickly left for his den, Stephanie in tow.

She sank into the chair he indicated, keeping one eye on the telephone, which was tantalizingly near, while Cade mixed a drink and took a seat behind the oak desk. She was glad he hadn't sat in the matching leather chair near her; there was a definite hint of menace in the brooding looks he cast at her. He didn't offer her a drink, merely staring at her through narrowed eyelids.

"I don't know how it happened," she tried to explain, but she stopped when he lunged forward, leaning his elbows on the desk.

"It's your job to know," he stated.

"I'll find out," Stephanie promised. "I was so paralyzed when it happened that I couldn't do anything." She forced herself to meet his piercing gaze. "And when you climbed up on the windmill, I was so afraid it was going to topple over and you'd be killed." She had been frantic, not knowing how she could have stood it if he had fallen and been seriously injured.

Cade searched her face, and she buried her head in her hands for a minute to compose herself. If he would just quit looking at her that way! She didn't know what he was thinking, and she was afraid to ask, almost as afraid as she had been of the risk he had taken earlier.

"I'm sure you were worried that my family might sue you if I were killed because of your negligence," he finally condemned her.

"Don't you ever give me credit for having feelings?" she cried out. "It was so terrible, and I couldn't stand it." She caught herself before she humbled herself any more in front of him. "At least," she finally was able to report, "it didn't fall."

"It still might."

Stephanie looked up at Cade. He was standing now with his back to her, gazing out the window at the pasture hidden in the darkness of the night.

"But you repaired it."

"Possibly." Though he did not turn to face her, she could tell he was physically spent. His broad shoulders sagged in spite of his effort to stand straight. "The damage wasn't as bad as I thought it

might be, and I think it's all right, but I'll feel better
if it's reinforced with metal plates. As it is, it might
not take the strain of a strong windstorm."

"We do have full insurance, you know," Stephanie reminded him, "and if you'll allow me to use the
telephone, I'll contact our attorney in Los Angeles
and have him get in touch with the insurance company. Our policy will cover the complete cost of
repairs."

He pushed the phone toward her, and she shakily
dialed the number after looking it up in the book
she carried in her purse. With his eyes on her she
could barely speak steadily enough to give the operator the necessary information for charging the call
and then to report what had happened to the attorney. Even with the time difference, she was lucky to
find him in his office. He had been working late and
was on his way home, he told her. The attorney
promised to handle everything immediately and to
have an insurance representative contact them the
next day.

Stephanie hung up the telephone but picked the
receiver up again immediately and started to dial the
hotel number. She had only three of the digits completed before Cade's hand came down on the phone,
severing the connection.

"I told you this is one night you're not going to
run back to your lover."

"He's not my lover, and I'll call him if I want to."

"Not on my telephone you won't."

Cade picked up the instrument and pulled the cord
from the connecting jack in the wall. He opened a

double drawer in his desk, set the phone inside and locked the drawer.

"This is outrageous," Stephanie defied him.

"And so are you, my beauty."

"I'm not staying here—" she turned toward the door "—if I have to walk all the way back!"

He was between her and escape in an instant. "And I say you're not going."

Mrs. Martin knocked on the door and announced dinner, but Stephanie blurted out that she wasn't hungry and asked if she could accompany the housekeeper to her own living quarters in another part of the house, to rest for a few minutes there. Surely there was another telephone that she could use.

"Of course," Mrs. Martin agreed, obviously puzzled by such an unusual request, but Cade interrupted.

"I'll take care of Stephanie and see that she has an opportunity to lie down. Why don't you call it a day, Eve? I think that husband of yours might need some tending himself. He's had a long day."

Mrs. Martin nodded and departed, after insisting that Cade leave the dishes in the sink, where she would wash them the next morning. Stephanie watched her go, feeling that her only hope was now out of her reach. She sank back down in the chair, too weary to fight.

She was aware of Cade's movements, of his departure from the room and his return a few minutes later, but still she sat numbly. He stood for a while, she knew, looking at her. She could feel his piercing eyes on her, and the tingling sensation on the nape of her neck could come only from Cade, but still she didn't move.

Slowly she began to think, to try to remember where she had seen other telephones in the house, to wonder if she could make her way to the Martins' section without Cade's noticing her. How could she? He was everywhere at once. Even now she felt him moving closer to her, until his strong hands took hold of her shoulders, forcing her body to shudder convulsively.

"I'm going to take a shower and get into some clean clothes." He spoke slowly and deliberately, his voice husky. "And I want your promise that you won't try to leave." His fingers dug deeply, arousingly, into her tender skin. "Do I have your word, Stephanie?"

"No." It was a defiant no, and she wasn't sure she could back it up.

Gliding with the swift movement of a cougar, and with an expression just as menacing, he was around the chair, facing her. "You are going to stay here until I return if I have to lock you in this room," he ordered. "We have a few more things to discuss, but right now I'd like to get cleaned up before I engage in one of your petty rows." He traced a finger slowly across her cheek. "Now, do I make myself clear?"

She nodded, but not before she dropped her head. "I'll be here," she whispered, "to hear what you want to tell me. But then I'm leaving."

He didn't argue, but simply strode out of the room, closing the door firmly behind him.

Cade's mood was milder when he rejoined her.

The shower seemed to have washed away the rage as well as the dust, but he was still tired, Stephanie could see, and she didn't want to tangle with him. She wanted him to rest, to go to bed and get a good night's sleep, to revive into the robust man she loved so much.

"Would you like to take a bath?" he asked.

"No," Stephanie responded. "I need to be leaving soon." She looked up at him. "Please, Cade, let me call the hotel. Brad can come for me if you don't want Jon to pick me up. I need to get back, and you should go to bed. You're tired."

"Yes, I should go to bed," he acknowledged, "and you, too."

She chose to ignore any possible double meaning in his words, saying instead, "Then I can call the hotel?"

"Not yet. Let's have a sandwich and talk awhile."

"I'm not hungry, Cade. I just want to go." There was a note of resignation in her voice, in spite of her determination to defy him.

Observing her weariness, Cade didn't argue with her; instead he went on to discuss the accident and the additional repairs that would be made to the windmill. To Stephanie's surprise, he actually complimented the quick thinking of the crane operator and the skillful work of the carpenters. He then went on to ask her about plans for the final filming in Dallas.

"Jon has it all worked out," Stephanie began, but Cade's eyes flashed a warning not to speak of the director, so she talked about the scenes to be done and the schedule instead. She had a feeling that Cade wasn't giving her his full attention, but she continued to explain the plans and to go into great detail on even the technical problems facing them.

"You're quite good at your job, aren't you, Stephanie?" Cade finally commented, surprisingly sincere, and she sat up straight, shocked at the remark.

"I work at it," she said, a happy thrill in her voice at the thought that he was pleased about something she did. "I try to be good at my profession."

He pulled her to her feet, holding her at arm's length, where he could see every flicker of expression on her face. "Then why don't you rely solely on your talent to succeed? Why do you have to use your beauty to get ahead?"

In an instant he'd undone every good thought she'd had about him. "I've told you before that I don't use looks or sex to get ahead. I work long hours, and that's the reason I have my job."

"That's why Jon hired you?"

"Originally he hired me as his secretarial assistant because he knew me. We had been childhood friends in New York." Why did she have to explain to Cade anyway? He chose not to understand, but she wanted him to know the truth. She needed him to realize that she wasn't the kind of woman he believed her to be. "I worked hard, and Jon kept giving me more and more responsibility. And that's the only reason."

Stephanie stared at him for a minute, wanting to understand him as much as she wanted him to understand and appreciate her. "Why do you always believe the worst about me?" She had moved out of his grasp, but he pulled her back, pressing her close to his body as if he didn't want her to look into his eyes. There was no sense of affection in his embrace, no caressing; he was simply shielding her from seeing whatever it was he felt he couldn't help revealing in his face.

"There was a woman once," he told her. "A beautiful woman. She wanted a career in show business, but I wanted her to be my wife." He paused for a moment, but Stephanie remained silent. She was mesmerized by the fact that, for the first time, he was revealing something of what made Cade Steele tick. "She told me she could have both, but I quickly found out which was more important. She got some small parts in television shows filmed in Dallas. Nothing big, but she thought they would lead to fame and a Hollywood starring role." His hand tightened on Stephanie's back. "Do you know how she got those jobs, Stephanie?"

Stephanie didn't dare respond.

"She got them by going to bed with the producer." His voice was harsh. "And she expected me to understand. After all, she told me, that's how all actresses get their start."

"It's not true," Stephanie whispered. "Only a few go about it that way."

"I find that very difficult to believe."

He let her go and strode to the window, again looking out into the darkness. Stephanie watched him for a minute before she spoke. "The woman," she finally said, "looked a lot like Kara, didn't she?"

His eyes darkened as he turned to face her. "Some," he admitted.

She wanted to add, "And that's why you're in love with Kara," but she couldn't. If she said it out loud, he would agree, and she didn't want to have the truth flung so violently in her face.

It hurt so much to look at him, torn from a love that had failed and now finding love again with someone else who would once again reject him. Maybe she shouldn't have helped Jon and Kara. Cade needed Kara; it would destroy him to have another woman walk away from him. But Jon loved Kara, too, and he needed her as much as Cade did. Someone had to get hurt in the struggle over Kara, as hurt as Stephanie already was.

If Jon had lost out, she would have tried to comfort him, but who would listen to Cade's heartache? She didn't know his friends, and evidently he kept his personal life to himself, since not even his housekeeper knew exactly what had happened with Merilee. Stephanie was glad he had told her, moved that he felt he could confide in her. Perhaps he didn't dislike her as much as he seemed to most of the time. Maybe they could at least have a cordial relationship. That would be better than this stinging anger he usually directed at her, which tore into her soul.

"Cade," she suggested in a soft whisper, "I'd like to be your friend."

He flinched as she spoke. Was it that terrible, she couldn't help thinking, to have her as a friend? Cade acted as if he were taking a strong dose of castor oil.

He thrust his hands into the pockets of the dusty

gray slacks he wore with a lighter gray shirt. "What if I want to be more than a friend?" he asked hoarsely, and her mind flipped back to the day he had tried to make love to her in the lush meadow.

Did he mean he still wanted her body? That he wanted her as a mistress—a lover in the physical sense? Undoubtedly that was what he was asking: he thought she might be friendly enough to share his bed while he waited for Kara to agree to a marriage proposal. A tear caught at the edge of her eye. Couldn't she ever make him believe the truth? Wouldn't he ever know that friendship didn't always mean sex—that friendship was a step toward love? That she had already passed over the plateau to the deeper emotion?

"I'm offering my—my friendship," she stuttered, "and I'd like to know that we could talk without quarreling, that we could have a casual relationship, the way that I do with...." She stopped, knowing that if she named Jon, the cynical look would appear in his eyes. "The way I do with the other people in the film company," she amended, "the way I do with your mother and your housekeeper." She extended a hand for him to shake, but he ignored it.

"Friends?" he asked. "You want friendship with nothing else?" There was a hard glint in his expression that bored into her, but she swallowed hard and lied. "Nothing else," she told him. "Just friendship."

Cade unlocked his desk, removed the telephone and plugged it in. "Do you want to call Jon, or do you want me to take you back to town?"

"I'll call," she said, but her fingers trembled so badly she couldn't dial the number, and Cade had to take the phone from her and complete the call. She heard him explain to Jon that she had been left behind when the others departed, and she listened halfheartedly while the two men discussed the accident at the windmill, the repairs, the insurance. Jon must have mentioned that he had been trying to call, because she heard Cade explain that the telephone had been unplugged. At one point Cade looked at Stephanie, and she knew she was again the topic of conversation.

"Of course she can stay here overnight," Cade agreed. "There's plenty of room, but I believe she wants to go back to the hotel." He listened for a moment before extending the receiver to Stephanie. "Jon wants to talk to you," he explained.

"How in the world did you get left?" Jon asked. "I thought you must have taken the bus or I never would have gone on. Cade said there was nothing we could do once the carpenters helped put the brace in place, so I brought the men back to town."

"It was my fault, Jon," Stephanie apologized. "I was watching the repairs, and I simply didn't see everyone leaving."

They talked a few minutes longer, with Jon trying to convince her to spend the night. "It's so late now; I'll come get you first thing in the morning," he suggested. "I need to come out and talk to Cade about the damage anyway. It would save a long drive, Stef."

She glanced at Cade, who was lighting a cigar and listening intently to every word she said.

"I don't think it would look right for me to stay,

Jon," she claimed. "I know the Martins are in the same house, but...." She paused to listen to Jon, then glanced upward at Cade. How could she explain that the electricity in the air was so alive she wouldn't be able to sleep; she'd be wanting to crawl into Cade's bed and feel the warmth of his body against hers.... She didn't want them to be just friends: she wanted him body and soul.

It took a while, but she finally got Jon to agree to come for her, and she hung up the phone with a sigh of relief.

"I thought you'd be happy to get away," Cade commented wryly. "Our friendship doesn't seem to last into the night."

She walked past him through the living room and out onto the front porch, where she could wait for Jon. There was no swing or chair, but she sat down on the top step, clutching her knees to her chin and trying to occupy her time by counting the stars in the clear sky.

Cade joined her, sitting close beside her but not trying to engage her in conversation until he noticed that she was looking at the sky. Then he pointed out constellations, telling her not only the names but also the folk tales about them. The stars looked much brighter without any city lights to dim their luster. Stephanie had never been especially interested in astronomy; in New York and Los Angeles it was much more difficult to count the stars. Cade's knowledge of the subject and of the old Indian stories about the constellations opened up an even more complex part of his personality.

The time passed quickly, and it seemed that barely
a few minutes had gone by before they saw the lights
of a car approaching in the distance.

"That must be Jon," Stephanie announced, almost sorry now that she had begged him to come.
"I'll say good-night and run out to meet him so we
can get on back and you can get some rest."

She didn't look at Cade, but he took her hand to
keep her from leaving. "If we're friends," he murmured, "I should give you a brotherly good-night
kiss, don't you think?" His lips settled on hers briefly, warmly, leaving a melting hunger in her body
when he lifted his mouth. "Good night, Stephanie,"
he whispered, turning her from him and giving her a
push toward the waiting car. She didn't want to go,
but she ran as quickly as she could, while she was still
able to tear herself from him.

CHAPTER THIRTEEN

THERE WAS ABSOLUTELY NO REASON for Cade to visit the set in Dallas, and Stephanie didn't really expect him to show up. But she looked for him every day anyway.

Her work wasn't as difficult now that the filming was being done indoors, so she had more time to think, to recall his flutter of a kiss, his kiss of friendship. She almost preferred his former debasing attitude to the platonic air he had chosen the last night she had seen him. He wasn't her brother, and she didn't want him to act like one.

He never appeared, and if he contacted Kara in the evenings, Stephanie wasn't aware of it. She hoped he hadn't, because she didn't want to know he had been stung by the truth about Kara and Jon; she had terrible nightmares about Cade proposing to Kara, only to have the actress tactfully reject him. Cade wasn't a man to reject lightly—he was a man to take seriously...to love.

Even more depressing to Stephanie was watching Kara and Jon. Their happiness was difficult to hide from the crew, and only Stephanie knew how much effort they put into acting as friends and not lovers. Already making plans for the wedding and the gown she would wear, the actress was impatient for the picture to be completed, and she was the first on the set in the morning and the last to leave at night to ensure that she was never the cause of even one hour's delay.

When Mrs. Steele called to inquire if she and a friend could visit the set, Stephanie wondered whether the woman knew her son was hopelessly in love with the picture's leading lady. But she didn't drop any hints, simply making arrangements for passes to be issued. Cade's mother was excited at the opportunity of showing her friend around the studio and introducing her to Kara and Robert, so Stephanie couldn't refuse when she was asked, as well, to be their escort.

Mrs. Steel bombarded her with questions. She couldn't figure out how they had trained a dog to kiss Kara on the cheek in the scene they were shooting, and Stephanie explained that the dog was actually licking the dab of butter that was smeared on the actress's face. Then she wondered why the man who operated the clapper board always hit the arm of it against the main part of the board. "It looks as if all you need to do is film the board with the information showing about what scene it is and what take you're shooting," she stated.

Stephanie had to explain that the clapping sound was essential for editing purposes. It helped synchronize picture and sound when they were put together. The camera photographed the striking of the arm of the clapper board at the exact moment that the recorders picked up the sound. The editor then matched the sound to the picture.

"It's all too involved for me," Mrs. Steele laughed.

"I prefer to look at the costumes and see how the makeup people do their job."

They spent all morning at the studio, and when the crew broke for lunch, Mrs. Steele asked Jon if it would be all right to take Stephanie to her condominium for the afternoon as a means of expressing her appreciation for allowing her to visit. He could hardly refuse, so Stephanie accompanied the two women to lunch at a nearby café and then to the north Dallas area condominiums where both lived. The friend excused herself, leaving Stephanie to spend the rest of the day with Cade's mother.

Mrs. Steele's home was strikingly different from the ranch house where she had lived for so many years. Her living room was an eclectic combination of traditional and modern, done in shades of blue and brown. She was her own interior decorator, she explained when Stephanie complimented her on her taste. The few antiques were quite valuable, capturing Stephanie's attention from the time she walked in the door. She was especially intrigued by the grandfather clock at one end of the entry.

"This doesn't look at all like the ranch," Stephanie remarked, stunned by the subtle sophistication of the small condominium as compared to the homespun atmosphere of the big house where Cade lived.

"I was always a city girl at heart," Mrs. Steele explained, "but when I fell in love with Cade's father, I gave up life in town for the country. It was a small price to pay for years of happiness."

"Cade said that his father died several years ago," Stephanie responded.

"Yes, and when he did the ranch lost most of its meaning for me. I moved to town, and I've been here ever since."

"But Cade stayed...?"

Mrs. Steele smiled. "You couldn't drag him away from that place now. I think it's his first and only love."

Stephanie made no response, and her hostess indicated the plush sofa in the living room. "Let's quit standing around and be comfortable. Have a seat, Stephanie, and I'll get us a cold drink."

When the woman came back, carrying a tray with two full glasses of lemonade, she immediately returned to the topic of the ranch.

"My husband grew up there," she informed Stephanie, "and he never wanted to leave it. But he wanted his children to have a choice about their lives, so he encouraged them to go to college and explore other careers to make certain of what they wanted to do."

"You have other children?" Stephanie asked. Cade had never mentioned any brothers or sisters.

"A daughter," Mrs. Steele told her. "She's two years younger than Cade, and she lives in New Orleans, where her husband is a banker. They met at the University of Texas."

Mrs. Steele left the room for a minute and returned with a stack of photograph albums. "I'll be the typical proud mother and grandmother," she proclaimed, "and bring out all my pictures."

She began with recent snapshots, some of which tugged at Stephanie's heart. There was one of Cade leaning against a tall post on the front porch of the ranch house, and it was so true to life that Stephanie could almost reach out and touch him. His hair had fallen across his forehead, and he was smiling. He looked so wonderfully magnificent that it was all Stephanie could do to keep her hands off the picture. She wanted to slip it from the album and sneak it into her purse to take back to L.A.

His sister looked more like her mother—beautiful, confident and serene. There were a number of pictures of her with her husband and their two little girls, and Mrs. Steele bragged about how cute and smart the grandchildren were and moaned about how seldom she got to see them now that they were of school age.

The grandchildren kept getting younger as Mrs. Steele flipped through the album back to their baby pictures and then her daughter's wedding photographs. It wasn't until they opened the second book that there was a picture of Cade's father. Stephanie could tell where Cade had got his strong chiseled profile and dark good looks. He looked uncannily like the older man, and she could tell that he had tried to imitate his father. There were shots of the two of them together, when Cade was seven or eight, with the boy standing exactly as his father did, his head at the same angle and his hands thrust deep in the pockets of his blue jeans.

Stephanie was surprised to find pictures of Cade in high-school football and basketball uniforms, although she realized she shouldn't be. He definitely had athletic ability. It was just that she hadn't heard him mention sports or any interest of that nature.

There was so much she didn't know about him. She was only beginning to recognize how little she actually understood of this fine strong man she loved. How could you love a man so deeply, she wondered, when you hardly knew him? She hadn't known about his childhood, his interests, even the fact that he had a sister, and yet thoughts of him consumed her every moment, and when she was near him his warm masculine presence filled every fiber of her being. Mrs. Steele was cracking open a few of the doors to his hidden self, making Stephanie want to break all the barriers that kept the real Cade from her. She had to know more, and she had to express an interest without arousing Mrs. Steele's suspicions. It wouldn't do to let Cade's mother know she was in love with him, for Stephanie suspected that, like the housekeeper, Mrs. Steele was hoping for a marriage between Cade and Kara.

Stephanie looked at the photographs and commented calmly, as calmly as she could, "I didn't know that Cade took part in sports in school."

"Cade did everything," his mother assured her. "He went to a small school, and the bus picked him up out in front of the house every morning. He had to leave early because it was a long ride to school, but he had to get up earlier than most of the other children because he had to do his chores."

She smoothed the wrinkled corner of a picture as she talked. "He had more jobs to do when he got home, and it was always late because he stayed for football practice, basketball practice, baseball practice, track practice, whatever sport was in season.''

Mrs. Steele told Stephanie that her son had gone to Texas A&M to study agriculture, knowing that he wanted to stay on the ranch. But his father had insisted he have a wider education, and so he had earned a graduate degree in business administration and worked two years for a company that sent him to Germany. He had been there, she explained, when his father became ill, and he had immediately given up his career, and a promotion that was weeks away, to come home.

"He simply took over," Mrs. Steele said proudly. "His father never had to worry about a thing from the day Cade walked back into the house."

When his father died, the ranch property was left jointly to his widow, his son and his daughter. Both women had wanted to sell the land; there were numerous offers, and a sale would have been highly profitable.

"But Cade wouldn't let us," Mrs. Steele remembered. "He said it had been built by his family and he wasn't going to let strangers have it. He didn't have a lot of cash, but he made arrangements for loans to purchase our interests."

She shook her head. "I would have let Cade have half of my share because he couldn't afford to buy it and someday he would have inherited it anyway, but he insisted on paying full value. He's worked twice as hard as he should have for the past several years to pay off his loans and to build up the ranch."

She closed the photo albums reluctantly, not wanting to give up her hold on the past. "I'm very proud of what he's done," she told Stephanie, who smiled and nodded. "He's his father's son, for sure. That's exactly what my Josh would have done."

Stephanie sat silently watching Mrs. Steele. She didn't know what to say, and her own emotions were almost at the breaking point, so moved was she at these unexpected revelations about Cade's character.

"It's a shame," his mother sighed, "that Cade doesn't have any children of his own to inherit the ranch from him. I thought for a long time that he was about to get married, but he didn't, and now I'm not sure he ever will." A little twinkle came into her eyes. "Although there might be hope again. He's showing more interest in the subject now than he has in years. In fact, we had a long discussion about how he felt about a certain woman before he flew to Houston the other day."

"Houston?" Stephanie asked. She hadn't been aware that he was out of town, and it was safe to ask about his travels. She couldn't question Mrs. Steele about the woman he had spoken of marrying. She knew the name anyway: they could only have been talking about Kara Warren.

"A business trip," Mrs. Steele explained. "Cade has some oil interests as well as the ranch." She looked at Stephanie's pale face. "Do you feel all right, Stephanie?"

It was the perfect opportunity to excuse herself, and Stephanie took advantage of it, glancing at her watch and mentioning that she needed to get back to the studio for the end of the day's filming.

"I imagine Jon will have some work for me to do," she explained.

"You work too hard, my dear," Mrs. Steele sympathized. "I told your director friend that this morning, and I also mentioned it to Cade when you were filming at the ranch. He said that he saw you every night around seven." She patted Stephanie's hand. "You should have been going home much earlier— that's too long a day."

"I'll get more rest when the picture's finished," Stephanie assured her. "Now I really must go. I had no idea I'd stayed so long."

In spite of Stephanie's offer to call a cab, Mrs. Steele insisted on driving her back to the studio, and she chatted happily all the way about her son and daughter and the two small grandchildren.

"I'm sorry they didn't get to come here to see the movie being made," she sighed. "I know they would have loved it."

"Maybe Jon can invite them to the premiere," Stephanie suggested. "He's planning to have the first showing here in Dallas."

"That would be wonderful," Mrs. Steele beamed. "And then you will get to meet them, too."

Stephanie's lips curved in a slight smile. "I doubt that I'll be here for the premiere," she said. "But Jon will make the trip and probably Kara and Robert, as well."

"You must promise to come back, Stephanie," Mrs. Steele insisted. "We all want you here."

Stephanie started to tell her she wasn't speaking for her son, but she didn't. She simply thanked the woman for the invitation and the ride to the studio and closed the car door gently when she got out.

As she watched Mrs. Steele pull away from the curb, she ruefully shook her head. *Poor woman,* she reflected, *you're going to be almost as disappointed as your son when Kara and Jon announce their engagement. You're counting on Cade's marrying Kara.* Then she turned and went into the studio to face the mound of paperwork that Jon had waiting for her.

When she returned to the hotel, she stretched out on her bed and let herself have the luxury of thinking about Cade. Soon she was going to put him out of her mind for good, find new interests to occupy her thoughts, perhaps date one of the men Jon was always introducing her to. She might even take a month off and go to Hawaii. It would be good to lie on the beach and soak up the sun.

But for now she was going to store up her memories of the rancher—and that wasn't difficult to do. She had merely to close her eyes and the compelling image of the man would dance crazily on her eyelids. She took the time to memorize every detail of his features, from the eyes that always captured her attention first to the straight nose and the firm chin with the tiny hint of a cleft in it. She smiled as she pictured the way his hair had covered more of his ears than usual the last night she saw him. He had needed a haircut, but she liked him better looking a bit disheveled. Otherwise his cool perfection was almost too much to take.

Though she wished she could be with him to offer

sympathy when he heard the news about Kara, she knew it would be more than she could bear. He would need a hand to hold on to, but it couldn't be hers. She had her own heartache to contend with. Fracturing her emotions even further by witnessing Cade's hurt would be inflicting too much punishment on herself.

Without even getting up for dinner, she drifted off to sleep as the image of the dark-haired man in her mind became less and less distinct...yet remained with her nevertheless, a presence both comforting and disturbing.

STEPHANIE SLEPT most of the next morning. She was grateful it was Saturday, because she hadn't set the alarm. The rest had done her good, however, and the face reflected in her mirror looked fresher than it had in days. She took a quick bath, dressed and departed for the dining room. Missing both dinner and breakfast had left her feeling a bit weak, so she took advantage of the all-you-can-eat salad bar and ordered a hamburger to go with the fresh fruit and vegetables.

She was supposed to join Becky for a shopping trip at a nearby air-conditioned mall, and she looked forward to the break from routine. Her friend joined her in the dining room shortly before Stephanie finished eating.

"I've got a long list of things to buy," she proclaimed gaily. "I hope you're prepared for some serious shopping."

"Anything to get away from the studio and the hotel," Stephanie agreed.

They were at the mall thirty minutes later, with Becky leading the way from store to store. Stephanie trailed behind, occasionally stopping to look at a dress on display but having little inclination to try anything on. She preferred watching Becky shop.

"I'll have to buy a new suitcase to carry all this stuff back to Los Angeles," Becky joked as she purchased her third outfit of the day. "I really ought to buy a pair of boots, too," she mused, "as a souvenir of Texas. How about you, Stef? Are you going to buy something to remind you of this trip?"

"No." She already had boots, and she didn't need anything else to remember Cade by. But she accompanied Becky to the shoe store and sat quietly while her friend tried on pair after pair of boots until she found the ones she wanted.

It required both of them to carry the boxes once Becky had completed her shopping, and they stood for a few minutes by the multicolored fountain in the center of the mall while deciding what to do next.

"My watch," Becky remembered. "I left it here last week to be fixed, and I'm supposed to pick it up." She set a couple of packages down and began rummaging through her purse, trying to find the claim ticket the jeweler had given her. When she had finally come up with the elusive piece of paper, she gathered her boxes again and directed Stephanie to the jewelry store at one end of the mall.

Protesting that her feet were beginning to ache, Stephanie refused to walk into the store, insisting that she'd rather sit on one of the benches just outside the jeweler's.

"It's one of the most expensive stores in town," Becky confided, "and the rings are absolutely exquisite. If I ever get engaged, I'm going to drag my fiancé here to buy the ring."

Stephanie tumbled the boxes onto the bench while Becky dashed into the store. She considered walking over to the little snack bar close by and buying a bag of popcorn, but she couldn't figure out a way of carrying everything without spilling popcorn all over the floor, so she sat and bided her time by gazing at the jewelry in the window of the shop.

Becky was right about it being beautiful. Many of the pieces appeared to be designer originals, and the price tags attached to them let Stephanie know that she could forget about buying anything at that store. The least expensive item she saw was far more than she could possibly afford.

She wished Becky would hurry, and she lifted her eyes from the window to look into the interior of the store. It was crowded with people moving about as they browsed. She wondered how many of them could actually afford to buy jewelry there. Most were probably like her, attracted by the beauty of the offerings but without means to purchase them.

The section with rings seemed to have the most customers, and Stephanie smiled as she watched a young couple eagerly admire the wedding ring a salesclerk held up to show them. They reluctantly moved away, only to be replaced at the counter by a man who decisively indicated to the clerk a particular ring he wished to see.

Stephanie didn't have to look twice to recognize

Cade. She whirled around quickly the instant she saw him, keeping her back to the store so that he would not be able to see her face if he looked up.

Not that he would. His attention appeared concentrated on the ring he wanted to inspect. Stephanie hadn't been able to see if it was an engagement or wedding ring, but it had to be one or the other. And it had to be meant for the one woman who would not accept it from him.

Someone had to tell him soon, she thought. He couldn't go on like this, loving Kara and thinking she might love him, too. He was so sure of her that he was already purchasing a ring.

Stephanie said a little prayer that Becky would come out of the shop before Cade did so they could leave before he discovered her, and she kept sneaking a quick look at the door of the store, silently urging Becky to make an appearance. Luck wasn't with her. They came out together, with Becky exclaiming, "Look who I found!"

Stephanie rose on shaky legs to face Cade, but she found it more difficult to talk to him than ever before. He had a right to know about Kara, but her mouth wouldn't form the right words. She wondered if Cade had actually bought the ring. He had nothing in his hands, and she couldn't tell if there was a small box in a pocket of the suit he wore.

"I thought we might talk Mr. Steele into giving us a ride back to the hotel so we wouldn't have to carry all this stuff on the bus," Becky confided in a stage whisper, deliberately loud enough for Cade to hear.

"I'll be happy to," he informed Becky while his

dark eyes swept appraisingly over Stephanie. Her hair was tied casually back from her face, and she wore a simple blouse with her dressy slacks. His gaze lingered on her blouse, and she flushed as she suddenly remembered it was the one he had removed with so little effort when he had lowered her to the ground in the grassy meadow on his land. Could he actually be thinking of that seduction scene when he had just been shopping for a ring for another woman?

Cade took some of the packages and showed the two women the way to the parking lot. "I was on my way to the hotel anyway."

To propose to Kara and give her the ring. He didn't say so, but he didn't have to. Stephanie wasn't dumb; she could figure out his plan. But she knew that Kara planned to be with Jon tonight. He had already left by now for what he'd told everyone but Stephanie was a business meeting, and Kara was going to meet him for dinner. She had shown Stephanie the dark wig she would wear as a disguise so strangers wouldn't recognize her. She planned to wait until she was out of sight of all the crew members before she donned it, however, so she wouldn't raise suspicions.

Now Cade was planning to interfere and ruin everything. He'd go barging up to Kara's room when she was getting ready to see Jon, and he would upset her by proposing. She'd be unable to concentrate on her own fiancé and would probably blame herself for the fact that Cade was in love with her. And Stephanie had to wonder how Cade would react. He wasn't a man to accept a refusal. Would he try to delay Kara from leaving? Would he insist that she stay and listen to his repeated proposals? Would he offer her the ring? Stephanie heaved a sigh and got into the car.

When they arrived at the hotel and Becky had taken all of her boxes and bags to her room, Stephanie watched Cade head for the desk to speak to the clerk on duty. To ask for Kara's room number, she more than suspected. She watched them talk for a minute while she made up her mind.

Seeing him turn from the desk, she knew what she had to do. Gathering her strength, she walked up to Cade and invited him to have dinner with her. He arched an eyebrow in surprise at her unusual request, and she hastily explained that she needed to ask him a few questions about the research she had done for the film. She wanted to make certain of some of the facts, she lied.

"I have to see someone right now," he told her. "Perhaps we can talk another time."

She nodded and turned away. There was nothing she could do to prevent what was about to happen.

Stephanie was in her room, pacing back and forth, when she heard the knock on the door. She opened it to find Cade standing there, his huge frame filling the opening.

"I'm free now," he calmly stated. "Would you like to go to dinner?"

She listened for the strain in his voice, but he hid his emotions well. His face was a mask—he had been handed a terrible shock, she was sure. She wanted to rush into his arms and tell him that she loved him, that he wasn't alone in the world, and she knew that if she stayed with him during the evening she would do just that. Cade might be able to hide his feelings, but she wouldn't be able to hide hers.

"I'm sorry," she managed to stutter. "Something has come up, and I have a dinner engagement."

He eyed her strangely. "I see," he said simply.

As quickly as he had appeared, he was gone.

CHAPTER FOURTEEN

STEPHANIE COULDN'T BRING HERSELF to ask Kara about her confrontation with Cade. It would have been too embarrassing. Instead she tried to put the entire ugly episode out of her mind. But every time she watched Kara perform before the cameras, she thought of what must have happened, what they must have said to each other.

She could almost picture the scene, like the climax in one of Jon's films. Kara would open the door, radiant with her newfound love, and Cade would think her glow came from seeing him. He would rush into the room, embrace her, press his lips against hers, stroke her hair, her neck, her shoulders, the way Stephanie knew so well.

Kara would be astonished, would try to break away, but Cade would hold her against him, murmuring silkily smooth words into her ear. Then he would let her go, but only to allow him to reach into his pocket for the ring box, to open it and display before her what must be a fabulous gem.

Kara would have to tell him the truth: that she was already engaged to Jon. Each time she got to that part of the scene, Stephanie shuddered and tossed it out of her consciousness. She couldn't take the image any further. Her mind wouldn't allow her to visualize Cade's face when he heard the news. He wouldn't be able to hide the initial shock, and it would be a few minutes before he could don the expressionless mask he had worn when he appeared at her door.

She should have gone with him. He had needed her, and he had come to her as a friend. She was too weak to do the one thing he had requested of her.

It was the final week of filming, and she spent much of her time winding up the loose ends that always came with the closing of actual shooting. She wished she could tie up her own loose ends as efficiently. Most of her time was spent in the little office provided for the director at the studio. She typed letters, compiled the bills to send to the accountant, made certain that Jon signed the checks stacked on the desk, and made arrangements for the party on the final day of shooting.

Jon's parties were always fun, but he wanted this one to be spectacular since he was using the occasion to announce his engagement, and it took Stephanie several days to handle the details to his satisfaction. He didn't like the menu she had planned so she had to redo it, and he made her increase the order for flowers as well as the size of the band. She pointed out that the extra expenses would send them over the budget that was allocated in the overall film production costs, but he didn't care, telling her he would pay the difference himself.

"This is going to be the best party we've ever had," he told Stephanie, "and I don't care how much it costs. Everyone's going to be there, too.

Make sure invitations go out to anyone who had any connection at all with the filming of this movie.''

He came back an hour later to insist that she issue invitations to all of Cade's employees as well as the rancher himself. Stephanie reached for the additional supply of envelopes and began addressing invitations. There was no point in telling him that Cade wouldn't want his employees to attend this particular party. She wondered if Kara had told Jon of Cade's proposal. More than likely she had kept that little happening to herself, not wanting to cause trouble between the men. She would wait until they were married to mention Cade's love for her. If she ever told him....

Everyone worked late on Thursday night to make certain of finishing early on Friday. There were no objections to the extra duty: they all wanted to be through so they could have plenty of time to don their party clothes for the evening festivities. And many of them needed time to pack because they were leaving for California on Saturday morning.

Jon and Kara planned to fly to Los Angeles on Sunday, and Stephanie, feeling absolutely unneeded, was booked for the same flight. There wouldn't be time to get any work done on the plane, she knew: once news of the engagement broke, reporters would no doubt besiege them, hoping to interview the celebrity couple. Kara had asked her publicity man to come to Dallas for the party and to fly back with her, but she hadn't told him that she would need his help in fending off reporters who tried to interfere too much with her privacy.

When Jon called the final "cut" shortly after noon on Friday, there was one large cheer and then a rush to box equipment and get the studio cleared. Nobody ever moved faster than on the last day of a film, and the trunks of costumes and other equipment going back to California were ready for the delivery service to take to the airport within two hours.

Stephanie gathered the last of her papers into her briefcase and made a final check of the office to be certain nothing was left behind. It was difficult to feel her normal exhilaration at the conclusion of shooting. She had done her job well, she felt sure, but she couldn't take pride in her accomplishments. Not when they had come at the expense of two broken hearts: hers and Cade's.

The party guests hadn't been requested to reply, but she had no doubt Cade would not attend. He had too much pride to choose to see Kara again after the humiliation he had suffered, and how could he honestly shake Jon's hand and congratulate the director on his upcoming marriage? Cade wasn't a hypocrite. He would not be there, which meant that she had seen the last of the rancher. There would be no reason for her to return to Texas now, and she certainly had no intentions of coming back for the premiere. Her last sight of Cade would be the one she remembered so well—him filling the doorway of her hotel room.

The image was in her mind as she boarded the bus to the hotel, and she sat alone, hardly aware of the chatter around her and the plans being made for smaller celebrations in the various nightclubs near

the hotel once Jon's party had ended. Her co-
workers were planning a long night of partying even
if most of them had to rise early on Saturday to catch
planes.

Stephanie was one of the last persons off the bus.
Her feet dragged, and she couldn't find the energy to
lift them off the ground. She hadn't had lunch, but
she didn't want to join the crew members who had
made a dash for the dining room. Their jovial banter
was more than she could take. She went straight to
her room and ordered a sandwich by telephone.

She wished she could get on a plane now and leave,
but she had no choice. Jon was expecting her to be at
the party, and she had to arrive early and stay late. It
was her responsibility to ensure that everything ran
smoothly, that there was plenty of food and drink,
that the music was exactly what the dancers wanted.

Jon's announcement would stun the group, she
knew. There hadn't been a single word of gossip or
speculation about the director and Kara, and that
was an accomplishment in itself. They had kept their
secret well.

After delaying as much as she could, Stephanie
bathed and dressed in a long silvery blue gown that
emphasized her curvaceous figure without flaunting
it. The fabric was delicate and soft, and the color
enhanced the honey tones of her complexion. She
added her silver slippers and evening bag and hunted
through her jewelry box for a necklace to complement the gown. Her fingers latched onto the gold
Texas charm that Cade had presented her, and she
threw it back into the box, closing the lid quickly and

deciding that her dress needed no jewelry after all.

She surveyed herself in the mirror, telling herself that she looked as good as possible under the circumstances. Her long hair was piled on her head in a Grecian knot, and she pulled a couple of strands down in small curls over her ears.

The party was in a large room in the hotel, so Stephanie had only to catch an elevator to the top floor to oversee final preparations. She was checking the hors d'oeuvres when Barry Logan, Kara's publicity representative, practically flew into the room. He rushed over to Stephanie, grasped her around the waist and practically swung her off her feet.

"Isn't it marvelous, Stephanie?" he cried, hardly stopping long enough for her to regain her footing.

She eyed him questioningly. "About Kara and Jon," he explained excitedly. "They confided the news to me a few minutes ago so that I could help with the announcement to the press." He surveyed the room. "I hope you don't mind, but I've put in calls to several reporters and photographers and invited them to attend."

Stephanie started to protest, but he stopped her with a raised hand.

"I know what you're going to say, but they won't be in the way, I promise. And they don't know about the engagement yet, so they can't tell anyone ahead of time."

She shrugged her shoulders. "As long as you've cleared it with Jon, it's fine with me."

They had to change the subject as the first guests

began to arrive, but Barry squeezed her hand enthusi- astically before he departed to watch for the news- men to arrive.

The room seemed to fill in an instant. The music was loud, but no one seemed to mind, and the dance floor was full of crew members, talent agents and others who had taken part in the making of *A Passionate Land*.

Jon made a point of arriving with both Kara and Robert, and their entrance sparked a cheer and a lull in the dancing. The director wanted to wait awhile, Stephanie knew, to tell the crowd of the engagement, but he was forced to say something, so he strode to the microphone and announced that it was custom- ary for the leading lady to dance first with her leading man, but he was going to usurp Robert's privilege for once and dance with Kara himself. Robert would have to cut in if he wanted a dance with Kara, he in- formed his male star.

Robert shrugged and turned to invite someone else to dance. It was Stephanie's misfortune to be stand- ing next to him at the time, and she had to smile and agree to accompany him onto the dance floor. At least he was sober. It was still early, however, and she feared he would be intoxicated before the festivities were over. Thank goodness Cade wasn't there and wouldn't be able to knock Robert to the ground with one punch of his powerful fist.

She would have thought that no one connected with Cade would be at the party, but Mrs. Steele was present along with Mr. and Mrs. Martin and four of the men who worked at the ranch. Their wives had probably insisted they come, she decided, in spite of Cade's wishes to the contrary.

"I'm going to be so sorry to see you leave," Mrs. Martin told Stephanie while they were standing by the table spread with a variety of snacks. "It was nice having you drop by the house every evening, and I've missed you these past few weeks."

Stephanie smiled and said nothing. There was nothing she could say.

Mrs. Steele was equally pleasant, urging her to stay on in Dallas and be her guest for a few weeks, insisting that Stephanie needed a vacation. "Cade's not as busy in the fall," she added, "and we might prevail on him to escort us to New Orleans. You could meet my daughter, and we could all go out and have a great time in the French Quarter."

She smiled sweetly at Stephanie, who wondered if Cade had told his mother about losing out to Jon. She might be trying to encourage him with Stephanie to ease his pain. Well, if that was the case, Mrs. Steele could quit trying right now. Stephanie had too much pride to accept anyone on the rebound.

She managed a smile. After all, it wasn't Mrs. Steele's fault that all of this had happened. "I have enjoyed getting to know you," she truthfully told the older woman, "but I do have to go back to California to help Jon with the final work on the film."

Mrs. Steele's gaze focused on the director, who was dancing with one of the women from the talent agency. "Yes, Cade said you were returning to California with Jon."

"Sunday," Stephanie explained. "We have a busy

few months ahead of us.'' She excused herself before she said too much to Cade's mother and walked over to catch Jon as he finished the dance. She placed a hand on his shoulder and whispered into his ear, asking him if he was ready to make the announcement.

He dazzled her with his smile. ''Just about,'' he concurred. ''Come stand by us while Kara and I break the news. I want you to get a good look at everyone's face to see if we really surprise them.'' He took her by the hand and led her off to find Kara while Mrs. Steele watched from the doorway.

The publicity man made them wait a few minutes until the photographers and reporters had gathered, and a few of the guests had already departed before Jon and Kara walked up onto the small stage where the band performed. Struggling to repress a grin, the director reached for the microphone.

''Ladies and gentlemen,'' he began, ''I have a couple of announcements to make before this party breaks up. First,'' he said, deliberately ignoring Kara, ''I want to thank all of you again for the hard work you put into this picture. You made my job very easy.'' He paused while the crowd applauded, then continued, ''I also want to introduce someone who's going to make my life much easier: my future wife, Kara Warren.''

There was a gasp of astonishment from the crowd as Jon embraced Kara. She responded with ardor, and the photographers were able to get several pictures of them kissing before they paused to answer questions.

Their joy was so contagious that the entire room

was caught up in the celebration, and smiles and cheers filled the place. Stephanie stood behind the lovers, seeing their happiness and contrasting it with her own failure. She knew she should join in the laughter, but she couldn't do more than frown at the flashbulbs that continued to pop in front of her while the photographers aimed their cameras at Jon and Kara.

Hoping nobody would notice, she sneaked off the stage and into the powder room, where she collapsed on the sofa and collected herself. *Oh, Cade,* she moaned inwardly, unable to hold back her longing for him, *I'll never see you again....*

She could hear women approaching the room. Their conversation about Kara and Jon carried through the heavy door leading to the hallway, and Stephanie quickly jumped to her feet and smoothed the wrinkles in her long dress. She walked out as they entered.

"Isn't it exciting?" one of the women called to her as they passed. "I think it's so marvelous. Do you know when they plan to get married, Stephanie?"

"No," she answered, "I don't think they've set a date. Jon has to finish editing the picture first."

She walked back into the ballroom as an informal press conference, organized by the publicity agent, was getting under way. The reporters, too, were eager to learn the couple's plans.

"We hope to be married Christmas Day," Kara was telling them, "if Jon gets through with the editing in time."

"I'll make sure the picture's completed by then,"

he laughed, covering her delicate hand with his. "I don't want work hanging over my head when we go on a honeymoon."

The questions and answers went on and on.

"No," Jon said, "we haven't selected a honeymoon location, but when we do we'll make certain it's kept secret from photographers!"

Kara was asked if she would continue to make movies, and she joked that she would only if she had a brilliant director like the one beside her. "Seriously," she told the group of reporters, "I do want to continue my career, but not at the cost of my marriage. If it means going out of town, I'll work only with Jon as the director, and I'll accept jobs in Hollywood only if he's in town at the same time."

"This will be no long-distance marriage," Jon agreed.

"Will you have a big wedding?" someone asked, and both Jon and Kara shook their heads.

"Not at all," Kara explained. "It will be very small and very private, with only our families and very close friends there."

At last the newsmen were satisfied and departed to write their stories.

"This will be in all the papers tomorrow," the publicity man exulted when the reporters had gone. "And I'll see that the picture is mentioned, too," he added. "You might as well get some extra publicity for the movie."

"No," Jon ordered. "Let them print what they have. If they mention the film, it's all right, but I'm not marrying Kara to promote this picture and I don't want it to appear as if I am."

"Of course," Barry agreed. "I didn't mean that."

"Excuse us," Jon told him. "I want the next five or six or maybe ten or twelve dances with my bride-to-be."

The party continued long past midnight, and Stephanie had to prop her head up with an elbow before the band finally replaced their instruments in the cases and the hotel staff began removing dishes from the room.

"Come have a drink with us," Jon invited as he and Kara prepared to depart.

"No," Stephanie refused. "You two deserve to be able to go out together without me in the way. I've had enough of being the third party in your little intrigue."

Kara gave Stephanie a big hug. "But you did a wonderful job," she exclaimed. "Jon and I might never have found each other if it hadn't been for you."

"That's right," Jon confirmed. "We might have gone along on our own lonely paths if you hadn't helped us."

Stephanie shook her head. "I don't believe that," she told them. "You would have found each other sooner or later." She surveyed the room to make certain her responsibilities were completed. "I'm a romantic at heart," she added, turning back to her friends, "and I don't think there's any way to stop true love forever."

Except in her own case. But she had the misfortune

of loving a man who didn't love her. Kara and Jon were different. They both loved each other, and their only problem had been that they failed to communicate their feelings and didn't realize their love was returned. Stephanie had no illusions about her own situation. She was lucky that Cade even wanted to be a friend.

It didn't do any good to dwell on the matter, however, especially at a time when Kara and Jon were so happy. She managed a brilliant smile and kissed them both, offering her congratulations again and telling Jon that she would check with him the next morning to see what work he had for her.

"No work, Stef," he informed her while he cuddled Kara close against his chest. "Tomorrow I'm spending the entire day with this gorgeous woman, and I don't even want to think about the picture. You take the day off, and we won't plan to meet until it's time to go to the airport on Sunday. Okay?"

Stephanie nodded, wishing she had known earlier that he wouldn't be needing her on Saturday. She could have flown back to Los Angeles with Becky and the others instead of spending an extra day in Dallas.

When she returned to her hotel room she checked with the airlines, but the flights on Saturday were full and she had to be content with her Sunday reservation. It would be a long wait until then, she knew, for packing wouldn't require more than an hour or two of her time. She couldn't stand to sit around the hotel the entire day and brood over what Cade was doing and how he was taking the loss of Kara.

By now his mother had probably informed him of the wedding announcement Jon and Kara had made. Or the Martins had returned to the ranch with the news. Mrs. Martin had been shocked by the announcement, and Stephanie knew why: the housekeeper had wanted Cade to marry the actress. Mrs. Steele had hidden any surprise she might have felt, instead returning to Stephanie before she left and renewing her invitation to be a guest in her home for the next few weeks.

At any other time the offer would have been tempting, but Stephanie couldn't stay anywhere there was a chance of running into Cade. She knew she would jump each time the doorbell rang, and she didn't think she could stand to hear his mother talk about the man or display more of his childhood photographs. She was grateful for her work in Los Angeles.

She set her alarm for early Saturday morning and also left a wake-up call with the hotel as extra insurance that she would not stay in bed. She wanted to get up and away from this prison. There were too many memories in the building, images of Cade looming in her doorway after he had visited Kara, even a vision of him sitting in the small chair in this same hotel intently listening to her tell the story of the picture the first day they met.

When the telephone rang and the alarm buzzed simultaneously at seven o'clock, Stephanie crawled out of bed and stood looking out the window at the tall skyscrapers of downtown Dallas for a few minutes before she dressed and prepared to leave. She didn't know where she was going or what she would do, but it didn't matter, not as long as she was away from the hotel and from people who might wonder why she seemed so unhappy. Anyone looking at her now might jump to the same conclusion as Cade and think she was mourning her loss of Jon to Kara.

She didn't even stop to eat in the dining room. There was too much chance of running into some of the crew members having breakfast before leaving for the airport. She rushed through the lobby and out the front door, heading for Jon's car in the parking lot. He had offered her the use of it, telling her that he and Kara would be able to go wherever they wanted to in the limousine that was still at the actress's command.

For a while Stephanie drove around aimlessly, soon losing herself in the network of freeways and not having any idea of where she was. It didn't matter. She could always find her way back when the day was drawing to a close, and she didn't much care where she was heading now.

She turned from the city, traveling the country roads that she had grown to love, slowly realizing now how much more she knew about the trees, the soil, the grasses and the native birds than she had the first time she made the trip to Cade's ranch. Despite his arrogance he had been a good teacher, and she had him to thank for her new knowledge.

Coming to a small town that looked vaguely familiar, she gazed at the old buildings as she paused at the lone traffic light, and her eyes came to rest on the little general store at one end of the main street. It was the shop where Cade had purchased the equipment to repair his engine, and she hadn't been able to go into the place because she was muddy and barefoot. Now it beckoned her irresistibly, and Stephanie responded by pulling her car into an open space in front of the nineteenth-century stone building.

The store was as enchanting as she had thought it might be the first time she saw it, and the elderly shopkeeper was just as entertaining. He showed her around cheerfully, pointing out the wide variety of merchandise, ranging from farm equipment to sewing goods to cosmetics to antiques.

Noting her interest in the older items, he displayed an antique churn, a brass bed and a collection of old irons, some of which were heated with coal placed inside the irons themselves. As Stephanie struggled to lift a couple of them, the proprietor chuckled, "You had to be strong to be a housewife in the old days," and Stephanie was forced to agree.

She looked around the store awhile longer, deciding now that she did want a souvenir, something that would remind her of her weeks in the state, something other than the gold chain Cade had so casually put around her neck. There didn't seem to be anything small enough to pack easily, however, and Stephanie was about to give up when she spied the porcelain shepherdess high on a shelf at one side of the store. She looked at it for a long time, mentally comparing it to the one in Cade's log cabin. They were virtually identical, and she wondered if this was a modern copy or an actual antique that had been lovingly moved thousands of miles to add beauty to a frontier home.

The man noted her interest and lifted the statue from the shelf, handing it to her as if it were a treasure to be cherished for a lifetime.

"You have an eye for quality," he complimented her. "This is the best antique I have in the store, and there's a long story behind how it got here."

Before he could even tell her how it had come from Pennsylvania through Virginia and into Missouri before arriving in Texas more than a century earlier, Stephanie knew she had to have the piece. It probably cost more than she could afford, but she would scrimp on buying clothes to make up for it. She didn't plan to do much socializing anyway, and she didn't need any new dresses.

The price was high, but Stephanie willingly agreed to it and asked if she could pay by check. She offered a variety of identification, and the store owner glanced briefly at the address on her driver's license. "Los Angeles, huh?" he commented, and Stephanie nodded. "You one of those people who were makin' the movie over at Cade Steele's place?" She nodded again.

That seemed to satisfy the man, and he began writing the receipt and finding a box to pack the statue in. As he worked, he talked about the filming.

"Been lots of interest in that movie 'round here," he informed Stephanie. "Everyone wanted to go out and take a look, but I understand only a few got into the ranch to see anything."

"Security has to be tight when we're filming," Stephanie explained. "We did have one day when everyone was let in for two hours to get autographs."

The storekeeper chuckled. "Yeah, I remember that. Cade was here that day. Said the folks 'round here were overrunnin' his place like ants swarmin' to a picnic." He looked up at her. "You get to meet Cade while you were there?"

"Yes," Stephanie replied without elaborating. She reached for the box that the man had obligingly packed so that the statue wouldn't break on the trip home.

"Nice man, that Cade Steele," he continued. "His father was one of my best friends, and Cade's turned out so well I wish the old man was still alive to see what he's done with that ranch."

"I'm sure he would be proud," Stephanie responded lightly. "The ranch looks very well kept."

"Best ranch in these parts, and Cade's become a wealthy man." The man watched Stephanie gingerly handle the box. "Now, little lady, I don't think that'll break, but you might want to carry it with you if you fly back to California, and not trust it to the baggage compartment."

"I intend to," Stephanie assured him. "Thank you for taking the time to show me around. I appreciate it."

Suddenly she was in a hurry to leave, irrationally afraid that she might run into Cade somewhere and have him ask what she had purchased. He would be aware that the statue was a reminder of him and his ranch.

She turned the car back toward Dallas, wanting to lose herself in the faceless crowds. Parking by a shopping mall she hadn't seen before, she wandered in, strolled through the Neiman-Marcus store and made a small purchase just so she could have a bag with the name of the famous store emblazoned on it. One of the Dallas people working on the film had mentioned that she did that occasionally and then carried her lunch in the Neiman-Marcus sack for days and days. It added a touch of status to her image, she confided, making people think she did all of her shopping at Neiman's.

Stephanie took her time at the mall. She went to a cafeteria for lunch and then walked through several other stores before deciding to take a busman's holiday and see a movie. When she stepped back out into the mall a couple of hours later, she couldn't remember very much about the picture she had seen, but the theater had been cool and comfortable, and she had been able to munch popcorn and stare mindlessly at the wide screen before her.

She glanced at her watch, thinking that she really should go back to the hotel but not wanting to be within the confines of its restrictive walls. Yet she also didn't want to be wandering around the city by herself once it was dark. She would have to return.

Stopping at a small bookstore in the mall, Stephanie purchased a couple of paperback novels to help her evening pass by. As she walked out of the shop, the newspaper rack at the entrance caught her attention, and she stopped to drop in a few coins and take out the Saturday edition of a Dallas paper.

The photograph was on the front page. It was large and very flattering of both Kara and Jon. They were in the foreground, exchanging loving glances, while a few people were shown in the background applauding and smiling. All except one. Stephanie stared at the reproduction of her own face. She looked somber, almost frowning in the picture, in marked contrast to all the other happy expressions. She hoped nobody connected with the movie would see the photo. Everyone would assume she was feeling the pang of rejection by Jon, and no matter how often she explained the truth, she wouldn't be believed. Every other woman fell for Jon—why should she be an exception?

She scanned the accompanying story quickly. It was well written, complete with quotations from both Jon and Kara about their plans for the future. There was one paragraph about the movie itself and about how it had been filmed in great part on the Steele ranch northwest of the city. Stephanie shuddered when she read that, knowing Cade wouldn't want his name included in a story about Kara's engagement to Jon.

Stuffing the newspaper into the bag with her books, Stephanie left the store and made her way to the parking area and the car. Reluctantly she turned back to the hotel. Getting there took a few minutes longer than she had expected, however, for the freeways still confused her and she had to stop once to ask directions.

When she arrived, she noticed the message light was flashing on her telephone, but she didn't call the operator to find out who wanted her. Instead she placed her packages on the bed and left again, this time for the hotel restaurant.

The room was crowded, but no one she knew was there, so Stephanie asked for a quiet table in the back and tried to amuse herself by watching the diners around her. It wasn't entertaining. There were too many young couples, bending their heads to each other, exchanging confiding looks, occasionally holding hands while they sipped their cocktails.

When her meal was served, Stephanie ate as rapidly as possible, signed her bill and left. She walked out into the lobby, quiet for a change, and stopped by the desk to pick up the messages her telephone had alerted her were waiting.

There were three in total, and they were all from Cade. The first message had come in the early morning, shortly after she had left her room for the day. The second time he called was at noon, and this time the operator had written the word "important" after the note to call him at the ranch. The last time was only an hour earlier, and this slip had "urgent" written across it in large letters that were underlined twice.

Stephanie crumpled the papers in her fist and tossed them into a nearby wastebasket. There was no reason to return his calls. She had completed all of her business dealings with Cade, and she had nothing else to say to him.

She knew why he was calling. He thought she might intervene on his behalf with Kara. No, she wasn't going to talk to Cade Steele again. Wearily, she took the elevator to her floor and walked down the hall to her room. She could hear the telephone ringing before she opened the door, but she still took her time unlocking it and entering the room. Stephanie stood staring at the ringing telephone until it finally stopped, and then she picked up the telephone and dialed the operator.

She left a message that she didn't want to accept any calls either that night or the following morning, and then she shed her linen pantsuit, donned a long silk robe and settled on her bed.

Stephanie wanted to open the box holding the porcelain shepherdess, to examine her precious purchase at leisure, but she didn't dare disturb the carefully packed antique. Instead she picked up the first of her paperback novels and began to read. The words danced fuzzily before her eyes, and it took a minute to realize that her vision was clouded by tears struggling to escape.

CHAPTER FIFTEEN

Jon teased Stephanie about the unflattering picture of her that had appeared in the paper, but she tried to ignore his flippant words.

"You looked as though you lost your last friend," he kidded her as they waited in the VIP lounge at the airport for their flight to Los Angeles.

"That's not true," she protested. She hadn't lost her last friend, merely her only love. "I was tired, and the photographer just happened to snap the picture at the wrong moment for me. But you and Kara looked happy enough to make up for it."

She was right about that. They were so happy they hadn't even been bothered by the photographers and reporters who crowded around them as they arrived at the airport. Stephanie, practically crushed in the group of reporters trying to get close to the celebrities, had been relieved when they reached the relative sanctuary of the VIP lounge. It was calm there, at least, even if she had to endure Jon's bad jokes.

They were flying first class, and Stephanie had a window seat. Barry was sitting beside her, and Jon and Kara were across the aisle. Stephanie hoped Barry wouldn't talk the entire way back to California. She couldn't stand too much of his good humor and exuberance at the amount of publicity his client was achieving this week.

"They'll be on the cover of a national magazine," he revealed to Stephanie as the plane's engines began to turn and the flight attendants checked to make sure all seat belts were fastened. Stephanie murmured an inaudible reply and stared out the window.

When the airplane swept down the runway and took to the sky, she couldn't resist a final panoramic look at the land she had vowed she'd never visit again. There was a lake beneath her, and both Fort Worth and Dallas were visible in the distance, one from her window and the other from the windows on the opposite side of the plane. Quickly orientating herself, she realized they were flying north from the airport that had been built between the two major cities, north over the trees and prairies beyond the city.

They must be going near Cade's ranch, she decided, remembering that they had been required to pause occasionally when shooting the film to wait for a plane flying overhead to get out of camera range. Her gaze was irresistibly drawn to the land below, but if the Steele ranch was in sight, she didn't recognize it. They were now too high to pick out specific features, and she felt a sense of loss that she hadn't gained a final glimpse of the property. With a sigh she leaned back in her seat and listened to Barry's monologue.

When they arrived in Los Angeles, there was another crowd of photographers, this group even larger than the one they had left at the Dallas-Fort Worth

Airport, but Stephanie managed to sneak through the press of people and stand to one side while Jon and Kara conducted an impromptu press conference, answering again the same questions they had been asked in Dallas.

The engaged couple was whisked away under Barry's direction, and Stephanie was left to fend for herself. Jon shouted back at her that he would be in the office the next morning, and she nodded and waved. Gathering her luggage and carefully holding the boxed statue she had carried in her lap the entire trip, she looked around for someone who could order her a cab. A hand reached out for the largest suitcase before she could find anybody, and she glanced up to see Morgan and his wife standing by her.

"I thought this would happen to you when I heard about Jon's and Kara's engagement," Morgan explained. "We figured you'd get left out in the cold, so Paula and I came down to give you a ride to your apartment."

Stephanie smiled gratefully at the couple. "Thank you so much. I wasn't expecting anything like this, and I really appreciate the ride. I've had a long summer in Texas, and I'm feeling the effects, I'm afraid." She pushed a couple of fingers inside her belt, showing Paula how many inches she had lost in the waistline while she was gone.

"I should have spent the summer in Texas," Paula laughed. "I wouldn't mind getting rid of an inch or two myself."

Stephanie invited the Andersons to stay for coffee once they had assisted her with getting her luggage inside her apartment and she had the air conditioning back on and the small room cooling again. She had been gone for so long she wasn't even sure she had coffee, but she had to express her appreciation in some manner.

They declined the coffee but did sit on the sofa that doubled as a bed for Stephanie and proceeded to talk about the film, about Kara and Jon and about Morgan's injuries, from which he assured her he was recovering.

"Aren't you sorry now that you thought Cade Steele and Kara were in love?" Morgan asked, a twinkle showing in his dark eyes.

Stephanie glanced quickly at Paula, who nodded and admitted, "Morgan confided in me, Stephanie. I hope you don't mind, but he tells me everything."

Stephanie stirred uneasily, crossing her legs and uncrossing them again. "I never said that Kara loved Mr. Steele," she protested, "only that he loved her."

She raised her eyes to meet Morgan's skeptical gaze. "He does, you know. I think he even...." She stopped, unable to tell him that Cade had likely proposed to the actress. "He tried to contact me at least three times yesterday, and I know he wanted to see if I could break up the engagement."

"Did he tell you that?" Morgan wanted to know.

"Of course not. I didn't even return his calls."

"Then how do you know what he wanted?" Paula asked gently. "Maybe he wanted to be with you on your last night in Texas."

"No," Stephanie assured her. "It was Kara. It was always Kara."

Morgan shook his head. "What are we going to do with you, Stef? You're more stubborn than our children on a bad day."

"What you can do," Stephanie retorted, "is forget about Cade Steele and let me get on with my work at the studio."

"The question is," Morgan continued to press his point, "can you forget?"

Stephanie averted her face, unable to meet his steady gaze. "Of course," she lied. "I'll have forgotten him in a week."

THERE WAS NO FORGETTING CADE, however. He was part of everything she did, until at last Stephanie gave up trying to forget and contented herself with the memories she did have of him. She pulled the china shepherdess out of its packing box and set it on the buffet in her little apartment, and each day she gazed at it and smiled a bit sadly. It was almost as if she were sharing in Cade's heritage when she looked at the piece.

He was with her at work, as well, in each task she completed that had anything to do with *A Passionate Land*. There were occasional letters from Jon to the rancher that she had to type and mail, and there was also the report from the insurance company about its investigation of the accident with the windmill. Once she had to place a long-distance call to the ranch, and her fingers trembled as she dialed the number and waited for Cade's deep voice to answer. Mrs. Martin was there instead, and Stephanie left Jon's message with her to be forwarded to Cade. She didn't ask how the rancher was doing because she wasn't sure she wanted to know.

She hung up the telephone in time to see the still photographer enter her office with a stack of pictures for Jon. The man flipped through them hurriedly, pointing out ones he thought would be particularly appropriate for publicizing the movie. He had done a good job of capturing the mood of the film, Stephanie could tell, and the prints were sharp and clear. She was especially interested in the ones he had done of the cattle-drive scenes and the ones showing the log cabin on Cade's land.

"This one doesn't belong," the photographer commented as he stopped to show her one picture, "and I'll take it back with me. I just couldn't resist snapping it when I saw the man and the horse, even if they weren't part of the film."

Stephanie practically snatched it from his hand. The photograph was a marvelous portrait of Cade. He was standing at the top of a hill, holding the reins to his quarter horse, and he had a commanding stance as he looked into the distance, over his property.

"No, don't take it back," she murmured. "That's the owner of the ranch, and Jon might want to send the photograph to him."

She held onto the picture until the man was gone, and then she slid it into the bottom drawer of her desk. Jon would never see that photograph. She was taking it home.

Stephanie had the picture framed, but she didn't have the courage to display it the way she wanted to do. There were too many friends and neighbors dropping by to ask questions about a photograph of a handsome man. She kept it in the top drawer of the buffet, directly below her porcelain statue.

Weeks turned into months as the editing of the movie continued. Jon spent hours with the editors, going over the film frame by frame, insisting on participating in almost every decision concerning it. He worked with the musicians, too, telling them exactly what he wanted for orchestration and listening to recording after recording before he was satisfied. He was out of the office a great deal, and Stephanie was grateful. When he was gone she didn't have to see his smiling face and be reminded of the happiness he'd found with Kara. He was uncharacteristically pleasant to everyone, and even though he made the editors and musicians work overtime, he never fussed or raised his voice at them. He was so agreeable, in fact, that at times Stephanie almost wished she had the old Jon back, the one who pounded his fist on the desk when things went wrong.

He procrastinated about the plans for the premiere of the movie, though, waiting to make certain that everything would be ready before he announced a date for the first showing. Initially he had planned to hold the festivities in Dallas, but later he decided to have the premiere in Los Angeles, where most of the movie critics were located. A mid-December date was set, one not long before the Christmas wedding. Jon explained that it was the earliest possible time for the showing and that he wanted to have the premiere out of the way before his wedding. ''So I won't have to think about it on my honeymoon," he explained to Stephanie.

By having its premiere before the end of the year, the movie also became eligible for Academy Award nominations, and Jon was hoping it would reap several prizes. "Some critics may say it's just a Western," he complained, "but it's so much more than that. It's the saga of an entire family, and I've got to make sure the critics realize that it does tell a dramatic story of a struggle to survive." He closed the door to his office while he thought out the problem, and Stephanie turned back to her typewriter, wondering if he had seen the half dozen notes she had left him at various times about her vacation.

She had decided to take a month off, beginning the day after the premiere. Jon would be busy with his wedding and honeymoon, and he wouldn't have any new projects started, so it seemed an ideal time. She knew that he was reading several proposed scripts for his next film, but it would be a while before production could begin even if he did make a choice.

Stephanie's vacation plans were indefinite. She could go back to New York, she knew, for a holiday visit with her cousin, but she still hadn't reached a decision two days before her holiday was to begin. She talked it over with Morgan, who dropped by to pick up premiere tickets for himself and his wife.

"Nothing sounds like fun," she complained. "I may just stay home all month."

"Now, Stef, you can't do that," Morgan ordered. "You've got to get out. I'll bet you haven't had a date since you came back from Texas."

She couldn't deny that. None of the men who had asked her out were the kind of people she wanted to be with. They were all in the movie industry, and they wanted to talk of films and stars and the work they were doing or were hoping to do. She didn't want to think about movies once she left the office. She didn't want to think of anything but the man she had left in Texas.

"Why don't you call him, Stef?" Morgan asked. "Invite Cade to the premiere."

"Jon sent him an invitation," she replied stiffly, "but he declined. I can understand why he wouldn't want to come here."

"You're being silly," Morgan protested. "Cade's not in love with Kara any more than you're in love with Jon."

Stephanie pulled some papers from her desk and shuffled them briskly. "I have some work to do now, Morgan, if you don't mind. With the premiere tomorrow, there's an awful lot to get done."

Morgan smothered an oath as he stood up, shaking his head disapprovingly. He tapped the envelope with his two tickets against his desk. "If that's the way you're going to be, Stef," he said.

"It is."

She inserted a fresh sheet of paper in the typewriter and lined up her tabs for paragraph indentions. Morgan didn't move, and she finally looked up to see him still standing over her desk.

"Stef," he asked, "is it possible for me to get another ticket for the premiere and the party afterward? One of my daughters might like to go."

"Certainly," she smiled, rummaging through her desk for the extra tickets. "I hope you do bring one of those pretty girls. You don't take them to enough parties."

"They don't need to be going to a bunch of Hollywood parties," he replied. "I don't want them getting interested in this business. There's too much heartache."

Stephanie nodded and turned back to her typewriter. She heard Morgan shut the door as he left.

By the time Jon returned from having a final look at the completed film, Stephanie had caught up with all the secretarial tasks and was clearing her desk. She planned to make the next day a very short one since she would be going to the premiere performance and to the party Jon was hosting afterward at his large estate in Beverly Hills.

"You do realize that I'm taking a month off," she reminded the director, who nodded distractedly.

"Stephanie, it's the best picture I've ever made," he told her. "I've just seen it all together for the first time, and I'm stunned by how good it really is."

"Well, thank heavens you're modest!" Stephanie laughed.

"Oh, I don't mean my directing," he corrected her. "The whole story flows beautifully. The writers, the editors, everyone did a simply fabulous job, and Kara looks delicious. It's her best performance, I think."

"You would, Jon," she joked again, but added sincerely, "I'm glad you're so enthusiastic. I know how important this movie has been to you."

"I couldn't have done it without your help. You know that, don't you?" He caught her hand. "And if you hadn't talked Cade into letting us film at the ranch, it wouldn't have been half as good. I should bring your name forward in the credits."

"That won't be necessary, Jon," she smiled. "I'm looking forward to seeing it tomorrow night."

"And don't forget the party, Stef," he reminded her. "I'll be sure to announce my appreciation to you then."

"You'll forget all about me, Jon, when you're standing there with Kara, and you know it," she informed her boss, kissing him lightly on the cheek as she prepared to go home for the night. "But I appreciate your thanks in private. That's all I need."

The next day was an absolute turmoil. Stephanie arrived late at the office to find the telephones ringing and people standing outside her door wanting tickets to the screening and to the party. By the time she had sorted everything out and settled all the requests, it was after three. She quickly asked the message service to handle any calls coming in for the rest of the day, phoned the girl who would be replacing her temporarily during her vacation, to remind her about office hours, and threw the cover onto her typewriter. She was out the door before Jon could ask another favor.

Normally Stephanie didn't dress up much, but she knew that as a part of Jon's executive staff she would be expected to make a special effort. She took a long leisurely bath, arranged her hair carefully atop her head, applied makeup with the skill of a professional artist and then put on a sleek blue gown that trailed to the floor. It was almost the same shade of blue as the hostess robe belonging to Mrs. Steele that she had worn the night she'd faced Cade for the first time in his den. She remembered the moment poignantly, but it did no good to recall what was gone and to think of what might have been. Stephanie pulled her shoulders back and surveyed herself in the long mirror.

If you could see me tonight, Cade, she told herself, *you might think I were as beautiful as Kara.* But of course he would never do that, so she blocked any further thought along those lines and walked moodily to her car just outside the door.

She had trouble reaching the theater because the crowd was so large, but at last she arrived close enough for a parking attendant to take her keys and allow her to step out. Kara and Jon had invited her to go with them, but she had declined, and she had also turned down Morgan's insistent request that she ride with him and his wife. She wanted to be alone, to sit in the dark theater and look again at the magnificent land she remembered. She didn't care about the performers the way Jon did. It was the background scenery she wanted to see, that and the animals. She wondered if by some chance Cade might have wandered into a scene, but she realized that was highly unlikely. He'd stayed well off to the sides when he visited the site.

Stephanie settled into her seat, one she had deliberately chosen because it was to the side, where there was less chance of someone talking to her and interrupting her concentration on the screen. Though she was hardly aware of the other guests who were arriving, she did see Robert make his entrance, to the sound of enthusiastic applause. But his reception didn't equal the claps for Kara and Jon a few minutes later. Hollywood loved lovers, and the guests showed their excitement at the fact that love had bloomed during the filming of a movie. They didn't know the love had been there earlier, waiting to be discovered.

When the lights dimmed at last and the opening title appeared on the large screen, Stephanie sat straight in her seat and stared at the words. She alone knew how true the title was. Texas *was* a passionate land, and the ranch was the most passionate site of all. A vision of a grassy meadow flashed across her mind.

One after another, names appeared on the screen—the stars and the other performers, the technicians and, last of all, Jon's name as producer and director. Stephanie checked each listing unconsciously. Part of her job was to see that everyone's name was spelled correctly, and she couldn't help going over them again, even though she had proofread them several times before.

But as the last of the credits disappeared from the screen, another statement appeared, one Stephanie hadn't been prepared to see. A dedication. Jon hadn't mentioned that; he must have inserted it at the last minute. Quickly she scanned the words on the screen: "Dedicated to the Texans who rebuilt their land after the Civil War and to the man whose life inspired this story—Joshua Cade Steele (1845-1917)."

Stephanie saw the movie, but she couldn't remember a single scene. Her mind whirled with confusing thoughts. No wonder Cade had allowed the film to be shot on his ranch. That was where it had all happened, where his grandfather or great-grandfather or maybe even great-great-grandfather had built a magnificent ranch out of the ruins of war. Thanks to the wild longhorns.

Now she knew why the animals were so special to him, why he had taken such pains to protect them during the shooting, why he had relented and given his blessing. He must have known that Carter Graham's novel was based upon the Steele ranch.

The picture was a success. She knew it when the lights came on to a roar of thunderous applause. There wasn't any need to wait for the reviews to come out. She stood and watched Jon accepting the congratulations of the opening-night audience, which gave him and the film a spontaneous standing ovation. Jon deserved the credit, she knew, but she wished Cade were there to accept part of the glory. He had earned his share by offering his land and his animals as well as the little log cabin. But he was home in Texas, and he wouldn't know how much his family's story had impressed the people seeing the film.

Cade remained on Stephanie's mind as she made her way out of the theater and waited for her car. People around her chatted, but she didn't listen, didn't hear what they said. She didn't know who was there and who wasn't. She simply stood dazedly until the attendant brought her car. Then she drove to Jon's home without knowing how she got there.

CHAPTER SIXTEEN

STEPHANIE COULDN'T STAND THE NOISE of the party. It was too festive, too full of goodwill, smiles and congratulatory remarks. It wasn't for her.

Wandering from room to room didn't help. There was no quiet area, no place to seek sanctuary from the din around her, so she unobtrusively slid the patio door open and stepped out onto the terrace.

A few people were lingering there, engaged in deep conversations about the movie industry, but Stephanie didn't want to talk about movies. She had to sort out the tumble of emotions rolling around in her head.

There was a grassy meadow beyond the terrace, a secluded section that separated Jon's estate from a neighboring home, and she made her way to the far end of the property, where the sounds of the party were only a distant background to the noise inside her. Moonlight filtered down through the sky, but there were no bright stars shining, not like the ones Cade had described to her in such detail back in Texas. She strolled back and forth along the fence that marked the boundary of Jon's home, knowing she should go back inside but unable to make herself turn toward the house. She would catch cold if she stayed here much longer. Southern California might be warm, but this night was cool, and her woven shawl did little to protect her from the evening chill. She rubbed her arms as briskly as she could and continued to gaze at the night sky.

She had made a mess of her life, first in New York, now in Texas, and she couldn't even pick up the pieces as she had done the first time. Jon had helped her then, offering sympathy and support, but there was no running to him now for comfort. Not even Jon could repair the damage that had been done this time.

"I never could stand noisy parties."

Stephanie didn't even turn. She would have known that deep voice with its Texas twang anywhere. But she couldn't bear to look at him. Her emotions were written too vividly on her face.

With desperate effort she applied a mask of calm and tranquillity and managed a bit of a smile. "It is a little noisy in there, isn't it?" she said lightly. "How are you, Cade?"

She pivoted to face him, her eyes sweeping across his tall body and swiftly turning away. His lean face, tanned even in the middle of December, brought back all the memories she had tried helplessly to bury.

He was silent, seemingly content to watch the play of expressions on her face as she fought to conceal her love from him. Each time she slipped, she relentlessly reapplied her mask. It wouldn't do to let him see how much she ached for him.

"I didn't think you were coming to the premiere,"

she remarked, needing to distract him. His gaze was far too probing.

He moved slightly, leaning against the fence and lifting his eyes to the cloudy night sky. "I flew in earlier today," he informed her.

"Jon didn't mention it," Stephanie replied. "I'm surprised to see you again."

She watched him light a cigarette and stare at the blazing flame of the match before he shook it in the breeze and extinguished the fire. "Jon didn't know I was coming," Cade said. "It was a last-minute decision."

"Well, I'm certain he's glad that you did make the trip." She didn't know what else to say. The conversation was stilted and awkward, but she couldn't be at ease with Cade. If she let down her guard even for a moment, it might mean humiliating herself with a declaration of love that would lead to his scoffing.

"Morgan called yesterday and insisted I come," Cade explained. "I told him I had no business being here, but he claimed it was important and refused to listen to any of my reasons for staying home. He and his wife met me at the airport a few hours ago, and I had only enough time to check in at a hotel and change clothes before going to see the movie."

Morgan! Why would he have done that? Surely he wasn't still trying to maneuver a romance between Stephanie and Cade? Stephanie was glad the evening sky was dark enough that Cade couldn't see the pink rising in her cheeks. She'd have a long talk with Morgan. Besides, it was cruel to coax Cade into coming to a place where he would see Jon and Kara lovingly holding hands and exchanging romantic kisses. She'd have a long talk with Morgan first thing tomorrow and tell him exactly what she thought of his actions.

But she couldn't apologize to Cade, express her sympathy for what he must be feeling. He didn't know she knew of his love for Kara. Instead she simply ducked her head for a moment and turned the conversation to the movie.

"I didn't see you at the theater, but I assume you were there. Did you like the film?" She realized for the first time exactly how important it was to her that he did approve of *A Passionate Land*. After all, it was the story of his family.

"Yes," he answered, moving closer to her, forcing her to take a step backward until she was flat against the fence. "You did a good job with your research, Stephanie. Everything was very accurate and true to history." In the dim moonlight she could see him smile as he complimented her, and she rejoiced inwardly while keeping a serious expression on her face.

"I thought everyone did well even though I don't know that much about how movies are put together," he added. "Jon seemed to know what he was doing, and Kara was particularly good, I thought."

Kara. For a brief moment she had forgotten, and she looked at Cade to see if his love for the actress showed. But any emotion was hidden behind the mask he wore, so she quickly changed the subject.

"I had no idea," she told Cade, "that the novel was based on your own family."

He shrugged. "There was no way for you to know. When Carter Graham did his research for the novel, he used a lot of my records, but I asked him to fictionalize it enough that it could also represent the hundreds of other Texas pioneers who faced the same hardships and conquered them."

"Why didn't you tell me the story was about your ancestors?" she wanted to know.

"It didn't seem important," Cade remarked, turning partially away to stare at the well-lit house in the distance. "Actually, I didn't plan to tell Jon. It slipped out one evening when he was staying with me at the ranch. We got to talking about Graham, and I mentioned his visit when he was doing the research."

He took a deep puff on his cigarette, and Stephanie had the uneasy sensation that he wanted to talk about something more intimate, possibly about whether Jon and Kara would actually be married. She wasn't going to offer any news on the subject, and the silence hung heavy between them.

"I'm going back to Texas in the morning," Cade finally told her.

Stephanie nodded. "I suppose you're busy, trying to get all your work done before Christmas."

"What about you, Stephanie?" he asked. "Are you through with your work for a while?"

"Yes," she replied, sighing with mingled relief and apprehension. "I start my vacation in the morning, and I won't be back in the office again for a month."

Cade asked about her plans, and she had to admit that she didn't have any. "I just want to get away for a while," she informed him.

Cade took hold of her shoulders, sending a chill through her that wasn't caused by the night air. "I know," he tried to comfort her. "It must have been terribly hard for you these past few months."

She looked up in surprise. "Actually, the work is easier when we're not filming," she told Cade. "I haven't been completely involved with Jon's editing of the movie. That's why I didn't know he had inserted the dedication."

"I don't mean the work." Cade seemed exasperated by the fact that she misunderstood him. "I mean about Kara and Jon."

Stephanie turned abruptly, and his arms fell from her body. "What are you talking about?" she asked.

"It must have hurt you to lose Jon to her."

"I didn't lose Jon." This man could be incredibly obtuse! "Jon's simply a friend. He always has been. I told you that a number of times."

"But I thought he was your...." Cade's voice trailed off, and Stephanie finished his thought.

"Lover, you mean." It stung her to know that he still thought the worst of her. "You always believed that, and you never believed me when I insisted you were wrong." She took a few steps toward the house and stopped to face him again. "Do you really think that if I'd been in love with Jon I'd have worked so hard behind the scenes to allow him some time alone with Kara while we were on location?"

Stephanie blushed at her revelation. She had admitted to Cade that she'd assisted Jon in winning Kara away from him. He would hate her for that, and she didn't want to see the disdain no doubt written on his face. She turned again to run up the hill, but Cade stopped her in two quick strides.

"What are you talking about?" he demanded to know, and the harsh hand around her arm told her he wasn't going to free her until she had given him the full story.

As briefly as she could, she explained what had happened: how Jon had asked her to pose as his date so that the crew and cast as well as the public wouldn't guess he was going out with Kara. She told him that Kara hadn't understood his intentions at first and how she had finally learned the truth.

"And that was why neither Kara nor Jon accompanied us to the museums that Sunday," Stephanie explained. She knew she was making Cade's pain more acute, but she realized he had to learn the entire truth about the love affair that had gone on around him.

Cade was so quiet that Stephanie wanted to cry out for him to respond, but she waited for the emotions to die down and allow him to speak.

"That was the reason you spent the day with me," he stated. Stephanie didn't acknowledge the remark: it wasn't the only reason, but she couldn't tell him that.

"I'm sorry," she did say, "that you didn't know about Kara and Jon. They should have told you earlier."

Though she wished he wouldn't look at her that way, she couldn't seem to break away from his hypnotic gaze. He didn't speak, but she could hear the air going in and out of his lungs with every deep breath he took. "I'm sorry," she repeated.

"You never were in love with Jon?" Cade asked, as if he couldn't believe what she was telling him.

"No, of course not. I've told you over and over that he's simply my best friend."

"And you weren't lovers?"

Her face turned crimson at his accusation. "I've never been anyone's lover." She couldn't bear to talk to him any longer. "Please go away and leave me alone."

"No." His tone was curt, reminding her so much of the way he'd spoken to her in the summer that she almost smiled in spite of her pain. "I'm not leaving you alone until we get all of this straight."

"What is there to get straight?" she asked. "It's really very simple. Both you and Jon were in love with Kara, but she chose Jon and you lost out." There, she had said it. The truth was cruel, but it was out in the open now, the way he had wanted.

Cade stared at her, his mouth half-open, leaving him with an astonished look instead of the scowling expression she expected to see.

"Where in the world did you get the idea that I was in love with Kara?" he asked, moving closer to her and lifting his hand gently to touch her neck.

Stephanie stepped back, away from his intimate caress. "Well, weren't you? You gave every indication, and I know for a fact that you were shopping for a ring for her."

Cade exploded in combined rage and laughter, and this time he didn't let her move away from his tantalizing touch, instead drawing her closer into the confining hold of his arms.

"I was looking at a ring, but it wasn't for Kara," he explained, taking Stephanie's chin in a strong hand and forcing her to look into his eyes.

"But you went to see her right after you purchased it."

"No, my dear, I didn't. And if you didn't jump to conclusions so quickly, you wouldn't have thought that."

Stephanie was insistent. "I remember it so well," she reminded him. "We came back to the hotel, and I knew Jon and Kara were going out together, so I asked you to dinner to keep you from interfering with their plans."

His eyes flickered for a second at her remark, and a hard line formed around his mouth.

"You said you had an appointment," Stephanie continued. "I knew it had to be with Kara because Jon had already left, and I assumed you were giving her the ring." She looked down at the ground, afraid to face him. "When you showed up at my door a few minutes later, I figured she had rejected you and you wanted to go out with me to take your mind off what had just happened."

Cade swiveled, gripping the fence rail so powerfully that it practically bent. It was as if he were trying to control a magnificent emotion building up inside him.

"My appointment was with Jon," he said huskily. "He had forgotten and left, so that was why I was free so quickly."

Stephanie stared at his back. "Are you telling me you were never in love with Kara?"

"That's exactly what I'm saying," he muttered savagely, refusing to face her.

"But I was certain you were. Even your mother mentioned that you had spoken to her about a woman you were interested in."

"It wasn't Kara." He spoke so low that Stephanie could barely hear him.

"You were with her a lot. You enjoyed her company." Stephanie's fingers kept twisting back and forth nervously, and at the same time she shifted her weight from one foot to the other. "And she looks a lot like Merilee."

Cade whirled around. "What does that have to do with it?" he demanded. "Am I supposed to love a woman simply because she looks like someone I once dated? I admit I was surprised when I first saw Kara because she looked so much like Merilee, but I never had any romantic interest in her."

Stephanie didn't answer, but Cade didn't appear to notice.

"It doesn't matter anyway, does it, Stephanie? I should never have followed you out here when I saw you walking away from the house. Now I'm going back to the hotel. I leave for home first thing in the morning. Tell Jon and Kara goodbye for me."

He started up the hill, and Stephanie couldn't stand to see him depart. Shielded by the darkness with the moon now hidden behind the clouds, she could allow her emotions to play across the features of her face. "Don't go," she called. It was a soft cry, almost a moan, but Cade heard and stopped.

He strode toward her, taking her by the shoulders

and staring into her face. "Why don't you want me to go, Stephanie? So you can watch me bare my soul to you? Tell you that I've wanted you for months? That I've agonized daily thinking you were having an affair with Jon? That I insisted he stay at the ranch simply to keep him away from you every night?" He shook her until her head flopped from side to side. "Go ahead, Stephanie, have your fun and enjoy my humiliation. But first I'm going to have one thing to remember you by."

His hand shifted to the nape of her neck, forcing her head backward as his lips descended to hers. She was powerless to move, and she didn't want to. There was no fight to escape his embrace: she welcomed it. Flushed with the knowledge that he loved her, she gave herself up to him, returning kiss for kiss and embrace for embrace. There was no time to admit that she loved him, too. She couldn't keep her lips from his long enough to speak.

Cade's touch was punishing at first, but she didn't mind. Her mouth ached from the force of his lips and tongue, but the feeling exhilarated her, raising her temperature to such a fever pitch that she didn't feel the cool breeze that had chilled her earlier. She clung to him, rejoicing in the erotic trail of his fingers across her shoulders and down the cleft between her breasts, and she pulled at the tie he wore with the formal tuxedo, trying to tear it from him so she could unbutton his shirt and rest her face against the soft curly hairs of his chest.

He was warm and sensuous, and she responded in full, thrusting her body tightly against his when his arms enveloped her waist and swept lower to contain her hips. Cade turned her lips loose long enough to murmur endearing words into her ear, phrases that stimulated her even more and made her reach for his dark head to lower it to her mouth another time.

When he set her completely free at last, he did it with a reluctance that racked both of them. Taking a step backward, he stared at her flushed face while she stood breathless, heedless of the hair falling out of the upswept style she had spent so much time working on, knowing only that he was walking away from her and that she couldn't let him go.

"I love you, Stephanie," he almost shouted. "I love you, and there's not a damn thing I can do about it. I've tried to get over you, and I can't." He shuddered almost imperceptibly. "I should never have come here. Seeing you again just makes it harder to bear."

She tried to speak, but he hushed her.

"No, don't say a word. I don't want to go away with your laughter ringing in my ears. Spare me that at least, Stephanie. Isn't it enough to know you've ruined my life? Do you have to take everything else? My pride? My dignity?"

Tears were rolling down her cheeks, but Stephanie made no effort to wipe them away. "Stop it," she screamed, "stop saying that! Stop even thinking it!" She covered her face with her hands. "Don't you know? Can't you tell that I'm so much in love with you I'm practically crazy with longing?"

He didn't believe her, Stephanie knew. But he took one tentative step toward her before he stopped.

"You hate me," he stated flatly. "You told me that once."

"I lashed out at you in frustration." She was determined that he should for once see the truth. "Oh, Cade, I've never hated you. I've always loved you—for so long I'm not sure even when it began."

He was by her side in an instant, gathering her weeping body into his arms and soothing her gently, softly massaging her back and crooning low sweet words that proved he cared.

"Are you sure?" he asked, so tentatively that she stopped crying long enough to laugh.

"I've never been so sure of anything in my life," she admitted.

"Then why didn't you tell me?" Cade questioned her. "Why did you let me go out of my mind for such a long time?"

"Why didn't you speak to me?"

"I was too stubborn," he admitted, sliding to the ground and settling her into his lap while he pressed her head against his chest in a loving gesture. "I was so quick to judge you...too hasty, I know." His lips grazed her forehead. "But I thought you were like all the show-business people I had heard about, that you had been sent to use your sexual prowess on me."

"I never did that," she protested, but he pressed her against him again when she tried to lift her head to speak.

"You have to understand. I was expecting a beautiful woman to be sent to the ranch, but when I first saw you I was overwhelmed. You were gorgeous, but you also looked so innocent and vulnerable with your pretty face covered with mud that for a minute I thought I might be wrong. I came to my senses quickly and decided that you were only there to seduce me.''

"You jumped to the wrong conclusions," she told him.

Cade nodded. "We both did. When I found you in Jon's room the day I called the hotel, I was so angry I couldn't stand it. The fence being broken and the horses escaping didn't bother me nearly as much as the thought that you were sleeping with him. And then the day I brought him the briefcase, you were there." His touch became harder as the memories rose to the surface. "How did you expect me to react when I kept finding the woman I couldn't help loving with another man?"

Stephanie enjoyed the sensation of his hard male body against hers, and she leaned closer to his chest, a smile flitting across her face as he spoke of his love.

"I thought you wanted Kara the entire time," she finally murmured.

Cade lifted her face and kissed her lightly on the lips. "Do you really believe I could have preferred her to you?" he asked tenderly. "She's beautiful, of course, and very nice, but she can't compare with you, my dear Stephanie. She doesn't have your ability to make my blood come to a boil just by being in the same room." His hand roamed down her neck to the curve of her breast. "Do you know how close I came to taking you that day in the meadow? And again the night you fell asleep by my barn? God, how I wanted you!"

"Do you know how close I came to giving in to you in the meadow?" Stephanie asked in return. "I wanted you, too, but I believed you only wanted me physically and that you were turning to Kara for your real love."

They cuddled for a few minutes longer, remembering the occasions when they had come so near to disclosing their feelings and moaning about the weeks and months of togetherness they had lost. Cade revealed it had been at his instigation that his mother had tried—unsuccessfully—to coax Stephanie into staying on in Dallas.

"I did decide to admit my love for you at the last minute," Cade confided. "But you never returned the telephone messages I left."

"I thought you had heard of Kara's engagement to Jon and that you wanted me to help you change Kara's mind. I couldn't have done that, Cade, not when I loved you so much myself."

Cade's hand entangled itself in the pins holding her hair in place, and he efficiently removed them, letting her hair flow long and loose in the gentle breeze.

"You wore your hair up the night Jon and Kara announced their engagement," he reminded her. "I like it better when it falls onto your shoulders, the way it was when I first saw you."

"How did you know?" she asked. "You weren't there."

"The picture in the paper," he explained. "I didn't see it for two days, but when I finally did, and noticed you in the background looking so forlorn, I felt you must be upset about losing Jon, and I didn't think I had any chance at all with you. That's why I didn't try to contact you after you went back to Los Angeles.''

"I wasn't sad about Jon—" she reported.

But he stopped her with a quick, "I know that now."

"It was just that they were so happy and I wasn't," Stephanie continued, determined that Cade should know every reason for her behavior, so that there would be no lingering doubts in his mind concerning her love for him.

Cade lifted Stephanie upward, bringing both of them to their feet, and caught her by the waist, swinging her around in exuberant joy.

"I'm ordering another plane ticket," he stated, "and you're going back to Texas with me tomorrow."

"Yes, sir," she giggled. "That's one of your orders I'll be delighted to obey."

His fingers throbbed against her temples for a moment while he searched her features in the dim light.

"Are you sure, Stephanie? Are you absolutely certain you love me?" he asked.

She answered with a glittering smile that even the night couldn't hide.

"You'd better be sure," he warned her, "because I'll never let you get away. I'll keep you so close you'll begin to think we're the same person."

"That's the way I want it," Stephanie assured him, raising a finger and lightly tracing the outline of his lips.

Cade enclosed her small hand between his firm

large ones. "I'm not going to let you out of my sight, Stephanie, until I get you back home. You might change your mind."

"I won't," she promised, her soft voice ringing with her newly discovered joy.

He walked along the edge of the estate with her, holding her hand as if they were school kids on a first date, both suddenly shy now, coming to grips with their emotions.

"I guess we have Morgan to thank for bringing us together tonight," Cade commented.

Stephanie laughed. "He's been trying to do that for a long time, and I've always tried to get him to stop. Remember when you thought I was flirting with him at the barbecue? He was busily making plans for us that night, and I couldn't get him to quit."

Cade glanced toward the house. "He's probably inside now. I'll have to shake his hand before we go." He squeezed Stephanie's hand hard, but she didn't even feel the pain. "I could practically kiss the man for what he's done for us."

"Oh, no," Stephanie protested with a pretense of being upset. "You're going to save your kisses for me."

"Are you going to be a possessive wife?" Cade asked her with a smile.

"Absolutely," she replied. "You can count on it."

"Good," he told her, "because I'm the same way."

As they approached the house the sounds of the party became more and more distinct. Cade stopped her before they reached the terrace. "I meant what

I said, Stephanie. I really can't stand noisy parties. Let's get out of here now. We can send them a telegram to let them know you're going home with me.''

"Morgan and Paula get the first one," she agreed.

They slipped around the side of the house without anyone seeing them and were at the front, where the parking attendant stood ready to retrieve cars for departing guests, when Cade remembered that he didn't have an automobile, having ridden to Jon's home with the Andersons.

"It's all right," Stephanie assured him. "I have my own car here." She handed the attendant the parking receipt, and they waited for him to bring the little sports car to them.

When he arrived and held the door open, Cade took a long look at the vehicle. "Are you sure you can drive this thing?" he asked. "After all, it may be muddy. We'd better not take the chance."

"You're being silly," Stephanie laughed. "Don't you know it hardly ever rains in southern California? We don't have mud." But she slid into the passenger's side and allowed him to take the steering wheel.

Before he pulled out of the circular driveway, he took her hand. "I meant what I said, Stephanie, about not letting you out of my sight until after we're married. Your place or my hotel?"

There was a momentary hesitation before she answered. "My apartment," she decided. "There are a couple of things I want you to see."

She directed him to the freeway that would take them to her home, then leaned back against the soft leather cushion of her seat, admiring Cade's profile. How could she ever have thought it was harsh? There was such a tenderness in the mouth when he turned to smile at her, and the eyes weren't cruel, as she had once thought. They were brimming with emotion.

Once inside her small apartment, Cade pulled her into the confines of his arms, as if afraid she might escape. "It's been so long since I've held you," he murmured. "At least thirty minutes, and that's more than twenty-nine minutes too long."

Stephanie shook free and darted to the buffet. Taking the porcelain shepherdess from its place in the center of the buffet and opening a drawer and pulling out the framed photograph, she offered both to him. "To prove to you that I didn't just start loving you within the last hour," she explained.

Cade tossed the picture aside, and, almost overcome with emotion, he cradled the statue in his big hands before he set it carefully on the buffet. "You don't need to prove anything to me ever again. Just stay close for the next fifty years, and then I'll see about renewing your option."

Smothered by his kiss, she let him lift her into his arms, not caring that her shoes fell off her feet, not wanting anything but the warmth of his body against hers.

He turned her around slowly while his eyes searched the room. "Don't you have a bed in this place?" he asked at last.

"Not really," she admitted. "Only the sofa. It opens up. The apartment doesn't have a separate bedroom."

Cade dropped her to her feet, and for a moment she thought he was angry. But he took her by the shoulders and gazed into her blue eyes.

"Where are your suitcases, Stephanie? I'll help you pack. I'm taking you out of here for good, and you're spending this night with me at my hotel." He tantalized her with his tongue against her parted lips. "There's a huge bed there, and I know it's much too large for one person."

She nodded and began to pack.

Stephanie had never packed so quickly in her life. She simply threw a few things into a suitcase and tossed some dresses into a garment bag, telling Cade that she would have Becky ship the rest of her belongings later. She didn't want to take time for mundane things like packing, not when Cade's nearness was making her bones cry out for his touch. But she did take time to set her shepherdess in a box filled with tissue paper and carry it with her.

An hour later she was still burning with desire as Cade unlocked the door of his room and led her inside. He hung the Do Not Disturb sign on the outside doorknob before he shut the door and bolted the lock.

Cade undressed her slowly, making the yearning even more exquisite, until she stood trembling in front of him. Then his patience and restraint ended, and before she could reach out her fingers to undo his tie, he had it off, had discarded his shirt and slacks and was carrying her toward the bed that was as large as he had said it would be.

Gently he laid her down so that her hair fell across

the pillow as her arms reached up for him. With an agonizing cry he was on the bed with her, stroking her smooth skin, arousing every nerve ending, causing her breasts to rise in taut towers in response to his electric touch. His fingers burned an exploratory path from her waist to her hips and beyond, and she uttered her own joyous moan and clutched at his body.

Stephanie couldn't keep her hands off his broad chest, her lips from his face. She knew that he was rising to the same peak of excitement that she was, and when he murmured, "Now," and claimed her, she let herself go, let the tension inside her build to such a level that she finally exploded with an intensity that shook her entire body.

She was left so limp she couldn't speak, couldn't move, could only lie listening to the beat of Cade's heart as he still clung to her. After a few moments he lifted his body from hers, fell exhausted on the opposite side of the bed and reached out to gather her to him. The warm expanse of his skin next to hers was comforting and exciting at the same time.

"This is a fine time to be asking this," he said into the darkness, and she could tell from the effort it took him to speak that he was virtually as spent as she was, "but you are going to marry me, aren't you, Stephanie?"

"The minute we can get a license," she agreed.

They were silent for a moment, thinking of the future, until he absently began to stroke her hand, his large strong fingers curling around her smaller ones.

"I never did buy that ring I thought would be so

beautiful on your hand, Stef. It has a single blue sapphire, and it made me think of your gorgeous eyes the first time I saw it. You're a rare gem yourself, you know.''

He propped himself up on one arm as he spoke. "We could wait until we get home to be married, and you could have that ring for your wedding band. Or we can marry here as soon as we can get the license.''

"I don't want to wait," she told him. "You might be the one to change your mind."

Cade slipped a hand over her mouth to cut off the words. "Don't you dare even think that," he ordered before allowing her to speak again.

"I don't care about the ring. I only want to be your wife, and any wedding band will do." She laughed even though she knew he was being absolutely serious. "How about using the band from one of your cigars?"

He turned from her to switch on the light and reach for the telephone.

"What are you doing?" Stephanie asked.

"Calling the airline to change my reservation," he explained. "There's no way I'm getting out of this bed at six in the morning to catch a plane." He snuggled her close against him. "I may stay in here with you the entire day. We have a lot of lost time to catch up on."

"You'll get no argument from me," Stephanie declared, sliding farther into the curve of his arm.

One hand was on the receiver, but he removed it

before he even picked up the phone. Instead he clicked the light off again and gathered her into both arms with renewed urgency.

"I'll call the airline tomorrow," he murmured, his lips nuzzling her neck. "I need you tonight."

Begin a long love affair with

SUPERROMANCE.

Accept LOVE BEYOND DESIRE, **FREE.**

Complete and mail the coupon below, today!

- -

FREE! Mail to: SUPERROMANCE

In the U.S.
1440 South Priest Drive
Tempe, AZ 85281

In Canada
649 Ontario St.
Stratford, Ontario N5A 6W2

YES, please send me FREE and without any obligation, my
SUPERROMANCE novel, LOVE BEYOND DESIRE. If you do not hear
from me after I have examined my FREE book, please send me the
4 new **SUPERROMANCE** books every month as soon as they come
off the press. I understand that I will be billed only $2.50 for each book
(total $10.00). There are no shipping and handling or any other hidden
charges. There is no minimum number of books that I have to
purchase. In fact, I may cancel this arrangement at any time.
LOVE BEYOND DESIRE is mine to keep as a FREE gift, even if
I do not buy any additional books.

NAME

(Please Print)

ADDRESS

APT. NO.

CITY

STATE/PROV.

ZIP/POSTAL CODE

SIGNATURE (If under 18, parent or guardian must sign.)

PR209

This offer is limited to one order per household and not valid to present subscribers.
Prices subject to change without notice. Offer expires March 31, 1983.

Now's your chance to discover the earlier books in this exciting series.

Choose from this list of great

SUPERROMANCES!

SUPERROMANCE

Complete and mail this coupon today!

Worldwide Reader Service

In the U.S.A.
1440 South Priest Drive
Tempe, AZ 85281

In Canada
649 Ontario Street
Stratford, Ontario N5A 6W2

Please send me the following SUPERROMANCES. I am enclosing my check or money order for $2.50 for each copy ordered, plus 75¢ to cover postage and handling.

☐ # 8	☐ # 14	☐ # 20
☐ # 9	☐ # 15	☐ # 21
☐ # 10	☐ # 16	☐ # 22
☐ # 11	☐ # 17	☐ # 23
☐ # 12	☐ # 18	☐ # 24
☐ # 13	☐ # 19	☐ # 25

Number of copies checked @ $2.50 each =	$_____
N.Y. and Ariz. residents add appropriate sales tax	$_____
Postage and handling	$____.75
TOTAL	$_____

I enclose_____.

(Please send check or money order. We cannot be responsible for cash sent through the mail.)

Prices subject to change without notice.   Offer expires March 31, 1983

NAME_____
(Please Print)

ADDRESS_____ APT. NO._____

CITY_____

STATE/PROV._____

ZIP/POSTAL CODE_____

20956000000